Miss Nightingale rose and gently pulled Madeleine's hands from her ears. 'What is it?' she asked quietly.

'I don't know, ma'am,' replied Madeleine. 'I can hear you perfectly, but at the same time there is a sound in my ears like – like hundreds of galloping horses, becoming louder all the time.' Her face was white and drawn as though with fear.

Some twenty minutes later the sound faded as suddenly as it had begun, but then behind her closed lids was Sebastian's face, in a flash so bright that her eyes flew open and she sat bolt upright. Just for an instant she had seen him as clearly as if he were standing before her, his face very deeply tanned, but taut and exhausted. Without realizing what she was doing, she held out her arms, but there was only the empty room, with the bright sun falling in hazy golden bars upon the wooden floor and the sounds of a Marseilles morning coming up from the street below.

PATRICIA CAVENDISH

Misunderstandings

GRAFTON BOOKS

A Division of the Collins Publishing Group

LONDON GLASGOW
TORONTO SYDNEY AUCKLAND

Dedicated with love to
the memory of my parents

Grafton Books
A Division of the Collins Publishing Group
8 Grafton Street, London W1X 3LA

A Grafton Paperback Original 1990

ISBN 0-586-20656-6

Printed and bound in Great Britain by
Collins, Glasgow

Set in Times

Contents

PART ONE
England, 1854

1

It was as she turned away from the graveside that she first noticed him: a tall man, standing hat in hand, beside the elegant brougham. His gaze was fixed unwaveringly upon her, and when she reached the grass verge he stepped forward to ask, 'Do I have the honour of addressing Miss Madeleine Brett?'

Madeleine raised startled, tear-drenched eyes to his face. He was expensively dressed, the centre panel of the brougham bore an escutcheon, the driver and horse were immaculate, and he had spoken with old-world courtesy. 'Why, yes, I am she.'

'Then I am delighted to meet you, Miss Brett, and only regret that I should do so in such tragic circumstances. I am Henry de Lacey. I believe you may have heard of me.'

Madeleine caught her breath sharply. Of course, papa's friend, Major General the Honourable Henry de Lacey, to whom he had written with the last of his strength on that fatal night. 'How do you do, sir? My father did indeed speak of you on the last night of his life, but I – I did not think to see you here today.' She spoke very softly, only just failing to keep the quiver from her voice.

Remarkable self-possession and a charming natural dignity, thought the General, but I can understand why Thomas Brett wrote, '*When you see her I think you will understand: there is an appealing tenderness about her which I fear may make her the prey of the first womanizing blackguard she comes across, and I beg you to care for her; she will not expect much.*'

'I set off as soon as I received the letter,' the General

told her. 'There is much that I wish to discuss with you. But first, may I drive you to your home?'

Again she was startled, wondering what this elegant elderly man could want with her and, as he saw her eyes widen, the General smiled slightly. 'Although I am a complete stranger to you, I believe your reputation will be quite safe,' he said quietly, 'for I am certainly old enough to be your father, if not your grandfather.'

Madeleine had never driven alone with any man except her father, but the east wind was bringing a flurry of snow and she desperately wanted to leave the huge cemetery with its crowded tombstones and soot-covered angels. 'Thank you,' she said gratefully, and allowed him to hand her into the brougham. As it moved off, she turned for a last look at the freshly covered grave with its single small posy of flowers. Oh, papa, darling papa, her heart cried, why did you leave me?

The General, noting her brimming eyes and tightly folded lips, gave her a few minutes, then he asked, 'How much did your father tell you about me?'

Madeleine swallowed hard. 'Only that as very young men you were friends and were together at Waterloo,' she said hesitantly.

'Your father saved my life and my honour at Waterloo,' the General said, his voice deepening with sudden emotion. 'It is a debt I have never been able to repay.'

She looked at him more intently then, her huge grey eyes widening. 'I did not know – papa mentioned nothing of that.'

'No, he would not. I know that very well. But it is the reason why I have come to talk to you. Ah, I believe we have arrived, have we not?'

Madeleine wondered briefly how he recognized the tiny terraced house and as he handed her down she said apologetically, 'I – I am afraid we have been quite unable to receive friends for a very long time.'

'I do understand,' said the General quietly, 'but we have much to discuss, so I hope, Miss Brett, that you will spare me a little of your time.'

She had to invite him in then. 'But you will find it so cold,' she added, turning aside to hide her deep blush as she led him into the front parlour.

The room was indeed icy and bare except for two chairs and a small rickety table. Only the darker patches on the walls indicated that once there had been pictures to give it colour and life. The General took in the whole room in a single swift glance, but his face remained impassive as he said, 'I can tell that life must have been very hard for you of latter months.'

Madeleine pulled at the ribbons of her bonnet. 'Yes, it was. Papa's illness started so soon after he lost all his money. Even so, we managed for quite a long time by moving again and again to cheaper accommodation and by selling our possessions. But now there is nothing.' The bonnet was off now, revealing rich chestnut-brown hair, smoothly parted in the centre and looped softly over the ears so that only their cold pink tips showed. She lowered her head as she blushed again, remembering the humiliation of standing in the queue outside the pawnbroker's shop with a picture or a clock or piece of silver hidden under her cloak, feeling the many hostile eyes upon her and having to return again and again until all the cherished family possessions were gone.

'Was there no one to help?' the General asked softly.

She shook her head. 'No one. I suppose one of the medical charities would have done so, but papa so hated the thought, and of course pride was all he had left. There was no family to turn to, you see, and I am an only child.'

The General decided to come immediately to the point. 'That is why your father left you in my care.'

The pale oval face was raised abruptly then, eyes wide

11

and soft lips parted in astonishment. 'In *your* care?' Madeleine whispered incredulously. 'I don't understand.'

'I had hoped that when he spoke of me, your father might have given you some indication of his wishes, because he made these very clear in his letter. That is why I am here now: to offer you a place in my home.' Only the slightest creasing of his fine dark eyes indicated the General's amusement as coolness replaced astonishment in the grey eyes which now looked shyly but directly into his own.

'May I ask in what capacity?' Madeleine asked cautiously.

'Not as the poor relation in one of Miss Austen's or Miss Brontë's novels,' he said, and now a smile visibly softened the stern lines of his face. 'But as part of my family, at least until you are of age. I have been a widower for many years; my elder sister, also widowed, lives with me and my daughter, Harriet, who is your own age. My son, like all the men in my branch of the family, is an Army officer and rarely at home. I am not a wealthy man, but' – he looked quickly around the room – 'I can offer you warmth, comfort and friendship.'

Without fully realizing what she was doing, Madeleine rose and walked to the empty fireplace, her hands twisting together. A very beautiful carriage and a most elegant walk, thought the General admiringly. For a few seconds she stood with her back to him, then when she turned once more to face him, her hands were still.

'It is wonderfully kind of you, General de Lacey,' she said decisively, 'and I do thank you from the bottom of my heart, but of course I cannot accept.'

The General had anticipated this reaction and also rose. 'May I say that I admire your spirit greatly,' he said, standing ramrod straight and with hands clasped behind his back. 'But I do beg you to look at your situation realistically: you have no money and no family, so it is

12

imperative that you find a position as a governess or lady's companion as soon as possible. I do not doubt that with your talents you could find such employment, but what a sorry existence yours would be: neither servant nor family. Then what would be your chances of making – as your father fervently wished – a marriage as happy as his own brief one had been? I repeat, I am not a wealthy man; I have no country estate and I live almost entirely in the City of Bath. But my name is an ancient and distinguished one, and if you were launched into society by me, as the friend of my daughter, I believe that your chances of making a suitable marriage – even without a dowry – would be very greatly enhanced.'

'But why, *why* should you wish to do so much for me?' Madeleine queried, her face troubled. 'I am a complete stranger to you!'

'And I to you,' the General replied quickly. 'So we have to accept each other on trust. For my part, I am happy to do so.'

Still she was not convinced. 'But surely whatever my father did for you does not warrant such generosity.'

'I think, Miss Brett, that you should let me be the judge of that,' the General said very quietly. 'I have not come here today without giving the whole matter a great deal of thought, and there is now no doubt in my mind. I beg you to let me repay my debt by consenting to my offer.' He paused to choose his words carefully. 'I give you my word as a gentleman that it is entirely honourable and I believe it is the best one you will receive this side of virtue.'

This side of virtue – she remembered at once the pretty horsebreakers riding in Hyde Park, impeccably mounted, ravishingly lovely, and papa, knowing she would be left alone in the world, had drawn aside the veil of secrecy and carefully explained about these young women. Then he had taken her on his rounds to St Giles and pointed out the other women, old, ugly and filthy, from whose toothless mouths obscenity streamed, and he had told her that this was how many of the beauties would end up . . . Madeleine shuddered and came back to the present. She had no food or fuel and the last of her money had gone to pay for the funeral; in two days the rent would be due and she was entirely, terrifyingly, alone in a hostile world. But her pride was as strong as her father's had been.

'Perhaps – perhaps I could bear your wonderful kindness in mind, and then if – if I am unable to find a suitable post, may I please seek your help?' she suggested hesitantly.

The General shook his head. 'Come, come, my dear,' he said gently. 'You are letting foolish pride blind you to reality. Why not accept my offer *first* and then if you do not care to remain with us indefinitely you can always seek a post later on. You will be quite free to come and go as you please.'

'Was it really what my papa wanted?' she asked wistfully.

'Oh, absolutely,' the General declared. She continued to look at him, her eyes deeply shadowed. Such a level gaze, he thought appreciatively, shy, yet calm and assured; the eyes of someone who is very used to listening and concentrating.

'But I cannot just live off you!' she protested, searching his face for the merest hint of insincerity and finding none.

'Oh, well,' replied the General, thinking rapidly, 'you might care to help with my correspondence and the cataloguing of my library, but most of all I should like you to be a companion to Harriet. She has many friends in and around Bath, but living with only my elderly sister and myself is rather lonely for her and I am sure you two would quickly become friends and enjoy many pastimes together.'

'Then – then, thank you, I – '

14

'Good!' he said, not hesitating to cut her short. 'I am delighted, and I can promise you that we shall do all in our power to make you happy. Now, to practicalities. Can you accompany me back to Bath tomorrow morning on the 9.45 train?'

Instantly she shied away. 'Oh, I – I believe not! There are still things to be attended to.'

He did not believe her, but was reluctant to say more in case she changed her mind completely. 'Well,' he said, 'Christmas is at the end of next week. I hope you will be able to join us by then?'

She was beginning to relax a little now and smiled shyly. 'Thank you,' she said again. 'I am sure I shall be ready by Christmas Eve.'

'Then, with your permission, I will ask my man of business to wait upon you tomorrow morning so that he can help you settle your father's affairs, and meanwhile I will arrange for coal and a hamper to be delivered.' The General came forward to take her small cold hand in both of his. 'Until Christmas, then,' he said, smiling now. 'We shall look forward to helping you begin a new and, I trust, a much happier way of life.'

2

The ever increasing opulence of the capital was much in evidence around Paddington station, where the many fine new squares and spacious streets almost bore comparison with those of Belgravia. It was obvious that the Departure side was not quite ready, while the roof and Arrival side still required much work to be done. Nevertheless, despite the noise, dust and extra congestion caused by the workmen, there was a definite atmosphere of bonhomie throughout the station on this Christmas Eve of 1853. Some travellers even paused to drop a farthing into the grimy hand of one of the many ragged children and beggars who cowered in the entrance. The trouble was, of course, that one was immediately surrounded by the filthy creatures, who, as everyone knew, were expert at picking pockets, lifting watches, and even snatching parcels and small valises, if one did not remain very alert and keep a tight hold on everything. Gentlemen often had to lay about them with their walking sticks, for although the railway police were very efficient, they were also very distinctive in their dark green uniforms and leather-crowned top hats; a glimpse of even the scarlet stripe on their trousers was enough to make all the varmints melt into the crowd. Still, it was necessary to try and maintain a Christian attitude, and the strains of 'God Rest Ye Merry, Gentlemen' from a group of carollers vying with the German band's rendering of 'Silent Night' were pleasant reminders that it was almost Christmas.

There was one young woman moving across the station who did not share the festive spirit, but felt only apprehension. Madeleine Brett, one hand clenched tightly around her valise and the other as tightly within her muff, was acutely conscious of being unaccompanied and hoped that she appeared more confident than she felt. London, *her* London, was harsh and full of tragedy, yet it was familiar and she wished desperately that she could remain. The General had promised her warmth, comfort and friendship, yet his was an unknown world and so much had already gone wrong.

Mr Lethbridge had insisted upon giving her three sovereigns to purchase 'necessities for the journey', as he tactfully put it, and she had hoped to buy new boots, a bonnet and material to make a dress and mantle. It was only when she had chosen the latter that she had found the side of her reticule neatly slashed; although she had neither seen nor felt anything, the tiny inside purse with the three precious sovereigns had, of course, been extracted. So instead of a neat new outfit to boost her confidence on this most momentous journey of her life, she was wearing her usual rusty black dress, mantle and bonnet. The previous evening she had spent hours sponging and pressing the outfit, but nothing could make it look other than thin and worn out. It was the same with her bonnet: she had washed the ribbons and steamed and curled the feather before replacing them in a more fashionable way, but the bonnet remained shabby, even slightly battered.

Then there had been the General's letter telling her that his son would be escorting her on the journey, but there had been no word from Sebastian de Lacey. Mr Lethbridge had clucked concernedly when he called the previous evening with her ticket. 'Dear me,' he said, plainly embarrassed, 'I am afraid Captain de Lacey is a young man with – er – many friends in town, and I can only assume that he has been away from his quarters and therefore has not received his father's instructions.' As Mr Lethbridge debated whether he should offer to escort her himself, Madeleine said, 'Please do not worry, Mr Lethbridge. I am very used to going out and about alone and am perfectly capable of making the journey unescorted.'

Mr Lethbridge still hesitated. The whole of the large de Lacey family, including the Earl of Wells and his sister, the Duchess of Wessex, were clients, and for some unknown reason this poverty-stricken young woman was being taken under the family's wing. The last thing in the world Mr Lethbridge wanted was to anger General de Lacey, but he had promised to take his own family to the theatre on Christmas Eve. 'Are you quite, quite sure?' he asked Madeleine, thinking fleetingly of how impossible it would be for his own daughter to travel alone.

Madeleine smiled, sensing his dilemma. 'Quite sure,' she said decisively.

A most unusual girl, thought Mr Lethbridge. She appears to be so fragile and vulnerable yet has great assurance. 'Well then,' he said aloud, 'I would suggest a seat in the "ladies only" compartment; go straight to the platform, show your ticket to the passenger guard – he will be wearing the company's dark green livery, so you will easily identify him – and he will direct you. But perhaps you are already familiar with railway travel?'

Madeleine shook her head. 'Not really. I did travel by train ten years ago when my father sent me and my governess on holiday to Brighton, but our own carriage was put on to the train and we travelled in that.'

Mr Lethbridge shot her a keen glance from under bushy white brows. Seeing her in such destitute surroundings, it was difficult to believe she had known any other existence; yet her voice, her bearing and everything about her indicated that she had been gently reared, and as a solicitor he knew only too well how easily the sudden death of the breadwinner could reduce a family's circumstances. So his voice held a hint of real warmth as he said,

'Ah, well, perhaps I should at least accompany you to Paddington and see you safely aboard?'

Madeleine, with nerves tightly strung through grief and apprehension, wanted to scream No! No, no! Just leave me in peace! But such behaviour was unthinkable, so clasping her hands together she said calmly, 'That will not be at all necessary, although I do thank you, Mr Lethbridge, for all your help and kindness.' As he still wavered, she quickly held out her hand. 'Goodbye,' she said, smiling a little, 'and may I wish you and your family a very happy Christmas.'

There was nothing for it but to take her hand, reciprocate her good wishes and hope that her journey was comfortable. It was only as he stepped thankfully into his carriage that Mr Lethbridge realized that for the first time in his life a chit of a girl had terminated an interview with him.

Madeleine tried to remember all Mr Lethbridge's instructions as she approached the platform; the passenger guard was certainly there, speaking with great authority and pointing with his short brass and ebony baton. When at last she was able to present her ticket, he looked at her speculatively. She was very shabbily dressed, yet had a delicate beauty and the proud carriage of a duchess. Moreover, she had a first-class ticket, so his tone, which had been distinctly hectoring at first, quickly changed to one of quiet respect as he said, 'The "ladies only" compartment, ma'am, is the one next to the engine, right at the end of the platform, if you please, ma'am.'

The walk along the platform was another ordeal for her since there were many people standing beside the open doors of their compartments and she was only too aware of their curious glances. She forced herself to walk without panic, looking straight ahead, and only hoped that in the dim light her deep blush would not be seen.

She first noticed the man because, against all regulations, he was nonchalantly smoking a cigar; then she saw that he was extremely tall and his figure, clad in a heavy caped ulster and outlined against a swinging lamp, was powerful, even menacing; his beaver was tipped forward over one eye and there was about him an air of careless authority and privilege, and a devil-may-care attitude towards the world in general. He was also extremely handsome, with the dark, slightly rakish good looks so favoured by current lady novelists, but even in the dim light his clean-shaven face bore signs of dissipation in the strong lines scoring his cheeks and around his long mouth. With a start Madeleine realized that he was looking as intently at her as she at him. As she came nearer, his narrowed eyes suddenly raked her boldly, as though, she thought in deep humiliation, he is seeing me without my clothes on! Her step faltered very slightly and hot blood suffused not only her cheeks but her whole body as the thought came to her that he only dared look at her like that because she was alone and poorly dressed. Instinctively she raised her chin in a small proud movement, but even after she had passed him she felt his eyes boring into her back. Then at last the magnificent engine was in sight, with its driver and fireman standing beside it in their white fustian. Immediately behind the engine were the neat first-class carriages and, yes, there was the "ladies only" compartment with a corner back-to-the-engine seat just as Mr Lethbridge had recommended. After a curt nod from an affluent matron confirming that the seat was free, Madeleine sank gratefully into it, carefully arranging her skirt so that it took up the least amount of space.

'This is a first-class compartment, you know.'

Madeleine looked up quickly. It was the large matron in the opposite corner who had spoken, her small eyes, as dark and hard as her swinging jet earrings, looking aggressively at Madeleine. 'Thank you, that was what I understood,' the young girl replied quietly, returning the woman's gaze before glancing at the other occupants. All were expensively dressed in either velvet or the finest merino, with muffs and tippets of fur, the latest bonnets, and long earrings of garnet, topaz or amethyst. They were all looking at her with frankly hostile curiosity, and one florid woman in a sealskin cape and magenta ensemble appeared almost mesmerized by Madeleine's boots. Hastily she tried to tuck her feet under her dress, but it was impossible. After so much tramping in the filth of the slums, she had been forced to shorten the skirt, and her boots, their uppers patched, their soles paper-thin, were always clearly visible.

Her composure was very nearly cracking when she looked through the window and saw the tall man just about to walk past. He, too, was looking straight at her, and as her eyes met his a smirk of pleasure and invitation animated his whole face. Not even in the Leicester Square soup kitchen or the alleys of St Giles had the ruffians and cutthroats looked at her like that, and she half rose, preparatory to jumping from the train, away from these hostile, condemning people who knew nothing about her yet appeared to consider her worthless. But as she moved, the door was slammed from the outside, followed by the sound of other doors being closed all down the train. Then a whistle blew, and the train jerked and began to move. Slowly Madeleine sank back in the seat. She had left it too late and now was launched on this lone journey into the unknown.

3

Although Madeleine knew the words by heart, she unfolded her father's letter, which had lain in her clenched hand like a talisman. Instantly the spidery, uneven writing swam before her eyes.

My beloved Child,

I must humbly beg your forgiveness for the action I am about to take, because by the time you find this letter I shall have died by my own hand, leaving you alone in the world and almost penniless. This must seem a heartless way of repaying all your devotion and care over these last years but, my darling, it is simply because you *are* alone that I am taking the overdose of laudanum. This agitated paralysis from which I am suffering is incurable, and no progress has been made with it since Dr Parkinson first wrote of it as far back as 1817. I only know that I will deteriorate rapidly and finally become as helpless as a baby. This I could bear if it did not also mean the sacrifice of your youth and beauty. Over these past three years I have watched you struggle against increasing hardship and the disintegration of our home, and what magnificent courage you have shown! I have been so proud, but at the same time so heart-broken that such a sacrifice should be demanded of you. If I were to continue to live, I know there is *nothing* you would not give up for my sake, and this I will not allow.

We have been so happy together, you and I, and I selfishly wanted no one else, but now I bitterly regret the absence of good friends who would look after you and ease your grief. I can only think of one person to whom I can appeal; I have not seen him for many years – in fact, not since we were young ensigns together at Waterloo – but the letter I was so anxious for you to post this evening was to him: Henry de Lacey. Do whatever he suggests; he is a man of great integrity and comes of a very distinguished family. I know he will do what is best for your future.

Do not, I beg of you, my darling, grieve or mourn for me. Even though I die by my own hand, I trust in the love and mercy of Our Lord. I look forward with great joy to being reunited with your blessed mother, and I pray that you may find a marriage partner to bring you as much happiness as I had in mine. Always remember that you come of good, honourable stock, so hold your head high, but love and pity the humble and the sick no matter how foul their mouths or how stinking their sores, for they, too, are the Children of God.

That God may ever bless and keep you, that the love of Our Lord Jesus Christ may enfold you all the days of your life, is the fervent prayer of

Your devoted father,
Thomas Fitzmaurice Brett.

Madeleine folded the thin, crumpled paper and replaced it in her reticule as grief threatened to overwhelm her yet again. But I must not – will not – cry in front of all these people, she thought, blinking hard and keeping her face turned determinedly to the window. Now that they were out of the thick soot-laden air of London, the light was much stronger and the countryside beautiful, but Madeleine looked at it with unseeing eyes. Instead, she was back in the elegant house in Hertford Street on the evening she had seen Mr Meadows emerging from her father's study.

He had come forward at once, smiling ingratiatingly, eyes darting everywhere, and even at sixteen she had instinctively disliked him. Yet papa had trusted him implicitly and said: 'With these new investments which Meadows is making for me, life will be rather different – oh, not for you, my dear, but I shall be able to give up the practice and concentrate on what I have long wished to do.' Sitting at his feet, arms hugging her knees, she listened avidly as he outlined his plans: there would be more than sufficient money for her coming out in two years' time, her dowry and eventual marriage; even for an allowance after her marriage, and for himself to work among the destitute – 'not the respectable poor who are frequently referred to me at Guy's, but the real outcasts of society who live and die in the filthy dens around Clerkenwell and St Giles. I want to start a surgery somewhere, perhaps the first of several, and it is my fervent hope that in due course I may persuade some of the new young doctors now training at Guy's to devote time to these people, for there are equally appalling slums in Southwark and Seven Dials.'

And he had carried through the plan, becoming increasingly immersed, so that within six months he had given up his appointment as one of Guy's specialists in order to spend more time at his new surgery. Then came the terrible evening when he emerged from his study ashen-faced. Terrified, Madeleine had led him to a chair and he had sat down stiffly, like a very old man. 'We are ruined,' he had said at last. 'Quite ruined. Meadows has swindled me out of every penny and has decamped to America. Oh, my God, what have I brought you to, my poor darling child?'

At first she had no idea just what he meant, for she was sixteen and had been surrounded by comfort all her life. But within weeks she *did* understand, and in that short time she grew up, learning to appear calm and cheerful even though terrified, and to take the initiative, for shock had expedited the first symptoms of her father's illness, which he diagnosed at once. By then all the servants had gone. 'We shall sell the house and move to something smaller,' Madeleine said bravely, although the thought of leaving the only home she had ever known filled her with sadness. But the house had only been rented and it was necessary to sell a lot of the furniture before they *could* move. It was she who found the three small rooms near the Strand and she who organized the move.

Then, as Dr Brett was determined to continue his surgery for as long as he could walk, Madeleine insisted upon accompanying him. He had always been adamant in his refusal before, but now he could not manage without her. 'You will be very shocked,' he warned her, 'for the conditions are totally indescribable and the people have been brutalized by life. They are very, very deeply mistrustful of strangers; I have only just begun to gain a small measure of trust for myself, but I think you will understand why I must continue. . .' But of course she had not been prepared for the filth, the smells and the people's hopelessness: life was less than cheap, it was worthless, so what did it matter if babies and children and the very old lay dying or dead in the gutters? There were untold numbers of others still able to walk or crawl, and a pennyworth of gin brought oblivion and a semblance of warmth for a few hours. To Madeleine it was a nightmare world full of hideous deformities and disease-ridden beings who, although they walked on two legs, behaved much more like wild, four-legged creatures. Yet the stinking courts and alleys teemed with life; even the standpipes of foul river water – the only source available – could not completely decimate the population, and there were always great packs of ragged, barefoot children swarming through the narrow streets and ancient, crumbling tenements.

It was then that Madeleine saw her father's greatness, for his manner was simple and kind, his hands gentle with all his patients. 'And this is my daughter, who has come to help,' he would say, with his tired smile. So, for his sake, Madeleine swallowed her nausea and hid her shudders. Instead, she learned to swab and bandage the great gaping sores and not faint at the sight of maggots, lice and fleas. When his hands started to tremble uncontrollably, it was Madeleine who measured out the medicines or pounded the ingredients into powder with pestle and mortar, watched by Dr Brett.

She came to realize that through inexperience she had let the best of their furniture go for a song, and she learned to bargain over each item, but with all except the barest essentials now sold, they could no longer afford to make up the medicines or even to buy rags for bandages. Dr Brett could now only advise his patients, and many abused him, not caring that it took all his strength and Madeleine's to get him there and back. When his legs finally became too weak for him to get beyond the house, he acknowledged defeat and they moved to the tiny terraced villa off the Harrow Road, where the rent was cheaper.

'May we not apply to one of the medical charities for help?' begged Madeleine.

'No!' His voice was adamant, its tone stronger than for months. 'Not while we are still able to manage.'

So Madeleine began her regular visits to the pawn-broker with their few remaining ornaments. Her physical and mental resources were now entirely concentrated on trying to obtain sufficient food to keep them alive, and for the first time there was heart-warming kindness from neighbours who, although almost as poor as herself, yet tried to help the young girl whose courage they admired. They had all waved her off this morning: the fourteen children of the Italian family next door running to hug her, their mother kissing her on both cheeks; Mr Silber-mann, who played the violin in the orchestra at the Cremone; even the butcher, who had often given her marrow bones to make broth, had emerged from his shop, wiping his hands on his huge apron and saying, 'Gawd bless 'ee, luv. Look arter yerself naow . . .'

Madeleine started and came out of her reverie. The train was drawing into Swindon and all her fellow passen-gers were preparing to alight. Madeleine looked at them coolly now: they were what papa called 'new rich' – merchants' and shopkeepers' wives who had become affluent through ever increasing trade. 'And some of them are still not accustomed to having so much money,' papa had said. 'I am afraid you would find them rather vulgar, but the next generation will be very different.'

Once alone, Madeleine began to relax at last. The padded seats were very comfortable and the compartment, with its papier mâché panels, lights above the door, and roller blinds, was extremely well appointed. I am lucky, she thought, her spirits suddenly lifting, extremely lucky. The General has been wonderful and I must look forward to this new life. After all, as papa said, we come of very good and honourable stock, so perhaps I might even meet someone in Bath, perhaps a physician like papa, who would want to marry me. How wonderful that would be – to have a husband and children to love and care for. Of course, I would not want to be mollycoddled, only loved, and if he were a physician I would like to help him in his work.

At that moment the tall man passed by and Madeleine was unable to take her eyes off his broad back; there was so much power, so much physical strength in his tall figure . . . How wonderful, she thought wistfully, to be loved and protected by someone like that. There would be nothing to fear from life then. In an amazingly quick movement, he had turned and was looking directly at her, his fine dark eyes sparkling, a wide, rather wolfish smile revealing strong white teeth. Confused and surprised, Madeleine lowered her eyes at once, quickly untying her reticule and fumbling inside it in an effort to hide her embarrassment. She thought she heard a smothered guffaw from somewhere nearby, but when at last she raised her eyes, he had gone. Yet she had the strangest feeling that he thought they were both playing some kind of game . . .

It was already dark when the train puffed and wheezed into Bath station. Lights, like a myriad glow-worms, gleamed in the hills, but the station itself was dimly lit and within minutes had emptied, leaving Madeleine alone, her valise at her feet. As she peered through the soft mist, it was at once evident that there was no one to meet her. But there must be a good reason, she told herself firmly, even as her heart began to thump loudly in her ears. I will just wait quietly here until the General comes.

'Are you in need of assistance?' The voice came from just behind her and made her start, but she turned eagerly – only to step back in dismay, for it was the tall man, smiling down at her in that wolfish way and barely raising his hat from his head.

'Thank you, sir, but I do not require assistance,' Madeleine said coldly as she turned her head away and pretended to look into the middle distance.

He was quite undeterred. 'Then what are you doing here?' he asked curtly.

Madeleine's head swung round, her huge eyes shining in the dim light with anger and tears. 'I hardly think that is any business of yours, sir!' she said, hoping her tone sounded as curt as his.

'True,' he acknowledged surprisingly, 'but Bath is not like London, you know. There will be no cabs cruising around, and if you do not know your way . . .'

Her head drooped slightly at that and her fingers began to twist the cords of her reticule. A brave little thing, trying hard not to show her fear, he thought with a spark of admiration. Now that he was close to her she looked much smaller, more vulnerable than when she had passed him on the platform. 'Come now,' he said, softening his voice, 'tell me where you are going and I will see that you get there.'

'I am going to Royal Crescent,' said Madeleine, and immediately bit her lip. Why had she told him? Why hadn't she insisted that he leave her?

'To Royal Crescent,' he was repeating, surprise in his voice. 'You are taking up a post there?'

'Indeed I am not, sir!' Madeleine answered frostily. 'I am going to stay with friends.'

She gasped and looked up at him as he suddenly guffawed derisively.

'Oh, don't be stupid, sweetheart,' he said, laughter still in his voice. 'I'll admit you're good, damned good. Your speech is perfect and in decent clothes you could fool anyone, but people in Royal Crescent do not have friends dressed like scarecrows! Your real destination is more likely to be in the region of Walcot Street, isn't it?'

Anger was beginning to replace her earlier fear, yet reason told her that this man, although so odious, was obviously a gentleman and therefore should be her natural protector – if only she could make him believe her. 'Sir,' she began, speaking with great earnestness, 'I know nothing of Walcot Street, but although I am alone and poorly dressed, I am a respectable woman and would ask you to treat me as such.'

'Oh, but why be so dull? Life is so much more exciting.'

'I am the daughter of a physician,' Madeleine continued, hardly hearing his words in her desperation, but he only laughed even more loudly.

'Really? Then no doubt he is a Dr Quack, peddling his one universal cure about the streets!'

She knew then that she could expect no help from him, and she turned to face him fully, still having to look up even though her spine was stretched to its utmost. 'I assure you nothing could be further from the truth,' she said quietly. 'However, since you choose not to believe me, I should be obliged if you would respect my wish to be left alone!'

But he stood there like a rock, actually looking as though he was thoroughly enjoying himself. 'I suppose you have been told many times that you have a lovely mouth?' he queried lazily.

At that her composure snapped and she spun on her heel, skirts flaring, to reach for her valise. 'I find your manner offensive in the extreme, sir, and I will not remain – '

'That's enough now, my girl,' he said, suddenly decisive. 'This play-acting has gone on long enough. I hear a carriage approaching and it must surely be mine.'

'Or mine!'

Once again he laughed. 'By God, you're a cool one! I have to admit I admire your nerve, but we both know that no carriage will be coming for you, so why not just tell me where you want to go?'

'Why, sir, just as far as possible away from you!' Madeleine retorted, goaded into unthinkable boldness. 'And I am neither your sweetheart nor your girl!'

'Ah, but I should so much like you to be,' he said, taking a step nearer. 'We could spend many happy hours together, and I always bring champagne – I know all you girls have a weakness for it.'

As she realized the full implication of his words, Madeleine was rendered speechless. But at that moment an elegant light carriage bowled across the square to stop just in front of them.

'Cap'n Sebastian, sir!' called a voice apologetically, and the tall man stepped forward. 'Ah, Sam, good fellow, you're here at last!'

'I be sorry ter keep yer waitin', sir, but Bess, her cast a shoe jus' as we was ready ter start an' us had ter put Daisy in – '

'That's all right, Sam. But now let's get out of this infernal damp!' He turned to Madeleine once more. 'Last chance,' he said softly.

'Please – just go!' she said, not quite able to keep the tremor from her voice.

'All right,' he answered. 'But we'll meet again – no one ever gets away from me, you know!'

'Beggin' thy pardin, Cap'n sir, but where be the young laidy marrster says thee was bringin'?'

The Captain uttered a crow of delighted laughter. 'The devil he did! He's not in the habit of suggesting I bring my friends to visit with me and I know nothing – '

'Sir, it be a young *laidy* – a Miss Brett – thee was ter escort.'

Relief and dismay battled for supremacy in Madeleine's tired mind and it needed all her poise to step forward without haste and say quietly, 'I am Madeleine Brett.'

But if she had expected her companion to be jolted out of his arrogance she was disappointed. He merely remained silent for a few seconds, and when he did speak it was with a terrible quiet coldness. 'Miss Brett, there appears to be some confusion. I am Sebastian de Lacey. Do I understand that my father expects you?'

Madeleine inclined her head slightly. 'That is so, Captain de Lacey,' she said demurely.

'May one ask in what capacity?'

'Why, I have been invited to make my home with your family.'

She heard his sharp intake of breath and then he said, 'Indeed? Well, we shall see about that. I have a young sister at home!'

'I do not understand you, sir.'

'Oh, but I think you do!' And in that he was correct, for his meaning was only too obvious: he thought her unfit to be under the same roof as Harriet de Lacey. His tone had ranged from curtness to banter, but now there was no mistaking the grim, even threatening note, and he held out his hand with evident reluctance. 'Allow me to hand you in, and then you must tell me just where and how you met my father.'

With equal reluctance Madeleine put her hand in his,

31

and was totally unprepared for the way her palm fitted snugly into his, for the warmth penetrating her cotton glove, and the tingling feeling which, just for an instant, extended even to her finger tips. It was gone before she had time to turn her head to look first at their hands and then up at him. His expression remained grim as he said, 'If you could bring yourself to hurry . . .'

She moved so quickly then that she stumbled a little against the top step, and instantly his hand moved to grasp her arm just above the elbow, pressing her forward. He thinks I do not know how to get into a carriage, Madeleine thought, flushing in the darkness, but of course I *do* know perfectly well; it is only because I am so tired and so frightened that I stumbled.

'Now tell me.' It was a command rather than a request, voiced from the darkness of the corner opposite her, and so compelling was Sebastian de Lacey's personality that Madeleine at once began nervously to recount the events of the past two weeks. He remained completely silent throughout, and as she only caught infrequent glimpses of his face from the dim street lights, she had no way of judging his reaction.

As the carriage came to a halt, her heart began to thud loudly again and she wondered if he could hear her fluttering breath. He leapt lightly to the ground, saying, 'You certainly tell a good story,' and she realized that was just what he thought it: a mere story, a fabrication. He held out his hand once more, but Madeleine ignored it. With one foot on the top step, she straightened so that she stood erect, shoulders back and head up. It was permitted to show one's boot but never one's ankle, so she only slightly lifted her skirts in both hands as she stepped effortlessly down to the lower step and then to the ground. Beside her she heard the faintest whistle of derisive admiration, but by then she had paused and was looking around in surprise and delight: she was facing an enormous crescent of magnificent stone houses whose huge Ionic columns supported a continuous Palladian-style cornice from end to end. Soft lights streamed from dozens of long windows and these, together with the total silence, added to the scene's enchantment.

'Why, how beautiful it is!' Madeleine exclaimed, fear and tiredness momentarily forgotten.

'Of course,' retorted Sebastian de Lacey laconically. 'It is the most perfect in Europe. Shall we go in?'

The door was opened by a liveried footman, to whom Sebastian handed his hat and gloves. 'Good evening, Timothy. Please tell my father that Miss Brett and I have arrived.'

Madeleine barely had time to note the splendid marble-floored hall and elegant curving staircase garlanded in swags of holly and scarlet ribbon before a girlish voice called out delightedly, 'Sebastian! Oh, how good it is to see you!' and a slender figure rushed forward with arms outstretched, closely followed by a King Charles spaniel yapping excitedly.

Sebastian's hands spanned the girl's tiny waist and he lifted her off the ground in a whirl of silken skirts and lace-edged petticoats. 'Harrie, my darling!' he exclaimed, his face alive with animation, 'how are you?'

'Oh, I am well and I have so much to tell you,' the girl said, clinging to the lapels of his coat. 'I have followed your advice and it is all turning out splendidly.'

Sebastian set her down on her feet and covered her hands with his own. 'Really? Are congratulations in order then?'

'No, but soon, very soon now, I can tell!' she cried, flinging back her fair ringleted hair.

Brother and sister had entirely forgotten Madeleine, who stood motionless and forlorn, except for the little dog. After a cautious sniff, he began to gambol around her, tail wagging as she bent to him, hand outstretched.

Then the General's voice boomed out behind her and she turned gratefully.

'Ah, Madeleine, Sebastian! Here you are at last. Madeleine, you see before you my daughter Harriet, and both she and Sebastian appear to have forgotten their manners!'

Sebastian and his sister had also turned, but Harriet only moved at her father's last words. She came forward slowly with hand outstretched. 'How do you do?' she said, her eyes bright with curiosity as they ranged over Madeleine's shabby figure. 'Please forgive me, but I see my brother so seldom. My father has talked a great deal about you and I am pleased to meet you. We thought you would be tired after your journey, so we have put back dinner for an hour in order that you may rest.'

The words were formal and did nothing to reassure Madeleine. 'Thank you,' she murmured, too deflated to find anything else to say, but feeling gauche and uncomfortable.

'Then Timothy shall carry up your valise and Ellen here will show you to your room,' said Harriet, stepping back.

A maid appeared from the rear of the hall and bobbed a brief curtsey to Madeleine. 'If you will follow me, please, miss.'

It was the General who walked to the foot of the stairs with her and took her hand briefly within both his own. 'I am so glad you are here at last, my dear,' he said, his voice very deep. 'Come and join us when you are rested, but meanwhile Ellen shall bring you whatever refreshments you wish.'

'Thank you,' Madeleine said again, managing a grateful smile. 'You are all very kind.' Then, conscious of the three pairs of eyes upon her, she straightened her back and held her head high as she followed Ellen up the curving staircase.

The sight of the bedroom, with firelight dancing on blue

walls and highly polished furniture, raised her spirits at once. As Ellen hurried to light the three pairs of candles, Madeleine looked around and thought she had never seen a more luxurious room: the furniture, small and delicate, was from the previous century, and the dainty canopied bed was covered with blue brocade to match the curtains. And there were roses everywhere; they garlanded the porcelain candlesticks, rambled over the delicate basin and ewer and were finely embroidered on the pin cushions. There was even a bowl of them on the dressing table, and as Madeleine exclaimed and bent over them, Ellen said, 'From the hothouses at Norton St Philip. Miss Harriet drove over farr them this mornin'.' Then, as Madeleine still appeared dazed, Ellen continued, 'The General thought as how yer might like a baf, miss, arter that nasty dirty train.'

A bath! It was a half-forgotten luxury, and Madeleine, thinking of the countless mornings when she had stood, naked and shivering, in an icy room and washed with equally icy water, now came to life. 'Oh, yes please, Ellen!' she exclaimed, smiling and pulling at her bonnet and cloak ribbons. 'That is, if it would not be too much trouble.'

It was the maid's turn to look astonished. ''Course not, miss,' she said abruptly, already rather suspicious of this strange guest who was reacting so differently from all the other young ladies she had attended. Swiftly she pulled a large shallow zinc bath and crowded towel horse from behind a lacquered screen and placed them before the fire. 'Do yer wish me to unpack farr yer 'fore or arter your baf, and do yer evening gown need pressin'?'

'My evening gown?' Madeleine echoed, animation leaving her abruptly. 'But I do not have one!'

Ellen shook out a towel with a flourish. 'The family always dress farr dinner,' she said and paused to enjoy Madeleine's embarrassment. Then moving briskly to the mahogany wardrobe, she added, 'But 'tis all right, the Gen'ral thought you might need a gown an' sent Miss Harriet to git this.'

Colour flared in Madeleine's cheeks as Ellen lifted down a delicate lavender blue gown. It was simple and plain, but the material was heavy silk and the bodice, cut in a vee to the waist, was filled in with bands of finest lace. 'Is it Miss Harriet's?' she asked in a stifled voice.

Ellen's tone was derogatory. ''Course not, miss! 'Tis bran' new an' come from Miss Harriet's own dressmaker.'

'How lovely,' said Madeleine, and she turned aside to hide the tears that threatened to spill over.

A soft knock sent Ellen hurrying to the door, where a very young maid stood bent under the weight of two large copper pails. Ellen motioned her forward. 'Make haste now, Annie, an' bring the others 'fore the wa'er gits cold!'

'Them's yere, outside,' gasped Annie as she struggled to empty the steaming water into the bath and at the same time look at Madeleine.

'Tha's all,' said Ellen, as Annie, having brought in the other pails, was lingering. There was no mistaking Ellen's tone, and the young girl gave a quick bob and scuttled away. 'Now, miss,' said Ellen commandingly, 'I will help you wif yer baf.'

'Oh, thank you, but I can manage.'

'Manage alone!' exclaimed Ellen, sounding genuinely shocked. 'Indeed you can't, miss! Wha' ever would the Gen'ral say if you was to slip an' he heard I wasn't yere?'

Madeleine was too tired to argue and gave in gracefully. 'Very well then, Ellen, if you will help me, please.' She began peeling off the layers of petticoats, acutely conscious of Ellen's critical gaze, which missed nothing. Only astonishment kept the maid silent; she did not know what to make of this guest whose underwear was of cotton, washed to paper thinness and actually patched in places. All the young ladies she had attended had worn silk or

36

the finest lawn, elaborately goffered and with yards of lace trimming. Then, as Madeleine stepped out of her chemise, Ellen saw that the white body, although perfectly proportioned, was pathetically thin, with hollows at the base of the throat and clearly discernible ribs. Ellen folded her lips tightly, resentment replacing criticism. This was a *person*, not a young lady at all, and therefore not eligible to be waited upon. Ellen wanted to fling the large sponge at her and tell her to get on with it, but instead she said coldly, 'My ladies always has soap in their bafs, bu' I don' s'pose *you* wan' – '

Madeleine turned to smile gently at the maid. 'Yes, I also like soap, Ellen,' she said quietly. 'You see, my father was a physician and he believed that warm water alone was not enough to clean the body, that one day everyone would use soap. And now that the tax has been removed . . .'

'Very well,' Ellen replied, as with barely concealed anger she slapped the sponge against Madeleine's back.

Madeleine sighed wearily. She wanted to cry out, 'I'm not an imposter and it was not my wish to come here', but instead she sank lower into the bath. The water was softer, cleaner and less evil-smelling than she was used to and the soap frothed in it deliciously. As Ellen continued to slap her with the sponge, Madeleine roused herself to try again. 'Have you been with the family long, Ellen?'

'Since I were eleven.'

'Really? That is *very* young. And – your husband?'

'I got no 'usband,' Ellen muttered reluctantly.

'Oh, I'm sorry, I – I noticed the wedding ring and thought . . .'

'Will you stan' up now, miss?' Ellen asked, holding the towel at arm's length. Then, as she wrapped it about Madeleine's body, she continued, 'He were took by the press gang as we come out o' church.'

Madeleine turned quickly to face the maid. 'Oh, Ellen,

how dreadful! I'm so sorry. Was it a long time before you saw him again?'

'He nefer come back 'cos he were kilt at Trafalgar wif Lady Frensham's husband. Tha' be the only reason why us was allowed ter marry, 'cos the admiral knowed my Stan.'

Then Madeleine uttered the words which were to make Ellen her devoted admirer: 'Forgive me, Ellen,' she said quietly. 'I truly did not mean to pry.'

No one had ever asked Ellen's forgiveness before; no one had shown any interest or understanding of her emotions, and in an instant all her resentment vanished, to be replaced by protective care and a total unquestioning loyalty which was never again to waver.

4

'. . . very shabby and not even a mourning ring or brooch.' The high girlish voice carried distinctly through the heavy mahogany doors, making Madeleine pause uncertainly. Would it be tactful to go in at once if they were discussing her? And yet, if the doors suddenly opened she would appear to be eavesdropping.

'All the more reason,' boomed the General clearly, 'why she should be looked after.'

'The family are in the drawing room, miss. Shall I announce you?'

Madeleine whirled to face the elderly butler, who had come to stand silently behind her, his eyes wary. She felt warm colour rush to her cheeks. 'If you please,' she said, pressing a hand against her suddenly racing heart. Putting on the beautiful dress, with its accompanying fine underwear, silk stockings and satin slippers, had bolstered her confidence, but now she felt uncertain and shy.

The double doors were opened wide. 'Miss Brett, m'lady!'

Madeleine was aware of a large, high-ceilinged room devoid of fashionable clutter but brilliantly illuminated by candles and firelight which danced on the glass-like surfaces of the delicate Regency furniture. A large Christmas tree, lit by tiny tapers, festooned with gilded fruits and surrounded by parcels, stood between the two long windows, and all the huge family portraits lining the pale walls were garlanded with holly. The group around the fire had become suddenly silent, then the two men rose, elegant in fine black broadcloth and immaculate white linen, and the General came forward, hand outstretched.

'Ah, Madeleine, my dear, come in,' he said heartily. 'Harriet and Sebastian you know, but you have not yet met my sister.'

Madeleine put the tips of her fingers on his hand and allowed him to lead her slowly forward to the woman who sat ramrod straight in a high-backed chair.

'Thea,' said the General, with the merest trace of warning in his voice, 'may I present Miss Madeleine Brett? Madeleine, this is my sister Dorothea, Lady Frensham.'

Madeleine sank in a curtsey of rustling silk. Effortlessly graceful and with natural elegance, thought the General approvingly, and what a transformation the gown has made!

Lady Frensham raised a gold-rimmed lorgnette to her eyes. 'Madeleine?' she queried unsmilingly.

'Yes, your ladyship, for my mother.'

'Your mother was *French*?' If she had been a Hottentot, Lady Frensham could not have sounded more shocked.

Madeleine lifted her head proudly. 'My mother's family were Huguenots who fled to this country after St Bartholomew's Day,' she said, looking shyly but very directly at the older woman.

'Come now, Thea,' interposed the General bracingly. 'The war has been over *thirty-eight years*!'

Sebastian de Lacey spoke from where he lounged against the Adam fireplace, one arm negligently leaning along its length: 'Our guest is looking puzzled and I suspect she is wondering about the origin of our own name,' he said, his voice laconic and bored. 'Confess now, Miss Brett, am I not right?'

Madeleine felt the hot blood surging to her cheeks, 'Well, I – '

'We were *Norman*!' interrupted Lady Frensham imperiously, 'as my nephew knows perfectly well! Our ancester, Marc de Lasci, came over with the Conqueror, and

40

later came to the West Country in the train of John de Villula, his physician. Afterwards, William gave the see of Wells to de Villula and the earldom to us.'

'But,' said the General, with a laugh in his voice, 'you see before you only the cadet branch of the family.'

'And,' continued Lady Frensham, as though her brother had not spoken, 'we have continued to serve England through all the centuries, mainly in the Army, although *I* married into the Navy. My husband, you know, was an Admiral of the Blue and died at Trafalgar.'

The General suppressed a chuckle with difficulty. His sister had been the one plain member of an otherwise handsome family, and when Admiral Frensham had offered for her, everyone – including Dorothea herself – had felt only relief. Nevertheless, she had made no secret of her delight when her bluff, elderly husband was recalled to the Navy; it was only after his death that he had become a much loved hero to her.

'It must have been a great honour to serve and die in such a battle, but so terrible for you,' murmured Madeleine. She had not known what to say and had spoken instinctively, from the heart. She was conscious that across the room Sebastian's brows had risen and his mouth twisted cynically.

Lady Frensham inclined her head graciously, and for the first time a tiny smile softened her long thin face. The lorgnette was raised again. 'What a very becoming gown,' she said, changing the subject abruptly.

Madeleine turned impulsively to the General. 'Yes, and I do not know how to thank you for such a beautiful gift,' she said earnestly and almost stammering in her nervousness.

The General bowed very slightly. 'Say no more, my dear. It was our pleasure, and if you are pleased, then so are we. Is that not so, Harriet?'

'Why – yes, of course, papa,' answered his daughter, looking and sounding far less certain than her words.

'Thank you, too, for choosing the gown, Harriet,' said Madeleine, once more blushing shyly.

Harriet, wary and already a little jealous of this beautiful, mysterious girl to whom her father paid so much attention, returned the smile dutifully, but Sebastian did not attempt to hide his anger.

The butler's quiet voice broke up the tableau. 'Dinner is served, m'lady.'

The General gave a tiny sigh of relief and decided to take immediate charge. 'Thank you, Perry,' he said, before his sister could answer. He turned commandingly to Sebastian. 'Will you take in your aunt and allow me the privilege of escorting the two prettiest girls in Bath?'

Sebastian bowed. 'Of course, sir,' he replied unsmilingly.

The dining room was on the ground floor and, like the one they had just left, was high-ceilinged and perfectly proportioned, the plain soft green of its walls contrasting with the white stucco and delicate gilt beading of the frieze. A long table, covered now in spotless damask, dominated the room. Table lights of Waterford glass, their pear-shaped drops and delicate crystal canopies glittering, stood at either end, while in the centre, instead of the fashionable, fern-laden epergne, there was a large plain *tazza*, each of its three tiers filled with grapes and rosy, highly polished apples. Against a side wall stood an elegant sideboard loaded with silver-covered dishes.

'I am afraid you will find us very old-fashioned,' said Lady Frensham, 'because we still prefer candlelight to a gasolier, which is so very unbecoming to one's skin, do you not agree?' She had meant to patronize the young girl by asking her opinion, but Madeleine could only nod and manage a small smile, for the cramps of hunger were knotting her stomach. Her face whitened as saliva flooded her mouth, and for an instant her head swam. Then, acutely conscious of Sebastian's sardonic gaze, she made a great effort to regain her poise.

The General lost no time in helping to put her at her ease. As soon as his glass was filled, he raised it. 'Welcome to our city,' he said, smiling warmly at her.

As his family dutifully raised their own glasses, Madeleine said shyly, 'If it is all like this crescent, it must be most beautiful.'

'Bath,' said Sebastian, cutting in smoothly, 'is like a woman who was the most lovely, the most fascinating of her time, but is now slightly raddled and deserted.' His eyes bore into Madeleine's, and despite herself a small shiver shook her.

'Oh, come now, Sebastian,' said the General bracingly. 'That is putting it a little too strongly. It is true that some parts have been allowed to become run-down, but plans are afoot to alter all that. Already we have got rid of those confounded Saturday night markets, and while I agree that the area around Poultney Bridge is badly in need of attention, I think that with the hills and all the orchards, we still have one of the most beautiful cities in the country, *and* in one of the most superb settings.'

'If only they had not taken away the balustrades,' said Lady Frensham plaintively. She turned to Madeleine. 'This crescent and the surrounding area once had the most delightful balustrades, you know, and now they have been replaced by these hideous iron railings and spikes.'

'And what about the people who insist on painting their front doors and window frames in colours different from the rest?' put in Harriet, suddenly looking animated and mischievous.

Even Sebastian was smiling a little as he said to Madeleine, 'You will have realized that this is a well-worn subject of family discussion.' He paused and, as his eyes swept boldly over her, his expression hardened. 'One

43

thing I can tell you with absolute certainty, Miss Brett, is that you will not find excitement in Bath. There is a great shortage of young men and a preponderance of eligible young females.'

Madeleine, fortified by food and a little wine, was determined not to let him embarrass her. 'Really?' she asked politely. 'But happily this will not bother me for I am not here to seek excitement.'

A small silence fell, which even the General seemed at a loss to break. Then Lady Frensham said dreamily, as though half to herself, 'Lady Nelson lived here for some time.'

'So did Lady Hamilton,' said Harriet, dimpling.

Her aunt sniffed audibly. 'As a servant gal.'

'As an adventuress,' murmured Sebastian, his eyes on Madeleine.

This is what he considers me to be, she thought, while colour flared in her cheeks. She lowered her head to hide the rush of tears, but then her father's words came back to her: 'Always remember that you come of good, honourable stock, so hold your head high.' And I am not an adventuress, she thought with sudden anger, nor did I ask to come here. She raised her head proudly and returned Sebastian's look. 'Surely Lady Hamilton's circumstances as a girl made her appear an adventuress even if she were not.'

He had noted the drooping head, then its proud lift and the huge eyes dark with hurt, and had thought it a brilliant performance. 'Perhaps you have a fellow feeling for her?' he suggested, his voice like silk in the absolute silence of the room.

'Sebastian!' growled the General. 'You are being insufferably rude, sir! I believe an immediate apology is called for!'

'No!' The young voice rang out, bell-like in its clarity, electrifying the group by its decisiveness. 'I should like to answer Captain de Lacey's question. It is true that I do have a fellow feeling for the young Emmy Lyon, for she was very poor and I know how terrifying it is to be either very young or very old when one has no money, no resources, no support. I also know' – Madeleine paused briefly, her eyes locked with Sebastian's and suddenly as contemptuous as his own – 'what it is like to be exploited by the rich and the idle.' Across the table she heard Harriet's gasp of amazement, but anger sustained her. Trembling yet ramrod straight, she sat in her chair with head flung back and eyes jewel-bright in the candlelight.

By contrast, Sebastian lounged very much at his ease, a finger and thumb playing with the stem of his glass. 'When you say you know, are we to take it that this knowledge comes from your own personal experience?' he asked with quiet hostility.

The General, crimson with anger, was about to speak when Madeleine replied, 'Indeed it does!'

This time Harriet's hand flew to her mouth, but Madeleine continued, her voice now as quiet as Sebastian's, 'I know because my father took me with him to his surgery; I saw the carriages of the young and beautiful in the park and the hovels of the old and worn-out behind the Haymarket and in St Giles. In addition, over the last three years papa and I became increasingly poor, and in the end were very nearly destitute . . . Does that answer your question, Captain de Lacey?'

Sebastian nodded slowly, reluctant admiration showing in his eyes. 'It does indeed,' he said evenly. Then he picked up his glass and very deliberately raised it to her.

Lady Frensham, made drowsy by the rich food and extra glasses of claret necessitated by this problematical guest, had barely followed the exchange, but looked from one to the other with eyes rolling sleepily. In the sudden pause she now roused herself to ask, 'Of course, you will have visited the Exhibition with your father?'

'Why no,' Madeleine said quietly, 'I am afraid we were never able to do so.'

'Not visit the greatest Exhibition the world has ever seen!' exclaimed Lady Frensham, astonishment making her suddenly alert.

Madeleine lowered her eyes. How could these elegant people ever understand just what poverty was like? Would they ever believe that it had been impossible to find the fare for the omnibus, let alone the entrance fee of one shilling? Would they ever, even in their worst nightmares, dream that there were human beings who scratched a living from what they found in the sewers; or parents who sat up all night to stop the multitude of rats from devouring their sleeping children? Theirs was a totally different world, and there were few if any bridges to link the two.

The General cleared his throat and said hastily, 'No doubt your father was even then too ill to make such a tiring excursion. And of course you could not leave him.'

Madeleine smiled gratefully at him. 'Yes, he was incapacitated by then, but we – we spoke often of the Exhibition, as my father was a great admirer of the Prince, who he considered has done a great deal for this country.'

'Such a pity he is a foreigner,' sniffed Lady Frensham.

'Oh, really, Thea!' exclaimed the General, exasperated.

Harriet turned to Madeleine. 'My brother serves with the Eleventh Hussars, you know, Prince Albert's Own.'

'My dear, the Prince is associated with many regiments,' began the General, but Harriet, excited now by a favourite theme, broke in quickly, 'But it *was* the Eleventh who escorted him from Dover when he returned here for his marriage, and because of that the officers and men are the only ones in the whole of the British Army

46

who wear pantaloons in the Saxe-Coburg-Gotha colours. Am I not right, papa?'

The General nodded. 'Yes, although in my day we were known as the Eleventh Light Dragoons.' He took a sip of wine before adding, 'It was your father's regiment, too, Madeleine.'

'So your father was a military man,' said Sebastian silkily. 'Strange, I had quite thought him to be a physician.'

Madeleine returned his challenging look, determined not to let him overwhelm her. 'He had intended to make the Army his career, but after witnessing the suffering at Waterloo he decided on medicine instead.'

'How very commendable,' drawled Sebastian, sounding bored.

The General stirred impatiently in his chair. 'Perhaps, Thea, if you and the girls have finished . . .'

Lady Frensham knew that when her brother spoke in that tone he expected immediate action from her, and she therefore roused herself once more. 'We will withdraw at once,' she said, nodding first to Harriet and then to Madeleine, and swaying very slightly as she stood.

The General waited until the door had closed behind them and he had nodded a curt dismissal to the butler and footman before he turned furiously to his son. 'What the devil do you mean by behaving in that disgraceful fashion?' he demanded, only to be countered by Sebastian asking icily, 'Father, you surely cannot intend keeping that young woman here indefinitely with my sister and aunt?'

'Just what are you insinuating, sir?' barked the General, his face turning an even darker shade of red. 'And how dare you remind me of my duty towards *my* daughter and *my* sister! I consider Madeleine to be an entirely suitable companion for Harriet and able to take her place in our family circle with ease and grace.'

47

'But we know so little about her.'

'Nonsense! Her father was a very old friend.'

'Whom you had not seen since you were very young men. You do not know what he turned out to be.'

'Ah, there you are quite wrong!' said the General, relaxing slightly. 'Do you think me such a greenhorn that I did not bother to make enquiries? I discovered that Thomas Brett was no ordinary sawbones, but a very fine physician who had studied not only in London but also in Edinburgh and Paris, and was a man of the highest integrity. He had a great reputation and a most lucrative practice in addition to being one of Guy's specialists. It was only when he had made a quite considerable fortune that he gave up his fashionable patients to devote all his time to the poor, for whom he felt great compassion. He established a surgery in the heart of the East End, where the most dubious characters came to respect him; he is credited with saving many lives.'

'A pity he did not lavish as much devotion on his daughter.' Sebastian's tone was coldly disdainful.

'Thomas Brett was entirely devoted to Madeleine! But if he had a fault, it was an entire lack of business acumen, for within six months a rascally solicitor had defrauded him of his entire fortune. That is how he and Madeleine came to such a low ebb.'

'Father, can you honestly say that you believe Madeleine Brett to be an innocent young girl after the extraordinary speech she made at this table?'

'Yes,' said the General decisively. 'I grant you that she has much more worldly knowledge than gently brought-up girls are given, but I *know* she is as innocent of actual experience as any of them. Dammit it, man, I've had more dealings with women in general than you'll ever have! You confine your activities to the demimondaines and are so cynical that you consider every young woman a potential whore. It was because of the likes of you that

48

Thomas Brett told his daughter so much, for with her startling beauty he was afraid that she would be the prey of every rakehell in town!'

Sebastian had seldom heard his father speak with such conviction and he regarded him with speculative interest. 'Yet I believe, sir, that you might think differently had you seen her walk alone along the platform at Paddington today, as I did.'

'Had you been escorting her that would not have happened,' his father retorted.

Sebastian merely shrugged. 'Yes, well, I have explained about that. But the fact remains that Madeleine Brett walked along the entire length of that platform with all the confidence and poise of a thoroughly experienced, worldly woman! I ask you, can you imagine Harriet being able to do that?'

'No, but Harriet has never been in the unfortunate situation of having to go anywhere unescorted.'

'But it was not *only* that; I tell you, father, she looked me over very coolly.'

'I grant you she has a most unusual, level gaze,' conceded the General, 'but I find nothing bold about it. Rather it is courageous and honest – a most refreshing change from the usual simpering and head-hanging pose adopted by so many young girls of today.'

Sebastian shrugged again. 'Well, time will tell . . . Would you care to bet, sir, that we eventually discover her to be a charlatan, a consummate actress?'

'No, I would not!' was the furious answer. 'And I'll thank you to keep a civil tongue in your head when you address her and to remember that by offering her a home I am discharging a debt of honour which affects our whole family.'

Sebastian looked at the old man, suddenly alert and deeply curious. 'May one venture to ask – '

'No, one may not!' retorted the General, glaring back.

'And I now wish to consider the matter closed. Let us speak instead of this war between Turkey and Russia; we shall be drawn into it sooner or later, you know, and when that happens the Regiment will most likely be involved. If you wish to be with it then, I suggest you begin concentrating your mind on release from your present War Office posting.'

Madeleine's ordeal was not yet over, for the General, on entering the drawing room, sensed the tense atmosphere and said at once, 'Harriet, my dear, will you not play for us?'

His daughter rose dutifully. 'Of course, papa. Shall it be your favourite, or some carols?'

Before the General could answer, Sebastian cut in smoothly, 'Ah, but I should so much like something from our guest.'

'I'm sure Madeleine is much too tired,' snapped his father, his colour beginning to rise again.

But Madeleine, realizing that this was yet another challenge, met Sebastian's cold stare with hauteur. 'Certainly I will play, if you will forgive me being very out of practice.'

'Oh, please, Madeleine!' begged Harriet impulsively. She played indifferently and had little voice, so any opportunity to escape was welcome. 'I'll show you the music, and shall Sebastian turn the pages for you?'

Madeleine stood effortlessly erect, her slender body one straight line. 'Thank you, but neither will be necessary,' she said, answering Harriet but looking at Sebastian, and in that look was disdain and a totally unconscious allure. Sebastian caught his breath, not seeing the young girl clinging to her poise, but the extremely fascinating woman she would become.

The General gestured towards the grand piano. 'The

stage is all yours, my dear, and we await with pleasure,' he said courteously.

Emotion stormed through Madeleine as she sat at the piano, flexing her fingers. She knew that she had considerable musical talent and her playing had always delighted her father. Memories arose of firelit evenings when he settled comfortably in his favourite chair and she chose the music to match his mood: Mendelssohn or Mozart for the happy days, Chopin for the nostalgic, Beethoven for the inspired when he had battled for a life and succeeded. She knew now that she could not trust herself to play the works of these composers, but there was one other piece she had learned when all hope of Dr Brett's recovery was gone, and she had played it constantly to bolster their flagging spirits. The piano had been sold many months before, but she could remember every note and – surprisingly – her fingers did not feel too stiff. Her hands fell to the keys; she would play the tarantella as a tribute to her father's memory and to convince the odious Sebastian de Lacey that she was no cheap adventuress but a talented, well-brought-up young woman.

The faultlessly played music, gay, lively and fast, filled the room, setting all feet tapping and causing the last vestige of drowsiness to leave Lady Frensham's eyes. When Madeleine's hands at last fell back to her lap, there were a few seconds of silence and then, 'Bravo!' said the General. 'That was splendid!' And, led by him, his family clapped enthusiastically.

Harriet, saucer-eyed with surprise, turned to Sebastian, always her first source of information. 'What was it?' she whispered.

'It's a tarantella by a Hungarian called Stefan Heller and is very fashionable,' answered her brother, reluctant admiration in his eyes.

'Oh, I *wish* I could play like that,' said Harriet wistfully, and then Sebastian spoke the words which were like a slap across Madeleine's face, 'No, do not wish that, Harrie dear, for it is positively vulgar to play so well when one is only an amateur. Such expertise should be left to the professionals!'

Madeleine rose with difficulty, her whole body trembling, and as she turned the room swam. She clutched the piano, but nothing could prevent her legs from buckling or blackness enveloping her as she slid slowly to the ground.

When she opened her eyes, she found she was lying on the brocaded sofa, with Ellen kneeling before her and Harriet leaning over the back, chafing her hands.

'Take another sniff 'o this, miss,' said Ellen, waving the vinaigrette bottle beneath her nose.

'I think a very small portion of brandy would be in order,' said the General. Both he and Sebastian had retired to the end of the room out of Madeleine's sight, but he stepped forward now, holding out a glass. 'Thea, will you be so kind?'

Madeleine took a sip from the proffered glass but could not refrain from grimacing with distaste. 'Thank you all so much,' she said, attempting to sit up. 'I am quite recovered now and must apologize for being so stupid.'

'Not at all, my dear,' answered the General, still from the rear. 'It is our fault for allowing you to entertain us when it was obvious you were exhausted.'

'I suggest you retire immediately to bed,' said Lady Frensham, looking as though she longed to go there herself. 'Ellen, tell Annie to warm Miss Brett's bed at once.'

As Madeleine attempted to put her feet to the ground, an immense shadow suddenly loomed over her, then strong arms swept round her, lifting her effortlessly, and she could only stare up mutely at Sebastian's dark face.

'I am quite able to walk,' she said at last in a very small voice, but he only tightened his hold.

'Nonsense,' he replied decisively. 'You might fall on the stairs and injure yourself. I shall carry you to your room.' As her eyes widened even more, he grinned wolfishly. 'And my sister shall light us.'

The General followed them to the foot of the stairs. 'I wish you a very goodnight, Madeleine,' he said, concern still furrowing his forehead.

Harriet was running nimbly ahead, the candle held high, and Madeleine, cradled expertly in Sebastian's arms, ventured to look up at him. Without the sardonic expression his face was extraordinarily handsome, dark and lean, with the lines of dissipation still only faintly etched between the fine straight nose and long mouth. Even his eyes, now that they were no longer narrowed and taunting, were large, brilliant, and finely set under thick straight brows.

Once more emotion stormed through Madeleine. She had thought him the rudest, cruellest man imaginable, and yet now, with her head against his chest, hearing the strong beat of his heart, smelling the lemon verbena of his toilet water, she felt not only a tingling excitement but the most perfect sense of security. Slowly her taut limbs relaxed until she lay limply in his arms, and then he looked down at her from the corner of his eye and winked broadly. The magic moment was over; colour flared in Madeleine's cheeks as anger and a strange feeling of hurt overwhelmed her.

'I wish to be put down at once, if you please, Captain de Lacey,' she said, trying hard to keep her voice steady.

'But I do not please,' Sebastian retorted, sounding happy, 'and instead I suggest you put your arms around my neck.'

'Oh, but that is the last thing in the world I would ever want to do!' Madeleine said, goaded for the second time that day into uncharacteristic boldness.

Sebastian bent his head until his mouth was close to her

ear. 'Ah, but you will one day, my love,' he whispered. 'And you will wait longingly for me to hold you as close as a man can hold a woman. I promise you that!'

'Are you all right?' called Harriet from the shadows above.

'Yes, we are fine,' replied Sebastian lightly, as he suddenly sprinted up the last of the stairs and walked without hesitation into Madeleine's room. He put her down on the bed but kept his arms around her, and with his face inches away he locked his gaze with hers. Overwhelming physical attraction, freely acknowledged by him, unknown to her, flared between them, and for a few seconds they were oblivious of the servants hovering and Harriet standing at the foot of the bed. Then Sebastian reluctantly withdrew his arms and slowly straightened. He looked again at her slightly parted lips, her wide eyes and hurried breathing, and did not bother to hide his desire, but smiled, mockingly triumphant. 'Sleep well,' he said softly, and with the smallest of bows, turned and walked from the room.

'And I will say goodnight too,' said Harriet, setting down the candle hastily. She felt bewildered and only wanted to get away from something she did not understand, but which vaguely disturbed her.

Not so Ellen, who had been brought up in a tiny cottage, surrounded by farm animals, and knew all about sex. Tha' Cap'n Sebastian, she thought now as she bustled forward to help Madeleine, he ought ter be decently married an' keepin' such looks for 'is wife, instead o' leadin' the life 'e does. Echoes of monumental rows between father and son and rumours of Sebastian's love affairs returned readily to her mind, and in her newly protective feelings towards Madeleine, she vowed that yere was one young woman 'e would not be allowed to 'arm. Over my dead body, thought Ellen, folding her lips

54

tightly as she undressed Madeleine and noted her almost trance-like state.

When Madeleine was alone at last, enveloped in the luxurious softness of the feather mattress, she stared into the darkness, her body trembling and full of new sensations. But as Sebastian's whispered words echoed again and again in her ears, she knew them to be true, for in those few seconds when his face had been so near, her arms had almost risen to go around his neck. She *had* wanted him to be close, as close as a man and woman could be . . .

5

'We always give the servants their presents on Christmas Eve,' said the General the next morning after he had led his family in prayer, 'but we do not exchange our own until Christmas morning, so will you now come with us into the drawing room?'

'May I just go to my room for a moment?' asked Madeleine, anxious to be alone for a short while. She had slept fitfully, her dreams full of Sebastian, and had come down for morning prayers feeling both excited and apprehensive. But he had not appeared and there had been only the veiled stares of the servants to endure.

The day before she left London, Madeleine had sold her bed, the last table and two chairs in order to purchase small gifts for the then unknown family: a silk cravat for the General; Cologne water for Sebastian; a sovereign purse of gold net with a mother-of-pearl handle for Lady Frensham; and Miss Yonge's latest novel for Harriet.

'Of course, I did not know your tastes,' said Madeleine shyly as she offered the small parcels and was unprepared for the enthusiastic reaction, necessitated by perfect manners and genuine pleasure. The General, having seen her poverty-stricken state, was particularly touched, but they had all been more than generous in return. There was a roll of white muslin, minutely embroidered in an all-over design of tiny flowers, from Lady Frensham; a Honiton lace fan with gilded ribs from the General; and wrist-length gloves of softest white kid from Harriet.

Madeleine was overwhelmed. 'I have never received such beautiful presents since I've been grown-up,' she said with touching simplicity as she looked from one to the other.

'And I, too, have a token,' said a laconic voice from the doorway, transfixing Madeleine. Sebastian came forward with his extraordinary light step, a bandbox in one hand. He held this out to her with a slight bow. 'My compliments for a very happy Christmas, Miss Brett,' he said smoothly. She took it mutely, astonishment making her devoid of speech and conscious only of his presence and the loud thudding of her heart.

'Oh, Madeleine, do open it!' begged Harriet, excitedly bustling about.

As Madeleine still appeared incapable of movement, Sebastian stepped forward. 'Allow me,' he said, straight-faced but with a laugh in his voice. He lifted off the lid to reveal a bonnet nestling in folds of tissue paper, and once again he held out the box to Madeleine.

'Oh,' she breathed, scarcely above a whisper, and then as she lifted out the bonnet, 'Oh – how lovely.' It was an exquisite winter bonnet of soft grey velvet lined with ruched white chiffon over palest pink silk, and on either side, tucked under the brim, was a white rose and a cluster of the tiniest pink velvet flowers.

'Why not try it on?' suggested Sebastian, and as Madeleine, trance-like, complied, he took the long satin ribbons in his hands. 'I claim the right to tie them for you,' he said nonchalantly, standing very close to her so that she was overwhelmingly conscious of his nearness, his splendid height and his masculinity. He was only too aware of the devastating effect his proximity had upon women of all ages, and now he took his time, allowing his long fingers to brush her throat as he tied the ribbons. When these were at last to his liking, he tilted his head to one side while his eyes slowly travelled from her throat upwards until he held her gaze with his own. Once again it was as though they were the only two people in the room: she, tremulous, with breath fluttering through softly parted lips, and he very much the hunter, sure now of his quarry and totally in command.

'Sebastian!' thundered the General menacingly, but his son, unabashed, turned at once towards him. 'Do you not think our guest looks absolutely ravishing in the bonnet, sir?' he asked smoothly.

'Whatever I think is irrelevant, but I *know* you are making her embarrassed by such fulsome language,' retorted the General, glaring. 'And I suggest you turn your attention elsewhere.'

'But how did you get the bonnet?' demanded Harriet. 'You surely could not have brought it with you.'

'Indeed not, Harriet dear, but your own milliner is always ready to oblige me.'

'Surely the shop was not open this morning?' Harriet persisted.

'No, but she lives over the shop and I just hammered on the door until she appeared and then waited while the bonnet was trimmed.'

His words roused Madeleine at last. 'Thank you very much for such a beautiful bonnet,' she said primly, hoping he would not realize how foolish and bewildered she felt.

Once again Sebastian bowed. 'The pleasure is entirely mine, Miss Brett,' he said, dark eyes sparkling with laughter.

'You must wear it to church this morning,' said Harriet, gathering up the tissue paper and replacing it neatly in the bandbox. She turned to her father, 'Papa, shall I tell Madeleine about the ball now?'

The General made an effort to shake off his brooding thoughts. 'I will,' he said decisively. 'But, Harriet my dear, you must remember that it is not really a ball; the invitation clearly states that it is a musical evening, followed by dancing to celebrate the new year.' He turned to Madeleine. 'It is being given by very old friends of

58

ours, the Templecombes, who would be delighted to welcome you too.'

'Oh, but I am in mourning!' exclaimed Madeleine, astonished that he should have forgotten.

'How long is it since your father died?' demanded Lady Frensham, unexpectedly joining the conversation.

'A little over – two weeks,' Madeleine said very softly, just failing to keep the sudden tremor from her voice.

'H'm,' murmured Lady Frensham, looking at her brother for guidance.

'Would you like to go?' asked the General, brows once more drawn together, this time in concentration.

'Well, I – I – ' She caught a glimpse of herself in the magnificent Adam mirror and thought how incongruous the fashionable bonnet looked with her shabby black gown. Her own face, looking back at her, was white, strained and bewildered against the background of the luxurious room with its exquisite moulded ceiling, its Hepplewhite, Sèvres and brocade. What am I doing here? she asked herself frantically. I don't belong with these kind but alien people. 'I don't think I should attend,' she said aloud, near to tears.

'Have you ever been to a dance, Miss Brett?' asked Sebastian softly and, as her eyes were reluctantly raised to his, he continued, 'There will be music and laughter, dancing and gaiety; all the things of which I believe you to be very much in need. Am I not right?'

'Perhaps,' she murmured uncertainly, her thoughts chaotic.

'I do not believe in the long period of mourning which present-day society demands,' said the General forcefully, and Lady Frensham at once nodded assent. Although they both paid lip service to convention, they had been reared in the tradition that as aristocrats they were above this and could do whatever they wanted. This had been their family's way of life down the centuries, and they secretly scorned the strict moral code of their own age.

'I distinctly remember the Admiral telling me that white is the colour of mourning in the East,' said Lady Frensham, allowing a slight smile to soften her long face. 'So if you were to wear white, you could attend the dance and still honour your father's memory.'

Harriet clapped her hands delightedly. 'Oh, aunt, how clever of you! You *must* come, Madeleine!'

Unexpectedly it was the General who said, 'Of course, there *is* more to mourning a loved one than merely wearing a particular colour.'

Instinctively, but without fully realizing what she was doing, Madeleine turned to Sebastian, who said softly, 'Whether it is a musical evening, dance or ball, I really do think that, like Cinderella, you should attend.'

At once the doubts and fears of a few moments before vanished. She looked at the four smiling faces and the corners of her own mouth lifted. 'Then – then I should love to go, if I may,' she said shyly.

'Excellent!' boomed the General. 'That is all settled then.'

'Yes, and tomorrow I will take you to my dressmaker to have this material made up,' said Harriet, now looking as excited as Madeleine.

'Oh, but I think I can make it myself.'

'You can make a ball gown!' exclaimed Harriet, once more round-eyed.

'Well, perhaps not a proper ball gown, but one suitable for an evening party, because the material is so pretty that only a simple style is needed.'

'Then I'll help you,' said Harriet, who was fast becoming enthralled by this girl who seemed able to do everything. 'I have lots of fashion plates from *Le Petit Courrier des Dames*, and although Sophie Clefton says the new Empress of the French will bring about great changes in

60

fashion, I don't suppose these will be too apparent for some time.'

Madeleine did not know who Sophie Clefton was and wondered why Harriet, as she spoke the name, should turn her eyes solemnly towards Sebastian. But he, apart from raising his brows in his usual supercilious way, appeared unmoved, and a few minutes later he even smiled as he said, 'I can tell that you two will need little entertainment between now and New Year's Eve.'

The happy, relaxed atmosphere remained throughout the day, and that night, after she had blown out her candle, Madeleine drew back the curtains and paused to look out at the tranquil scene. It was a night of brilliant moonlight and far distant twinkling stars. Directly in front of her the common, on which sheep grazed by day, was lightly covered with snow, and beyond, set in a slight hollow, lay the heart of the fine old city. Lights still glimmered there and in the hamlets on the surrounding hills. A church clock began to strike the hour and was immediately followed by others in every parish; they had a ponderous medieval sound, unhurried and unchanging. During the day the city would be full of the noises and smells of all large towns and cities throughout the country, but now in the silence of night, lightly powdered with snow and bathed in soft moonlight, it had a magical quality.

I am so lucky to be in this lovely place, Madeleine thought as she slipped into the warmth of her bed, but seconds later as her eyelids drooped, her thoughts were of Sebastian: how he had looked as he tied the ribbons; how his voice had deepened when he said she should go to the ball. Life had suddenly become wonderfully exciting and she smiled as she drifted into sleep.

Then suddenly she was wide awake, trembling and with heart racing. She lay quite still, listening to the sound of someone moving very quietly across the room. The footsteps made hardly any noise, but there was the unmistakable sound of material brushing against carpet . . . A

61

shaft of moonlight fell across the room, and as the figure moved into it Madeleine felt the hair on her nape rise. But, as her eyes became fully accustomed to the dimness, she gasped with relief: the figure was that of Lady Frensham and she was sleepwalking. Still trembling a little, Madeleine slipped out of bed and approached her. She knew how important it was not to waken a sleepwalker abruptly, but the older woman's skin felt very cold, so with an arm around her waist and a hand on her shoulder, Madeleine turned her very gently and guided her out of the room. Lady Frensham did not waken until she was back in her own room, and then she sighed and asked sleepily, 'Where am I?'

'It is all right,' said Madeleine soothingly. 'You came into my room by mistake and I have just brought you back to bed.'

'Silly of me,' murmured Lady Frensham, still very drowsy, and she allowed Madeleine to lead her to the large half-tester just visible in the fading glow of the fire. Once more Madeleine sighed with relief, this time thankful that the older woman had accepted the brief explanation and was now allowing her thin legs to be raised on to the bed. She sank back on her pillows with a little gasping snore, and Madeleine smiled as she smelled the claret on her breath. She hoped very much that Lady Frensham's recollection of the incident would be hazy enough to save her embarrassment in the morning.

It was as she was making her way back along the corridor that she came face to face with Sebastian. She had heard his quick light footsteps on the stairs, and as he came towards her she shrank into a shallow recess, hoping that he might not see her in the darkness. He was softly humming the melody of the tarantella she had played the previous evening, and in the flickering light of his candle she could see that he looked relaxed, with a tiny smile lifting the corners of his mouth. Then instinct warned him that he was not alone. He stopped abruptly, a frown replacing the smile as he raised the candle and looked about him. Astonishment crossed his face as he realized who was flattened against the wall, and instantly his eyes swept over her, noting her dishevelled hair loose about her shoulders, her bare feet, and the fact that she was wearing only a nightgown.

'I – I was just returning to my room from – from – seeing your – '

'So I observe.' His eyes had flicked beyond her along the corridor and now came back to her, dark with fury. 'And how does my father?' he drawled, his voice ferocious in its icy smoothness.

It was Madeleine's turn to look astonished. 'Your father?' she queried, half turning to look back behind her as he had done. Then, as some realization dawned on her, she drew in a quick shuddering breath and whirled to face him. 'Why – you – you – ' a mixture of emotions rendered her speechless, but as her hand came up to slap his face, he seized her wrist and pressed it back against her breast.

'Oh, you mustn't do that,' he said softly, his tone of exaggerated concern belied by the snarl on his lips, 'for it spoils an otherwise faultless performance. But perhaps you've yet to learn that no well-bred young lady slaps a gentleman's face. Only whores and cheap little adventuresses do that! But don't try it on me, sweetheart, or I'll break every bone in your body!'

He towered over her, standing so close that she could smell the faint aroma of cigar from his velvet smoking jacket. He still held her wrist in a vice-like grip and she had little doubt of his menace and power. But anger was overriding astonishment and hurt now as she looked up at him. 'You dare to call yourself a gentleman, Captain de Lacey, a *gentle man* – when all you can do is snarl, insult and threaten!'

'How else am I to react when a little whore treats me

63

like an imbecile by pretending innocence, even when she is seen coming from the direction of my father's room – in her nightgown?' he demanded furiously.

For all her efforts, Madeleine could not quite suppress the quiver in her voice as she said, 'You may insult me as much as you wish, but do not dishonour your father, who has done nothing – *nothing* – except to try and take the place of my own father. I was sleeping when your aunt came in, sleepwalking. I have just taken her back to bed. If you ask her in the morning, she should have some vague recollection of it.'

For a few seconds Sebastian continued to hold her, studying her chalk-white face and the tears sparkling in her eyes. Then he released her wrist and stepped back. 'Is this true?' he asked very quietly.

She was beginning to tremble, and only pride kept her from bursting into tears. But she lifted her head in the way which he realized was very characteristic of her. 'Yes,' she said evenly. 'Absolutely true.'

He hesitated only very briefly. 'Then I believe I owe – '

But now it was her turn to cut in icily. 'I do not wish you to apologize, Captain de Lacey, for I know it would mean nothing. You are convinced that I am some sort of adventuress and it seems that nothing will alter that opinion. But I would ask you to remember that I did not seek to come here, nor did I want to do so; I only agreed because it was the wish of our two fathers that I should. If *I* could have a wish, it would be that I might never have to set eyes on you again!'

His shout of laughter was loud in the silent house. 'You are astonishing,' he said amicably. 'In fact, quite the most astonishing young female I have ever met!' Then he very nonchalantly bent down, took her chin in his hand and kissed her lingeringly on the lips. 'And you do have a very beautiful mouth,' he said softly as he straightened, the usual wolfish grin slowly spreading across his face. 'I bid you good-night, Miss Brett,' he said, and sauntered away as easily as if from a friendly meeting, leaving her too shaken to move or speak.

6

'I'm not very expert, but I think I could stitch some of the seams,' said Harriet eagerly as she watched Madeleine cutting out the ball gown. Both girls were kneeling on the floor of Madeleine's bedroom with the delicate muslin spread all around them.

'Oh, thank you, that would be a great help,' replied Madeleine, twisting round awkwardly in her dragging skirt to cut the deep curve of the neckline. 'There! That's the end of the cutting-out, thank goodness.' She sat back on her heels and held up two long pieces. 'If you're quite sure you don't mind, could you please stitch these together? I'll get on with the bodice. Of course, it'll have to be boned at the front, sides and back, but once that is done, I don't think the rest will take long.'

Madeleine felt she had to keep moving and talking to combat the great lassitude which threatened to overwhelm her. When Sebastian had left her, she had rubbed the back of her hand furiously across her mouth, while silently raging at him. Yet it had been her first kiss, and it had held a hint of tenderness which aroused new and all-powerful emotions in her. She was frightened at what was happening to her, and even while she told herself how odious Sebastian was, she could not stop thinking about him and waiting with a mixture of tingling fear and longing to see him again. But he had not appeared, and she had spent the day alternating between a dream-like state and acute nervous tension every time she heard a footstep.

'Well,' Harriet was saying happily, 'this *is* a nice change from Berlin work or making shell boxes, or even water-colouring. Tell me, Madeleine, don't you *honestly* feel a tiny bit bored sometimes?'

'Oh, I've not been here long enough to become bored, and my life in London was very different. But now – now that your brother is here, I expect you will be going out with him.' The words, although spoken with elaborate casualness, had been uttered against her will and she looked anxiously at Harriet, sure she would realize the real meaning behind them.

But Harriet, with a beatific smile on her face, was pursuing her own dream. 'Sebastian?' she answered absently. 'Oh, he went off at first light to Gloucestershire. He rides to hounds with the Berkeley, you know, and has gone to stay at the Castle. He never remains here very long – I think he finds us all rather dull and provincial.'

Madeleine bent her head over her sewing to hide the tears which threatened to spill over. The totally unexpected feeling of disappointment was the most devastating she had ever known. She wanted to be alone to pace about nonstop, to cry, and to think again and again over the night's events; but instead innate poise kept her sitting quietly on the floor, with a billowing mass of material on her lap.

'Of course,' Harriet was saying, 'it will be different when we're married. Madeleine, don't you *long* to be married?'

'Well, I – I – oh yes, but there's been no one to want to marry me.'

'Oh, but I'm sure there will be – you're so pretty, Madeleine. I expect someone will appear very suddenly, as Willie did to me.'

'But surely you've known him all your life?'

'Yes – and no. Being Aunt Thea's nephew on her late husband's side, and with all the family living so near at Norton St Philip, I had met Willie when we were children and had always known *of* him; but when we met again last spring it was the first time for fourteen years. It was very surprising the way we met, too, for it was not here, you know, oh no, it was on a Drawing Room Day at the Palace! I was to be presented – by Aunt Thea – and when we arrived we were greeted by two young men. One was in evening dress and the other – oh, the other looked absolutely gorgeous in the full-dress uniform of the Bengal Lancers, and it was Willie, home on furlough from India! Obviously Aunt Thea recognized him at once and he stayed with us all the time. We talked as easily as if we really had remained close friends all our lives and I think I fell in love with him there and then . . . Have you been presented, Madeleine?'

Madeleine, remembering the near destitution in which she had lived for the previous three years, could not help laughing a little, and as she shied away from the sad memories, she shook her head and asked, 'Was it exciting – being presented, I mean?'

'Yes, very. Even though the waiting *is* very tedious. Just when you think your legs will give way, you find the pages are spreading your train with their ivory poles and you hear your name announced – and you go forward, terrified that you'll fall when you curtsey, but of course you don't, and you suddenly realize that a very small white hand is being held out to you. That's the tricky part, for you have to keep your balance and put your own hand under the Queen's and very lightly kiss the back of it. Then you rise and back away – or rather, sidle away – and that is *the* most difficult of all because you have to handle your train with one hand and keep your bouquet in place with the other. As soon as you're out of the room, a page gathers up your train and throws it over your arm, and it's only then that you realize it is all over! You've kissed the hand of the greatest Queen in the world, in the very heart of the greatest Empire . . .'

Ellen, entering quietly, found both young girls with needles in mid-air, gazing into the middle distance as though bemused. Moonstruck, the pair of 'em, thought

Ellen disapprovingly, I can see I'll 'ave ter 'elp wif the dress if it's ever ter be ready in time, but 'oo'll escort my lamb ter the party?

This was a question which Lady Frensham had just put to her brother.

'I don't know, Thea,' the General replied worriedly. 'I confess it is causing me some concern.'

Lady Frensham took a generous sip of Madeira before she said, 'I suggest – not Sebastian.'

'Most definitely not Sebastian!' answered her brother decisively.

'How wise,' murmured Lady Frensham, with an approving sniff. She took two more meditative sips and then said, 'The last time I was at Norton St Philip, William introduced a most pleasant young man who was staying with him. I believe his name was Arbuthnot, Harry Arbuthnot. Now *he* would be most suitable and must surely have an invitation to the Templecombes' party; it would be ideal if he could accompany William to dinner here first, and then we could proceed together. Should we propose ourselves for luncheon today in the hope that you would be able to have a quiet word with him?'

'Excellent, Thea! Excellent!' said the General, his brow clearing. 'The girls are busy with their sewing, so we shall be able to slip away. I'll order the carriage immediately.'

Once at Frensham Park, it did not take the General long to approach young Mr Arbuthnot and ask him abruptly, 'Are you nesting, boy?'

'Why n-no, sir,' answered the startled youth, flushing deeply.

'Then my sister and I would very much like you to come to dinner with us on New Year's Eve and later accompany us to the Templecombes' party. We have a young girl staying with us who is charming and very pretty but she knows no one in Bath. Will you escort her?'

'I should be honoured, sir,' answered young Mr Arbuthnot, even as his heart sank. There *must* be something wrong with the girl, but he did not dare refuse the General, whose embarrassment made him appear unusually fierce.

The General flicked his handkerchief over the ends of his small clipped moustache and looked critically at himself in the splendid Adam mirror. His still handsome face – an older version of Sebastian's – gazed back at him and, except for a slight adjustment to his stock, he felt satisfied with his appearance. Not bad for an old un, he thought jovially, and winked at himself.

All his plans for the evening had worked out beautifully and he was feeling extremely content, having just risen from a magnificent dinner and more than his usual amount to drink. He normally ordered Perry not to be too lavish with champagne, but tonight was, of course, a special occasion: it was New Year's Eve, and he was about to accompany two radiantly pretty girls to an elegant evening party, and the young men escorting them were all he could wish for. To crown everything, Willie Frensham, within minutes of arriving, had asked his permission to marry Harriet. He had readily given this, knowing how besotted his daughter was with Willie. He'd never been able to understand why, since to him Willie appeared a very ordinary, none too bright young man. Still, he came of a fine old family and would make Harriet a very good, stolid husband, and any husband – even a bad one – was better than no husband at all. It was a matter of intense relief to any father to know that his daughter would be protected and provided for, since the fate of a single woman without money was indeed a sorry one.

Darling Harrie, the General thought fondly, how well she had turned out and how like her mother she was, both in character and colouring, while Sebastian, of course, was entirely a de Lacey and therefore too much like himself to make for an easy relationship. How different would Sebastian have been, wondered the General, if Margaret had lived? The ten-year-old boy had certainly been heartbroken by her death, and packing him straight off to Eton might have been a mistake.

'Ah, Margaret, Margaret,' murmured the General, remembering how she had quietly slipped away following Harriet's birth. He had never forgotten her and never found anyone to replace her, even though there had been numerous affaires over the years, plus a very accommodating little widow in Bristol. He remembered that he had been quite attached to her; she knew none of the tricks of her professional sisters, but had striven to please. When the purchase of Sebastian's commission and the expense of Harriet's début had forced him to give up the widow, she had cried silently with every show of sincerity, but had not made a fuss. Very infrequently he wondered what had become of her and once, when he was hurrying to catch a train at Bristol, he thought he had glimpsed her youngest son selling matches and bootlaces. There had seemed to be a gleam of recognition in the lad's eyes, but it had not really been possible to be sure through all the grime and tattered clothing, and the train had been about to depart. On his few subsequent trips to Bristol he had never remembered to look for the boy.

Thank God, the need for women was not nearly so strong now and he could look forward to a serene old age. But an occasion like tonight should be shared by a wife, and suddenly he felt the prick of tears in his eyes. Damme, I'm getting maudlin, he thought disgustedly, and with an impatient tug at his brocaded waistcoat he turned and strode into the hall. He came to an abrupt halt, his sense of wellbeing immediately fading, for Sebastian, in the full-dress uniform of his regiment, was standing there, clearly awaiting the ladies.

71

'Sebastian, *you* here!' rasped his father, his face a study of amazement. 'And in full fig, too! What does this mean?'

'Why, that I am attending the party of course,' replied Sebastian smoothly.

'Not quite your style of entertainment, is it?' remarked the General acidly. 'And I cannot remember your willingness to attend in previous years.'

'Ah, but then there was not the same inducement,' said his son, eyes never leaving the top of the stairs.

'Well, I'm afraid you'll be superfluous to our party,' continued the General, too angry to even try and be civil. 'But no doubt you will find your entertainment elsewhere.'

'No doubt,' agreed his son equably.

Harriet had whispered her good news to Madeleine, who had impulsively hugged her, and they now came into view laughing together. They were halfway down the stairs before Harriet caught sight of her brother. 'Sebastian!' she exclaimed delightedly. 'How wonderful to see you! We did not think you would be here tonight!'

The eyes of both men were on Madeleine, who had halted momentarily and then continued down the stairs very calmly, only the sudden whitening of her face betraying the shock she felt.

'Oh, I assure you that wild horses would not have kept me from joining you this evening,' Sebastian said, answering his sister but keeping his eyes still fixed on Madeleine. As she reached the foot of the stairs he took her hand and bent over it. 'May I say how truly beautiful Cinderella looks in her ball gown,' he told her softly, his eyes alight with admiration.

'Thank you,' whispered Madeleine, hardly able to look up at him and wondering if he could hear the painful thudding of her heart. She felt both dazed and dazzled for there was no doubt that Sebastian, wearing the full-dress uniform of the Eleventh Hussars, was a most spectacular sight: the dark blue tight-fitting jacket was almost entirely braided and fastened in gold across the chest; the cherry-coloured trousers, with a broad gold stripe on the outside leg, were strapped under the instep of his shining ankle boots, while from his left shoulder was slung a fur-bordered blue pelisse, heavily embroidered with gold. His head was held proudly above the high collar and he stood immensely tall and ramrod straight, broad shoulders and trim waist emphasized by the tapered jacket, and powerful thighs moulded by the close-fitting trousers. White gloves and long-necked silver spurs completed the uniform, which would have made even an insignificant man look handsome; on Sebastian de Lacey the effect was magnificent and totally dazzling.

He took a bouquet of white roses and lily-of-the-valley from a side table and held it out to Madeleine. 'And may I offer you these white roses – "for a heart that has never known love" – which I believe is the correct message, is it not?'

'Quite correct,' she said composedly, not hearing the mockery in his voice and looking up at him now with delight touching her lips and eyes.

Already she is half in love with him, groaned the General despairingly to himself. But I will not, most definitely not, let him break her heart.

She is all mine, thought Sebastian triumphantly as his eyes devoured the long slender throat, the white shoulders and the fluttering breast. And I want her – my God, how I want her!

'Why, Madeleine, now you have two bouquets, for surely Mr Arbuthnot brought you that posy of pink roses. What shall you do with two?' asked Harriet.

Acutely aware that all eyes were upon her, Madeleine gathered up the remnants of her poise and replaced Sebastian's bouquet on the table. Then she picked up the smaller one of pink roses and said calmly, 'I believe I shall be able to use both. If you will excuse me?' And she started back up the stairs.

The General hastily pulled out a thin gold half-hunter, compared its time with that of the long case clock in the corner, and said, 'We must leave in ten minutes, Madeleine.'

She managed to smile down at him with a serenity she was far from feeling. 'I shall be back in good time,' she said, forcing herself to a slow and graceful ascent. But once out of sight at the top, she gathered up her skirts and dashed into her room, which Ellen was still tidying.

'Ellen,' she said a little breathlessly, 'will you please help me undo these flowers so that I can put some in my hair.'

Ellen put her head on one side and considered; she had washed and brushed Madeleine's hair into shining smoothness, then arranged it in a thick plait which stood up like a halo around her head. 'Yes, miss, I think I can do tha',' she answered, and began ruthlessly cutting the ribbons and gold paper from around the flowers.

'I must be ready in ten minutes,' said Madeleine, sitting down at her mirror in a puffball of skirts.

'Plenty o' time,' replied Ellen soothingly. Expertly she snipped off the few thorns and began threading the long stems through the plait so that behind each ear lay a cluster of pale pink rosebuds.

'Oh, lovely, lovely, Ellen!'

Ellen stood back to survey her work. 'Yes, reely lov'ly, Miss Madleen, an' how abou' tuckin' these few lef' over buds in the fron' o' yer bodice?'

'Yes, please, if we have time, but I promised not to keep the General waiting.'

Once more Ellen snipped off the thorns and then bound the stems with their ribbon and tucked the whole into the

74

centre of the neckline, securing it with pins inside the bodice. 'How's tha' then, miss?' she asked triumphantly.

Madeleine turned to hug her impulsively. 'Ellen, you are a darling!' she exclaimed, excitement suddenly bubbling within her. She was going to her first dance and knew she looked pretty.

In the corridor, Lady Frensham, in ruby velvet and with diamonds circling her brow and throat, was making her slow progress towards the stairs. She had never commented upon the sleepwalking incident, but since then her manner towards Madeleine had imperceptibly warmed, and she now stopped, raised her lorgnette and surveyed her silently.

'I – I hope you approve of my gown,' said Madeleine, made suddenly nervous and uncertain by the older woman's stare.

Lady Frensham unhurriedly closed the lorgnette. 'Quite delightful,' she pronounced at last, still poker-faced. 'But a suitable covering is needed.' Without turning, she said to her maid, who was hovering just behind her, 'Wilson, bring my pink velvet cloak immediately!'

When the maid scurried back with the cloak, Lady Frensham ordered imperiously, 'Place it around Miss Brett's shoulders.' It was a beautiful garment of deep rose velvet lined with paler pink silk and embroidered around the edges with a wide border of rosebuds in white and pink.

'Oh,' exclaimed Madeleine, 'it is most lovely, but of course I cannot – '

'You will oblige me by not being a foolish gal,' interposed Lady Frensham at her most autocratic. 'I wish you to wear the cloak, and that is the end of the matter. I suggest we do not keep my brother waiting any longer.' She had already resumed her stately progress, leaving Madeleine to stammer her thanks and follow in her wake.

Downstairs in the hall, Harriet, surrounded by the men

of their party, was saying excitedly, 'Yes, and to mark the occasion papa has given me mama's circlet – Willie dear, is it not pretty? It is mounted on plaited brown velvet and, look, the leaves are of green enamel and the tiny orange blossoms are of very fine porcelain; it is almost identical to one given by the Prince to Her Majesty, you know, and there are brooches and long earrings to match, but aunt says I may not wear these until we are married.'

'Certainly not,' Lady Frensham interjected, effortlessly joining the conversation. 'Long earrings on a young gal would be entirely unsuitable, but the circlet is very becoming on your fair hair, Harriet.'

There were murmurs of assent from everyone, and Mr Arbuthnot, a young man with a huge voice, whose vocabulary appeared limited to 'By Jove!' and 'I say!', now boomed out emphatically, 'By Jove, Miss Harriet, I do agree!'

Madeleine stood a little apart from the others and Sebastian moved so that he was beside her. She was instantly conscious of his height and power and, quietly, like a worm in the brain, came the thought that it would be wonderful to be loved by him, to know that all that strength and power were for, rather than against her. There would be no more terrors, no more doubts and fears to face then! As though reading her thoughts, he slipped an arm around her waist, and involuntarily she leant against it in a moment of surrender and longing. She turned her head to look up at him, and the magic shattered as she encountered the triumphant look in his eyes, the thin smile on his long mouth. She gave a tiny, strangled sound of hurt, but almost at once she straightened her spine and lifted her head as she deliberately moved away from him.

Sebastian regarded her through narrowed eyes, and for the first time felt a twinge of regret that she was only an adventuress playing a deep and very careful game, for now she looked so vulnerable, so genuinely hurt. By God, though, she was desirable! It was not only her undoubted beauty, but the extreme fragility of her body, the feeling that he could break it, that aroused him; he wanted to kiss the unfashionable but endearing hollows at the base of her throat, to pull the demure gown from her shoulders so that he could caress her breasts until they swelled. How would she be in the throes of passion? he wondered. Her soft mouth had sensuous curves to it, but she had not responded to his kiss. He wanted to see her with her long neck thrown back, her eyes half-closed, and those lips parted for him – he wanted to devour her!

The General, who had watched the whole incident from under beetling brows and interpreted his son's thoughts fairly accurately, now set about mobilizing his party. As the last of them left the house, he turned furiously to Sebastian. 'Why don't you get out of that uniform and take yourself off somewhere to cool your hot blood? I am sure I do not need to tell you where to go!'

As always when his father raged at him, Sebastian became ice-cold. He inclined his head and said suavely: 'No, indeed not, sir! And I shall undoubtedly take your advice – after the party!'

The General glared at him but knew he was defeated. As the footman put his cape around his shoulders and handed him his silk hat, he said, 'Well, there is no room in the carriages for you. You will have to make your own way to Marchmont Court.'

Sebastian bowed. 'As you wish, sir.'

'And may I remind you, sir,' barked the General, drawing on his white gloves with hands that shook despite his efforts to control them, 'that while Madeleine Brett is our guest, she is entitled to our complete protection – *as gentlemen* – for her happiness and well-being. Anything less than this would be a dishonour to our name. Do I make myself clear?'

Sebastian bowed again. 'But of course, sir.' His tone was impeccable. Then, in complete contradiction to his words, he smiled cynically at his father while devil-may-care lights sparkled in his eyes.

'Damn your bloody insolence!' roared the General as he stormed out.

Marchmont Court, home of the Templecombe family, was a magnificent Palladian-style mansion standing on high ground, with terraces and gardens falling away in a graceful sweep. On that New Year's Eve lights blazed not only from windows of the central house but also from its massive wings, and a never-ending stream of carriages bowled along the drive to deposit their occupants beneath the shelter of the splendid Corinthian colonnade. Inside, logs blazed beneath a great marble overmantel, elaborately sculptured, and the myriad tiny candles on a huge Christmas tree vied with the lights from the central chandelier and numerous wall sconces. A marble staircase curved elegantly upwards to where Lord and Lady Templecombe awaited their guests. Beyond them, open double doors revealed a huge drawing room where rows of small gilt chairs were set out facing a raised dais, banked with flowers.

In the warmth and brilliance of the scene, Madeleine's emotions, which had been in a turmoil, began to lighten. On all sides people were greeting the General and his party and introductions were being made: 'May I present Miss Madeleine Brett, who is our house guest?'

'Sir George Cholmondeley.'

'Admiral and Mrs Mainwaring.'

'The Honourable Frederick Allan.'

'Lord and Lady Clefton.'

'Why, Sophie!' Harriet exclaimed delightedly as she moved to embrace a tall woman with hair the colour of a newly minted sovereign. 'What a wonderful surprise. I did not think to see you here!'

Madeleine could not take her eyes off Sophie Clefton, like most people meeting her for the first time, but she was so dazzled that she was never able to remember her beauty in detail; she was merely conscious of flawless skin, startlingly white against pale gold hair; of plump, fashionably sloping shoulders rising above a froth of green, and of large eyes full of sweetness.

'Sophie, I must tell you that Willie and I became engaged this evening,' Harriet was saying breathlessly.

'Why, my dearest Harriet, what wonderful news! I am so very happy for you,' said Lady Clefton, embracing her once again before turning to Willie. Her long white-gloved arm was extended to him. 'May I offer you my congratulations?' she said, looking him straight in the eye with disarming candour. Then she turned and greeted the rest of the party, her limpid gaze resting on each in turn, her perfect rosebud mouth – so much in fashion – smiling and uttering a pleasantry to one and all. 'But where is Sebastian?' she asked at last. 'I had heard he was home on furlough.'

'Where else should I be but beside the most beautiful woman in England?' There was no mistaking the drawl, and Sophie Clefton whirled with a great sweep of skirts and a drift of Rose Thé perfume. 'Why, Sebastian, you devil!' she exclaimed laughingly as she tapped him on the chest with her fan. 'I might have guessed you would be here all the time – and still given to *the* most fulsome compliments. I can tell you have not changed one little bit.'

Sebastian bending over her hand, looked up at her from under his straight black brows. His eyes were full of dancing lights and his smile distinctly rakish as he said, 'No, I've not changed. Have you?'

It seemed that even Sophie Clefton's poise was not

equal to this, and it was left to Harriet to break the sudden silence. 'Sophie, what a wonderful gown!'

Sophie turned at once to smile and give her entire attention to Harriet. 'Yes, isn't it? I got it in Paris at Maison Gagelin, where there is an amazing Englishman named Worth who designs the most heavenly clothes. Then dear George gave me the emeralds to match. Are they not beautiful?' She moved her head prettily from side to side so that the light caught the deep colour of the gems dangling from her ears.

'Oh, yes,' breathed Harriet, sounding quite in awe.

Sebastian had been openly looking at the large square emerald which, suspended on a thin link of diamonds, lay between Sophie's full breasts. 'This is particularly fine, I think,' he said, straight-faced but with laughter in his voice.

Madeleine heard the General mutter, 'My God!' under his breath, and then Lady Frensham said in her most imperious tone, '*Do* let us move into the drawing room.'

Sebastian was still bending over Sophie. 'I do hope you will spare me a dance, if your programme is not entirely full.'

She detached the card from her wrist. 'Why, of course, Sebastian! And there is so much you must tell me.'

'H'm, but I see all the dances are already bespoken, except the first one.'

Sophie turned to the portly red-faced man, who so far had been entirely silent. 'Oh, that one is reserved for my dear George!' she said, giving him her sweetest smile.

Sebastian, too, turned to Lord Clefton. 'My lord,' he said, bowing, 'would you deny a childhood friend just one dance with your most exquisite wife?'

Lord Clefton guffawed as though vastly amused, although the others did not even smile. 'No, indeed not!' he exclaimed as he clapped Sebastian heartily on the back. 'Anything to keep a gallant soldier happy and a pretty woman amused!' But, Madeleine watching numbly, thought she saw fury in his small eyes.

Sebastian bowed again. 'I shall await it with the utmost impatience, but first we have to endure the concert!'

Moments later Madeleine, seated between the General and Mr Arbuthnot, began trying to sort out her thoughts. Seeing Sebastian with Sophie had suddenly made her aware of her own feelings towards him; she had convinced herself that she disliked him as much as he appeared to dislike her, yet she had thought constantly of his kiss, waited every day for his reappearance and felt only half alive when he was absent. Surely I cannot be falling in love with him, she thought miserably now, for how foolish, how hopeless that would be when he obviously adores Sophie.

Sebastian had not seated himself with his family, and Madeleine turned her head from side to side, only half realizing that she was looking for him. He was sitting with the Cleftons, just behind her across the centre aisle, leaning slightly towards Sophie as she whispered to him behind her fan. But his eyes were fixed on Madeleine with a look of such depth and intensity that it was as though he had pinned her to the wall, as a butterfly is pinned to a board, she thought distractedly. Quite unknowingly, she showed all her wistful longing in her huge eyes.

She was totally unable to concentrate on the music and hardly a note registered with her, although she applauded automatically when everyone else did. When the recital finally ended and the major domo announced that supper was served, Madeleine rose with the others, and only then realized how stiff her entire body felt with the tension of knowing that Sebastian's eyes had been constantly upon her. With the utmost difficulty she refrained from turning in his direction as she heard the General say, 'It is our host's duty to tell us which lady we shall each have the privilege of taking into supper, but I've no doubt he will have selected Mr Arbuthnot for you, Madeleine.'

'Oh, but I say, sir – ' began that young man, when another voice cut in smoothly:

'Indeed not, father! Lord Templecombe has asked *me* to take in Miss Brett!' And there was Sebastian, grave-faced but with triumph in his eyes as he looked at her.

The General whirled angrily to face him. 'This is most irregular! Mr Arbuthnot is in our party, not you. What – what did you *say* to Templecombe to make him choose you?'

'Why, I merely pointed out that as Miss Brett is said to be rather shy and is not acquainted with anyone here, I thought she might feel happier if I were to escort her. And his Lordship was in total agreement.'

The General turned back to his guest. 'Arbuthnot, this is the most deuced situation and I can only apologize for my son!'

Mr Arbuthnot, growing ever pinker, nevertheless rose magnificently to the occasion. Bowing, he said, 'I quite understand Captain de Lacey's sentiments and while I am naturally disappointed, I shall look forward to rejoining you all and dancing with Miss Brett after supper. Now, if you will excuse me, sir, I will go to escort Miss March-mont, as his Lordship has already requested.' It was undoubtedly the longest speech of his life, and with his acceptance of the situation General de Lacey knew there was nothing further he could do. He stood aside, furious but silent, as Sebastian bowed and offered his arm to Madeleine.

She hesitated, suddenly conscious of her simple muslin gown and her uncertain status, knowing that to be escorted by the most desirable man present would make her the cynosure of all eyes. Then Sebastian said very softly so that only she could hear, 'Come, don't falter now. This is the greatest chance you'll ever have: you've been presented by my father, chaperoned by my aunt and are now to make an entrance with me. Play it well and you'll be accepted by everyone.'

Madeleine was too bewildered to analyse his words or motive, but only knew that he had asked for her and that she must not let him down. So she moved to his side, tucking her hand just within his elbow and adjusting the bouquet in her other hand so that she held it gracefully. Then, as she fell into step with him, she raised her head shyly but with growing confidence, and so great was his charisma that many actually stood aside to let them pass. Many, too, in that glittering company looked with curiosity, envy or admiration at the handsome, gorgeously attired man who exuded such power, vitality and maleness, and the mysterious girl whose fragile beauty, made her look so vulnerable.

In the dining room, round tables for eight or ten persons were set in a huge circle, while at the far end a line of liveried servants stood behind a splendid buffet table, its damask-covered sides beswagged with flowers and ribbons, its top displaying every imaginable cold delicacy, all set out in the family's magnificent old silver dishes.

As the meal progressed and the champagne flowed ever faster, light-hearted chatter and laughter filled the room, but at the de Lacey table conversation was spasmodic. The General was brooding, Madeleine was completely overawed by the magnificence of everything, and Lady Frensham, who had slept through the entire recital, only to be startled into sudden wakefulness by the final applause, had not recovered sufficiently to be sociable.

Sebastian said softly to Madeleine, 'You are very quiet, Miss Brett. Are you perhaps dreaming of the day when you might become the chatelaine of a house such as this?'

Madeleine turned to him, smiling at such an absurdity. 'Why, such a thought never occurred to me.'

The black brows lifted. 'No? But there *is* an heir who is said to be looking for a wife, and already this evening he has asked about you. As he is Aunt Thea's godson, you will undoubtedly meet him.'

Madeleine laughed outright then. 'Forgive me, Captain de Lacey, but I fear you are being somewhat absurd. I am a stranger here, without family and' – with a little gesture of her hand, she indicated all the beautifully gowned, highly eligible girls around the room.

'Very good . . . very *jeune fille* . . . very convincing,' Sebastian murmured enigmatically, even as the major domo rapped his tall white cane three times for silence.

'My lords, ladies and gentlemen,' he intoned solemnly, 'pray rise for the Loyal Toast!'

The guests stood instantly, all the stiff taffetas, the supple satins and jewel-deep velvets rustling and whispering as their wearers moved. Then Lord Templecombe raised his glass high. 'The Queen, God bless her!'

'The Queen!' everyone echoed, then drank, and as glasses were lowered, the great ormolu clock on the mantelpiece began to strike, followed by all the other clocks in the house, from tinkling chimes to heavy sonorous booms. Everyone stood immobile except for the footmen who moved silently from table to table replenishing glasses. As the twelfth stroke began to fade, bells from the Abbey and other churches all over the city rang out.

'My friends, it is 1854 – Happy New Year to you all!' shouted Lord Templecombe, and the greeting was immediately taken up as glasses were clinked and toasts drunk.

Sebastian, touching his glass with Madeleine's, whispered, 'To us!' and drank, his eyes holding hers with dark intensity.

Then the double doors were flung open and a small orchestra playing 'Auld Lang Syne' as they walked, advanced smilingly into the room. Instantly people moved between the tables to link hands and form a huge circle, all singing heartily as formality was momentarily forgotten. But Madeleine, her hands linked with those of Sebastian and the General, felt sudden tears rise to her eyes, for something was not quite right; she did not know what, only that Sebastian's words held some kind of vague threat. Yet as the singing ended, he bent low to kiss her finger tips. 'Happy New Year, Madeleine,' he whispered, letting her hand go with seeming reluctance.

When dancing was announced people began to move to the stairs, their laughter and chatter muffling sounds of the music, and soon the ballroom was like a living bouquet from the adjoining conservatory, so many and varied were the colours of the gowns. And everywhere the silver lace of flounces, the mother-of-pearl of fans and the diamonds encircling foreheads and throats were all caught in the light of hundreds of candles.

Mr Arbuthnot immediately claimed Madeleine for the first dance, which required his full concentration. It was only at the end that he ventured an enthusiastic: 'I say, Miss Brett, you do dance well', which was more than could be said of him, poor fellow, as he seemed to have exceptionally large feet and only a very vague idea of what to do with them. Madeleine was glad when the dance ended, but within a short time the music began again and then, unbelievably, it was Sebastian himself who was bowing and saying, 'This is my dance, I believe, Miss Brett.'

Never for a moment had she thought he would wish to dance with her, and she could only look up at him and ask stupidly, 'Are you sure?'

'Of course I am sure,' he replied impatiently. 'I marked your card before we left the house. Come, you will surely not deny me the pleasure of this waltz – "The Love

Song"?' The familiar mocking look was back in his eyes, the sarcastic tone in his voice.

Madeleine rose, uncertain and trembling, and as his arm encircled her waist she stumbled a little. Instantly his arm tightened until she was pressed against him. 'I do not think you should hold me so tightly,' she said, trying to rally herself against the sudden lethargy of her limbs.

'Indeed, I shall hold you as I want,' he retorted, as arrogant as ever.

'Then I shall refuse to dance!' she replied, and stood still.

'Are you trying to quarrel with me, Madeleine?' he asked softly, instantly demolishing all her defences.

'Why no, I – I – '

'Or are you using this as an excuse because you do not really dance the waltz?'

That brought her eyes up to his, huge and astonished once more. 'Of course I dance the waltz!'

'And do you reverse?' he persisted in the same mocking tone.

Real anger rose then, stiffening her spine and making her raise her head proudly. 'Try me!' she said defiantly.

His laugh was deep and delighted. 'Oh, I shall, I shall!' he exclaimed, and suddenly smiled at her with real warmth. She just had time to notice how different his eyes looked when they crinkled at the corners into a real smile, and then he was whirling her into the rhythm of the dance and she forgot everything except the sparkling music and the delicious feeling that she was floating.

Sebastian was a superlative dancer, very light and quick; he guided her expertly and smiled when he felt the rigidity go from her spine and her small hand begin to rest trustingly in his. She was feather-light in his arms and as her steps began to match his in perfect rhythm, his desire for her was renewed. When he saw her head tilt back on her long neck and her eyes half close with sheer delight in the moment, he whirled her quickly and expertly out of the ballroom and into the huge conservatory.

There, in the shadows, he pulled her roughly against him and his mouth came down harshly against hers. For a few seconds she could not take in what was happening to her: she had been lost in the music of the dance and it was inconceivable that in a public place she should suddenly be almost lifted off her feet and crushed against the length of his body; that she should feel a hand intimately cupping her breast and another holding her at the nape, with long fingers caressing her throat. Then his lips moved to nibble her ear before descending to linger on her neck. She felt his powerful frame shake as he murmured huskily, 'I want you, sweetheart, I want you more than I've ever wanted any woman – to make love to, day and night . . .' His wide shoulders and black head were very close; it would have needed so little effort to wind her arms around his neck, to rest her cheek against his hair, and the shattering knowledge that she wanted to do so made her even more rigid. Then his mouth was back on hers, hungrily parting her lips and driving the remaining breath from her body.

But gradually, through the haze of his desire, Sebastian became aware of her total lack of response. He tore his mouth from hers and lifted his head to look at her, his black eyes opaque and narrowed. 'Come now, love,' he drawled, suddenly once more in command of himself, 'I am sure your other lovers have taught you to respond better than this.'

She was totally shattered and could only whisper, 'But I have not had any other lovers.'

Sebastian gave a bark of derisive laughter and thrust her away until he was holding her at arm's length. 'Oh, really? Well, I assure you *that* is no problem, for I am entirely at your service and shall be a most willing teacher!'

At last some reality was returning to her. 'Are you mad?' she whispered, thinking they were still in the ballroom and looking wildly around her.

'Ah, come on now, Madeleine, this silly play-acting has gone on long enough! Stop it at once and tell me you'll come back to London with me in the morning. I still have two weeks' furlough and we can be together the whole time.' He pulled her back so that once again she was crushed against him. 'You and I belong together and can give each other many hours of wonderful pleasure – I can promise you that!'

Panic was now beginning to make Madeleine desperate. 'Oh, let me go, let me go!' she whispered frantically, trying to push him away. 'How dare you treat me like this – and in a public place too!'

He released her so suddenly then that she reeled against the wall. 'You know,' he said casually, 'your act is really very good and I can quite understand how you've come to hoodwink my poor fool of a father.'

Mention of the General and the thought of her debt to him rallied Madeleine as nothing else could have done at that moment. 'Your father is a kind, honourable man who deserves a son with – with a sense of decency!' she exclaimed, trying not to stammer. 'Not a – a savage beast who only wants to hurt and destroy! And – and so reckless too! If – if anyone had walked through here just now your life would have been ruined and your family disgraced.'

He shrugged indifferently. 'I hoped it might be worth the risk.'

'And – what of my reputation?' demanded Madeleine, anger just managing to keep the tears in check.

Lights danced in his black eyes as he slowly and suggestively let them rake her body. 'Your – er – reputation?'

'Yes, my reputation,' she retorted with spirit. 'I do have one, you know, and it is not my intention to lose it!'

'Well said, my dear, and with every appearance of sincerity too! You really should be on the boards – but perhaps you have been?'

'Why?' she whispered. 'Why do you persist in thinking so ill of me? What *could* I have done to make you consider me so worthless?'

What indeed? At that moment he might have begun to doubt his judgement, but then he remembered Sophie and *her* apparent sweetness and candour – and he knew only too well what a complete charlatan Sophie was. So again he shrugged and said bitterly, 'I know your type very well and you are all the same.'

'But you know nothing, nothing about me at all!' Madeleine protested passionately. 'And I did not ask to join your family.'

The heavy brows went up at that. 'No?' he queried. 'What proof have we that you and your father did not carefully plot the whole thing when you both realized he was dying?'

She looked up at him then, shaken to the depths of her being and profoundly shocked. 'You really believe that possible?'

'Why not?' he queried again. 'It's been done before.'

Heartbreak made her suddenly exhausted and totally defeated. Her eyes closed fleetingly and then she said very calmly, 'I see it is hopeless. You only believe what you want to believe, so think what you will of me, but please stop – stop tormenting me and just leave me alone!'

'Why, certainly my dear, if that is what you wish,' Sebastian drawled. And with a complete change of manner which made her gasp, he bowed perfunctorily, turned on his heel and walked casually away.

Madeleine gazed after him open-mouthed. Having whisked her out of the ballroom in front of hundreds of curious eyes, he had now left her to make her own way back unescorted. For a second she wanted to rush forward and beat her fists on the broad, immaculately clad back, but then her arms dropped to her sides; it would have no effect whatever and there was nothing for it but to return alone and face them all. Agitatedly her hands moved to smooth her hair, and then she realized her gown was torn at the neck and hung very low over one shoulder; hastily she pushed it up to match the other side, but it immediately fell again. With something like despair, she knew that she would either have to leave it lopsided or else pull down the undamaged side, but that would leave much of her breasts and back exposed. She looked wildly around her, but there appeared to be only one exit from the conservatory, and that led directly into the ballroom; she would have to cross the vast floor alone to reach the General's party on the far side. And in a dress which might fall to her waist if she were not careful! I cannot do it, she thought wildly, but I cannot stay here either.

For a few moments panic took over completely, but then she suddenly quietened. I have done nothing wrong, she thought, and I *will* walk across that room and will *not* let my gown fall down! It was then that she remembered the pins Ellen had used to secure the rosebuds inside her bodice, and with shaking fingers she removed the flowers and pinned the tear so neatly that only close scrutiny would reveal it. Then she shook out the flounces on her skirt, straightened her spine and stepped forward.

It was unfortunate that almost at once the music should stop and the dancers begin dispersing, so that by the time Madeleine was crossing the ballroom she found herself alone in the middle of the huge floor. Her step faltered as the thought came unbidden to her mind that she was an unknown orphan, wearing a pinned-together homemade gown, crossing one of the most elegant rooms in the country under the eyes of a fashionable and curious crowd. It would have been easy then to panic once more, to cover her face with her hands and rush blindly into the nearest corner, but instead Madeleine moved forward, her back a straight, slender line from the top of her head to where her skirt billowed at the waist. And there were many who admired the tall, willowy girl with the cameo-like features and elegant walk as she progressed slowly across the floor. Only the bright spots of colour under her cheek bones betrayed her feelings, and even Sebastian, watching her through narrowed eyes, felt a twinge of admiration. He made a move to go to her, but his father forestalled him, striding quickly across to bow and offer his arm with all the courtesy he would have given a Princess of the Blood.

'Ah, there you are, my dear,' he said gently as he smiled down at her.

'I – I just felt I needed a little fresh air,' she whispered hoarsely. She tried to smile but her face felt stiff.

The General pressed her hand briefly against his side. 'I understand,' he said. 'But now, do come back to us because we have missed you.' And his eyes locked with those of his son across the room in anger and contempt. Damn you, thought the General, damn you for ruining her evening and jeopardizing her reputation.

Madeleine was still trembling as she sank gratefully on to a chair, hardly hearing Harriet say excitedly to her, 'Madeleine, you must remind me to tell you all about Sophie Clefton's meeting with the Empress Eugénie – she had a private audience and they talked fashion all the time. It sounds *fascinating*!'

The General was plainly concerned about Madeleine's now chalk-white face, but people were moving on to the floor for the lancers and he said, 'I am engaged to Lady Templecombe for this dance, so I must leave you, but I suggest Mr Arbuthnot fetches you a glass of white wine, my dear.' Not waiting for her reply, he turned to the young man, who was hovering uncertainly. 'Arbuthnot – would you mind?'

'Sir!' exclaimed Willie. 'May I dance again with Harriet, as we are engaged to be married?'

For once even the General was indecisive and stood with head bent, jingling the loose change in his pocket as he considered.

'Oh, please, papa, *please*,' begged Harriet, round-eyed and with hands clasped imploringly.

The General chuckled and patted her cheek. 'Oh, get along with you then and dance!' He turned smilingly to Willie. 'I warn you, William, you are marrying a little baggage who knows exactly how to get her own way.'

'I know, sir, and it makes me the happiest of fellows,' replied his future son-in-law as he took Harriet's hand and moved forward with her.

'Decorum!' boomed Lady Frensham, whom everyone had forgotten. 'Decorum must always be observed!'

Sebastian's bark of laughter was derisive. 'Yes, of course. Like that unbroken line from the Conqueror, it must never be forgotten.'

Lady Frensham remained sitting stiffly in her chair and continued to stare straight ahead. '*You* of all people, Sebastian, should remember that,' she said coldly.

He acknowledged the rebuke with a deep bow. 'My dear aunt,' he said deferentially even as his eyes met hers mockingly. He was, in fact, in somewhat of a quandary: Madeleine had begged him to leave her alone, yet the next dance was his and he wanted overwhelmingly to hold her in his arms again. Silently he acknowledged that there had been something very courageous about the way she had walked alone across the room, and he knew he had behaved very badly. Now, to his intense surprise, he wanted to make up for that and to hold her, not roughly or with passion as before, but gently, protectively, and to watch her come sweetly to life again; to see soft colour in her cheeks and those remarkable eyes become luminous with reflected light. How better to do that than in the dance? Although she was clearly furious about his conduct, surely she would prefer to be with him rather than that – that baby boy they had teamed her with. So he moved to Madeleine and bowed. 'Shall we dance?' he asked pleasantly.

She looked at him over the top of her fan, eyes blank with amazement at his effrontery. 'If you will glance at your card,' he suggested, and watched her eyes darken until they resembled the winter sky outside.

'I have no need to look at my card,' Madeleine replied quietly. 'I do not wish to dance.'

'*What!*' It was the first time he had ever been refused, and he stared at her unbelievingly.

'I think you heard me,' Madeleine said, clenching her hands in her lap to keep her composure.

'But of course you must stand up with me!' Sebastian retorted, anger now beginning to replace that first hint of tenderness.

Oh, would the beast never go, she thought wildly, as she heard her own voice say calmly, 'I am indisposed.'

The frowning black brows rose mockingly. 'Indeed? And yet you look – radiant.'

Madeleine raised her head so that her eyes gazed into his very coolly and levelly. 'Captain de Lacey, please understand that I cannot and will not dance with you.'

All his suspicions returned with a sudden thought and he smiled rakishly at her. 'So, if you are indisposed, you will no doubt wish to be escorted back to my father's house.'

She snapped her fan shut, her composure almost cracking. 'I most certainly do not! And if I did, I would rather go alone than with you.'

But he had the last word after all. 'I do not believe I have offered to escort you,' he said coldly.

It was Lady Frensham who rescued Madeleine. 'Sebastian,' she said in her usual imperious tone, 'I do think you should pay your respects to Miss Llewellyn Morgan, who appears to have just arrived with her father.'

'Ah yes, you are quite right,' Sebastian drawled. 'I must certainly hasten to greet my future wife. If you will excuse me, ladies?' He saw Madeleine's eyes become blank again and he smiled dazzlingly at her as he bowed and turned away, unconcernedly aware that the eyes of most women in the room were upon him. The eternal hunter, he stalked females of all ages and types, bedded them, used them and very soon left them. Immensely successful as a lover, he accepted admiration and acquiescence as his due and was genuinely amazed that Madeleine had not capitulated.

Oh, thank heaven, Madeleine thought exhaustedly as she watched him stride away. She saw him tower over a short figure in an exquisite white satin gown, and within minutes he had whirled her into the dance. As they approached and she saw them conversing animatedly, the girl flushed, Sebastian's attention seemingly riveted upon her, new emotion swept through Madeleine. His *future wife*, he had said, and at once she remembered the strength of his arms about her and the feel of his lips on hers. Surely I cannot be jealous, she thought dazedly; but the thought of anyone else being in his arms was unbearable. I must be going mad, she thought, and when Harry Arbuthnot approached with her wine she almost snatched the glass and drank avidly.

'Mr Arbuthnot, I, too, require a glass of white wine,' announced Lady Frensham, fanning herself languidly while turning a large black eye upon him.

'Why, of course, your Ladyship, please forgive me,' stammered the unhappy youth as he departed once more.

Madeleine wondered how much Lady Frensham had heard of the exchange between Sebastian and herself. For all their anger, they had both spoken quietly; the music was loud and she was separated by two empty chairs.

There was nothing wrong with Lady Frensham's hearing. Snapping her fan shut, she tapped it against the seat next to her. 'Come and sit here,' she commanded, without turning her head.

With a sinking heart Madeleine complied, and at once Lady Frensham said, 'My nephew behaves appallingly, but you must not blame him entirely. Growing up, he was always reckless, but the cynical heartlessness only began when Sophie Clefton threw him over. They'd grown up together, d'you see, and he was madly in love with her. Everyone thought she was with him too, but then Clefton appeared and she dropped my nephew like a red-hot brick. Of course, Clefton doesn't have a brain in his head, but he is worth his weight in gold – several times over – and Sophie had never had any money. Actually, it was the best thing that could happen as she and Sebastian could never have lived on love in a cottage – they both have very expensive tastes – but ever since he has been completely wild and treats all women with contempt, even though the poor fools continue to throw themselves at him.'

'D-do you think he still loves Sophie?' Madeleine heard herself ask, and it was as though the words had been uttered of their own volition.

'Of course not! In fact, I think he despises her, but he *pretends* so that one day he can hurt her by showing what he really feels. All that sweetness she exudes is a complete sham, you know. In reality she is a most calculating, cold-hearted woman, but she manages to hide this very well, which is another reason why Sebastian never has any faith in a woman.'

'But I thought Lady Clefton was a family friend; Harriet seemed so pleased to see her.'

Lady Frensham sighed. 'Harriet is such a *child*. I fear adult emotions are still unknown to her.'

Madeleine's thoughts were chaotic. 'Why are you telling me all this?' she asked in a small voice.

The answer came without any hesitation: 'Because I know that you are already half in love with him, and it will not do! If you had had any money you might have been the one to tame him, but as it is he will marry Catherine Llewellyn Morgan in his own good time. It is plain that she dotes upon him, and rumour has it that she has refused a number of other better offers. Of course, he will break her heart, but she will have her good works to console her and no doubt he will give her a child a year – now, now, there is no need to colour up, my gal. I know your father told you much more than he should about life, and perhaps it was as well since Sebastian clearly has you within his sights. But just remember, he thinks of women as prey and himself as their stalker, and once the chase is over, he loses interest. No, it must be left to Catherine to continue our line. Of course, they are very *nouveaux riches* – the father owns half the mines in Wales – but she has been well educated, and with the de Lacey name and her father's money, she will be received *everywhere*.'

Lady Frensham suddenly paused as though lost in thought and then she added, 'Besides, our home will then be restored to us; Summerleigh Manor, where the Llewellyn Morgans live, had been in our family since 1209 until my grandfather gambled it away. He'd been a very successful gambler in his youth, but then in his old age he lost everything. The day after the house went, he was going to try and redeem it, but instead the old fool fell down the stairs and killed himself. Evan Llewellyn Morgan bought it years later when he first began to acquire his wealth.'

Lady Frensham fell silent again and Madeleine finished the last of her wine. She felt cold and devoid of all feeling except for a wild desire to giggle at the thought of a de

Lacey daring to die in such an undignified way. As she felt the wine warming her, she found sufficient courage to say, 'Thank you for telling me, Lady Frensham, but I can assure you that even if your nephew were the last man on earth, nothing would induce me to marry him.'

'Poppycock!' exclaimed Lady Frensham, before turning to smile upon Harry Arbuthnot, who had appeared at her elbow. 'Ah, thank you, Mr Arbuthnot, how kind!'

The young man beamed as though she had bestowed an accolade upon him and, greatly encouraged, said to Madeleine, 'Miss Brett, if you are not engaged for this dance, may I have the honour?'

Oh, why not? thought Madeleine. She felt exhausted and drained by all these people, but at least to dance would be preferable to remaining in Lady Frensham's dragon-like presence. 'Thank you, Mr Arbuthnot,' she replied, giving him her hand as she rose. From across the room she suddenly became conscious of Sebastian's furious gaze upon her and instinctively she smiled at Mr Arbuthnot, hoping to appear serene and happy, but the tight clenching of her free hand betrayed her inner conflict.

After that, a seemingly endless number of young men asked her to dance, yet she was always to remember her first dance as a nightmare that went on for ever. But when release came at last and she sank into her bed, sleep eluded her. Instead, she felt Sebastian's arms around her in their vice-like grip, his hands exploring her neck and breast, and his whispered words which brought the warm blood surging through her. She told herself that she hated him and pitied Miss Llewellyn Morgan, yet deep within her she knew that she wanted to be in his arms again, that the thought of his marrying anyone else was unbearable.

'He must be right – I am a wanton,' she whispered in the darkness, for had not papa explained the difference between true love and something which he had called 'mere lust'? 'True love between a man and a woman is a most wonderful thing,' he had said quietly, 'and there should always be passion too, but with real love the passion is accompanied by tenderness and the wish, the very greatest wish, to give happiness and protection to one's partner; without love, there is only the thought of gratifying one's own desire, with or without the partner's consent, even if this involves brutality.' There had been no tenderness, no thought for her in Sebastian's embrace, and this knowledge brought the bitter tears pouring from the corners of her closed eyes.

When at last she slept, her dreams were all of those moments when she had been locked in his arms, and she moved restlessly in her lonely bed, moaning softly.

7

Madeleine awoke and was immediately racked by conflicting emotions, one half of her longing to see Sebastian again, the other shying away from his hard, cynical gaze. She need not have worried, for only the General and Harriet were seated at the breakfast table.

'Good morning, Madeleine. I hope you slept well?' The General spoke with his usual courtesy, but seemed preoccupied. He was unsmiling and, while his colour was high, the skin around his eyes and mouth looked white and strained. When Harriet began, 'Madeleine, wasn't it simply wonderful – ' he rose hastily, murmured a quiet, 'Excuse me, my dears', and strode quickly from the room.

Harriet, who had obviously been lost in a dream of her own, became quickly alert and leaned forward to whisper, 'I'm afraid papa is not in a very good mood this morning and I'm sure it has something to do with Sebastian; they had the most terrible quarrel last night after we all returned home. I know, because I came down to get an apple and I heard their voices in the library. I could not catch everything they said, but I did hear papa shouting about Sebastian being a disgrace to his regiment by behaving so cadishly, and when Sebastian demanded to know if papa wished him to leave the Army, papa replied that he only wanted him to conduct his affaires with discretion and to behave like an officer and a gentleman and to remember that he belonged to one of the very best regiments in the Army. Then Sebastian suddenly dashed out of the room, looking absolutely black with fury, and leapt up the stairs as though the devil himself were after him. He slammed the door of his room so hard that all the windows rattled – didn't you hear the noise? I peeped into the library; papa was sitting at his desk with his head in his hands, so I just crept back upstairs. It must have been something Sebastian did at the ball, but I didn't see anything untoward, did you?'

Madeleine knew only too well, but now she merely shook her head.

'And now – ' Harriet broke off as the footman appeared, silver salver in hand. 'Yes, what is it, Timothy?'

'Beggin' yer pardin, Miss Harriet, but Miss Llewellyn Morgan's footman has jus' brough' this for yer an' is waitin' wif her coachman for a reply.'

Harriet read the note quickly and then looked up, smiling. 'How nice, Catherine has invited us both to tea this afternoon. Shall I say we will be delighted to accept?'

'Are you sure she means me as well?' asked Madeleine. 'After all, she and I only met very briefly last evening.'

'Yes, she says, "And I do hope Miss Brett will be able to accompany you."'

Madeleine suddenly wanted very much to see the de Laceys' ancestral home, where Sebastian would eventually live with Catherine Llewellyn Morgan. 'Yes,' she said, with only the merest catch in her voice, 'yes, I should like to go.'

Harriet rose with her usual flurry of skirts. 'Then I will go at once to ask papa's permission and write an acceptance. Timothy, be sure and see that Miss Llewellyn Morgan's servants are given something hot in the kitchen.'

'Yes, Miss Harriet,' murmured Timothy, poker-faced. He had left the two men tucking into heaped plates of the kidneys, bacon and sausages only just removed from the sideboard. Which meant that only the kedgeree and kippers would remain for the de Lacey servants, just when they had been hoping for plenty of leftovers, what with the General eating so little, Miss Brett nothing at all, and Lady Frensham still happily snoring upstairs.

* * *

Harriet had told her that it was a small moated manor, dating mainly from the Tudor period and built over a much earlier fortified farmhouse, but Madeleine was unprepared for the sheer beauty and romance of the building. First there was the long straight drive, lined with magnificent old oaks, and at the end the massive gate-house, flanked on each side by square towers, their parapets crenellated, their walls slit by narrow lancet windows. The grey stone walls were softened by controlled growths of Virginia creeper, ivy and cotoneaster, while to the side could be seen the tall twisted chimneys and sloping red roofs of the Tudor addition.

The carriage clattered over a drawbridge and there was a glimpse of the moat below, its water almost entirely obscured by lily pads. Then they were in the courtyard, and Madeleine gasped as she descended from the carriage, for the building was pure Tudor: timbered, high-gabled, with huge mullioned windows and massive doors of ancient oak. The black and white walls were laced with the bare wood of a carefully trained wisteria and on each side of the entrance were barrels containing bright pink camellias, sheltered from the frost and cold of winter, and already in full bloom.

'Do you like it?' asked Harriet.

'Like it?' echoed Madeleine. 'I think it is the most beautiful house I've ever seen.'

'Yes, and to think that we lived here for so many hundreds of years, and now our only trace is in the quarterings on the windows.' Harriet sighed. 'If only Sebastian would hurry up and marry Catherine, it could be our home again. She loves it, too, and I must say she and her father have restored it wonderfully well. I wish, oh, I *wish* Willie and I could be married in the chapel and stand with papa to receive our guests in the great hall; there would be musicians in the minstrels' gallery and long tables with refreshments on the terrace and – and yes, our house flag would fly again from that pole over the gatehouse.'

Harriet's voice was so wistful that Madeleine impulsively hugged her, even though for herself the magic had been shattered. 'Perhaps it may still be like that,' she said gently, but Harriet shook her head.

'No, I'm sure Sebastian has no intention of asking Catherine immediately, and even if he did, theirs would be a very grand wedding needing months of preparation. But as Willie has to return to India in the autumn, papa has said that we may marry in June.' Her voice suddenly lifted, 'And of course that will be wonderful too!' she exclaimed, smiling again. 'Now, do let us go in; Evans has been standing beside the door for at least five minutes and must be wondering what is the matter with us.' She raised her voice. 'Good afternoon, Evans, how are you?'

The elderly butler's bow was creakily deferential. 'Good afternoon, Miss Harriet. Thank you, I am well, and may I say what a pleasure it is to see you, miss.'

Harriet smiled with just the right degree of warmth. 'Thank you, Evans. And this is my friend, Miss Brett. Will you please announce us to your mistress, who is, of course, expecting us.'

Catherine Llewellyn Morgan awaited them in the drawing room, where a bright fire blazed in the huge stone fireplace. She rose at once and came forward to kiss Harriet on both cheeks. 'Harriet dear! How lovely to see you,' she exclaimed, 'and Madeleine too – may I call you that? Please do come in.' A small hand was extended to Madeleine, its grip surprisingly firm. 'Come and sit down. Evans, we shall take tea at once, if you please. Oh, Madeleine, will you not come a little nearer the fire and take a more comfortable seat?' Catherine was smiling almost apologetically as she continued: 'My father and I have tried to keep the Tudor atmosphere throughout the

102

house, but seating of that period was not at all comfortable, so we have made a concession with these winged chairs.'

Madeleine had briefly met Catherine and her father at the ball, where they had only just managed to conceal their curiosity about her. But now it was impossible not to respond to Catherine's warmth and friendliness. Although not a beauty, her smooth brown hair, translucent skin and softly rounded figure, simply and elegantly clothed, gave the overall impression of attractiveness. But her real charm lay in the sincerity of her quiet manner, the lifted corners of her firm mouth and the softness of her large forget-me-not blue eyes. Seeing her effortlessly dispense tea from splendid silver, Madeleine had to admit that Catherine would make an admirable hostess for Sebastian. The knowledge depressed her and made her realize what she was: a complete nonentity without even the status of a poor relation. She took no part in the conversation as Evans handed round cups of old, exquisite Meissen and tiny iced cakes, but Catherine was too good a hostess to leave her excluded for long.

'I see you are studying the panelling, Madeleine,' she said. 'It is the original, and is inlaid with black bog oak and apple wood. Tell me, do you admire old buildings or is contemporary architecture more to your taste?'

'Oh, I much prefer the old and historic,' Madeleine replied. 'And, if I may say so, I think this house the most beautiful I have ever seen.'

Catherine was clearly delighted. 'Oh, how I agree! I was only a small girl when my father bought the Manor, but I have always loved it as though my family had lived here for generations and I really would not ever want to leave it.' Catherine paused and then flushed prettily. 'Oh, Harrie dear, forgive me, this must cause you pain.'

'Ah, but if we cannot live here, then there is no one we should prefer to have the house than you, Catherine,'

Harriet said, and then could not help adding impishly, 'But how will you feel when you marry and perhaps have to move elsewhere?'

The blush deepened, but Catherine replied serenely, 'Perhaps I may not marry, or, if I do, perhaps it will be to someone who would be happy to live here too. My father has always said he will return to Wales, if and when I marry.'

Harriet sighed. 'Oh, I do wish Sebastian – '

But even Catherine's poise was unequal to what her friend might have added. She interrupted with just the faintest hint of agitation, 'Ah, yes, how is your brother? Did he enjoy the ball?'

'I don't know. I did not see him before he left this morning.'

Harriet, despite her euphoric state, could not fail to note that both heads immediately snapped round. She heard Madeleine draw in her breath sharply, but it was Catherine, with teapot in mid-air, who said, 'Left? But I thought he was not due back at the War Office for another two weeks. I am sure he told me – '

'Yes,' Harriet sighed again. 'But you know what Sebastian is! He quickly becomes bored with everything and I know he finds Bath very dull. After we returned from the ball, I understand he packed his bags and left almost at once – goodness knows where to.'

There was a sudden stunned silence, broken only by the crackling of the fire, then Catherine rallied to hide her disappointment. 'Madeleine, perhaps you would like to see some of the house after tea – the long gallery and the tower rooms, where the view is quite magnificent?'

Madeleine, making an equal effort, inclined her head. 'That would be lovely,' she said, wondering why her voice sounded so unsteady and hoarse.

The next moment all three young women started as a furious knocking began on the double doors. 'Good gracious!' exclaimed Catherine. 'Whatever is happening? Evans, will you . . .?'

The ancient butler made his slow, stately way down the long length of the room, but hardly had his hand touched the knob when the door was flung open by a dishevelled, panting figure.

'Timothy!' cried Madeleine and Harriet simultaneously, and all three young women rose apprehensively.

The young footman dashed unceremoniously into the room. 'Miss Harriet, come quick; the General, he's took reel bad an' Lady Frensham said yer was t'come a' once. The doctor doan' 'old out much 'ope.'

Harriet was turned to stone and could only gaze back at the servant, quite unable to speak. It was Madeleine who came forward to ask quietly, 'Timothy, what exactly has happened?'

But Timothy, who had rather enjoyed his moment of high drama, now remembered that Lady Frensham had told him he must return to Bath with all speed, and he knew what her temper would be like if he delayed. 'I got ter go, miss,' he said obstinately, 'I come on a hired horse from the White Hart an' Lady Frensham – '

'Just tell us, Timothy,' Madeleine insisted very quietly.

'Well, miss, all I knows is tha' the Gen'ral come out the lib'ry clutchin' his ches' an' fell down in the hall, moanin'.'

'Oh, no,' cried Harriet, coming out of her shock to clap her hands over her ears. 'Oh, no, not papa – it can't be, it just can't be.'

As Catherine moved to put an arm around Harriet's shoulders, Madeleine said, 'Thank you, Timothy, you may go now. Please tell Lady Frensham that we shall return as fast as the carriage can travel.' She turned to Catherine. 'The carriage . . .'

Catherine nodded over Harriet's bowed head. 'Evans, order Miss Harriet's carriage immediately and tell them in the stables that it is a matter of the utmost urgency. Madeleine, shall I come with you? My father, who is a magistrate, is sitting on the bench at Bristol and will not be home until late.'

Madeleine glanced at Harriet, who was now weeping bitterly and still murmuring that the news could not be true. 'I think perhaps until we know exactly what the situation is, it might be best if you did not come. Later, I am sure Harriet will be greatly comforted by your presence.'

'I understand,' Catherine said quietly. 'I will send over tomorrow for news. Please give General de Lacey my very best wishes and tell Lady Frensham that I shall be only too happy to help in whatever way possible. Harrie dear, try and compose yourself a little. You know how the servants always exaggerate, and I am sure you will find the situation not nearly so bad . . .'

But in reality it was far worse. Three black broughams, unmistakably doctors' were drawn up outside the house, two of whose owners were on the point of departure. Harriet, seeing the family physician in the act of bowing farewell to his eminent-looking colleagues, almost fell from the carriage and dashed forward. 'Dr Richards, what has happened? How is my father?'

The doctor was maddeningly calm. 'Ah, there you are, my dear! I am relieved to see you. Now, if you will just step inside and join Lady Frensham in the drawing room, I will be with you in a few minutes.'

As Harriet stood irresolute, Madeleine took her arm. 'Perhaps we should do what he says,' she suggested, and Harriet allowed herself to be propelled forward.

Madeleine caught a glimpse of Lady Frensham sitting, as always, bolt upright in her chair, her face expressionless but chalk-white. Harriet dashed over to her. 'Oh, aunt, what has happened? Whatever has happened?'

Lady Frensham, frozen and implacable, said without

any preamble, her voice toneless, 'Harriet, you must prepare yourself for a very great shock: your father is dying.'

Harriet's outraged shriek of 'No! Oh no! No, no!' could be heard throughout the house and brought Dr Richards hurrying forward.

'Lady Frensham, please! I must insist,' he said with great authority.

The drawing-room door closed abruptly and Madeleine, who at the last minute had hung back, was left alone in the upper hall. She sank on to a chair, feeling suddenly faint and stricken. That the General should be dying! The kind man who had plucked her out of abject poverty and treated her like a daughter; the gentle, courteous man; the man who had been her papa's dearest friend. The grief of her father's death, which had been blunted by so many other emotions, now returned with all the accompanying despair. Once more her world was falling apart, and she did not even look up when the door opened and Lady Frensham emerged, followed by Harriet, who had reverted to a state of frozen shock. They went quickly up the second flight of stairs, and only the doctor spared a passing, professional glance at Madeleine's small huddled figure.

Afterwards she never knew how long she sat there, or how long she would have remained if the doctor's quiet figure had not come to stand beside her. 'Miss Brett, General de Lacey is asking for you.'

She raised surprised, tear-filled eyes. 'For me? Are you sure?'

The doctor nodded. 'Quite sure. I understand you are a physician's daughter, and I must ask you to try and be as composed as possible, not only for the General's sake, but for Harriet's; she has taken it extremely badly and will need considerable help. I had no idea that Lady Frensham would break the news to her so, er, abruptly.'

107

Madeleine rose stiffly. 'How – how is General de Lacey?'

Dr Richards paused only very briefly before he replied, 'The General suffered a major heart attack earlier this afternoon and another attack is feared. I regret that there is very little hope for him, and all we can do is help his life to move peacefully towards its close.'

Ice enveloped Madeleine then and she swayed slightly, pressing her hands against her mouth. Automatically the doctor moved to support her, but she shook her head. 'I am all right,' she said very calmly, 'and I shall not make a fuss. Shall we go now?' The stairs were surprisingly difficult to ascend, for her legs felt like lead, and she had to cling to the banister for support. Once inside the General's bedroom, Madeleine clenched her hands in the folds of her gown and pressed her lips tightly together to keep from crying out. She had not expected him to be so altered in appearance. Although propped up by many pillows, he was shrunken and extremely old and reminded her poignantly of how her father had looked in his last hours. Lady Frensham was seated on one side of the bed, while on the other Harriet was kneeling, with her cheek pressed against her father's right arm. She looked totally broken-down and grief-stricken.

The General's tired dark eyes looked steadily at Madeleine and he managed to smile faintly. 'Thank you for coming, my dear. I do apologize for causing you and all my family so much trouble.' As Madeleine moved to speak, he very briefly raised a flaccid hand. 'And for you, Madeleine, it must open the wound of your father's death . . . but I have asked for you because I have a proposition to put to you.'

'Oh, anything, anything I can do to help you! Please tell me!'

'Good. Then I want you to marry me at once.' The General thought tiredly that if he had suggested they

108

should fly to the moon together, his words could not have caused greater astonishment. Lady Frensham uttered a gurgling, incoherent sound, Harriet slowly raised her tear-drowned eyes to gaze at him dully, while Madeleine, poor Madeleine, seemed turned to stone. Even Dr Richards was sufficiently thrown off his guard to let amazement show through his professional mask.

At last Madeleine murmured as though from a great distance, 'I – I don't understand. I think I have misheard you.'

The General sighed. 'No, of course you do not understand! But in a few hours I shall be dead – ah, now, Harriet my darling, please do not scream so. It is a fact, a very hard fact, but we must all try to face it, and you have always been my brave girl. Please bear up for my sake. Yes, that's better! Now, Madeleine, I have already discussed their future with my sister and Harriet: Thea will go to her brother-in-law at Norton St Philip and Harriet must marry William within the next three months – I've always considered the obligatory year's mourning period to be nonsensical – and I forbid her to abide by it. But this leaves your future in jeopardy, and I am afraid, so very much afraid, that you will have to face great difficulties.'

Again, as though from a great distance, Madeleine heard her own voice say, 'Thank you, but please, please, do not concern yourself. I am sure I shall be able to manage.'

'Other gals have to do so,' interposed Lady Frensham, returning to life with fire in her eyes.

Her brother turned his head to her. 'Yes, but at what cost! Would you let it happen to Harriet, if their situations were reversed and if you could do something to alleviate it?' Without waiting for her reply, he continued, 'You surely cannot deny that anyone bearing our name, even if only by marriage, would have far greater chances than someone unknown. And do remember that Madeleine has no relations whatsoever.' Dying though he undoubtedly was, the General knew he had triumphed over his sister, who had always placed so much store by their name and therefore would be unable to contest his words.

'I dare say you are right,' Lady Frensham conceded with one of her strongest sniffs of disapproval.

The General felt desperately weary and his voice was weakening, but willpower drove him on. 'Perhaps you do not know, Madeleine, but ours is a very large and still quite influential clan; apart from my nephew, who succeeded to the earldom last year, we have three Members of Parliament, one bishop, two canons of the church, and a first secretary in each of our St Petersburg and Paris embassies. Then there are my two brothers; the younger is Her Majesty's Ambassador to Vienna and the elder is an ex-ambassador to the French and still resides in Paris. So with all these connections by marriage, I know that a lot of help will be given you. And, my dear, you will need it!'

As Madeleine continued to gaze at him mutely and in a trance-like state, he added, 'Of course, the marriage will be a nine days' wonder, but when the facts are known, no blame will be attached to you.' He paused and even chuckled a little. 'Although, no doubt, everyone will assume me to be suddenly in my dotage to even suggest such a circumstance.'

'I confess, Henry,' boomed Lady Frensham, quickly returning to battle, 'that you make me wonder whether you have taken leave of your senses!'

The General shifted his gaze to Dr Richards, who had been standing at the window, looking out, hands linked behind his back. As though feeling his patient's eyes upon him, he half turned. 'I can assure you, Lady Frensham, that there is nothing wrong with General de Lacey's mental powers.'

'Thank you, Richards,' said the General. 'Now, what is

the time?' he tried to move his arm to reach for the small pouch hanging on the wall beside him, but was too weak, and his arm flopped like a stone to his side. Harriet rose to her feet unsteadily and handed him his gold half-hunter from the pouch. 'Papa,' she whispered, her voice quavering. 'What about Sebastian? He knows nothing of this – of your proposal.'

'Ah, Sebastian!' sighed the General. 'If only he were different, I would be so happy to leave Madeleine in his care, but I know that he is a rakehell with all the fascination of a wild animal – a man from whom no woman is safe. But I think that even he would treat a stepmother with a certain amount of respect. Now, let us waste no more time! Parson Johnson must be sent for at once. Madeleine, will you please ring for Perry? And a special licence will be needed, but Llewellyn Morgan will issue that without any difficulty, I'm sure.'

Lady Frensham suddenly shot to her feet. 'There is no need to get Perry. I will go myself for Mr Johnson and the licence.'

'Now, Thea, really – '

'Do you not see, Henry, that I could bring Mr Johnson here so much quicker? I could explain at once why he is needed, whereas if Timothy were sent, Mr Johnson would not know precisely and might just shillyshally. And of course the same applies to Mr Llewellyn Morgan. After all, he is not likely to issue a special licence at the request of a mere footman, is he?'

The General looked searchingly at his sister, a frown between his brows, but she returned his look with none of her earlier animosity. At last he said wearily, 'Very well, Thea, but you will be sure to hurry, will you not?'

His sister inclined her head very briefly before moving briskly to the door. 'Madeleine, be kind enough to ring for Perry to have the carriage brought round at once. I shall be down directly.'

Rather to everyone's surprise, Lady Frensham returned very quickly with a young clergyman trailing slowly behind her. The General, who had been dozing, opened his eyes and at once frowned upon the young man. 'And who are you, sir?' he demanded with the merest echo of his usual authority in his voice. 'Where is Mr Johnson?'

The clergyman stepped forward. 'My name is Parsons, General de Lacey, and I am Mr Johnson's new curate.'

'Parson Parsons?' gasped the General, the laugh in his throat turning into a fit of coughing. 'How – how very absurd!'

Mr Parsons waited until the coughing ended and Harriet had given her father a sip of water. Then he said, 'I am the Reverend Hubert Parsons, sir, and I understand you wish me to conduct a marriage ceremony.'

'Yes, yes!' agreed the General impatiently. 'This young lady, Miss Madeleine Brett, is to be married to me. You have the licence?'

Mr Parsons held up a paper. 'Yes, but I am afraid it is all somewhat irregular,' he began, when the General cut him short: 'Oh, get on with it, man! It is only a marriage of convenience – this time tomorrow you will be preparing for my funeral.'

Harriet screamed at that. 'Oh, no papa, no! You must not leave us, not now, not ever!'

'Harrie darling, in a few months you will be going to India, and even if I were still alive, we should be separated for years. Have you thought of that?'

'But that's quite different!' she protested, between sobs.

'Perhaps not so very different,' replied her father softly. 'Now, if you please, Mr Parsons.'

But this time it was Madeleine who protested. 'General de Lacey, I do very greatly appreciate your thoughtfulness, but I cannot – really, I cannot – agree to this marriage! But, please, I beg of you, do not worry about me; I shall be all right. As Lady Frensham said earlier, other girls have to do so and – '

The General sighed and closed his eyes briefly. 'I am so tired,' he murmured, 'so desperately tired. If only you would all do as I wish, I could sleep . . .'

Dr Richards came to place his fingers on the weak pulse. Then he looked round at them all. 'I must insist that this business is resolved at once, one way or the other,' he said with quiet but absolute authority. 'General de Lacey is most urgently in need of rest and quiet.'

The General, weak and exhausted as he was, nevertheless recognized his cue. 'But I cannot sleep with a quiet mind until the marriage has taken place,' he declared, his dark eyes fixed unwaveringly upon Madeleine. She began to wring her hands in an agony of indecision and at last turned appealingly to the other two women. 'Lady Frensham – Harriet – what shall I do?' she begged, very near to tears.

Harriet burst out at once: 'Oh, please, Madeleine, do as papa wishes! Please! Please!'

Even Lady Frensham's head moved in the slightest inclination and Madeleine, numb now with grief and shock, whispered hoarsely, 'Very well.'

Mr Parsons began to speak quietly, even hesitantly, and then, unbelievably, Madeleine heard a voice saying, 'I, Madeleine Angèle, take thee, Henry Augustus, to be my lawful wedded husband . . .' She heard Mr Parsons say something about a ring and watched, as though in a trance, as the General slipped the signet ring from his little finger, and a moment later she felt the weight of it on her own third finger. Then Mr Parsons was mumbling words that sounded like 'I pronounce you man and wife . . .' and she was being asked to sign something; she wondered aloud which surname she should use and then wrote shakily, her signature scrawling and uneven, like that of a very old person. She saw Lady Frensham and the doctor signing as witnesses, and then Mr Parsons was offering her a limp hand and murmuring some congratulations before departing rather hastily.

Madeleine turned back to the General, to find that he was looking at her with a mixture of sadness and humour in his fine dark eyes. He managed an exhausted smile as he said, 'Poor little Madeleine! Poor little bride! I vow that in all the long history of our family, there has never been a stranger wedding. But always remember, my dear, that it has been brought about so that your second wedding shall be conventional and, I hope, much grander, with you as a proper bride and marrying the man of your choice.'

As Madeleine began to shake her head, he continued firmly, 'Oh, there *will* be another marriage. A mysterious and beautiful young widow, not yet twenty, and bearing one of the oldest names in England, should have no difficulty in finding a suitable husband. But choose carefully, my dear, for I know you have a tender heart and a great capacity for love. Choose someone who will not only protect you but cherish you as you should be cherished.' He held out his hand to Madeleine and she at once clasped it lovingly between both her own.

'Whatever my fate is to be,' she said, just managing to hold on to her composure, 'I shall always remember your wonderful kindness, and I do thank you with all my heart for . . . everything you have done. If I could find someone like you . . .'

Feebly he raised her hands to his lips. 'God bless you, my dearest girl,' he murmured, sinking down against his pillows, eyes closing in exhaustion. 'I pray that you will find true happiness. And now . . . I should like to sleep a little . . .'

Two hours later Henry de Lacey, soldier and English gentleman, died as he had lived: quietly and with dignity.

8

'The women in our family do not attend funerals,' said Lady Frensham the following day. 'But we shall, of course, accompany my brother's body to Wells for interment in the family vault and later a memorial service will be arranged.'

'I – I will stay here,' said Madeleine, whose remaining courage was instantly sapped by the thought of meeting the family en masse.

Lady Frensham gave the smallest inclination of her head. 'As you wish,' she said, rising. Earlier she had asked Madeleine if she wished to take over the household management at once, and a quick gleam of satisfaction had shown briefly in her hooded eyes when Madeleine begged that everything should continue undisturbed, with no mention of her strange marriage being made to anyone for the time being, not even to the servants. She felt that everyone was too stunned by the suddenness of the General's death to accept any further shocks. Nor did she feel capable of bracing herself to meet any new situations. There had been one long and devastating storm of tears, followed by hysterical, hiccoughing laughter as she realized that she was the Honourable Mrs Henry de Lacey, widow of a major general, and Sebastian's stepmother. When at last the tears and the laughter ceased, there was a total draining of emotion and complete exhaustion. Yet willpower and a sense of duty kept her on her feet and at Lady Frensham's disposal, an offer of which the latter took full advantage. Madeleine was kept busy running errands, sending telegrams and collecting patterns of mourning clothes, so that at night when at last she was able to sink on to her bed, she slept as though drugged until being roused to face another day.

Lady Frensham herself remained at the centre of all the activity, directing, writing numerous letters and holding the household together by her implacable will; but while the strictest mourning was observed, no tears or other hint of emotion was allowed.

No one could do anything with Harriet. On being told of her father's death she had become hysterical until heavily sedated by Dr Richards, and after awakening from that she had refused to leave her bed or to eat. No amount of ordering by her aunt or cajoling by Dr Richards had any effect; Harriet remained dry-eyed and staring into space in her darkened room. 'Send for William,' ordered Lady Frensham, and Madeleine herself dashed to Norton St Philip to explain the situation to him. Harriet refused to see him. Catherine Llewellyn Morgan arrived bearing fruit and flowers and remained a long while in the silent room, before finally emerging to frown and shake her head. Even Dr Richards was defeated. 'All she will say is that she wants Sebastian,' he reported.

'But he cannot be found!' exclaimed Lady Frensham with just a hint of exasperation in her voice. 'When my brother became ill I telegraphed at once to the War Office, but the reply was that his whereabouts were unknown because his leave does not expire until early next week. If only he were with his regiment, it would be so much easier, but some months ago Sebastian was seconded to the War Office and the Eleventh are in Ireland.'

'How very, *very* unfortunate,' murmured the doctor, 'I suppose his many friends – '

'No one has seen him,' answered Lady Frensham, who was agitated enough to rise and take a quick turn about the room before coming to face the doctor. 'I've no doubt he is ensconced in some sordid love nest and will only emerge when he has to return to duty. But meanwhile, something must be done about Harriet!'

In the end it was Madeleine who walked boldly into Harriet's room, closing the door firmly behind her. The air smelled stale and the light was so dim that Harriet's body was barely visible. Madeleine strode to the windows to pull back the curtains and raise the sash a little.

'Oh, don't,' groaned Harriet, flinging an arm across her eyes. 'It's cold and my eyes hurt.'

'Then I suggest you get up and close the window yourself,' Madeleine answered calmly.

Harriet gasped with astonishment and the stirring of anger; no one had ever spoken to her like that. She raised her arm slightly and looked at Madeleine through swollen and sullen eyes. 'What do you want?' she asked rudely.

'I? Why, nothing, nothing at all,' retorted Madeleine, keeping her voice calm and equable. 'But I have come to tell you about life . . . and death.'

'No! No! I don't want to hear!' Harriet shouted, head tossing from side to side in torment.

'Nevertheless, I shall tell you,' Madeleine said, as she sat down on the end of the bed. Then, very softly and calmly, she began to speak of all the misery, the grief and the heartbreak she had witnessed in the stinking courts and alleys of London. She told of babies dying of starvation at their mothers' dry breasts; of men, women and children dropping and left to die in the ordure of the narrow streets because they were too weak, too ill, or just too hungry to move; of children and babies hardly old enough to stand upright who wandered, crying piteously, while they scavenged and ate unspeakable filth; of whole families wiped out by epidemics caused by the deadly water of the river. And because the scenes and the stories were imprinted with such great horror on her own mind, Madeleine was able to tell of them with great eloquence.

When she finished speaking there was silence in the

117

room and Harriet, who had been forced to listen, was now staring at Madeleine, open-mouthed and round-eyed with horrified revulsion. Madeleine had half expected her to demand what it all had to do with her, and had planned to end her homily by drawing a comparison between the General's death and that of so many others, of Harriet's own grief and the stupendous suffering of so many other young girls; but she now saw that this would not be necessary. Harriet, she was sure, was about to rise above her grief and self-pity.

Madeleine stood up. The pale winter sun was streaming into the room, and through the open window came talk, laughter and all the sounds of bustling life.

'Ellen will be up with your bath water in ten minutes,' Madeleine said as she moved to the door. 'Why not let her wash your hair as well, and then have a light meal on a tray before you come down?' She did not even wait for Harriet's reply before slipping out of the room, closing the door softly behind her.

And Harriet did come down, deathly pale in her black dress and with her fair hair in a soft, still damp cloud about her face; and there in the hall, by the greatest good fortune, stood Willie, bouquet in hand. Harriet stopped, and for a long moment the young couple looked into each other's eyes, then with a little sobbing cry she was flying down the remaining stairs and into his arms.

'The servants will, of course, be travelling to Wells for the funeral, so you will be alone in the house, but I have ordered a cold collation to be left for you,' said Lady Frensham, managing to make it sound like a great favour.

'Thank you,' said Madeleine quietly. She bit her lip as she felt the hot blood surge to her cheeks. Did Lady Frensham have no feelings, no inkling of how arrogant and obnoxious her manner was? She had certainly never troubled to mask her antipathy and now treated

118

Madeleine as a poor relation. Harriet, too, had now developed a distinct reserve in her manner, and several times Madeleine had looked up to find the other girl gazing at her with frowning puzzlement. So it was with a sigh of relief that Madeleine went to an upper window to raise the blind slightly and watch the family's departure. The hearse, its glass panels bordered in black, each of its four corners topped by a black plume, was standing outside; the heads of its four magnificent black horses, also plumed, were being held by a coachman in deepest mourning. Even as she watched, Madeleine saw the feather men and pages move to line both sides of the short distance between the house and the pavement; then the coffin appeared, covered in a pall of black velvet, its corners lavishly embroidered in silver bullion, and over it all the family flag with the General's dress sabre and his medals on a velvet cushion. Immediately behind the hearse stood Sam, the family coachman, holding the General's horse, from whose sides, in reverse order, hung a pair of riding boots. So much pomp, so many trappings, Madeleine thought sadly, for the laying to rest of a kindly, honourable man to whom she had been *married*! She was seeing the body of her *husband* being taken away!

For the first time she acknowledged the full implication of her bizarre marriage, and an hysterical laugh bubbled in her throat, only to be cut off abruptly as she saw a tall figure emerge with a heavily veiled figure clinging to each arm. He was bare-headed, his dark hair stirring in the brisk wind, and his face looked haggard, the vertical lines running from eyes to jaw seemingly carved out of the taut skin. He handed in the two women and then, as though feeling her scrutiny, suddenly looked up. Instantly his eyes narrowed with a look of such fury and contempt that Madeleine actually reeled back a step. She knew at once what it meant: he had been told of the marriage and,

119

convinced as he always had been that she was an adventuress, now believed that she had contrived the situation.

'Surely they will tell him how it really was,' she whispered to herself. 'Surely they will be fair . . .' But what could anyone expect of Lady Frensham's desiccated personality; and Harriet, the adored and adoring only daughter, might there not be an element of jealousy in her grief when she realized that her father's last conscious hour had been devoted almost entirely to Madeleine? Suddenly, the most important thing in the world was to explain it to Sebastian; no matter what else was said or happened, he must be told what had really transpired. But what if he returned directly to London after the funeral? 'Oh, please dear God, please let him come back here. Please let me be able to tell him,' Madeleine whispered in her distress.

The day seemed endless. She walked for hours around the city until cold and hunger forced her to return. The house was utterly silent and, because of the drawn blinds everywhere, quite dark. Hungry as she was, Madeleine found she could only peck at the food left for her, and it was impossible to sit alone in the large cold drawing room where the General's personality was so strong.

Eventually she went to her room, lit the candles and made up the fire. Then she washed off the dust and grime from her walk, put on her nightgown and sank on to the chaise longue. The room was wonderfully warm and cosy, and within minutes Madeleine's eyes had closed.

She slept until the slamming of a distant door brought her bolt upright on the chaise, heart hammering. She listened intently for a few minutes, but only the crackling of the fire and her own loud heartbeat disturbed the silence. Had she dreamt that a door had slammed, or had the noise come from one of the neighbouring houses? Thick as the walls were, some sounds from other inhabitants of the crescent were inevitable from time to time.

Eventually, Madeleine took her candle and went on to the landing, where everything remained silent; she peered down to the first floor, then descended so that she could see the hall; all was in order, with the front door closed. She let out a taut breath and returned to her room. She felt surprisingly fresh and had no wish to get into bed. Instead, she poked the fire to greater brightness and took out her mending basket.

As the clock in the hall struck ten, Madeleine finished the last darn and tossed the garments aside restlessly. She still felt too wakeful for sleep and knew she should be thinking about her future, but whenever she tried to concentrate on this, her thoughts shied away and reverted at once to Sebastian. Perhaps if I read for a while I shall not be so fidgety, she thought, but then realized that she had only the Brontë sisters' novels, and their work, brilliant though it was, was perhaps not the best reading for someone alone in a large silent house. Miss Austen's dry wit and the civilized behaviour of her characters would be more appropriate, and Madeleine remembered that there was a complete set of the novels in the library. It took some minutes before she overcame her reluctance to leave the warmth and brightness of her room, but sternly telling herself not to be so childish, she swept a large shawl around her shoulders, picked up a candle and set off.

But how quiet it was! In London there would still be the roar of iron-rimmed wheels grinding over cobbles, but here it seemed that the inhabitants of Royal Crescent retired early, for there was not a sound inside or out, and Madeleine's nerves were already tingling as she opened the library door and saw the brightly burning fire. She stood quite still, heart thudding; no one had told her there would be a fire in the library, and how could it still be so bright when it had not been made up during the day? She raised the candle and looked apprehensively around the large room. The far corners and deep wing chairs remained in shadow, but there was no movement and the only sound was the loud ticking of the clock on the mantelpiece. Bracing herself, Madeleine stepped resolutely into the room; she knew exactly where the Austen novels were, and she would just take the first one which came to hand. She had put the candlestick on the mantelpiece and turned towards the tall bookcase when a voice drawled, 'Well, well, if it isn't the bride herself!'

Madeleine made a deep gurgling sound in her throat as she whirled, backing against the bookcase, hands pressed against the wood in fear.

A dark figure rose from the chair on the far side of the fireplace. 'Now, Mrs de Lacey, there is no need to be so frightened! It is only I, your devoted stepson – surely you heard me come in an hour or so back?' The voice was quiet, even silky, and she knew it could only belong to Sebastian; but the shock had been too great and her knees began to buckle. Instantly he was beside her, his figure huge against the firelight.

'Why, you're shaking!' he exclaimed, as though genuinely surprised. 'Here, come and sit down.' A steel-like arm went round her and a hand grasped her waist firmly as he led her the few steps to a small sofa, where he pressed her into one corner, solicitously arranging the cushions at her back. Then he brought the glass from beside his own chair and, sitting down very close to her, said, 'You must drink this – it will stop the faintness.' But her hands were trembling too much for her to take the glass, so Sebastian held it to her mouth; her teeth clattered against the rim as she took a sip. Then she pulled away, grimacing.

'Oh, but you must drink it all,' commanded Sebastian, and again held it to her mouth. Through her shock and chaotic thoughts, she was dimly conscious of his closeness, of his arm along the back of the sofa, and of how comforting all this was. Obediently she drank the remainder of the brandy and felt its fiery warmth flood through her body. 'That's a good girl,' Sebastian said, as though speaking to a small child. 'Better now?'

Madeleine nodded. 'Yes, thank you. I – I'm sorry I behaved so stupidly, but I truly did not know you were in the house . . . and I just came down for a book. Now – now I must go back.' She tried to move but found she was wedged between the arm of the sofa on one side and by Sebastian on the other. A hand on her shoulder pressed her down.

'There is no hurry, is there?' he asked equably.

'But – I'm not dressed!' Madeleine exclaimed, blushing hotly as she became conscious of her thin cotton nightgown and inadequate shawl.

'Neither am I!' retorted Sebastian, and almost added, 'Isn't that lucky?' but just managed to bite back the words. Madeleine saw then that he was wearing a floor-length velvet dressing robe, elaborately frogged, its collar and cuffs luxuriously quilted. 'Why not stay here awhile until you feel stronger?' he asked gently. 'Besides, it's cosy here, isn't it?'

That made her giggle a little. 'Cosy is not a word I would ever associate with you,' she said, trying hard to cling to coherent thought.

'Oh, but I can be very cosy,' Sebastian assured her. 'When I'm happy. And I'm very happy now.' In fact, he was more than happy, he was triumphant: she was here, virtually a prisoner – although she had not realized it yet – and they were alone in the house, just as he had planned. And he was finding her intoxicatingly desirable: her profile, etched against the firelight, had all the delicacy of a fine cameo, and without her petticoats and enormous skirts she was unbelievably tiny. It was requiring all his self-control to proceed slowly, but he was determined that she would not leave the room before he had taken her; yet if she realized this intention too soon, he knew she would fight him all the way – and this time he wanted her to consent and participate fully. Besides, when swapping stories of sexual prowess with fellow officers in the mess, he had always maintained quite truthfully that it had never been hard for him to obtain a most willing assent.

Madeleine, with the brandy rising to her head, relaxed against the cushions as a feeling of total wellbeing swept over her. Sebastian's powerful body was close and, she felt, entirely protective, and he had been speaking to her so gently, so normally, without the hateful mocking drawl or the wolfish grin on his face. Yet she frowned; there was something she knew she should tell him without delay; what . . . oh, yes, of course, the marriage! She turned her head, and the strange thing was that although her head felt so heavy, it seemed to turn too far and the room turned with it. 'Ooh!' she groaned, putting her hands up to her temples.

'It's perfectly all right,' said a softly caressing voice close to her ear. 'Just relax now.'

With the last of her willpower she tried to pull away and to fight the lassitude which was threatening to overpower her. 'Sebastian,' she said, quite unaware that she had called him by that name, 'I must tell you how I came to be married to your father. It was not – '

But his mouth was already brushing hers as he whispered, 'I am imagining how it would be if you were married to me.' Then his hand moved to cup her cheek, his fingers to thread their way into her hair as his mouth came down on hers, softly, tenderly, to rise teasingly for a second before returning to kiss her more deeply. Her head fell back against his shoulder and her heavy lids over her eyes when at last timidly, hesitantly, she began to return his kisses. He slid his hand inside her nightgown to hold her breast, and felt her lips part in a soundless gasp;

124

she tried to pull her mouth away from his, but he would not let her and instead bore down hard, feeling her lips part again for his tongue. When her breasts began to swell, he started very gently to ease the nightgown off her shoulders. He wanted to rip it away, but instinct told him that this might just bring her back to reality . . . With the delicate pointed breasts and their rosebud nipples bare at last, he snatched his mouth from hers to cover them with butterfly kisses. She shuddered then as waves of delight swept over her. One tiny corner of her brain registered that this was shameful, but she wanted it never to end, and when his lips closed around a nipple, she pressed his head close to her, burying her fingers in his hair, as the ecstasy became almost unbearable; when his mouth came back to hers, she kissed him as hungrily as he did her, and whimpered softly in protest as he tore himself away at last. Then, still held in his arms, she felt herself sliding forward until she lay on the rug before the fire, with cushions behind her head and her nightgown gone.

Sebastian stood briefly to toss aside his robe, and the clean, beautiful lines of his splendid body filled her with quivering delight. Without realizing what she was doing, she held out her arms to him, and at once he was beside her, mouth and hands demanding total possession. As the last of her reticence dissolved and she responded whole-heartedly, brief soundless laughter shook Sebastian. He was bringing to life the passionate woman he had always known to be present behind the mask of demureness, and now her need was as great as his own. But at his thrust she cried out, and he raised his head, frowning a little, to look at her. A virgin? Surely not! Yet pain as well as ecstasy showed in her half-closed eyes, and he forced himself to wait. He was aware that in certain London establishments he was known as 'the Stallion', and for the first time in his amorous life he now tried to be patient, but as he felt her back arch and her arms tighten around

125

his neck, the last of his self-control snapped and he let passion take over.

Sebastian had the reputation of being an immensely powerful lover with great stamina, but although never cruel or sadistic towards his partners, he was not known for his tenderness. Yet, when at last he lay beside Madeleine, he felt not only complete happiness, but an aching tenderness for her. 'Don't leave me,' she had begged, arms trying to hold him fast, and he had wanted to remain for ever. 'But, sweetheart,' he had said, laughing a little, 'I'll break every bone in your body if I let my whole weight rest on you.' 'I don't mind,' she had replied recklessly, hands slipping over his back as he moved away.

He raised himself on an elbow to look at her, his eyes lingering with delight on the small but perfect breasts, the tiny waist, narrow hips and long, tapering legs. 'By God, you're beautiful,' he murmured and, bending low over her, he began to cover her body with kisses, his lips clinging hungrily to her warm flesh. By the time he had kissed each toe, she was trembling and holding out her arms, and he came back to her mouth. 'Why so shy?' he whispered, and as she hesitated, not understanding, he took her hand and guided it; when she turned her body towards his, he moved at once. 'This time it will be wonderful,' he told her softly, feeling her strong hold closing around him as she, too, strove for oneness. He snatched a cushion and put it under her and then gave himself to her completely, laying his whole length against hers, thigh to thigh, breast to breast, mouth to mouth, in a hunger and passion so great that it was to bind them together for ever . . .

So this, she thought, when they once more lay side by side, this is the true love that papa spoke of, this total sharing of each other's secret places, this total belonging to each other – oh, but she would never have believed anything could be so wonderful, or that there could be such love, never have believed lips and hands and bodies capable of creating such wonderful sensations which culminated in a total wave of feeling that engulfed, almost drowned her, so that she had cried out against Sebastian's mouth, even as a muffled shout burst from his own lips.

It was she who now turned to bend over him, her hair falling like a curtain around them. His eyes were like black velvet, crinkling at the corners as he looked up at her. With a feather-light touch her fingers traced the line of his straight brows, lifted a damp strand of curling hair from his forehead, and then moved to follow the outline of his long mouth, which was just beginning to curve in a smile of real tenderness.

'I love you, oh, I love you,' she whispered, her eyes echoing her words with a wonderfully soft luminous light. She heard him draw in his breath sharply, felt his body stiffen, and then to her bewilderment he leapt to his feet in one lithe movement.

'Love?' he queried harshly, 'what has love got to do with it?' He began pulling on his robe. 'Pleasure, yes, marvellous pleasure, and another de Lacey bride well and truly bedded. Your performance, my dear, was superlative, and I enjoyed your technique of shy innocence. But take my advice: never spoil it by alluding to love, for nothing enrages a man more after he has just spent a light-hearted hour than to have his partner become mawkish.' As he unhurriedly fastened the frogging on his robe, he looked her over coolly, making her immediately conscious of her nakedness. 'Here, put this on,' he said, picking up her nightgown and tossing it so that it landed, none too gently, on her stomach. 'We shall do very well together, so long as you remember that love – the roses-round-the-door kind, with samplers of HOME SWEET HOME and hordes of puking babies – is not for the likes of you and me.'

He picked up the brandy bottle and moved towards the door. 'I trust I was a satisfactory substitute for my father,' he said, turning to look at her once more. He seemed to waver then, for she had sat up, long legs bent and curving to one side, and was holding the nightgown against herself with both hands; her head and shoulders were outlined against the fire with her face in shadow, yet he could see that it was frozen with shock. She appeared incapable of speech, and only her eyes, huge and dark, showed the intensity of her pain and bewilderment. Sebastian was immediately reminded of his first shooting trip as a boy when, by mistake, he had shot and wounded a tiny, elegant doe; when he raced to administer the *coup de grâce*, he had seen the same terrible agony in the doe's beautiful eyes.

The memory faded; Sebastian shrugged, and his mouth twisted in the familiar cynical grin as he said casually, 'Run off to bed now. You must be tired. And thanks for livening up a dull evening.' Then he went out, not even bothering to close the door behind him. She heard his light footsteps leaping up the stairs, followed by the crash of a door. It reverberated through the house, and the noise roused Madeleine. She rose slowly and painfully to her feet, and carefully put on the nightgown, smoothing it down over her hips, while her mind remained quite blank. All Sebastian's words and everything that had happened would be burnt deeply into her consciousness for ever, but the transition from total happiness and delight to total hurt had been too sudden, and for the present she could not take in the reality of the situation; her only thought was that she must be in the throes of some terrible nightmare.

The darkness of the hall and stairs seemed to confirm this, and it was only when she was back in the light of her room that her frozen state began to melt at the edges. Gazing dully into the fire, it was as though a heavy curtain

128

was raised at one corner, allowing her to remember that she had left this room to fetch a book; that within minutes Sebastian was making love to her; that she had willingly surrendered, had let him know and touch every inch of her body; that his cruel words had turned something natural and wonderful into a dirty and degrading incident; that it had all been just a trick to humiliate her. She shook her head, as though to refute this knowledge, but then as the curtain lifted a little more, she remembered that he had always hated and despised her, so how had she let him . . .?

'Because I love him and wanted to think that he loved me,' she whispered, then shook with brief laughter as she thought, why, I was like the proverbial duck taking to water! And from being ice-cold, she suddenly burned as she remembered how she had acted – how *abandoned* she had been in the throes of passion. 'A superlative performance', he had called it. It had meant nothing, nothing, *nothing* to him; he had led her on so that he could confirm his opinion of her: that she was just a cheap adventuress, to be used and tossed aside . . . She wanted to rush into some small dark place like a little animal to hide her shame and degradation, and she would have cried then if it had been possible, but although there was pain behind her eyes and her throat felt closed, no tears came. Instead, there was the single feeling that she could not bear to meet Sebastian face to face again, that she must leave at once, go right away; she had no idea where. The grief, like the humiliation, would remain with her for ever, but so long as she did not actually see him, perhaps she might just be able to exist without him.

But first there was the need to wash away the smell of him. She poured cold water into the wash basin and began to scrub herself from top to toe until her skin was red and sore. Then she washed her hair and wrapped it tightly in a towel; it would not be dry by the time she was ready to leave, but that didn't matter – nothing, nothing mattered, except to get as far away as possible from the house and the de Laceys. She put on all the clothes in which she had first arrived, and packed her small valise, leaving the General's gift of the silk dress, the petticoats, slippers and soft kid gloves in the wardrobe and drawers. There was a moment of intense pain when she saw the bonnet Sebastian had given her, but then she turned quickly from the wardrobe, closing the doors with a slam. The wish to be gone was becoming more and more urgent, yet to leave like a thief in the night without any explanation – wouldn't that reinforce his bad opinion of her? Reluctantly she sat down at the small writing table and pulled paper and pen towards her. She sat for a moment with head in hand, trying to focus her chaotic, darting thoughts, then began to write:

Dear Lady Frensham,

I have decided that, after all, I must try to make my own way without the help of your family, and so I am leaving at once. As you know, I only consented to marriage to General de Lacey because he wished it so earnestly, and I shall always remember how wonderful he was to care so much about my future when he was so near to death. He was a great man, and I shall cherish his memory with love and very deep gratitude. I will leave his signet ring with this letter.

Thank you for [here Madeleine paused; she had been about to thank Lady Frensham for her kindness, but when had the strange, cold woman ever shown her any real kindness?] all your hospitality, which I have much appreciated.

Yours sincerely,
Madeleine Fitzmaurice Brett

Madeleine looked at the heavy signet ring with its finely engraved arms and the motto 'Amor et Fidelite'. Then slowly she drew it from her finger and placed it against her lips. '*If I could find someone like you,*' she had

130

whispered to the General, and within a few days there had been his son, in whom she had sought comfort and love. Hastily she pushed the letter and the ring aside. There was still Harriet, who *had* been kind to her. Sighing, she began to write again:

Dear Harriet,

As I have just written to Lady Frensham, I feel I must make my own future without any further help from your family, but I cannot leave without wishing you every happiness in your marriage. I do hope life in India will be just as you have so often spoken of it.

Thank you for your friendship over the past ten days; I am sorry these should have ended in such grief and sadness for us all.

Please convey my very best wishes to your fiancé.

Madeleine

She paused again, suddenly overwhelmed by her thoughts. Would Harriet, on her wedding night, know the sublime joy of total giving and taking, of a oneness so deep that for an instant time and the stars in their courses must surely have stopped? Yes, Madeleine thought, Harriet will have the opportunity to experience all that, not just for *one* hour, *one* night, but all the nights of her married life; she will be a cherished wife, the bearer of children conceived in love and wedlock, and Willie's arms will always be about her; there will be nothing for Harriet ever to fear, 'neither the sun by day, nor the moon by night'. Oh, lucky, lucky Harriet, if only it could have been like that for me!

Deep, dry sobs tore at Madeleine with a terrible despair. Only the urge to be gone made her rise and begin to bind her hair; then she put on her old black bonnet, picked up her valise and the letters, carefully blew out the candle and walked from the room. As she reached the hall, the longcase clock struck four. She put the letters on the table, her fingers lingering very briefly on the ring.

Goodbye, she said in her heart, and opened the front door.

The cold damp air of the early January morning hurt her lungs, but she closed the door at once and looked quickly about her. Royal Crescent, in all its grace and beauty, still slept, and Madeleine's worn-out boots made no sound on the flags as she walked away on stiff, exhausted legs.

9

The main characteristics which Bertha and George Sharpe
shared as brother and sister were greed and ambition.
Their road to success had been long and hard, but
everything they had achieved had been due to their own
efforts, aided by tenacity and complete ruthlessness. Nor
were they content now that George had become head of
the Avon Shipping Line and Bertha had been transformed
into Madame Berthe, Milliner to Ladies of Quality, with
the most attractive shop in Park Street. George was
anxious to branch out into other forms of commerce, now
that Liverpool had definitely taken over from Bristol as
the country's main port, while Bertha was determined to
achieve the same personal success as Mary-Ann Disraeli.
For had not Mary-Ann also been a milliner in nearby
Culver Street, and had she not met and married the
handsome and wealthy MP Mr Wyndham Lewis from that
same shop? Of course, everyone knew that her second
husband, Benjamin Disraeli, was nothing but a dirty Jew
turned Christian for expediency, but nevertheless he had
become Chancellor of the Exchequer, which meant that
Mary-Ann moved in the very best circles. The fact that
she was dainty and beguilingly feminine was lost on
Bertha, who considered that with her large gentle eyes
and long bunches of curls on each side of her face, she
resembled nothing more remarkable than a spaniel.

So Bertha waited, with supreme self-confidence, for her
own wonderful destiny to materialize, and ignored the
fact that she was already well past thirty and needed the
most stringent corseting to control the rolls of soft fat
produced by her greatest weakness – food. Perpetually

hungry as a child, she was now completely unable to resist the gargantuan meals which local hostesses vied with each other to produce. The necessary corseting caused permanent dyspepsia and, no matter how carefully Bertha breathed, there was always an internal gurgle accompanied by a creak from one of the many whalebones confining her. Bertha chose to suffer the one and ignore the other. She was always perfectly and expensively gowned in silk, her hair elaborately coiffured. Until the recent past, when an application of henna had become necessary, she had always worn a profusion of her favourite gem, the garnet. Unfortunately, the dark red had clashed with the auburn of henna, so Bertha had immediately sold her collection of garnets and invested in golden topaz.

One of the many abilities on which she prided herself was of being instantly able to judge a person's class and occupation, yet the young woman standing before her definitely puzzled her: from one sweeping head-to-toe look Bertha noted the bedraggled bonnet, the shabby, rain-soaked dress and mantle, and decided that here was a seamstress, either seeking work or begging. In this she was partially correct, but the young woman spoke with an effortlessly cultivated accent very different from any ordinary seamstress, and there was a certain air of breeding and gentility about her; she *said* she was a physician's daughter, and appeared to have other accomplishments beyond the scope of Bertha's workers, or even of Bertha herself, whom she considerably disconcerted by initially speaking in rapid, obviously fluent French. Bertha was so startled that she forgot her own careful enunciation and said roughly, 'Us only speak English yere.' Then quickly recovering her poise, she demanded, 'Why aren't you a governess?' She thought this would make the young woman stammer out an excuse, but instead she answered very calmly: 'To obtain such a post would take time, madame, and I am in urgent need of employment and shelter.'

'You say you was – hm, *were* stayin' with friends and have had to leave suddenly through a bereavement?'

'Yes, when the father died last week, it was decided that his sister and daughter should remove to other relations.'

Ah ha! thought Bertha triumphantly, so she was the old man's doxy and was turned out! Yet again she was not absolutely sure: there was something about the level gaze and proud set of the head which belied this. 'Well,' she said at last, 'there's no work yere; there's great unemployment in Brisle, y'know.'

'Yes, so I have found,' said Madeleine, pride alone keeping the despair from her voice. 'Thank you, madame. I – I am sorry for having taken up your time.' She managed a small tired smile before turning to the door.

Bertha, who knew all about poverty, reluctantly admired the younger woman's courage and also her beautiful carriage and elegant, graceful walk. She prided herself on her own carriage – 'Like a ship in full sail,' her brother had once said; and thinking of him now had suddenly given her the germ of an idea. She ground her teeth together, a sure sign that she was thinking deeply and rapidly, and as Madeleine was about to close the shop door, Bertha said, 'There may be somethin'. Come back in ten minutes.'

'I couldn't wait here, could I?' asked Madeleine, whose legs felt as though they might give way any minute.

'Good heavens no!' exclaimed Bertha in a shocked tone. 'Whatever would my ladies say if they saw you yere?'

'Yes, of course, I'm sorry,' said Madeleine humbly. She supposed she must be looking quite awful by now. She had been walking the streets of Bristol the whole day in a fine drizzle which eventually had saturated her thin

135

mantle, while the skirt of her dress was caked with mud
to which wisps of straw stuck. There was a slight but
unmistakable smell of horse dung; she wrinkled her nose,
not only in distaste but hopelessness. She *had* tried to
keep her skirts clean, but the streets of Bristol were even
more filthy than those of London, and the crossing
sweepers appeared quite unable to cope. In addition, the
iron-rimmed wheels of every passing vehicle sent up a
spray of liquid mud which Madeleine, exhausted and
unfamiliar with her surroundings, had not always been
quick enough to dodge.

It was with something like joy that she heard Bertha
say on her return, 'Take this letter to my brother, Mr
George Sharpe, in Corn Street. He may have somethin',
but you'll have to hurry because he's got a dinner party
tonight an' will be leavin' the office early.'

'Oh, thank you, madame, thank you so much! Could
you very kindly tell me how to reach – '

But Bertha had seen a carriage drawing up outside.
'Yere, quick, out the back!' she exclaimed, moving with
remarkable speed for someone so large. 'Doan let them
see you!' She propelled Madeleine through a tiny dark
back room and almost thrust her out of the rear entrance.
Then she drew a deep breath, patted her hair and sailed
back into the shop, where she immediately sank into a
creaking curtsey. 'Why, my lady, I did not think to see
your Ladyship out in this inclement weather!'

Madeleine never really knew how she got to Corn
Street. She asked first an organ grinder and then a woman
selling garden produce at the kerbside, yet could understand neither because of their heavy accents. When she
approached a respectable-looking woman with, 'Please,
could you – ' the woman, thinking her a beggar, shielded
herself with her open umbrella and hurried past. But,
driven on by desperation, Madeleine eventually turned
into Corn Street as the clock on St Werbugh's Church was

striking five. She saw an imposing colonnaded building with strange objects which looked like flat-topped tables. Business was apparently being transacted around these, and Madeleine hurried across the congested street, only to find that the building was the exchange and not the one she wanted.

The head office of the Avon Shipping Line was immaculate and silent; all the clerks were bent diligently over their books when Madeleine at last found her way into it. A large board on the wall facing the entrance announced in bold red letters: WE ONLY DISCUSS BUSINESS HERE, while beneath it a stove glowed cheerfully. It was some minutes before one of the clerks reluctantly rose and sauntered over to Madeleine. 'Yes?' he queried offhandedly.

'I have been asked to give this to Mr George Sharpe,' said Madeleine hoarsely. It was thirteen hours since she had drunk a last glass of water in her room and now her voice was failing. As the clerk turned the sealed wafer over uncertainly, she made a last desperate effort. 'The note is from Mr Sharpe's sister and – and I was told to wait for an answer.'

That galvanized the clerk into action. He knew that Madame Berthe only wrote to her brother on matters of importance and he had vivid memories of her tongue-lashing – in the most colourful language – when delay had been caused in the past. 'Wait,' he said brusquely and darted away to an inner office.

Madeleine's lips parted in a sigh of heartfelt relief; her legs were literally trembling with exhaustion, but terror and willpower kept her on her feet. She had resolutely refused to think of where she was going to spend the night, but the terror was there at the back of her mind: she was almost penniless and knew only too well that if she collapsed in the street she would remain there until able to crawl to shelter or get back on to her feet.

'Brett!' The word shouted across the large room, made her start. She cleared her throat quickly, 'Yes – sir?'

'Come!' It was a barked order and she quailed inwardly as she hurried forward under the covertly inquisitive eyes of the clerks.

George Sharpe had gone to stand before his open fire, hands clasped behind his back under his coat-tails. As Madeleine hesitated in the doorway, he said impatiently, 'Well, come in an' shut the door, can't you?' His voice was naturally loud, the words being barked out in a harsher tone than his sister's, but they shared many other similarities: the same short weighty body – already running to paunchiness in his case – the thin-lipped concave mouths and small boot-button brown eyes which could strike fear into those whom brother and sister considered their inferiors.

He took his time now, looking over the young woman before him. She was certainly rain-soaked and the soot-laden air had clung to her wet face, giving it a fine coating of dirt, yet there was something about her – George Sharpe could not define it – but he knew that here was the genuine article: a lady, if ever he saw one, and passionate too, by the look of her beautiful mouth. His eyes roved slowly to her breasts, sharply outlined by the wetness of her mantle. Too small, he decided. He liked a big squashy handful that he could pummel, but at least hers were high and pointed with youth. Her waist, too, was exceptionally tiny and she was tall; he had no doubt that under all those skirts would be long, slender legs. He licked his lips. Good old Bertha, he thought. Unlike himself, she had never mastered the written word, yet she had got her meaning across; ''Corse er story may not be tru peraps shes a thief but somehow I dont think so & if Im rite she could be useful to you make er your housekeeper & companion to Dora mebee she could learn Dora a thing or 2 Gawd nos she needs it & wen the kids are older you will ave a governess 3 for the price of one yeres er adress in London get your solicitor to telegraf & find if it & the story is reel but meentime ang on to er cos if she goes now you may nefer find er again & shes reel diffrent.'

'I want a housekeeper,' Sharpe said now without preamble, 'and someone who will be a companion to my dear wife. Hm, she's not been too well since the birth of my son' – the useless, whey-faced bitch, he thought – 'and I'm willin' ter give you a try for two weeks, even though you've had no experience. If yer no good, you'll be out, no matter what time of day or night it is, but if you are – er – satisfactory, I'll keep you on with meals, yer own room and one candle a week, all provided. My staff is happy, the office outside is the cleanest, warmest one in Corn Street, if not the whole of Brisle, 'cos I give 'em a good stove and each clerk brings a bag of coal to feed it. I also bought 'em brooms, scrubbers and soap, and they get yere a half-hour early every marrnin' to clean all through. If I keep you, yer wages will be eleven pounds per annum – ' He broke off as Madeleine continued to stare at him, wide-eyed. He knew the wage was absurdly low; he gave his cook one pound more and she was underpaid by the current slowly rising rate, yet he was expecting Madeleine to do two jobs. 'Well,' he said curtly, 'take it or leave it; I haven't got all night.'

'Oh yes, yes please, I do want to take it, sir,' Madeleine said eagerly. She had hardly been able to believe her luck: she was being offered shelter and food, the two essential ingredients for survival, and for the time being the spectre of the dreaded dosshouse was removed. 'May I start straightaway?'

'Yes. I'm givin' a dinner party tonight, got the Lord Mayor, Chief Constable an' some of the biggest bankers comin', so I'm leavin' now. Come!' he barked as a discreet tap sounded on the door.

'Carriage is yere, sir,' said a clerk, sliding quickly into

view and then, as he hesitated, his employer shouted: 'Well, don't stand there, dolt, get my coat an' hat!'

The man scuttled to do his bidding and as he was heaved into his greatcoat, George Sharpe turned his small eyes to stare at Madeleine. 'An' what are you waitin' for?' he demanded.

'I do not know where you live or how to get there,' Madeleine faltered.

He came to stand in front of her and wag a thick finger in her face. 'First thing you got to learn, my girl, is that all my staff call me "Sir". I'm payin' for good work and respect, y'know.'

'I beg your pardon, sir,' Madeleine said humbly, even while the hot colour rose to her cheeks. 'I meant no disrespect.'

'I should think not!' was the barked reply. 'Come, I'll take you up with me – can't waste time givin' you directions.' He strode from the room, and as he passed through the outer office all the clerks rose hastily and intoned 'Goodnight, sir!' which was acknowledged by a curt nod.

At the open street door he suddenly stopped and Madeleine, who had found some difficulty in keeping up with him, almost cannoned into his back. 'Isn't she beaut'ful.' It was a statement rather than a question, and he was looking straight ahead at a light, graceful carriage drawn up outside.

'Oh yes, very elegant,' said Madeleine, wondering if he had really meant that she was to accompany him in this.

'Saw the model at the Exhibition, y'know, an' ordered one from Mulliner of Northampton. It's called a pilentum and it's the only one yere. Usually has a crowd admirin' it.' He swept forward, flailing to left and right with his cane at the small ragged urchins who had suddenly appeared with hands outstretched. 'Yere! Get off, the lot of you, good for nothin' little varmints!' He leapt into the vehicle and sat down heavily. Then as Madeleine stood hesitating, he roared: 'You deaf or jus' dull? I told you I haven't got all night!' He made no attempt to help as she stammered an apology and hoisted first the valise and then herself into the carriage. 'You'll have to look sharp, y'know,' her employer told her, with a hard stare. 'Got no time or money to waste on dozy workers!'

Madeleine bit her lip to keep back the tears of exhaustion. There was no doubt that her new employer was an aggressive boor and her heart sank as she thought of all that her duties might entail. How was she ever to be a satisfactory housekeeper to such a man – and what would his wife be like? She stole a timid sideways glance at him as he sat with arms akimbo and beaver tipped over closed eyes. Whatever happened, she must be sure to obtain a good reference from him as any future employment would be impossible without one. It was strange that he appeared to have accepted her statement that she had never worked before, even though this was, of course, the truth.

The journey seemed to take a long while, partly because of the congestion in the streets and then, a little later, because the horse was struggling up a steep incline. The city centre had been left behind and they were driving through an elegant residential neighbourhood of Georgian houses in whose long windows lights were beginning to appear. Then they were drawing up in front of a tall terraced house which was in darkness except for a dim light showing through the fanlight and side panels of the front door. This time, when her employer leapt from the carriage, Madeleine was at his heels. He tugged at the bell and then hammered on the door with his cane, muttering a violent oath, before spinning round and glaring at Madeleine.

'I'll expect you to see that the damned girl answers the door at once,' he said, even as the door opened a crack and half a female face became visible. With another oath, George Sharpe thrust the door open, flattening the maid against the wall. 'How many times 'ave I got to tell you, this door must be answered at once!' he shouted, 'an' why aren't there any lights showin'?'

The maid just had time to bob hastily before his coat and hat were flung at her. 'Please, sir,' she said in a snuffling voice, 'I thought yer said no lights until yer come home.'

'Only when we've not got company comin',' was the angry reply. 'I s'pose the mistress is upstairs dressin'?'

'Naow, sir, her be in drawin' room.' It was too dim for Madeleine to see the expression on the girl's face, but the malice in her voice was unmistakable; so the girl hated her mistress. Madeleine just had time to hope that Mrs Sharpe was less odious than her husband before George Sharpe flung open a door and shouted, 'Why aren't you dressed yet?'

In contrast to the hall, the drawing room was brilliant with the yellow light of a huge gasolier, and its brightness fell harshly on the pallid face of the woman reclining on a large red plush sofa.

'I can't, George, I can't. I feel ill, reel ill.' The words were spoken in a low whine, but although her face was twisted in obvious fear, she did not move.

With a roar Sharpe leapt forward. ''Course you're comin'!' he shouted, seizing both her wrists and hauling her to her feet so roughly that one of her slippers flew off. Then, transferring his grip to her upper arm, he strode forward. 'My slipper!' she protested, but he paid no heed and she was forced to follow, walking awkwardly, her unshod foot constantly catching on the hem of the skirt. When they reached the hall he thrust her forward with such force that she crashed full-length on the first stairs. She lay there, completely winded, but he continued to hound her mercilessly. 'Now get up!' he ordered. 'Unless you wan' me ter take my strap ter you.' It was obvious that she had knowledge of this, for she uttered a whimpering scream and began to drag herself up the stairs on hands and knees.

'Oh, dear God,' whispered Madeleine, cringing against the wall. Beside her she heard the maid snigger, and turning her head saw that the girl's face was animated, eyes shining and thick lips parted in the travesty of a smile. Can it be that she is actually enjoying all this? Madeleine wondered, appalled and sickened. She wanted to rush from the house, but outside darkness had fallen and she had no idea where she was. If she left now, she might have to face worse nightmares in which she could quite easily be victim rather than onlooker.

At that moment Sharpe became conscious of Madeleine and the maid. 'Well, wha' the hell are you two standin' there for?' he shouted, glaring from one to the other.

Madeleine moved away from the wall and drew herself upright, even though her heart continued to thud in her ears. 'I am just waiting, sir,' she said evenly, 'to know what you would like me to do first.'

Her quiet tone seemed to calm him somewhat. 'Why, to help my stupid cow of a wife to dress, o' course,' he said, actually lowering his voice a little. 'An' then get downstairs an' see that the dinin' table an' food is all proper.'

'Very good, sir, but may I first wash and change?' As he appeared about to roar a refusal, Madeleine hurried on, 'I – I just don't think that I should enter a lady's bedroom or be anywhere near food without washing.'

He made an impatient gesture with his hand. 'Five minutes then,' he said grudgingly, before turning into the drawing room and flinging the door shut.

Madeleine turned to the maid. 'I am Madeleine Brett, the new housekeeper,' she said quietly. 'Will you please show me where my room is.'

143

The girl laughed outright then. 'New housekeeper, are you?' she queried mockingly, 'Well, Gawd help us all then!'

'That's enough,' said Madeleine. 'Now, please show me – '

'At the top of the back stairs, firs' on lef',' muttered the girl as she turned away.

'I have a valise and I shall need a candle and water to wash. I cannot carry them all,' said Madeleine, letting authority creep into her voice. 'So I shall require you to lead the way.' As the girl looked about to refuse, Madeleine added quietly, 'At once, if you please.'

'Aw, all right then,' said the girl sullenly. 'Bu' I can't stop ter heat no wa'er farr you.'

'Cold will do for now,' conceded Madeleine, 'so long as there is a good jugful.' She regretted not having insisted upon hot water when, five minutes later, she stood in the attic room and looked around her. It was desperately cold and cheerless, with only a bed, plain deal table and washstand with enamel jug and basin. The straw mattress was covered with paper-thin cotton which might once have been white but was now grey and stained. There was one thin blanket; the plain floorboards were devoid of linoleum or mat and the one small window set in the sloping roof was uncurtained. There was no looking glass, but on the wall facing the bed a framed sampler worked in crude colours sternly admonished the room's occupant to PREPARE TO MEET THY GOD, the words being encircled by unlikely-looking flowers, and with a trumpet-blowing angel floating in one corner.

A weak, hysterical giggle rose in Madeleine's throat at the sight of it, but the next instant this had given way to great heaving sobs as despair and exhaustion claimed her and she wondered if there could be any worse shocks in store for her on this dreadful night. She sank down on to the bed, but its very hardness roused her. She must not

144

be turned out into the street – hadn't the terrifying man warned her that she would be thrown out, regardless of time, if she were unsatisfactory? She dragged herself off the bed and began feverishly to unpack her valise. She had only one other dress, a sprigged cotton and quite unsuitable, but it would have to do. Swiftly she pulled off her mud-caked skirt and underwear, had a quick but thorough wash in the cold water, and with teeth chattering, redressed, fingers fumbling with buttons and hooks as she tried to hurry. Her house shoes, not worn since she left London, had huge holes in the soles, and this time there was no paper to stuff into them. Instead she took out two of her treasured fashion plates; the styles illustrated were outmoded, but she had always been able to adapt them. Ruthlessly now she cut the thin board into the shape of her feet and pushed it into the shoes.

As she did so, there was a distant roar from the lower floor: 'Brett!' Madeleine rushed from the room, smoothing her hair as she went; there had been no time to take it down and redo it and she could only hope that it looked fairly tidy. As she emerged from the back stairs on to the front landing, Sharpe was standing in shirt sleeves outside a bedroom from which brilliant light streamed. 'In yere,' he commanded brusquely, and as Madeleine paused on the threshold, Dora Sharpe saw her reflected in the dressing-table mirror.

'Who's she?' she demanded.

'This is Brett, our new housekeeper, who will also act as a companion ter you, Dora.'

Instantly Dora's rather slack features tightened into wariness. 'But I don' wan' no companion.'

'Well, you're goin' ter have one, like it or not,' her husband announced as he struggled into his black cutaway. 'An' mebbe Brett can tell you how to behave – as the wife of one of Brisle's leadin' businessmen!'

With a movement startling for so lethargic a woman,

145

Dora swivelled to face him and said with passionate appeal, 'George! Don' make me come down – don' show me up in fron' of all them people! You know I can' tark ter them, you know they laugh at me – jus' as they do at you, behind yer back. Us don' belong in this big house – or with all them grand business folk. Us should be back in Bedminster. Let's go back, George, jus' you an' me an' the kids, back to our roots – an' I swear I'll try an' be a dootiful wife!'

It was as though her husband had not heard her, for he went to stand before the long cheval glass, first to straighten his waistcoat then to turn from side to side in self-appraisal, whistling softly all the while through his teeth. When at last he spoke his voice was quiet, even silky. 'Why, Dora love, you can go back ter Bedminster this minute, if you wan'. But mind, if you do, you don' never come back!'

And that's why she has to bear it all, Madeleine thought with sudden insight, for if she leaves him she will be an outcast without money or a home, and even her children will be denied her. So, monster though he is, she is better off with him, for he provides food, shelter and the status of a married woman.

'Dozin' agin, Brett?' The voice was still quiet, but to Madeleine's frayed nerves it held even more menace than his earlier ranting. But mercifully he was now striding to the door. 'I'll not have it, y'know – jus' you remember, I'll not have it!'

Before Madeleine could think of a reply a loud wail came from Dora Sharpe. 'He's goin' ter send me packin'. I knewed it all the time, I did! I did! Even though I done my best, he don' wan' I no more!'

Madeleine went forward slowly, stirred to compassion by the broken-down figure before her. Then, as Dora continued to sob noisily, Madeleine sank to her knees and put a tentative hand on the woman's shaking shoulder.

'Surely he would do no such thing,' she said soothingly. 'You are his wife and the mother of his children, and think how his reputation would suffer if he were to send you away.'

The sobs ended abruptly as Dora raised a tear-drenched face to gaze at Madeleine. 'Who *are* you?' she asked hoarsely.

'I am Madeleine Brett and I am here to help you run this large house, as I believe you have not been very well.'

'Yes – yes.' Dora's voice sounded almost eager now. 'I been ever so ill; the doctor, he said it were touch an' go, but' – her face crumpled again – 'no one cares if I lives or dies. I got no friend in the world.'

'I should like to be your friend, if you would let me,' Madeleine said gently.

The ravaged face was raised once more, but now the eyes were narrowed. 'You always tark like you got somethin' in yer mouth, or are you jus' puttin' it on?'

'Why, I believe this is my normal voice,' Madeleine replied, wondering if she dared smile. Dora's unwavering stare was embarrassing and even vaguely disturbing; that she was physically ill was obvious, but it was the expression in her eyes which sent the merest shiver down Madeleine's spine, for she knew instinctively that the other woman's mental balance was precarious.

As though in confirmation, Dora's face tightened once more as she said suspiciously, 'Wha' makes you wan' ter be my friend? The likes o' you nefer have!' The last words were spat out with sudden venom, but Madeleine forced herself to remain calm.

'Perhaps – er – madam, we are not so different, for I, too, feel very alone and have no friends in this city . . .' Her voice trailed into silence as Dora continued to stare mutely.

Then suddenly Dora smiled and drew her hands together as though about to clap. 'Yes! Tha's wos us'll be

– reel friends an' you can tak me down ter the Hot Wells for the wa'er an' to Park Street, 'course' – her voice sank to a whisper – 'he nefer gives me no money, bu' us can look.'

Madeleine wondered fleetingly how she was ever going to fit in all her duties, but she tried to speak with real warmth: 'That would be very nice, but now, madam, perhaps you should dress for your party?'

Dora had obviously forgotten about the evening for she exclaimed and sprang up so suddenly that Madeleine fell back on her heels. 'Get my dress,' ordered the other woman imperiously, pointing to where a blue satin gown lay on an elaborately lacquered and canopied bed. When Madeleine complied, Dora threw off her wrapper to reveal underwear of plain cotton, greyish, none too clean, and even torn in places. Then, as Madeleine lifted the gown over the spare bony frame and fastened the many tiny hooks from neckline to waist, Dora leaned forward to open a large jewel box. 'Pretty, aren't they?'

Madeleine, who had all the feminine woman's appreciation of jewellery, replied enthusiastically, 'Oh yes, very.'

'I expec' you'd like ter have some jools too, wouldn' you?' The words were spoken softly, but something made Madeleine look up and meet Dora's eyes in the mirror: they were narrowed with suspicion, even though her mouth smiled. Madeleine forced herself to say lightly, 'Diamonds do not go well with cotton dresses, madam, and whoever heard of a housekeeper wearing jewellery?'

'Still, wif tha' face I expec' yer're hopin' ter find a rich husband, aren't you?' Dora did not wait for a reply before adding obscurely, 'But Mr Sharpe isn' rich, y'know – everythin's on tick, the shippin' line is only third-rate an' he isn' reely one of Brisle's leadin' businessmen.'

I can believe that, Madeleine thought dryly, but why is she telling me? Surely she doesn't think I would ever want him? The idea was so absurd that she almost laughed, but instantly there came the memory of Sebastian, whom she *did* want with all her heart, and the laugh in her throat changed to a hastily suppressed sob.

'Yere, help me with this.' Dora's voice had resumed its normal grating tone and her expression was stony as she held out a diamond pendant.

How will I ever be able to keep up with her constantly changing moods? Madeleine wondered despairingly. But when Dora stood before the cheval glass and asked, 'How do I look?' compassion made her say gently, 'Very nice, madam; the gown is pretty and the blue complements your eyes.'

Dora was childishly delighted and peered closely at herself. 'So it do!' she exclaimed, laughing and even pirouetting as she continued to gaze into the mirror.

'Your gloves and fan, madam?' queried Madeleine, and realized just too late that she had said the wrong thing, for Dora's animation ended as abruptly as it had begun. She stood quite still. 'I got no fan or gloves,' she said, sounding like a forlorn child.

'Well, never – ' began Madeleine, and then gasped as Dora started rushing about the room, trying to tear off her gown.

'I can't go down – I can't, can't, *can't*!' Her voice rose to a screech, but when taken by the shoulders she quietened long enough for Madeleine to say authoritatively, 'Do not upset yourself, madam! You are in your own house and may wear what you wish. The other ladies will just follow your lead, so please compose yourself and come down now.'

'You reely – '

'Yes. And tomorrow we shall ask Mr Sharpe to let you purchase gloves and a pretty fan for when you return your guests' visit.' Somehow she managed to get Dora out of the room and heading for the stairs.

'You come too,' Dora begged, as though their rôles

had become reversed, but before Madeleine could assimilate this, Sharpe appeared on the stairs.

'Wha' the hell d'you think yer doin' yere?' he demanded.

'Why, er – er, sir, I am escorting Madam down to the drawing room,' Madeleine stammered, nerves jangling.

'Not down these stairs, you aren't! The back ones are for the likes o' you, m' girl, jus' you remember tha'. An' now, be orff ter the dinin' room, d'you hear me. Be orff!'

I'll never be able to stand it, Madeleine thought as she turned and ran down the servants' stairs. Why, even the rogues in the alleys and rookeries of London, despite their shouted obscenities and half-savage way of life, have more natural kindness than this man, and I believe that she, poor soul, is half mad.

The dining room was a revelation and looked like a set piece from the Great Exhibition, with its Turkey carpet, ornate mahogany furniture and dark, heavily patterned wallpaper. The long window was shrouded and beswagged in red velvet, but it was the table which immediately drew Madeleine's eye: enormous, and covered in white damask, it was set with gold-plated cutlery and a dinner service of Crown Derby, its red and blue clashing with the claret and deep blue of the Bristol glass. Three elaborate gold-plated epergnes, loaded with fruit and topped with maidenhair fern, stood at regular intervals along the centre of the table. The whole effect was vulgar and garish in the extreme, yet it all represented a great deal of money. What kind of household was this, Madeleine wondered dazedly, where the mistress wore satin and diamonds but dirty underwear; where the cutlery was gold-plated but incorrectly placed and looked as though it had been slapped down carelessly? She thought of the simple elegance of the de Laceys' table: the heavy Georgian silver, delicate crystal glasses and old, flower-patterned Meissen service with the family's crest in the centre of each plate. But, she chided herself, it was no use thinking of the past; if she was to survive at all in this household, she would need to focus her entire concentration on the present. She went round the table then, putting the cutlery in its right order and straightening everything.

But the kitchen was the worst of all: smoke-blackened, its floor littered with vegetable peelings, it smelled pungently of hot, unwashed bodies and cooking. The large deal table was covered with elaborate dishes of chicken galantine, plovers' eggs garnished with aspic jelly, and lobster mayonnaise, together with raised pies and ham with truffles. Madeleine gasped and saliva filled her mouth. She had eaten nothing but a hot potato purchased for a farthing from a street seller hours before; the sight of so much food made her feel faint with hunger and she quickly grasped the table for support. A huge woman in a filthy apron had turned from the roaring range and was regarding her with tiny, hostile eyes. Madeleine straightened and attempted a wan smile. 'I am Madeleine Brett, the new housekeeper,' she said hesitantly.

'Oh ah,' said the cook, pushing back her dirty cap and vigorously scratching her head. This done, she looked in a leisurely fashion at the scurf under her nails and set about scraping it out with a thumb nail.

Madeleine swallowed a sudden feeling of nausea and asked quietly, 'And you, of course, are the cook, Mrs . . .?'

'Boot,' said the woman, pretending to concentrate on her scraping and ignoring Madeleine. What a very appropriate name, thought Madeleine wryly, for she looks as tough as old boots; but, anxious not to antagonize the woman, she said, 'You have a wonderful array of dishes here, and some hot ones too, I see. May I take a look?'

Mrs Boot shrugged. ''elp yerself.'

Madeleine moved to the blissful warmth of the range,

on which a dozen copper pans stood. She carefully lifted the lid of the nearest and saw a great quantity of clear vermicelli soup simmering; the smell was delicious, but then as she looked more closely, she saw that the inside of the pan was green with verdigris. Once more she gasped with shock and hastily replaced the lid, but when she looked into the other pans of beans and potatoes, they were all in the same state. She turned to the cook and said almost apologetically, 'The pans look as though they are in need of relining and appear covered in verdigris.'

'In wha'?' asked the cook loudly, beginning to show signs of belligerence.

'The green inside, surely it will spoil all your lovely food and give it a very metallic taste?'

'Haven't nefer bin no complaints,' shrugged Mrs Boot and then, as Madeleine hesitated, uncertain about asserting her authority, the cook folded short fat arms across her huge breast and took the initiative. 'An' now, Miss Clever Cat, you can get out o' my kitchen double quick an' not come back.'

'But,' Madeleine protested, 'if I am to housekeep, we must work together.'

Mrs Boot rushed forward and, in a fair imitation of her master, she whirled Madeleine around and began pushing her towards the door. 'Out! Git out!' she shouted viciously. But just when she thought she had won, Madeleine turned.

'Take your hands off me, you filthy old woman!' she said, not raising her voice but speaking with such authority that the cook actually stopped with hands in mid-air and gaped at her. 'And,' continued Madeleine, 'I want all those pans cleaned with lemon skin dipped in silver sand and salt until every spot of verdigris is removed. If this is not done, I shall go straight to Mr Sharpe.' Then she quietly walked out of the kitchen and up the stairs, glad that the cook could not hear her painfully thudding heart. But Mrs Boot was not overawed for long; as Madeleine walked tremblingly along the passage, she heard a burst of raucous, derisive laughter followed by the violent slamming of the kitchen door.

There were still the two waiters to be dealt with. Madeleine discovered they had been hired for the evening, and when she attempted to find out if they knew their duties, one came to stand very close behind her, while the other faced her. He was so near that she could smell his fetid breath when he leered at her. As the man behind fumbled her skirts, she darted away from them both. 'Keep your hands to yourselves,' she said furiously, 'or I'll see that you leave without your wages.' Both men hissed obscenities at her then, not daring to raise their voices, but Madeleine walked calmly from the room. Such language was not unknown to her and, although she trembled with anger, she knew she could deal with it – it was far less menacing than fumbling hands.

It was hunger which eventually drove her back to the kitchen. After the ladies had retired to the drawing room and the gentlemen were lingering over their port, Madeleine descended once more to the basement, where Mrs Boot and three other women were seated at the table, piled plates in front of them. A sudden silence fell as Madeleine appeared, until Mrs Boot said rudely, from a full mouth, 'Wha' yer wan' now?'

'Some food,' Madeleine replied briefly. No one volunteered to tell her where a plate and cutlery could be found, but all eyes were upon her as she moved calmly around until she found what she needed and then began to help herself from the many dishes of food returned from the dining room. 'The guests do not appear to have eaten very much,' she remarked, and glanced up just in time to see a look of triumph pass between the cook and her companions.

Madeleine paused in the middle of spooning *chaudfroid* of chicken on to her plate. What if Mrs Boot deliberately left the pans in a filthy state, knowing that the food would be largely inedible and would then be returned to the kitchen? It would not be too difficult for the staff to then scrape off the sides and bottom of food and so remove most of the verdigris. Madeleine sat down and began to do this to her own food under the silent scrutiny of the four women. Despite her efforts, the food tasted distinctly metallic and she wrinkled her nose fastidiously, but hunger forced her to continue eating; indeed, it required all her willpower not to bolt each mouthful, so ravenous had she become.

Afterwards she wondered if anyone would have spoken to her at all if a quiet knocking on the street door had not then been heard. 'Emmy,' said Mrs Boot, and the scullery maid hastened to the door. 'Do 'ave some wine,' Mrs Boot suddenly suggested to Madeleine, smiling ingratiatingly. 'When it come down from the table, us always finishes it orff. Red or white?'

'Some white, please,' said Madeleine, curiosity making her keep her eyes on Emmy, who was silently handing two large bags to the unseen caller. Madeleine bit her lip: food was being smuggled out of the house, and she supposed that as housekeeper she would be expected to stop it. No doubt Mrs Boot's sudden attempt at civility had been made to divert her attention; over the rim of a mugful of wine she met the cook's eyes. Mrs Boot continued to smile, revealing blackened and broken teeth, but her eyes remained hostile. Well, thought Madeleine philosophically, there's so little to choose between master and cook: they're both equally awful, and if the smuggling has been going on for ages, why should I interfere so long as the pans are cleaned? Perhaps the food is for someone who really needs it: heaven knows, I've seen enough beggars and ragged children in this city today.

Her thoughts were suddenly interrupted by a vibrant hiss of 'The marrster!' from Mrs Boot. Emmy closed the street door, forgetting in her panic to do this quietly, but George Sharpe's attention was entirely centred upon Madeleine.

'Can you sing an' play the piano?' he asked anxiously, his face red and a small tic below his left eye very noticeable.

'Why, yes.'

'Come on then!' he shouted, already turning away. 'Come an' entertain the guests!'

'Oh, but – '

'*Will* you come on?' demanded Sharpe impatiently, 'or do I have ter drag you there?'

She had to comply, of course, even though she shrank from having to face a roomful of people. When she had been tidying Dora Sharpe's bedroom she had caught sight of herself in the glass and was horrified at her appearance: not only was her face white and pinched, but the black circles under her eyes were like large bruises, and her hair, which had been put up while still half wet in the early hours of the morning, looked wispily untidy. As she followed George Sharpe into the drawing room, he announced loudly: 'My dear friends, may I present Miss Madleen Brett, my dear wife's companion, who will now entertain us with some songs an' piano playin'.'

Madeleine stood blinking in the sudden dazzle of the gasolier. There seemed to be banks of brilliant colours, of light-catching jewels and snow-white shirt fronts scattered about the room, and she realized there were some twenty people present, all gazing at her silently.

'Come, Madleen, m'dear,' said her employer silkily. 'You mus' not be shy!'

So Madeleine curtseyed to the assembly and moved to the grand piano, which stood, covered in deeply fringed velvet, between the two windows. What on earth was she

155

to play? As she flexed her fingers, she stole a quick glance at the few guests: they were all opulently dressed in the height of fashion, but there were few smiles and no signs of conviviality among them. George Sharpe was darting about, smiling and bending to say a word here and there, but his wife sat in silence, her expression mulish and her only movement a nervous pulling of one earring. They are all completely bored, thought Madeleine, and this gave her courage. She launched into the tarantella and followed it with two Chopin waltzes before George Sharpe called out: 'Sing us a nice ballad, Madleen!' She gave him a fleeting, ironic glance: 'Madleen', indeed! When before it had been a bawled 'Brett'.

So she sang them 'Meet Me By Moonlight', 'Barbara Allen' and 'Charlie Is My Darlin'', and her voice was just beginning to fail when one of the hired waiters announced that the carriages had arrived. The guests rose with alacrity; most had clapped her after each song, but there was no doubt that the party was a failure. Madeleine suspected that the guests were not only bored, but hungry. Only two men came forward to thank her for playing 'so delightfully' and when she curtseyed and thanked them in turn, George Sharpe at once bustled up saying, 'Come, come, m'dear, it is "My Lord Mayor" not just "Sir", and this other gentleman is Lieutenant Henry Fisher, our Chief Constable.' But both men immediately waved aside Madeleine's apology and even shook her hand before departing. One or two of the other men cast ogling looks at her, but their womenfolk ignored her completely.

Madeleine slowly closed the piano, and the memory, kept at bay until now by desperation, took over: the last time she had risen from a piano she had fainted and Sebastian had scooped her up in his arms. She remembered his race up the stairs with her, his rakish grin and the lights dancing in his eyes; most vivid of all was the feel of his arms still about her after he had laid her on the

156

bed, and the way his wide shoulders had blocked the candlelight. The memory was a searing pain which literally made her body shake.

'Brett!' The shout cut across her reverie, and she started nervously.

'Yes, sir.'

George Sharpe came striding back into the room, looking thunderous: 'I wan' a word with you, an' you, too, Dora,' he said, catching sight of his wife trying to slink up the stairs.

'I'm ever so tired, George,' she replied whiningly, but after he had given her one telling look, she said, 'Aw, all right then,' and came slowly back into the room, looking imploringly at Madeleine as she did so.

'The dinner was terrible,' said Sharpe, standing in his favourite stance before the dying fire. 'The dishes were hardly touched, an' by this time tomorrer all Brisle will know tha' my guests wen' home hungry.' He whirled suddenly to his wife. 'Why?' he barked.

Dora started visibly but then made a pathetic attempt at indifference. 'I dunno,' she said. 'It all seemed all right ter me. Perhaps they wasn't hungry.'

'Aw, don' try ter be more stupid than you are!' exploded Sharpe. His eye fell upon Madeleine. 'An' you, Brett? Yer lookin' very thoughtful an' I reckon you know the answer.'

Madeleine hesitated only briefly. 'Yes, I do know,' she said calmly. 'It was because all the copper cooking pans are full of verdigris. It gave the food a very metallic taste and it is also very bad for one's health.'

'Is tha' so?' Sharpe's voice had suddenly become silky. 'An' whose fault was it tha' the pans had this – verdy – verdy gree?'

'Why, the cook and the maids. But really your previous housekeeper should have supervised the staff more thoroughly.' To Madeleine's astonishment, this caused Sharpe to guffaw loudly before he swung back abruptly to his wife. 'Hear tha', Dora luv?'

Madeleine realized that Dora was now looking at her with both suspicion and hostility, and instantly understood: there had been no former housekeeper, and George Sharpe had used her as a means of venting his fury upon his wife. He strode now to the doorway and yelled, 'Boot!' When an answering shout reached him from the basement, he added: 'Git up yere with Emmy an' Jess!'

And Dora, her face suddenly contorted with blazing anger, hissed at Madeleine: 'I knewed you was lying about bein' my friend. I just knewed it all the time you was talkin' so sweet an' nice. You're nothin' but a schemin' bitch!'

There was no chance to explain, and later, as she trudged upstairs after yet another dreadful scene, Madeleine realized that she had now made a bitter enemy of Dora as well as the maids, and she had no doubt they would do everything they could to discredit her. It was a frightening thought, but she was too exhausted to care much. She just wanted to sleep, and told herself that it did not much matter if she never awoke.

A distant crash made the windows rattle and Mabel, the nursemaid, plodding up behind Madeleine, giggled: 'Thank Gawd for tha'! He's gone to his dolly-mop an' now us'll be able ter git some sleep. The missus doan like him in her bed, y'know, an' when he stays home, the air's blue with their yellin'. He used ter have a reel doxy but her give him a dose of clap las' year, her did.'

Oh, isn't there just one decent human being in this terrible house? Madeleine wondered as she dragged off her clothes in the icy room. She thought longingly of her luxurious room in Royal Crescent, then quickly tried to put this out of her mind. But it was as she lay shivering in the cold lumpy bed that her thoughts took over.

Exhausted as she was, sleep seemed to elude her, and instead all that she had experienced on this most dreadful day of her life processed like pictures behind her closed lids.

When she had left Royal Crescent, she was still dazed and with no clear idea of where she was going or what she intended to do. But the city was already beginning to stir: servants were cleaning brass door knockers and whitening front steps, drovers were arriving from the surrounding countryside with their produce, and she even saw sheep being shepherded into roadside pens. After she had almost been knocked down twice by Lurcher dogs pulling barrows, Madeleine tried to collect her thoughts. The dogs moved at a tremendous pace, stopping for no one, and if she were injured by them, or one of the horse-drawn carts . . . It was as she was passing the Greyhound Inn that she heard two drovers mention 'Brisle' and, on a sudden impulse, she stopped and asked if they would be returning to Bristol; when one confirmed that he was about to do so, Madeleine asked if he would take her up with him. He was young, with a round apple-cheeked face, clear eyes and an accent so thick that she could not hold even the simplest conversation with him, but he conveyed her into the heart of Bristol.

There she wandered, not knowing anything about the city but conscious that she must find the main thorough-fare. At one stage she thought she must have stepped back in time, so narrow were the streets and so ancient the buildings with their steep-pointed gables and over-hanging windows. Later, drawn by the clean tang of the sea, she suddenly came upon tall-masted sailing ships at anchor in what appeared to be docks in the centre of city activity. She also saw warehouses and churches, potteries, tanneries and banks. Then, rounding the corner of one narrow street, she was faced by a great number of enormous pigs advancing upon her with snorts and

159

squeals. They entirely filled the street and she had the terrible feeling that if she did not get out of their way they would simply trample her underfoot. Panic-stricken, she turned and ran until her heart seemed about to burst and her old valise was like a great stone weight in her hand. This fright, more than anything else, made her focus her thoughts coherently. Soon after that, she had reached Park Street and made desperate attempts to find work at one of the many shops . . .

Madeleine turned in the cold bed, longing for sleep, but the one thought she had resolutely held at bay now kept her awake: Sebastian! Had she really lain in his arms the night before? Had she really been so stupid that she had allowed him to use her? Already the whole incident seemed to belong to another life, and yet every detail was burnt into her memory. In the bright light of day she might fool herself into thinking that she hated him as much as he despised her, but here in the darkness her heart told her that she would love him for ever, that she longed for his nearness and that she would only ever be half a woman until he held her in his arms again. The thought made her burn with shame even as her reason told her that it could never be, she would never see him again, let alone be close to him – or to any man – for had not papa said, 'No matter how profligate a man may be, he always wants the woman he marries to be an untouched virgin.'

Then what is to become of me? she asked herself in terror, but, exhausted as she was, her spirit reasserted itself. She would leave this terrible household as soon as possible and find a job as a governess; it was what girls of her class always did, and with her fluent knowledge of French, she might even be able to work in France. That was it: an entirely new life where she could live quietly and, *perhaps*, in time the memory of that one night would fade, the night which had been both wonderful and totally heartbreaking.

So, at the age of nineteen, Madeleine thought her life was over. But of course it was to be quite different.

10

It did not seem as though she'd slept any time at all when loud movements from the next room roused her. Madeleine had no idea of the time, and the light filtering through the dirty window pane was dim, yet there was the sound of water being poured, followed by a short series of gasps and squeaks as Mabel, the nursemaid, performed brief ablutions; she whistled softly as she dressed and then began to make her bed. It was obviously time to get up and Madeleine dragged herself off the bed. The room was freezing and there was even a thin film of ice on the water in the enamel ewer.

It was as she lifted her nightgown that she felt it: a terrible nausea which had her rushing to the slop pail. Oh, those awful dirty pans, she thought dazedly when the vomiting and retching finally ceased. She felt hot, yet was shivering and faint. 'Fresh air,' papa had said, 'always remember that fresh air is most necessary'. So, pulling on a shawl, Madeleine tottered to the window. It appeared not to have been touched for years and the catch was actually rusted into place. But after a struggle she managed to raise the lower half. Freezing air, crisp and tangy, hit her like a blow, but Madeleine gulped it in until gradually her stomach settled. Then she stared in surprise at the scene before her: it was a deep, magnificent gorge, thickly wooded on the far side and with a broad silver ribbon of river curving along its base. It was beautiful, and only slightly marred by the tall, flat-topped brick towers standing on each side of the gorge, which appeared to have no useful function.

Madeleine was to see more of the Avon Gorge later

that day when Dora sent her down to the Hot Wells for a bottle of the famous spa water, but by then she was incapable of admiring the scenery, magnificent though it undoubtedly was. Dora had sent her first to High Street to buy meat, and as soon as she had trudged back to Clifton, she was sent down to Park Street to buy extract of elderflowers for Dora's complexion; then down again, this time to the Hot Wells, and the long, steep zigzag walk back on legs that were trembling with weakness. Several times nausea and dizziness forced her to stop, and she wondered how long she was going to be able to continue.

Nor was her torment over when she eventually returned to the house, for every few minutes, wherever she was, there would be a scream of 'Brett!' and when she got to the drawing room Dora would send her upstairs for a handkerchief, then back for smelling salts or a book – anything, in fact, which would keep Madeleine continually in motion. Always on her return Dora would look at her silently, but with eyes brightly malicious, and Madeleine knew she was being subjected to a campaign of petty cruelty. She had tried several times to win back Dora's confidence, but the woman refused point-blank to listen, even rushing from the room with a screech, hands clamped over her ears. Things might have been very different if she had listened, for with Madeleine's support and compassion, her fragile personality might have stabilized sufficiently for her to take some charge of her ramshackle household. Instead, friendless, abused by her husband and held in contempt by her servants, she found in Madeleine the perfect means of assuaging all her own pent-up hurt, bitterness and inadequacy. For the first time in her life she had absolute power over another human being and she used this with all the unremitting ruthlessness of the very weak.

When hunger and thirst eventually drove Madeleine down to the kitchen, all conversation immediately ceased and no one made a move to serve her. She knew that she should be able to have her food alone, but where – in the icy, cheerless attic? No other room had been allocated for her use and at least the kitchen was blessedly warm. But when the food was in front of her, she could hardly swallow it although, aware that all eyes were silently fixed upon her, she tried hard to do so.

It was almost a relief to start up at the now familiar bellow from the master demanding her presence. She found that she was expected to give a minute account of every farthing she had spent and he contested each item: 'You paid *ninepence* for meat?' he queried, voice registering extreme shock.

'It is the best cut, sir,' Madeleine answered quietly, hands clenched in the folds of her dress.

'I doan' care!' was the shouted reply. 'You'll have ter do be'er or you'll be out of yere!' It was to be a nightly inquisition: 'Wha's this, a pair of Dover soles for 1s 6d!' or, 'Are you reely tellin' me you paid one shillin' for a rabbit?' When Dora ordered her to buy salmon at 1s 4d per pound, she thought Sharpe would have a stroke so furious did he become, but by then Madeleine was beyond caring. She had come to realize that he expected the household to be run on a shoestring, which was why there was no butler and so few maids, but everything was for show: the rooms which visitors might see were elaborately and expensively furnished, entertaining was lavish in the extreme, and because competitiveness was as keen socially as in business, Dora had to be decked in satin and diamonds, and her fingers stiff with heavily encrusted rings.

Only the children brought a glimmer of light into the dark drudgery of Madeleine's life. She had asked Mabel why they were always so quiet, but the nursemaid had merely looked shifty as she shrugged and said, 'Aw, they sleeps a lot!'

It was some days before Madeleine even saw them, and then only by chance on a morning when she came upon a half-open door and glanced casually into the room. This was small and sparsely furnished, but it was the two cots which drew her attention: in one a small girl was asleep on her stomach, a thumb tightly held between her lips, while in the other a baby, just able to stand, was clinging to the rail. He wore no clothes except for a loose nappy, and he made no sound, even though his face was puckered in distress. He looked up at Madeleine with fear in his large blue eyes.

'Why, you must be Albert,' said Madeleine, advancing into the room and speaking very softly. But to her horror, the baby cringed away from her as though in terror. 'Oh no, please don't be frightened,' she whispered, and tentatively put out a finger to stroke the tiny hand on the rail; immediately the hand was whipped behind his back and his mouth opened in a whimpering cry.

Horrified, Madeleine bent down so that her eyes were on a level with his as she continued to whisper reassuringly to him. A few minutes later when she moved to touch his other hand, this was not drawn away. She stroked it very gently and then moved up his thin arm to the back of his neck, which she supported, her fingers in the soft gold curls at his nape. Could the monstrous George really have fathered this delightful-looking little child? Madeleine wondered. She could not resist picking up Albert, for he was cold, and she held him warmly, tenderness welling up in her. She pulled the thin, dirty blanket off the cot and put this around him; he snuggled against her breast and neck as though hungry for affection, and she was singing a lullaby when Mabel appeared. She looked startled and instantly apprehensive, but then demanded: 'Wha' yer think yer doin' in yere?'

'The door was open and Albert was standing up, looking very distressed. So I came in and picked him up

165

because he was cold. Why is there no fire and why is he not wearing a nightshirt?'

Mabel came and took the child none too gently from Madeleine. 'None o' yer business,' she retorted rudely. 'An' naow yer can git out – they chil'ren be nothin' ter do with yer!'

Albert had made only the tiniest sound of protest when he was taken from her. Madeleine frowned; she knew almost nothing about babies, but this did not seem natural and she was loath to leave him. 'His napkin needs changing,' she said, trying to delay her departure.

'I aren't stoopid, yer know,' said Mabel, glaring at her furiously, 'but I aren't goin' ter do nothin' about it till yer goes!'

'Why?' asked Madeleine calmly. 'Are you so bad a nursemaid that you are afraid to let anyone watch you attending to your charges?'

Dark red colour stained Mabel's fat cheeks as she said churlishly, 'Missus thinks I does all right.'

'Does Mrs Sharpe care about her children?' asked Madeleine, trying to sound casual.

Malice caused Mabel to fall immediately into the trap: 'Missus 'ates the chil'ren,' she said with a snigger. 'I reckons they reminds 'er of wha' 'er 'ad ter go fru ter get 'em.'

'So, therefore, she would not care whether you were looking after them properly or not,' retorted Madeleine, and as Mabel, realizing what she had let herself in for, was temporarily speechless, Madeleine continued: 'I want a fire lit at once and kept going, so that the room always has a warm, even temperature, and I want the children bathed night and morning and then kept properly clothed. Albert was very cold and I see that the little girl is not wearing a nightgown. Just why is she so sound asleep at this hour of the morning? She should be up and playing.'

Mabel went to the second cot and roughly shook the

sleeping child. 'Yere, cm'on, Looesa, the sergeant major yere says yer got ter get up!' Louisa hardly stirred and Mabel shook her again, until Madeleine said sharply, 'Stop that at once!' She bent over the cot, puzzled. Then, very gently she turned the little girl over on to her back and put her hand on the child's forehead; the skin was very cold, but instead of waking, Louisa whimpered fractiously, turned herself back on to her stomach and quickly replaced her thumb in her mouth.

'I don't understand it,' Madeleine murmured, more to herself than to the nursemaid. 'She feels very cold, so surely that alone should have made her wake, yet she hardly stirred.'

Mabel was smiling triumphantly. 'Mebbe her doan' wan' ter be bossed about.'

A distant scream of 'Brett!' reached them and Madeleine turned away reluctantly. At the door she whirled to face Mabel, her eyes like grey slate. 'See that you look after these children properly from now on or I shall call in a doctor on my own initiative!'

But as she went down the stairs she heard Mabel derisively trying to copy her voice saying, 'See tha' yer look . . . aw, go ter hell, Lady-Muck, I'll still be yere long after yer gone!'

Madeleine continued to visit the nursery whenever she could. This proved to be easier than she had expected because her continuing sickness precluded her from eating until evening. As soon as the nausea ceased every morning, she would creep down to the children and, no matter how wretchedly ill she felt, her heart always lifted at the thought of them. Very often they would be asleep and she would linger just long enough to ensure that they were warmly clad and the fire was burning well, but if they were awake, she would gather them into her arms, whispering and crooning gently to them. Little Albert soon came to know her and would hold out his arms in a

167

heartrending way immediately she approached, but his sister cringed away at first as though in great fear. Eventually, she too accepted Madeleine, but she never spoke and frequently after she had been held warmly for a few minutes, her eyelids would begin to droop and her small head to settle against Madeleine's shoulder. This, and the fact that Louisa appeared unable to talk, continued to worry Madeleine, for no matter how hard she tried to cajole her into speaking, the little girl continued to regard her warily and silently, thumb clamped tightly in her mouth; when Madeleine gently pulled it away, Louisa's face would pucker and within seconds of release the thumb would be back, being sucked hard for comfort.

There was something very wrong. At first Madeleine thought it was because the children were only taken out into the fresh air on Sunday afternoons when Mabel made a great fuss of putting them both into the perambulator and wheeling them on to the Downs for half an hour, after which they would be taken very briefly to see their father.

The answer came one morning when Madeleine happened to pass the nursery and saw Mabel spooning a dark liquid to each of the children in turn. When Louisa almost spat it out and Albert was reluctant to accept it, Mabel shouted at them so that both children whimpered and cringed. Madeleine strode forward angrily. 'What is that you are giving the children?' she demanded. 'It is obvious that they do not wish to have it, so why are you forcing them?'

Mabel started and looked apprehensive at the sudden intrusion, then she held out the bottle, shrugging. 'See fer yerself – it only be Godfrey's Cordial.'

The label did indeed confirm this, but still Madeleine was not satisfied. 'But why do you give it to them now? Surely in the mornings they should not be made more sleepy?'

'Yer fergit,' said Mabel surlily, 'I got ter do missus's bedroom every marnin' an' wha' with all tha' silver an' lace, it takes me more than two hour. I can't leave the chil'ren all tha' time.'

'I see,' said Madeleine reluctantly. Of course, in this penny-pinching household the nursemaid had to double as housemaid as well, and Dora's bedroom, since it was to be seen by visitors, was luxurious in the extreme. It was quite feasible that even by Mabel's slapdash standards she would need two hours to clean the room.

But still Madeleine was not satisfied, for it was not only in the mornings that the children were so sleepy. The next day, when Mabel was in the kitchen, Madeleine went to search for the bottle. It was half hidden in a mass of crumpled dirty clothing which had looked as though it had been tossed haphazardly into the cupboard. The bottle, which the previous morning had been almost full, was now down to a thin covering of liquid in the bottom and it smelt of treacle and something else – yes, surely, opium. The children were being kept in a semipermanently drugged state, no doubt to save Mabel effort!

'Oh, dear Lord,' whispered Madeleine, her mind in a turmoil. 'Whatever am I to do?'

The following day was Sunday; she decided to tell George Sharpe when the children were taken down to him. He would then be able to see for himself and surely even he, monstrous man though he was, would not allow such a practice to continue.

It was as well that she did not know at that stage what a dramatic effect the day was to have upon her own future. The first bombshell came when she went down to the kitchen for the evening meal. When it was put before her the now familiar nausea rose in her throat and she hastily put a handkerchief to her mouth as she tried to swallow.

169

'You've fallen, haven' yur?' said Mabel, suddenly lean-ing across the table and leering at Madeleine.

'Fallen?' queried Madeleine coldly. 'I don't know what you mean.'

This was greeted with a crow of cackling laughter from all the women. 'Aw, come orff it!' begged Mabel, 'I hears yur throwin' up every marnin', an' I were brung up wit' tha' sound, bein' the eldest o' thirteen. My ma used to suffer summit awful when her was expectin'.'

Madeleine suddenly understood and colour rushed to her face, only to drain away as quickly. 'I am constantly sick because of the filthy state of everything here,' she began, but was stopped by another guffaw from all around the table.

'Oh ah, Miss Oity-Toity be tryin' ter make believe 'er aren't nefer bin with a man! I bet yur was a cold fish though!' This was from Mrs Boot, mouth wide open in a knowing smirk.

'Who was it then, some toff in Lunnen wantin' a quick tumble? 'E done it reel good, didn' he?' said Emmy, eyes shining. 'But us can pull it out with a knittin' needle an' a bit o' Ergot.'

Madeleine rose. 'I think you are all disgusting,' she said, trying to keep her voice steady, 'and I am not staying to hear any more of your insults.'

Their laughter followed her up the stairs, but once in the attic room she collapsed on to the bed. A baby! Could it be possible? Feverishly she tried to remember all that her father had told her; it had been his longest explanation on life and at times her attention had wandered through sheer embarrassment, yet he had persisted, no doubt hoping to save her from a situation such as the present. Dates! She knew he had said these were vital, and she put her face in her hands as she tried to concentrate. When eventually her mind stopped its panic-stricken, chaotic whirling, her hands slipped slowly to cover her mouth.

She was three weeks overdue with her period and therefore it must be true: she was going to have Sebastian's
baby! Why had she never thought of such a thing? Surely
she should have known that a moment of such perfect
union could result in a child – but instead, because events
had crowded upon her with such rapidity, her main
thought had been for survival. Instantly, all the pain and
grief she had tried so hard to suppress overwhelmed her
like a great wave and she wept – for her father, for the
General, for the baby, but most of all for Sebastian. She
wanted him, needed him, longed for him with such
desperation that she felt she could not live without him;
being apart from him was like having her heart torn out,
and now, now that she was to have his baby she could not
go on alone.

Yet gradually, gradually, her spirit revived. She sat up
and blew her nose. Sebastian did not love her, never had
done – hadn't she told herself this dozens of times? So
why could she not believe it? And now she must fight, not
only for herself but for the baby, *their* baby, whom she
would protect and adore and never allow anyone to hurt
or take from her. She thought of Lady Frensham and her
obsession with the 'unbroken de Lacey line'; she thought
of herself, having married the father but now pregnant by
the son, and little hiccoughing laughs burst from her until
at last exhaustion claimed her and she slept.

The fact that she was going to have a child made
Madeleine all the more sensitive to the needs of the
Sharpe children, and she was hovering in the hall when
they were brought to the drawing room the next day.
Mabel held Albert aloft in her arms, not bothering to give
him any support, and Madeleine caught her breath as she
watched his small head wobbling on its thin neck. Louisa
was left to toddle uncertainly behind the nursemaid,
clutching at her skirts.

George Sharpe's voice boomed out: 'Well, an' wha'

have you two bin doin', eh? Cat got yer tongue, has it, Louisa?' The little girl hung back against Mabel as she gazed up dumbly, thumb in mouth. Her father bent and took her arm, 'Come on naow, come an' sit on my knee.' But she instantly drew back, bursting into tears, and he let her go. 'Oh, all right then, yer silly little bugger,' he said roughly and turned to Albert. 'Naow you, my son, will come to papa, won't you?' He lifted the child, but Albert, as though taking his cue from Louisa, screamed and struggled. Sharpe almost threw him back at Mabel. ''ere, take him, take both o' em out of my sight! Stoopid, tha's wha' they are, stoopid little halfwits, the pair!'

'No!' Madeleine strode forward, her face white with anger. 'Your children are neither stupid nor halfwitted, Mr Sharpe! They are just worn out because they are being kept in a semi-permanently drugged state. Can't you see how exhausted they are? Just look at them – they can hardly keep their eyes open. And don't you *know* why Louisa doesn't talk? It's because she cannot do so – she doesn't know how because no one ever talks to her.'

George Sharpe advanced on Madeleine menacingly. 'Jus' wha' are you sayin'?'

Madeleine stood her ground and returned his look unflinchingly. 'I am saying that this – this so-called nurse-maid keeps spooning a mixture of treacle and opium to your children to keep them quiet, day and night, so that she can get on with her other work in this house, but mainly, I suspect, to save herself the trouble of caring for them.'

'She's lyin'!' Unexpectedly this was from Dora, not Mabel. She swung her feet off the sofa and sat up, pointing a finger at Madeleine. 'I tell you she's lyin' cos she's goin' ter have a babby an' she's bin wormin' her way into the nursery in the hope tha' she wouldn' be sent packin' when she couldn' hide it no more!'

''Tis true!' screeched Mabel, coming in on cue. 'I heard

her throwin' up every marnin' since she's bin yere, jus' you ask her if tha' aren't true.'

'Well?' thundered Sharpe, standing with legs apart and hands on hips.

'Yes, it is quite true,' Madeleine said calmly. 'But I assure you this has nothing to do with what I've been saying.'

'Nothin' ter do with it!' repeated Sharpe, his face crimsoning. 'Yere you are, tryin' to blacken my servant's name when all the time you're nothin' but a trollop yourself – aw, take 'em away, do!' he shouted to Mabel as both children, alarmed by his raised voice, had started to scream loudly. She withdrew with obvious reluctance.

'Git rid of her, George,' said Dora, madness glittering in her eyes. 'She's bin no damn good anyway!'

'You're right,' replied her husband, agreeing with her for probably the first time ever. He turned back to Madeleine. 'This is a respec'able household, an' to think tha' after takin' you in an' feedin' an' keepin' you, you should repay our kindness by bein' a loose woman!'

Madeleine was stunned by the way the tables had been turned on her, but pride prevented her from letting this odious couple see how afraid she was. 'And may I remind you,' she said quietly, 'that I have worked for fifteen hours a day to earn your so-called kindness! And far from being respectable, your household is filthy, hypocritical and disgusting from top to bottom!'

George Sharpe looked as though he might have a stroke and could hardly speak for fury. 'Git!' he roared. 'I wan' you out this house in five minutes, understan'?'

Madeleine inclined her head. 'Perfectly. And I shall be only too pleased to leave, but what about your children?'

Amazement showed on Sharpe's face as he looked from Madeleine to his wife and then back. 'None of your bloody business,' he shouted. 'An' naow git out! Git your bags packed at once an' git!'

So once again she was standing in the hall, valise in hand, but nothing had been said about her wages and she was determined not to leave without them. The drawing-room door was open and Sharpe was standing in his favourite position before the fire. Contrary to general custom, he made no effort to smoke away from the reception rooms, and now stood drawing on a large cigar, eyes narrowed. There was no sign of Dora. His eyes swivelled round to Madeleine and, still keeping the cigar clamped between his teeth, he demanded, 'Why haven' you gone?'

'I think you have forgotten that you owe me three weeks' wages, Mr Sharpe,' said Madeleine, advancing into the room.

The tiny, boot-button eyes opened to their very limited extent. 'Do I hear you right? You're askin' me for wages when you've bin a complete washout?'

'I have worked long and conscientiously, and done everything you and your wife have required of me, so I am saying that I am entitled to be paid for my labour.' Madeleine just managed to speak calmly, although her composure was almost cracking.

Suddenly his manner changed. He came to stand close beside her and actually removed his cigar before he said, smilingly, 'It doan have ter end like this, you know, darlin' – you're a pretty piece an' your figure' – running his eye critically over her – 'ain't too bad. I could be good ter you, if you was good ter me; could set you up in a nice li'le place in the city, an' come an' see you mebbe every night; could be a reel li'le luv nest. Wha' you say to tha', eh?'

Madeleine wondered if she were going mad and gazed at him wide-eyed until she felt his arm slide around her waist, then with one swift movement she was standing in front of him. 'Do I understand you correctly? You are offering to make me your mistress and to install me in some rooms here in Bristol?'

The cigar was back in his mouth. ''S right,' he said as, hands in pockets, he rocked gently to and fro.

'Even though you know I am – with child by someone else?'

The answer was barked out: 'Git rid of it!'

'I see,' said Madeleine, white to the lips. 'I knew you were the most revolting, the most hypocritical and brutal man I had ever met, but I just wanted to make absolutely sure so that I could tell you that never in a hundred years would I ever become your mistress; I'd – I'd rather die in the gutter!'

His face changed to its customary snarling look. 'An' you *will* die in the gutter, tha's farr sure! Farr you'll git no ref'rence from me an' withou' tha' you'll not git work!'

Madeleine's chin lifted defiantly. 'I'll take my chance on that. And now, if you will give me my wages, I shall be happy to leave.'

But he laughed in her face. 'Aw, no! You'll git no wages from me neither!'

'Then I remain here until I do,' replied Madeleine calmly, even though her heart was thudding loudly and unevenly. He came towards her, fists balled and face distorted. 'Lay one finger on me, and I'll go straight to the police,' Madeleine said, standing quite still, her level gaze holding his.

The very absurdity of the remark made him pause, fists in mid-air. Then he guffawed. 'The police indeed! An' whoever would take the word of a dismissed servant?'

'Perhaps the Lord Mayor and the editor of the *Bristol Mercury*?'

'Only your word 'gainst mine,' he said, but his eyes had grown wary.

'And of course I should tell how you abuse your wife, how your children are kept drugged, and how filthy your staff and kitchen are. Do you think your business friends would want to bring their wives here for dinner if they knew all that?'

Sharpe realized that she was not just threatening him, she would take action, and he had no doubt that some of the mud would stick. He could not afford to jeopardize his chances with the influential business community for, with the finding of gold in Australia, there had been a sudden huge demand for all kinds of supplies, especially prefabricated buildings of galvanized iron. He had gambled heavily on the manufacture of these being continued in Bristol, but only the previous year the firm had moved to London and he had lost the contract to transport the buildings. With war in the Crimea now imminent, he would need all the goodwill he could muster to obtain contracts for the shipping of war materials. He flung the cigar into the fire with barely contained fury, then he dug into his pocket and counted out a number of coins which he threw violently at Madeleine. 'Naow git out!' he said savagely.

Some of the coins had rolled under the furniture and it was necessary for her to go down on hands and knees to retrieve them; she did so silently, conscious that he was watching. When she had to stretch forward to pick up a shilling perilously near his boot she paused, reading his thoughts. She looked up, white-faced but with lips thinned in determination and her eyes quite steady, daring him to kick her. But he remained still and Madeleine rose gracefully to her feet. Without another word or look at him, she walked out of the room and out of the house.

Her courage lasted until she had left the immediate vicinity and then she began to shake uncontrollably and her legs to be in danger of buckling. She just managed to get as far as a bench in Church Walk before terror and despair swept over her once more. She was a nineteen-year-old girl without family or friends, and with only a few shillings between herself and starvation; even if she found an employer willing to take her without a reference, there was the baby; she knew enough about convention to realize that no establishment would keep her once her pregnancy became obvious. Vice, immorality and every kind of degradation could flourish just beneath the surface so long as respectability and the strict moral code were outwardly maintained; the stern Protestant Christianity practised by the majority did not extend to the 'fallen woman', 'the scarlet woman', or the 'wicked, wicked girl'. There was the Poor Law, of course, and Madeleine remembered the beautiful old black and white building in Peter Street which was the hospital for the poor, but she suspected that behind the fine façade the interior would be grim. Whatever am I to do? she thought wildly. Where am I to go?

It was then that Ellen found her. She almost passed the small, sagging figure in the bedraggled bonnet and rusty black clothing, but some instinct made her look closer, and then in one little running bound she was beside Madeleine.

'Miss Madleen – Miss Brett! Is it reely you, miss? Oh, ter think you bin found a' last!' she exclaimed joyfully.

Madeleine looked up fearfully, saw the familiar faded blue eyes and the seamed face now beaming in delighted surprise, and rushed into Ellen's arms in a storm of weeping. Ellen held her warmly, oblivious of the stares of passing nursemaids and their charges. 'There, there, me dove,' she murmured soothingly. 'Come an' sit down an' tell me all abou' it.'

And Madeleine did, omitting Sebastian's part, but ending with a sob and, 'I'm going to have a baby, Ellen.'

Ellen compressed her lips and her face flushed angrily. That selfish, unthinking young rake! She had suspected

177

the moment she walked into the library at Royal Crescent and found the scattered cushions on the floor. Her fears were later confirmed when Madeleine could not be found. The servants, who had all returned from the funeral in time to prepare breakfast, commented on Sebastian's happy mood; he came swinging down the stairs and Perry actually heard him humming under his breath. After a hearty breakfast he instructed that a tray of Miss Brett's favourite food be taken up to her, and he then retired to the library to sort the General's papers.

'Yes, Ellen?' he enquired, looking up at her with those splendid dark eyes dancing and even with a smile touching their corners.

'Please, sir,' said Ellen, watching him like a hawk, 'bu' do you know tha' Miss Brett has gone?'

'Gone?' Sebastian echoed, the smile fading. 'What do you mean?'

'Tha' her's lef', sir, all her clothes is gone an' her bed not slep' in.'

'What!' he shouted, springing to his feet and scattering papers everywhere. 'You must be mistaken, Ellen!'

'Won' you see farr yourself, sir,' she replied very boldly.

Without another word he had dashed from the room, astonishing her with the speed and lightness of his movements. She followed as he leapt up the stairs, and by the time she reached Madeleine's room he was gazing numbly about him. 'Her only took her own clothes, sir; everthin' tha' the marrster give her an' all her Christmas presents, her lef' behind.'

'Where could she have gone, Ellen? What would she do?' His voice had quietened and, like his face, registered amazement.

'I dunno, sir, bu' her did leave letters for 'er Ladyship an' Miss Harriet on the hall table.'

That galvanized him into action once more. He went

out of the room and down the stairs with such recklessness that she felt sure he would trip. But he was extremely surefooted and within minutes was tearing open first one and then the other letter. When he looked up at last his face was devoid of expression and the black eyes had become opaque. 'She's really gone, Ellen,' he said dully.

Ellen, who like all servants, was fond of sitting in judgement on her employers, now thought: Give him his due, he's reel cut up an' nefer bin like this before.

'Her couldn' have gone farr, sir,' she said consolingly, and this seemed to give him instant hope.

'You're right!' he exclaimed. 'And I'll find her. I *must* find her, wherever she is!' With that he shouted for Sam and dashed out.

Subsequently Sam related to an enthralled staff how their master, having arrived at Bath station, had leapt from the carriage, 'As if his life depended on it' and seized the stationmaster by the arm, 'pullin' him round like he be one of 'em rag dolls!' When the bewildered man had shaken his head, 'the Cap'n had grabbed the lapels of his frock coat an' looked about ter shake him too!' Eventually he had returned to Sam 'lookin' like a thundercloud' and dismissed him. When last seen he had been dashing in and out of all the shops in Milsom Street. 'Half orf his chump, he be,' ended Sam succinctly.

Ellen returned to the present, realizing that Madeleine was looking at her with fearful, tear-drenched eyes. 'It's not the end o' the world, lovey,' she said gently. 'But us have got ter think about wha's ter be done. I s'pose you . . . wouldn' consider tellin' the Cap'n?'

'Oh, no, no! Ellen, promise me, please promise me, that no matter what happens, you will never tell the de Laceys' about me.'

'All right, all right, dearie, doan you fuss yoursel' naow, but wha' us goin' ter do?'

'Should I – should I go to St Peter's, Ellen?' It was said

falteringly, huge grey eyes beseeching Ellen to dismiss this.

She did, with a shudder. 'Nefer tha'! 'sides, they wouldn' keep you in, mebbe jus' give you a few pence an' then send you ter some dosshouse!'

They both shuddered then, thinking of the reeking, overcrowded rooms, haunt of every kind of criminal, where disease flourished, and a bunk and a handful of filthy rags could be obtained for twopence per night. 'Yer not goin' ter one o' them!' said Ellen decisively. 'Naow, my new lady has a young baby, so her needs a good seamstress. Perhaps I coul' get you in there.'

'Oh, Ellen, that would be wonderful!' exclaimed Madeleine. But then her face clouded again. 'Could we keep the other servants from knowing about the baby?'

Ellen shook her head. 'No, it isn' possible ter keep any secrets, not with the sickness an' all. An' they'd tell on you, so tha' when you was put out one o' their people could come in. 'Tis the times, y' see.' Ellen's tone was apologetic. 'There be only one thing ter do, I'm takin' you ter me Mam; her's only got a li'le cottage, more like a hovel you'll think it, bu' her'll shelter you.'

'Oh, but Ellen, surely your mother would also be shocked by my – my condition?'

Ellen smiled. 'No, tha' her wouldn't. In the country, us knows how these things happen. Lots o' girls get into trouble – wha' with long hours workin' in the fields with the lads an' nice, warm haystacks ter fall into in the evenin's.' She stood and then picked up the valise. 'Come, lovey, us mus' make haste, for light's fadin' an' I got ter be back by ten. Can you wark? Good, then let's be orf!'

It seemed to Madeleine that they walked for hours and it was quite dark when a tiny, single-storey cottage became discernible in the bright moonlight. 'Yere us be a' last!' said Ellen, relief in her voice, as she marched up to the door and flung it open. 'Come you in then.'

180

Madeleine had thought that the cottage was in darkness, but now as she stepped inside she saw that it was lit by a single tallow dip and the glow from a small fire. Three seated figures turned and greeted Ellen simultaneously.

'Mam,' said Ellen to the smallest, 'I've brough' a young lady who needs help reel bad: her's in the family way an' got nowhere ter go!'

Madeleine was glad then of the dimness to hide her deep blush, but to her astonishment the family appeared to accept this without any adverse reaction. A very stooped elderly woman rose stiffly with a small, quickly stifled exclamation of pain and ran her eyes expertly over Madeleine's figure. 'You not be farr gone, then.' It was a statement rather than a question and uttered quite matter-of-factly.

'Just about six weeks,' Madeleine replied, almost in a whisper.

All three showed astonishment then, but it was at her voice, not her condition. 'Why,' exclaimed the mother, 'you be a lady!' and the other two figures rose as they would in the presence of a gentlewoman.

'I jus' told you, Mam,' said Ellen, her arm sliding protectively about Madeleine. 'Not goin' ter let tha' make no diff'rence, are you?'

Before the mother could answer, one of the figures came forward and Madeleine saw that it was a young woman with a terrible spinal deformity. 'How we goin' ter keep a lady yere?' she demanded, looking up at Ellen with difficulty.

'Naow, Ade – ' began Ellen, when Madeleine said quickly, 'Oh, I shall be able to work and help you all.'

Ada turned to her and Madeleine caught her breath, for even in the dim light she could see the delicate spun-silk beauty of Ada's hair and the bright periwinkle blue of her eyes, but her body was stunted and hideously twisted. She appeared to have no neck, her head resting very low on her shoulders, and there was a distinct whistling gasp to her breathing. 'Wha' can you do?' she asked.

'Cook, clean and sew,' began Madeleine, but Ada broke in at once: 'Tha's no good yere! You needs ter work in fields; ah bet you's nefer done tha'!'

'No, I have not,' agreed Madeleine, 'but I should like to try.'

'Tis terrible hard,' said the mother, shaking her head doubtfully.

Ellen turned to the third member of her family, a stocky young man who had been looking silently at Madeleine. 'Jem,' she said, with a hint of desperation in her voice, 'surely you could find some work tha' weren't too hard for Madleen?'

'Ar,' said Jem cryptically, and then after some seconds of ponderous thought, 'Ah can try.'

'Tha's be'er!' Ellen, visibly relieved, turned to Madeleine. 'Ade an' Jem are me harf sister an' brother as me mam was wed twice.'

Madeleine smiled at them all. 'Oh, but I could tell you were related as you all have the same lovely blue eyes as your mother.'

This was received in complete silence and Madeleine wondered if she could have offended them. It was not until much later that she realized the whole family had been at a loss as to how they *should* react; no one had ever paid them a compliment before and, with the exception of Ellen, they regarded Madeleine with some suspicion. Ellen broke the silence at last:

'I brough' summit,' she said, lifting her skirt unconcernedly and showing a small linen bag pinned to her petticoat. When she opened it and unwrapped a few slices of chicken and beef, there were exclamations of delight and fingers were outstretched to snatch at the meat. Ellen

182

put her hand under the wrapping and offered the contents to Madeleine. 'Crumbs from the rich man's table,' she quoted unexpectedly.

Madeleine shook her head. 'Thank you, Ellen dear, but I could not eat anything at present.' This was quite untrue for the long walk in the cold frosty air had made her extremely hungry, but she felt that she could not take even one slice of meat from these people who were obviously so poor.

Ellen turned to her mother. 'Madleen has a lot o' sickness in the marnin's, Mam. Can you help her with summit?'

The old woman nodded slowly. 'Ah reckon.' Her bright blue eyes seemed to bore into Madeleine. 'Warm yerself, missus, by fire an' do take orf your bonnet,' she said at last, and Madeleine moved gratefully to the fire, sinking down wearily on to the hard settle as she pulled at her bonnet strings. Ada and Jem joined her hesitantly while continuing to stare at her as though she were a being from a different planet.

Ellen and the mother had disappeared behind the ragged curtain which partitioned the room, but their vibrant whispering and a lot of rustling could plainly be heard. Eventually they emerged, Ellen brushing straw from her skirt. 'I mus' leave naow,' she said.

Madeleine rose, exclaiming in dismay, 'Oh, Ellen, so soon?'

'Yes, dearie, an' you mus' get ter bed, farr there'll be an early star' tomorrer.' She looked anxiously at Madeleine. ''Course, there be no bed yere, only some straw on the floor ter share with Mam and Ade.'

'But how lucky I am to have that!' Madeleine said at once, and then added earnestly, 'Ellen, do be careful on that long walk back in the dark.'

That produced laughter from all three and Ellen said, 'Why, there be nothin' ter be 'fraid of – not in the

183

country. Only poachers abroad naow, an' they'll not hurt us.' She began to tie her bonnet ribbons. 'I'll be back in a month's time when I gets me next harf day off.'

Madeleine went to hug her. 'Thank you, oh thank you so much, Ellen dear,' she said, tears of gratitude coming to her eyes.

'Naow, doan' fret yerself.' Embarrassment made Ellen pat Madeleine awkwardly on the back. 'An' tomorrer Jem will ask foreman if you can work with him in potato fields.'

The family's farewell was laconic in the extreme and no one rose to hug or kiss Ellen when she said brusquely, 'Nigh' then!'

The old woman replied, 'God be with you,' but Ada and Jem merely nodded, and Ellen's last look as she pulled open the door was for Madeleine.

Her departure was the signal for bed. Jem began spreading a bundle of straw in front of the fire and his mother held back the ragged curtain as she crooked a finger at Madeleine. Behind, on the bare floor, lay a large quantity of straw inadequately covered by one thin dark blanket. Mother and daughter quickly removed their skirts and dropped down on to the straw, huddling close together under the blanket. Then they watched in utmost fascination as Madeleine slowly took off her dress and chemise, and there was even a stifled exclamation from Ada as Madeleine put on her nightgown. Unable to bear their scrutiny any longer, she quickly pulled the pins from her hair and gave it a single long stroke with her brush. As she hesitated, the old woman lifted the side of the blanket and Madeleine sank down beside her. The straw was surprisingly thick and springy, but even so she could feel the damp rising from the mud-packed floor. She shivered, and at once a hand moved to tuck in the blanket carefully around her.

'Thank you,' she whispered in the darkness and folded

her hands over her flat stomach. The blanket smelled strongly of horse, but it was a covering, and in her desperate situation she could hope for little more. She and the child she was to bear were in shelter, and if these people seemed alien, she must remember that she appeared equally strange to them. And primitive though everything was, how much better than some filthy doss-house where she could have been robbed, raped or even murdered without anyone to care. But how silent everything was! To Madeleine, city bred, the utter silence of the deep country was unnerving, but then the family began to snore: great trumpeting sounds from Jem, whistling gasps from Ada and little snorts and sighs from the mother. Madeleine smiled and closed her eyes; even these sounds were comforting because they confirmed that she was no longer alone. She drifted into sleep, whispering yearningly, 'Sebastian . . . Sebastian.'

11

It was still dark when the family's movements awoke Madeleine. She cautiously raised her head and, as she did so, the old woman appeared holding a roughly fashioned ceramic cup. 'Can thee drink this?' she asked, smiling a little. As Madeleine took the cup and sniffed at the contents, she added, 'It be only herbs an' hot wa'er.' So Madeleine drank the concoction, which tasted of nothing she had ever known. 'Thee can bide yurr till Ah come back,' she was told, and was only too thankful to slide under the blanket once more.

When she eventually rose and dressed, she found, to her delighted surprise, that she felt only hunger. 'Good morning,' she said as she slipped out from behind the curtain. She felt awkward and tried to smile reassuringly at the family. They all stared back at her, then Jem and his mother nodded their heads, but Ada's lip curled.

'Jem,' said his mother, 'fetch wa'er for missus ter wash.'

'Oh, please,' said Madeleine. 'Please call me by my name: it is Mad-el-lane.'

'Ar!' said mother and daughter simultaneously, but neither attempted to pronounce it and many weeks were to pass before any of them ventured to do so.

Jem returned with an ancient bucket full of water. 'Doan' you dap it doon naow,' warned his mother, who then scooped up a small bowlful and put it behind the ragged curtain. Madeleine wondered how she was ever to keep even remotely clean if water was this scarce, but she determinedly thrust her hands into the icy liquid. She was to learn rapidly how desperate was the family's poverty and how primitive their living conditions: the only 'privy' was a hole in the ground at the rear of the cottage and dangerously near the well, which was their only source of water; they used wood for warmth and cooking, but it was left to the mother to gather this from the lanes and hedgerows. Stooped and crippled as she was with rheumatism she nevertheless went out daily in all weathers, only returning when a great sack of kindling was on her back. Jem, and all those who worked on the land, depended entirely upon the weather, for if frost made the earth too hard to work, or if it became waterlogged, the labourers received no wages; as these amounted to a mere pittance at the best of times, in a bad winter a family could be reduced to starvation level within days if they had no crops of their own. But on that early February morning Madeleine knew little of this and was concentrating on getting down the strange-flavoured broth, which appeared to be hot water with a few herbs thrown in; this was followed by coarse bread covered with a scraping of dripping. But, strange and unappetizing as it all was, she ate it and was not sick, nor did she even feel sick.

'Pin yer shawl over yer head an' frote,' advised Mam when they were all preparing to leave. 'An' Jem, can you look ter the missus an' see her doan' work too hard, naow.'

Ada spoke unexpectedly to Madeleine: 'Do yer wan' to touch me hump, then?'

'Why – why,' stammered Madeleine, embarrassed and uncomprehending, 'why should I want to do that, Ada?'

'Farr luck, o' course,' replied the young woman, and then added angrily, 'Ah weren't born with it, yer know; Ah got it when Ah were five year old, sewin' gloves an' pinned to my mam's apron ter keep me sittin' still. All the other babbies growed up straight, 'cep' Ah!'

'Thee can' do nout abaut it, Ada,' said Mam sharply. 'An' naow thee mus' be orf.'

Sounds of voices, even laughter, were heard, together

with the ring of iron soles as many clogs struck hard ground. Jem motioned with his head for Madeleine to follow him, and when she stepped outside she saw that a large crowd had gathered, mainly of women, with children of all ages. When they saw Ada a shout went up and there was a sudden surge forward to touch the great hump which jutted through her shawl. 'Oh,' gasped Madeleine in distress, 'how horrible!' but Mam caught her arm and put her finger to her lips. Madeleine nodded reluctantly; she remembered the effect her voice had had upon the family and was now a little apprehensive about how this crowd would react to it.

At last Ada had endured enough. 'Ge' orf, you buggers!' she screamed, laying about her with her short arms. 'Let Ah be!' It was to be over a hundred years before people began to realize that the handicapped had feelings just like themselves and certainly this crowd had no idea of their cruelty; many called out in puzzlement: 'Wha's a ma'er with you, Ade? You knows frost will give out if you brings us luck!' But Ada had already set off at a strange, awkward run, followed by jeers and raucous laughter.

Madeleine had seen Jem speak earnestly to a large florid man and then jerk his thumb in her direction; the overseer had looked briefly at her before nodding curtly, and now, as she felt Jem's hand on her wrist, she began to walk beside him. He had deliberately put her on the outside of the crowd, with himself as a shield between them, and Madeleine walked silently, with head lowered.

As they progressed the crowd began to disperse over various fields, and Madeleine ventured a look back to see what was happening to the children. She was, of course, very used to seeing children at work: in London the streets were full of them, begging, selling matches and bootlaces, holding horses' heads or assiduously gathering up dogs' excreta to take to the tanneries. But seeing the

188

children set to work in the fields tore at her tender heart: they looked so small to be weeding or stone-breaking or gathering acorns, while the youngest of all were left entirely alone, one to a field, to stumble through, rattle in hand, to scare off the birds. Their small faces all bore a look of resignation and endurance, but none of them smiled.

Madeleine followed Jem as he began to dig up potatoes, but wielding the heavy fork made her wrists ache and within minutes great blisters had covered her palms; half an hour later these were raw and bleeding, so she tore strips from her petticoat and bound them around her hands. But it was obvious that she would not be able to continue for long, and when Jem returned and saw blood dripping down the fork, he stared for a few minutes, then said ponderously, 'You can't dig tatties.'

'But there must be something I can do,' said Madeleine, who had begun to realize how desperately her earnings of a halfpenny a bushel were needed. So Jem set her on to hoeing and levelling the ground he had just finished digging; this work was being done all around by the older children, who appeared to manage very well, but for Madeleine it was still cruelly hard and she was soon panting. When at long last Jem produced a tin dinner can and handed it to her, she ached in every bone, and within minutes the sweat, which had coursed between her shoulder-blades and down the back of her knees, felt cold against her skin. She paused only long enough to eat two pieces of bread and a few strips of fat bacon before recommencing. Jem, meanwhile, had not stopped at all, but had begun filling her sack with potatoes.

'Jem, you must eat,' Madeleine said, but he only shook his head. His face was red with effort and the cold wind, yet he seemed tireless, and when at last it was too dark for them to continue, he walked many times to the cart, shouldering both Madeleine's and his own sacks of potatoes. All the other women carried their sacks on their backs, and Madeleine was grateful that the darkness hid her from their view. Yet she had worked to the limit and beyond of her endurance and needed Jem's help on the long walk home, for the paper-thin soles of her old boots had all but disintegrated in the thick soil, making every step an agony. The younger children were crying with exhaustion and Madeleine felt like crying with and for them; they received no sympathy from their mothers, only frequent shouts and slaps, until eventually the older children picked up the younger and carried them on their backs.

'Mam,' said Jem, even as he pushed open the door, ''er feet an' 'ands be scraged reel bad.'

The old woman bustled forward. 'An' you be shrammed too,' she said, taking Madeleine's hands and leading her to the fire. Then, with surprising gentleness, she unbound the strips of cotton and clucked at the sight of Madeleine's raw palms. 'Jem, set wa'er ter heat an' be quick!'

'Please,' begged Madeleine, 'I can manage – do let Jem rest, he has been so kind to me.' But the old woman only made a hissing sound of disagreement and, tired as he was, her son fetched the water at once and set it on the fire.

'Soon be be'er naow,' promised Mam, a smile touching the corners of her still bright blue eyes. And as soon as the water was hot, she put Madeleine's feet in one bowl and her hands in another. 'You keep 'em there, naow,' she admonished, and Madeleine was only too glad to do so.

'But where is Ada?' she asked eventually.

'Ade not be yere yet cos 'er's got a seven-mile wark from factory.'

'Seven miles!' exclaimed Madeleine, almost upsetting the bowl in her lap. 'But where does she work?' Then they told her: Ada worked in a bone factory and spent all

190

her working days surrounded by the putrefying feet of bullocks and horses, sheep and pigs. Her job was to scrape off the hair and then steep the hoofs in brine. Oh, dear God, thought Madeleine, feeling her stomach churn, poor, beautiful, tragic little Ada, what a terribly hard and merciless fate was hers!

It was late when Ada did appear and she was covered completely with snow.

'Snow!' exclaimed Mam, and there was real anxiety in her voice.

'Yes,' said Ada, gasping, 'an' it be comin' down reel hard.'

Jem went to the door and looked out. It was indeed snowing extremely hard, with a strong wind already turning it into drifts. It was to continue for four weeks during which time no agricultural work was possible. Only Ada continued to work, but as it was quite impossible for her to walk through such deep snow, Jem carried her on his back, morning and night. 'If her doan' go, there be plenty others ter take her place at factory,' Mam explained to Madeleine. But when Madeleine tried to make them take her few shillings, they all refused. Yet they were all hungry, and one night when she was awakened by the sound of the door closing and peeped through a hole in the curtain, Madeleine saw Jem come in holding a dead rabbit. He crouched in front of the dying fire, holding out his hands, and Madeleine realized he had been poaching. She bit her lip anxiously, wondering how he had been able to cover his tracks in the untrodden snow, until common sense told her that this was probably the least of his dangers. The next day mam made rabbit stew and Madeleine thought she had never tasted anything so good; it was the first meat she had eaten since her arrival and the family all made tiny sounds of appreciation as they tore it from the bones. There were no table knives or forks, only leaden spoons, but

191

Madeleine's hesitation was brief before she, too, picked up the meat in her fingers.

'That was wonderful,' she said, when they had finished and every plate had been scraped clean.

Mam smiled and said to Jem, 'Do thee remember that missus likes rabbit!'

A few days later there was a chicken stew, and Madeleine began to worry about what would happen if Jem were caught. She, like the other two women, relied on the silent young man, and if he were imprisoned she doubted very much whether they could exist without his help. She was also silently appalled by the paucity of their lives, and one day she said to Jem and Ada, 'I should very much like to teach you to read and write, if you would allow me.'

This appeared to have much the same effect as a thunderbolt on them and they were speechless. Eventually Ada said, 'Wha' goo' be tha'?'

Then, surprisingly, it was Jem who said shyly, 'Please, missus, could you learn Ah?'

'Oh yes,' cried Madeleine, delighted. 'Now, I have a pen and a few sheets of paper in my valise, but no ink.'

'Ar,' said Mam, and Madeleine turned to her eagerly; she had come to realize that, like many Bristolians, the family used this cryptic exclamation to cover almost every contingency, but Madeleine was still unable to interpret its meaning. A few minutes later Mam produced a small broken dish filled with a black, strange-smelling liquid. 'Yere be ink farr thee,' she said triumphantly, and Madeleine saw that it was a mixture of soot and vinegar.

So the lessons commenced, with Ada as sullen a pupil as Jem was eager. Then, almost overnight the thaw came, first in heavy rain, followed by soft, hazy sunshine. Work recommenced and Mam produced small leather pads for Madeleine's palms, which she tied around her hands and wrists. 'An' do pin this to your petticoat, it be farr the rheumatics,' said Mam, handing her a tiny object sewn up in linen.

'What is it?' asked Madeleine, who was becoming increasingly fascinated by Mam's knowledge of herbs.

'Brimstone,' was the answer. 'Ter hold in your hand when it hurt.'

Jem showed Madeleine how to pull up beet by its leaves and then to cut these off at their base. He was so expert that with a quick flick of his wrist he could lift the beet and cut its leaves in the second before it fell of its own volition into the cart. Madeleine, of course, took very much longer and was clumsy, but at least the work was not so hard on her hands, even though Jem warned 'Do be careful not ter cut orf thy fingers or thumb.'

Work generally increased in an effort to make up for the four lost weeks and, as she watched the ploughing teams with their great horses making their slow but steady progress through the fields, birds wheeling and dipping around them, a strange calm came to Madeleine. The year was awakening, and although the buds on the apple trees were still tightly folded, primroses were blooming in the hedgerows amid the tender green of new grass, and twig-carrying birds were busy with their building. Threshing and the drilling of spring wheat continued, and Jem worked round the clock. The hazy sun warmed Madeleine's aching back and her belly began to round softly.

On a fine Sunday morning Jem smoothed a small patch of earth beside the cottage and with a pointed stick laboriously wrote his first word: 'CAT'. 'Oh, well done!' exclaimed Madeleine, and he turned to smile shyly at her, adoration plain in his brilliant blue eyes. She realized then that he appeared to be slow and stolid because no stimulation had ever been given him; he had known nothing but dire poverty and unremitting physical labour, but he only needed this one tiny success to turn into a pupil avid for knowledge. From that day he spent every available moment trying to read aloud from Madeleine's Bible.

'But,' admonished Mam, 'thee can't work on Sunday – remember the man in the moon!' As Madeleine looked up in smiling wonderment at this, Mam said very seriously, 'He were sent ter moon cos he worked on Sunday!'

'That aren't work, Mam,' Jem protested. 'It be lahnin'.' The family took no part in organized religion, mainly because the nearest church was five miles away and no minister had ever shown any interest in them. Yet their lives were blameless: they lived close to the earth, totally dependent upon it for food, warmth and the medicinal properties of flowers, weeds and herbs, which mam gathered in great quantities and hung in bunches to dry. After their initial unease with her, the family had accepted Madeleine, even Ada grudgingly admiring her determination to work and add to their meagre resources. But it was to Mam that Madeleine became closest for the old woman was surprisingly sympathetic and gentle. When Madeleine developed a craving for something sweet, it was Mam who gathered dead nettle flowers and showed her how to suck the honey-like flavour from their tips, and it was she who instructed Madeleine in the use of orris root, betony, sage and a host of other herbs. And Madeleine tried her best to repay Mam's kindness. Realizing that the old woman loved the small nut found in the middle of thistle buds but that her fingers were too stiff to extract this, Madeleine braved the pain of peeling countless thistles, and when Mam complained of 'bein' all behind loike a cow's tail', it was Madeleine who prepared yarrow for Ada's toothache and spent hours rolling dried lavender, eyebright and coltsfoot between her hands until they were reduced to powder. It was tiring and monotonous, yet when Jem sat on the front step, his clay pipe filled with the mixture and the whole cottage permeated by the fragrance, Madeleine felt not only contentment but a sense of belonging to the family.

By midsummer all work was becoming increasingly difficult for Madeleine, and one night when she was walking home in the scented darkness, her child moved within her. She stopped abruptly, hands instinctively clutching her stomach, and it was at that moment that she finally realized what her pregnancy meant. Until then she had half denied it, her mind numbed by perpetual exhaustion, only registering that she ached in every limb, that her hands bled and her stomach continually rumbled with hunger. Although she remembered her past life, it was as though it had all happened not to herself, but to someone she knew very well; even though her body yearned unceasingly for Sebastian, he had assumed the dream-like quality of a Prince Charming, his insults and cruelty forgotten, his presence as unattainable as the stars. But now, with evidence that her baby was living within her, she suddenly became terrified that she would die in childbirth and that the baby would be sent to an institution; she remembered seeing children from the Ashley Down Orphanage, boys and girls dressed uniformly in blue smocks, walking hand in hand, their faces serious, and she edged towards hysteria at the thought of her baby being left to the mercy of strangers. Contrary to her initial wish, she made Ellen solemnly swear that she would not let this happen and that, in the event of her own death, Ellen would inform the de Laceys. After all, Madeleine reasoned with herself, the baby would be entitled to their assistance, and although she felt sure it would have only the status of a poor relation, this would be infinitely better than life in an orphanage.

'Bu' nothin' be goin' ter happen ter thee,' Mam assured her, and Ellen looked at her mother sharply. That Madeleine was undernourished was only too evident; except for her swollen belly, her face and body were

195

gaunt, her eyes sunken. Ellen began smuggling more and more food and Jem poached regularly, but this was the only meat they ate; even milk and butter were unknown to them.

Over the months Ellen's relationship with Madeleine had completely changed. Now it was she who was the wise counsellor, the one who was depended upon, and she had come to think of Madeleine as the daughter she had never been given the opportunity to produce. She secretly resolved that if Madeleine were to die and if the baby were rejected by the de Laceys, she would appeal to Miss Llewellyn Morgan, for whom all the General's former servants felt great respect. It had been common knowledge below stairs in Royal Crescent that she and Sebastian would marry. Remembering what little money the General had left, Ellen felt sure that his son would have marriage to the heiress very much on his mind.

But in this she was mistaken.

12

When he awakened after leaving Madeleine so brutally, Sebastian felt extraordinarily happy. He had successfully stalked his quarry and was quite certain that she was now entirely his property. He remembered her stricken face and felt quite a stab of regret, but then he shrugged off the thought, confident of being able to make her forget. Tonight, he mused happily, as soon as the household had retired, he would go to her, slip silently into her bed and take her immediately into his arms; between kisses he would murmur an apology for his cruel words and spend the entire night making love to her. The anticipation of this made him leap from his bed and wonder how he was going to get through the day. Seeing the empty brandy bottle, he was surprised not to have a splitting headache; instead he felt full of power and supercharged energy and sang lustily as he took his customary cold bath.

Then, as he dressed, he began to plan a future with Madeleine. When he returned to London, she would, of course, accompany him and he would at once set her up in a couple of small rooms somewhere in the capital. Unfortunately, it would not be possible for him to maintain her entirely, so she would have to work. A post as governess was the obvious solution, but quite unsuitable, as she would have to live in and naturally he would demand that she should be instantly available for him whenever he could come to her. No, it would have to be in one of the new emporiums, of which there were now quite a number in Regent Street: Peter Robinson, Jay, Liberty, Swan & Edgar and – yes, how about those very nice new ones out at Knightsbridge, Harveys and Harrods? The snag was that almost all the new shops employed mostly men and required their staffs to live in dormitory accommodation. Still, he had no doubt that Madeleine, with her looks and splendid impersonation of a lady, would be able to find employment somewhere. He would have to find some really decent rooms for her because she would be Mrs de Lacey, being visited constantly by Captain de Lacey, so what could be more proper and respectable?

The thought caused Sebastian to grin delightedly at himself in his shaving mirror. With this happy prospect in mind, he went leaping down the stairs, unconsciously humming until he met the butler's startled eye and remembered that he was supposed to be mourning his father's death.

He smiled knowingly when Madeleine did not appear for breakfast and wished he might have been able to find a white rose to put on the tray which he had ordered for her. Yes, he thought as he ate his own hearty breakfast, he would be good to her, but he would certainly not tolerate any more nonsense about love: it was pleasure, exquisite, perfect pleasure they had experienced together. He'd also have to remember that she could not be trusted an inch, for it had been quite amazing the way she had kept up that shy innocence – as though she did not know what to do! If he had not seen it, he would never have believed it possible for an experienced woman to sustain such a role in the throes of passion. But he had no doubt that she would be kind to him.

Of course, he thought as he rose from the table, he definitely would have to marry one day. Perhaps Catherine Llewellyn Morgan would not be such a bad bet, for her money would give him complete independence, and once she had produced an heir she could be left to her good works, while he would be free to spend nearly all his time with Madeleine. For no matter where his future lay, he would always keep her, and with an heiress's money he would deny her nothing: her own house, carriage, clothes, jewels, even a child if she insisted.

Ellen's entry into the library ended Sebastian's rosy dream and then had followed his frantic search throughout Bath.

It was not until the evening that Madeleine's disappearance was discussed, and by then grief, frustration and anger had made Sebastian revert to bitterness. 'Ah well,' he said with a shrug, 'she was only a cheap little adventuress who would no doubt have scuttled away as fast as she could when she realized there really was no money for her.'

Lady Frensham raised her lorgnette to survey him as though he were a new species for whom she had no great liking. 'Really, Sebastian,' she said in her cold voice, 'I find that statement quite extraordinary! I should have thought that even you would have enough sensitivity to realize that Madeleine Brett was a highly intelligent, well-brought-up gal who did not ask to come here, but when she did, she tried to fit in and never once moped over her father's death. I do not know the real reason for her sudden departure, but I *do* know that she was not an adventuress, for no one of that breed would leave even a handkerchief, yet Madeleine left clothes to which she was quite legitimately entitled.'

Sebastian turned to his aunt, heavy black brows drawn together ominously. 'Why, aunt, you astound me!' he answered curtly. 'I had no idea you championed Miss Brett and, in fact, I thought you did not care for her.'

'Then you thought quite wrongly!' retorted Lady Frensham with her loudest sniff. 'Actually, I admired her greatly at the ball when you treated her so abominably.'

'I *what*?' demanded Sebastian, but she broke in at once, 'Yes, quite abominably. Waltzing her out of the ballroom in full view of everyone and then only reappearing after at least ten minutes. As if that were not enough, you then left her to return quite alone – as though you were some ignorant clodhopper without any idea of etiquette. It would have been too easy for her to burst into tears or faint, but instead she walked across that vast floor with quiet dignity, and it was left to your father to go and offer her his arm.'

'Ah yes, my father.' Sebastian's voice was now silky. 'And no doubt you have an explanation for her extraordinary marriage to him?'

'Indeed,' Lady Frensham agreed, inclining her head in a stately manner. 'Your father insisted upon it and Madeleine only agreed because he was so obviously exhausting himself with persuasion.'

Harriet, who had been silently weeping, now raised tear-dimmed eyes. 'That is quite correct, Sebastian,' she said unexpectedly. 'And one of papa's main reasons was because he said you would not dare to treat Madeleine other than well if she were your stepmother!'

'Et tu, Brute,' Sebastian murmured, his mouth twisting. Even Harriet . . . who had always been his greatest ally in everything.

'Are you quite sure you had nothing to do with her sudden departure?' persisted Lady Frensham, her heavy-lidded eyes never leaving his face.

Sebastian felt himself flushing. 'Why should I?' he countered.

'Because you were the only one here yesterday evening, and surely even you must admit that it was very strange for anyone to leave in the early hours, unless they were a thief, and Madeleine Brett was certainly not that!'

'I can think of a dozen reasons,' Sebastian said coldly and quite untruthfully.

Lady Frensham suddenly gave up the fight. 'Well, I cannot, and I still think it a brave thing to do. I only hope she does not end up in the gutter. And now, I shall retire;

it has been a long and extremely trying day and I am very fatigued.'

It was with relief that Sebastian at last returned to the War Office, and he was soon back in his old routine: attending the theatre, opera and all the grand balls in Belgravia, where he was a much-sought-after guest, flirting outrageously and giving many an anxious mama reason to hope that he would choose *her* daughter. But several of those daughters reported petulantly, 'He suddenly seemed to lose all interest in me and, anyway, I had the feeling right from the start that he was looking at me and seeing someone else . . . and did you not notice, when he first arrived, how he looked around everywhere, as though searching? It was the same when he was at the theatre with us last week; he seemed to spend more time scanning the audience than the players, and didn't even bother to hide the fact.'

It was quite true. Everywhere he went he looked for her, growing more and more desperate, yet certain that she must be somewhere in this huge capital and that if he searched long enough he would surely find her. One day he thought he had done so. He was in a hansom being driven down Regent Street when he suddenly saw a tall slender figure entering Liberty's emporium; he caught only a glimpse, but she looked sufficiently like Madeleine for him to leap from the cab heedless of the driver's outraged shout for his fare, to zigzag between the great mass of carriages, cabs, buses and drays, mindless of the horses' hooves, the yells and general pandemonium he was causing. Rushing up to the young woman, he grasped her arm, exclaiming with a great burst of joy: 'Madeleine, oh, Madeleine, at last!' Only to find himself staring at a singularly plain and startled face. The young laird's wife on an infrequent visit to London blushingly accepted his stammered apology and could not suppress a quick stab

201

of envy of the unknown Madeleine, who was able to make such a splendidly handsome man look so miserably disappointed.

Sebastian then went to the tiny terraced house off the Harrow Road where Madeleine had lived with her father. All the Italians rushed out and started speaking at once, although they knew nothing of her whereabouts, and it was left to Mr Silbermann to tell Sebastian in halting English of their affection and admiration for the young girl who had battled unceasingly against overwhelming odds. Although obviously used to very different circumstances, she had not hesitated to go regularly to the pawnbroker; to run after the coal carts in an endeavour to retrieve the pieces that had fallen off; and even, on her last day, to load her remaining furniture on to a handcart and try to trundle it to the nearest second-hand dealer; halfway along, everything had slid to the ground, but Madeleine, although scarlet-faced, had merely dragged it all back on to the cart. 'I aff feared for die young girl,' Mr Silbermann concluded. 'T"ere is too much heart, too much tears – life, I tink, will boom-boom – nein, nein, escuse me, I mean batter her.'

'But were there no friends – young girls and their brothers, perhaps, to help?' asked Sebastian, even now reluctant to revise his opinion of Madeleine.

Mr Silbermann's large, almond-shaped dark eyes looked steadily into Sebastian's own and he shook his head so decisively that the long dangling ringlets on each side of his face tossed. 'No. I tink she need goot man to care for her – she made for Liebe – love, yes?'

Yes, thought Sebastian, yes, yes, *yes*! And she's mine! I want her with me always! It never occurred to him to analyse why he should want this so much; if asked, he might have shrugged indifferently, or at best have said that no woman had ever eluded him and he did not intend that a cunning chit like Madeleine Brett should do so

202

now. Always highly competitive, he did not easily acknowledge defeat, and when finally forced to do so, he told himself that it was only her satin skin and delicate, long-limbed body which had enslaved him; that there were countless others with such enticements – so what the hell? Madeleine Brett had vanished and good riddance! He determined to waste no more time or thought upon her and returned then to his favourite brothels, seeking out the youngest, most slender girls, but although they all gave him release and some even exhausted him, he remained strangely tormented by thoughts of Madeleine.

The declaration of war on 28 March forced Sebastian to concentrate on obtaining permission to leave the War Office. He had watched the departure of the Coldstream and Grenadier Guards the previous month, when all traffic had come to a standstill and people had even rushed out in their night attire to cheer the troops. There had been a carnival air to the occasion, and Sebastian was determined not to remain cooped up in a dusty office if there was any fun to be had elsewhere. The only snag was that no one knew precisely where the action was likely to take place, and for the time being the Army was going to Malta.

By mid-June Sebastian was free, and not even the announcement of Lord Cardigan's promotion to Major General and command of the Light Brigade could dampen Sebastian's enthusiasm. 'But why did they have to choose *him* of all people?' he muttered to himself. The mere mention of Cardigan's name had been sufficient to make General de Lacey's colour rise dangerously, and Sebastian remembered his own instinctive feeling of antipathy on seeing his lordship strut down St James's in the full-dress uniform of the Eleventh Hussars; at various stages there had been troopers waiting to salute their commanding officer, and it was said that Lord Cardigan paid them five shillings each to do this. But stupid and vain though he was, he had nevertheless made sure that the Eleventh was the best mounted regiment in the Army, as well as the most gorgeously uniformed.

And now that the regiment was to be commanded by John Douglas, thought Sebastian delightedly, things could only improve. He decided to spend his last night in London with Sal, whom he had met some five years before. He had been on the prowl near the Burlington Arcade and Sal, who worked in a drapery shop within the Baker Street Bazaar, had thought to augment her meagre wage by soliciting. She had been instantly thwarted by the dozens of full-time prostitutes in the area, who saw in her extreme youth and prettiness too great a threat to themselves. Sal had been chased away, and it was then that Sebastian, seeing her legs in their pink stockings and liking what he saw, had become her first customer.

That first night he had taken her to Kate Hamilton's establishment in Leicester Square. He knew that Sal would never have been admitted without him, for it was the most famous and luxurious house of assignation in London. But Sebastian was well known there, so although the Prince's Street entrance was guarded by huge doormen, it needed only the briefest look through the peephole before the door was swung open for him. Sal had been overawed by all the lights and the gilt – and by Kate's glittering mass of jewels – and it was from that night that she had acquired her weakness for champagne.

A most unlikely but very real friendship was formed from that time onwards; Sebastian, although he did not know it and would have hotly disputed it, was a lonely man. The emotional deprivation of his childhood and his subsequent rejection by Sophie Clifton, whom he had adored with all the intensity of first love, had turned him into a drifting pleasure-seeker. When he realized that he had an overwhelming effect upon women of all ages, he began to exploit this power in a ruthless but unconscious revenge on the female sex in general. With every new conquest, his cynicism increased; but with Sal he was at his most relaxed and generous. An uninhibited bedmate who made up in lustiness for what she lacked in finesse, she made no demands upon him and was a bright companion in the intervals between their lovemaking. He never questioned her about any other men, but she was always available whenever he unexpectedly appeared. The fact was that Sal had fallen completely in love with him on that first night and had not been able to bear anyone else near her. She dared not let him see how much he meant to her, so she always kept the atmosphere light and gay, even though she often wept afterwards. Sebastian had never told her his full name – 'Never let 'em know that, m' boy,' the General had warned him years before, 'nor your regiment, because if you do, sure as hell you'll have some little whore hanging around the barracks, or even the mess, at best asking for you, at worst rushing up to greet you.' So he had merely said, 'My name is Sebastian,' at which Sal had wrinkled her nose and replied, 'Funny, i'n'it?'

'No more so than your having started as Sarah-Jane,' Sebastian had said, his deep laugh ringing out.

''ere,' she had added, 'one of the girls in the shop 'as a sergeant, but I said I was sure you was a lieutenant. I'm right, ain't I?'

'Actually, I'm a captain, love,' Sebastian had said, laughing again at her brown eyes made huge by astonishment.

She had snapped to attention then and saluted him with great smartness. 'I shall call you Capt'ing,' she had said, keeping her face rigid, and he had shouted with laughter for she was wearing only her frilly drawers, and the sight of her shoulders thrown back and plump breasts outthrust had delighted him; with one arm around her waist he had swept her off the ground to nuzzle her until she squealed and he felt her nip his ear.

Whenever he wanted to see her, Sebastian would go into the shop and pretend to need help in choosing something for 'my sister' and they would go through an elaborate charade, under cover of which an arrangement for the night would be made. He knew that she was tremendously proud to have such a 'swell' for a lover and he always dressed with great care when he visited the store. On that last day he wore a black coat faced with silk, lined with scarlet satin and perfectly tailored across his massive shoulders; his linen, starched and very white, complemented the black and white check of his trousers, which tapered to strap under the instep of his highly polished ankle boots. Hat in hand, he advanced to Sal's counter. 'We all knows you're a reel toff 'cos you always takes orf your 'at and not many do that,' she had once told him, but of course he had done so automatically.

'May I help you, sir?' she asked now, eyes downcast, and Sebastian stifled his laughter with difficulty; her demureness and care with her aitches when she was 'on parade' always vastly amused him.

'Some ribbons for my young sister, if you please,' he said courteously, very much aware of the stares and whispers around him: 'Wot a toff!' 'Blimey, ain't he loverly?' 'Just like one of those great big glossy black 'orses you sees in the park.' So they thought him a stallion, did they? He half turned to the last speaker, smiling lazily and letting his eyes roam slowly and appreciatively over her in a look which said, how pleasant, how *very* pleasant to prove you correct!

'Er – wot colour, sir?' Sal was asking, her tone slightly sulky; she loved to hear such comments about him, but not for him to respond, which of course he always did.

'Oh, I think blue,' Sebastian answered seriously, while under cover of the ribbons he let his finger stroke the back of her hand. 'I'm off to the war, love,' he whispered, 'and I want to spend tonight with you – are you free?'

Oh, was she! She looked up, radiant. 'The whole night?'

'Naturally!' Then, taking pity on her obvious happiness, he added generously, 'But I'd like to take you somewhere nice first. Where would you like to go?'

Sal's eyes lit up. 'Oh, could we go to the Cremorne?'

'Of course.' It always pleased him to make her happy. 'I'll come and collect you – best bib and tucker, mind!'

Sal's day was made, and she lost no time in telling her colleagues that 'the Capt'ing' was a reel gent – instead of making her wait around for him at the Cremorne Gardens, where she would be the target for every unaccompanied male in the vicinity, he was actually coming to collect her. Thank Gawd it was Saturday and she would be able to leave the shop early – at seven o'clock – and she would wear her orange gown and bonnet; he would surely love her in them.

In reality, Sebastian had the greatest difficulty in suppressing his laughter when he saw her: the gown was almost luminous in its brilliance and each of its many flounces was edged with glittering paillettes, while the bonnet was a monstrosity of ruched orange silk covered in huge roses and topped by a giant feather which swayed and fluttered with her every movement. But beneath it Sal's extremely pretty little face was radiant. 'D'you like it?' she asked and pivoted for his approval, arms outflung at her sides.

'Wonderful, sweetheart,' Sebastian said heartily. He held out a posy of creamy peach roses, circled with gold filigree paper. 'And these are to complete the outfit.'

Sal was speechless; no one had ever given her flowers before, let alone a bouquet done up so elegantly. 'Oh, Capt'ing, you are a love,' she said at last, tears of happiness shining in her eyes. 'An' you look wonderful

207

yourself!' It was true; he was in full evening dress with an opera cloak flung carelessly around his shoulders, and the contrast between black and white, the superfine materials and expert tailoring all set off his tall figure to perfection. Sal thought her heart would burst with pride at such a splendid escort. Then she noticed the tight white rosebud in his buttonhole. 'Why d'you always wear a white rose, Capt'ing?' she asked, and at once his gloved hand came up to cover the bud in an instinctively protective gesture, even though he shrugged and said indifferently, 'Oh, I don't know.' But because she loved him, she was very perceptive to his every mood, and suddenly the magic of the moment had gone.

'Well, let's be off before I change my mind and take you to bed now,' Sebastian said, grinning at her with every appearance of gaiety. 'I've a cab waiting.'

They were both tipsy when they returned in the early hours and Sebastian was clutching a bottle of champagne, from which they both took frequent draughts. When Sal stumbled on the stairs, ripping the orange gown and giggling happily, Sebastian picked her up in his arms, taking the stairs two at a time in a swaying, precarious way.

'Ssh!' said Sal, finger waving about in an effort to put it before her mouth when they were both crashing unsteadily about her tiny room. Somehow this seemed the funniest thing in the world and they were both helpless with laughter.

'"First lesson of a gen'elman, m'boy"' quoted Sebastian hazily, '"is to learn to carry his liquor." Father always said, "m'boy . . ."' They collapsed once more into giggles before falling on to the bed, where they made boisterous love until, still entwined, they fell asleep simultaneously.

It was broad daylight when Sebastian first opened his eyes and then quickly closed them again. His mouth felt like a desert and his head like lead when he tried to move it. But then he became conscious of tiny, ineffectual movements beneath him and a voice beside his ear saying urgently, 'Please, Capt'ing dear, will you move – me ribs is breaking.' And there was poor little Sal looking up at him with real distress in her brown eyes. With a muffled exclamation of apology, Sebastian rolled away and on to his back, one arm flung across his eyes.

'Squashed like a bleedin' fly, that's wot I am!' Sal said, the laughter in her voice belying her words.

Sebastian was genuinely contrite. 'I'm so sorry, love,' he said, uncovering half of one eye to look at her ruefully.

Sal jumped off the bed and drew the curtain to shield him from the light. 'That's all right,' she said, slipping into her shift. 'I can't think of no better way of bein' squashed! Naow, 'ow about a nice drop o' tea?'

'Wonderful,' replied Sebastian, who would have preferred champagne. He watched her bustling about, thinking how characteristic it was that she seemed as bright and chirpy as a bird. 'Take that horrible shift off,' he commanded suddenly. 'It doesn't hide anything and I like you much better when you've not got it on!'

'If you say so, Capt'ing darlin'.' Instantly the garment was slipped over her head and tossed aside.

Sebastian whistled appreciatively; one of the things he liked most about Sal was her complete lack of any inhibitions, and she continued now to make the tea as unconcernedly as though dressed in layers of petticoats. Such a nice little body, he thought, so plump and full of roundness and with the prettiest legs. He remembered when he had first glimpsed them in those bright pink stockings and wondered if women's dress would ever change so that they could legitimately show their legs; he hoped so, for when, like Sal's, they tapered to the most slender ankles, they were certainly good to look at. His glance travelled lazily upwards to her tousled curls and then he said: 'What's happened to your hair? It looks much fairer than I remember.'

To his surprise, she actually seemed embarrassed. 'Yes, well,' she said slowly, 'I found a mule, didn't I?'

'A mule?' he echoed. 'What on earth has that got to do with it?'

'Mule water,' she said reluctantly, but Sebastian was completely mystified.

'I don't follow,' he said.

'Oh – y'know.' She was blushing and pleading for his comprehension.

Sebastian blinked. 'Good God,' he said blankly.

'It makes 'air ever so fair,' said Sal, some of her confidence returning with his seemingly calm acceptance. She paused briefly and then added, ''course I washes it out after with lots of Sunlight soap.'

'Yes,' he said, still dumbfounded, 'yes, of course.' She brought him a steaming cup and he raised himself cautiously on an elbow; the tea was so strong that he could hardly refrain from grimacing, but he had to admit that it was wonderfully refreshing, and when he had finished it he lay back, stretching luxuriously before putting his arms behind his head. 'What a night!' he said, grinning lazily at her as she came to perch on the other side of the bed. 'You're good for me, Sal, it's a long time since I've slept like that.'

Sal put her hand against her sore ribs. 'So I should 'ope,' she said with mock severity.

Sebastian's deep laugh filled the little room. 'No, silly, I meant it's a long time since I slept so well.'

'Yes?' she queried, eyebrows raised. 'Yet you kep' on an' on about being mad.'

'Being mad?' he repeated slowly. 'Why, what did I actually say?'

Sal shook her head. 'I dunno. All I could make out was "Mad, Mad" an' somethin' about bein' "lean" or "lane".'

His smile faded then and the lights ceased to dance in his eyes. So even in his sleep his thoughts were with Madeleine, and sufficiently strong for him actually to murmur her name.

'Wot did you mean?' Sal was asking curiously, but he shrugged, feigning indifference.

'God only knows,' he said casually. He stretched out his hand to touch her breast, where a bruise was becoming visible. 'I must have been rough, love, for you're bruised. I'm sorry.'

Sal smiled. 'Don' you worry, it's nothin'.'

Why should he then see another face looking up at him with wounded, stricken eyes?

'Would you say I was a cruel man?' he asked suddenly.

The blonde curls were immediately shaken from side to side. 'Oh no, never – ' She broke off abruptly and began frowningly to nibble a thumb.

'But . . .?' prompted Sebastian gently. 'Tell me, I shan't be angry.'

'Well,' said Sal hesitantly, 'I do think you can be crool with words an' you can look reel fierce wen you draws your lips back, like this.' She bared her teeth, thinning her lips in a caricature.

Sebastian gave a bark of laughter. 'By God, if I look like that at the Russian gunners, I reckon they'll turn and run without firing a shot!'

That reminded her that he was going to war. 'I do wish you didn' 'ave to go,' she said, suddenly serious.

'Oh, I'm looking forward to it and will be back in no time,' Sebastian said bracingly. He caught her wrist and pulled her over to him. 'Meanwhile, why don't we pretend that I'm a wounded soldier who can't do much, but is greatly in need of comfort.'

The blonde curls were just above him then, the brown eyes like velvet as she teased his lips with her own. 'Are you reely in need of comfort, Capt'ing dear?' she murmured throatily, moving so that all her soft curves covered his lean hard body.

'Ah yes, yes, in terrible need,' he whispered urgently. 'But lift up, sweetheart, so that I can come closer.'

'Like this?' she asked, raising herself and then returning to hold him fast.

'You're wonderful, wonderful,' he murmured, closing his eyes and giving himself up entirely to her pleasuring. And because he didn't want to think of another loving woman, see another pretty face, he cried out, 'I don't want this to end!' and clamped his arms around Sal until she was whimpering. Then suddenly he was in command again and with a lightning movement had turned her so that she was beneath him. When at last he drew away panting, he only remained still for a few minutes. 'I must go now,' he said abruptly, and in one lithe movement was off the bed and already pulling on his trousers.

Sal dressed too, silent and unhappy. She sensed that he had already gone away from her, and knew in that moment as never before that she really meant nothing to him – oh, he had a certain fondness for her, that was obvious, but it was the kind which he would carelessly bestow on a particularly loving puppy.

'Well now, love,' he said, swinging his cape around his shoulders, 'I'll see you when I get back, and meanwhile here is something to remember me by – ' He put into her hand a small velvet case. Then, as she appeared turned to stone, he put his arm quickly around her waist, gave her a lingering kiss on the forehead and was already out of the room and halfway down the stairs before she roused herself and rushed out on to the landing.

'Gawd bless you, Capt'ing,' she said, a catch in her voice, 'an' please, please, take care of yourself!'

He paused to look up at her, eyes dancing and the

familiar wicked grin creasing his tired face. 'Especially of some rather essential parts, eh, love?'

Her gurgling laugh was instantly appreciative. 'Oh, my Gawd yes!' she agreed, and he lifted a gold-topped cane to touch his silk hat, which was rakishly perched over one eye.

'I'll do my best,' he said, and then with a 'Thanks for everything, Sal!' he was gone. She rushed to the window in time to see him leap into a passing hansom, but he did not look back.

Sal was crying as she slowly opened the velvet case and her tears fell on the fine gold chain, from which hung a tiny enamelled heart surrounded by paste brilliants. Inside the heart was space for two minute portraits, but she knew it would always remain empty.

13

By August Madeleine was in her seventh month and, although exhausted in mind and body, she was as always driven on by her spirit. The cereal harvest was in full swing, with work continuing round the clock. So on that brilliant morning Madeleine took her place in the row of women who followed the scything men as they advanced in line across the standing corn. The women's job was to scoop the corn into sheaves and tie them with straw, ready for carting and stacking. As they worked, the whole crowd sang, for harvesting was paid by piece and they were thankful for the cloudless day, which might end with a ration of cider if the farmer thought they had done well. As the morning advanced, the men discarded their coats and waistcoats and the women tied their skirts under their knees, allowing their bare legs and clog-covered feet to move freely through the stubble.

Then, as Madeleine paused to put both hands to the small of her aching back, she looked up and encountered the horrified eyes of Catherine Llewellyn Morgan. For an instant the two young women stared at each other in astonishment, then Madeleine, with heart hammering, quickly turned away and resumed her work.

Catherine, who was sitting with her father in their open carriage, said to him urgently: 'Why, look, papa, I believe that young woman is Madeleine Brett!'

Her father, immersed in judging the state of the land which he was proposing to buy, said vaguely, 'Who? Where?'

'There, the one third from the left at the end of the

214

line; she is incredibly changed, but I *do* believe that it is Miss Brett!'

Evan Llewellyn Morgan saw a young woman, gaunt of face and body except for her advanced pregnancy, her skin unfashionably tanned and her untidy, windswept hair already stringy and dull with the heat. As Catherine folded her parasol and began to move, saying, 'I must speak to her,' her father quickly placed his hand on her arm.

'No, no, my dear, you must not,' he said quietly. 'See how quickly she turned away; she would not thank you for acknowledging her, especially as she is in – er – a delicate state of health.'

Nothing could have sounded more ludicrous, and even Catherine, who was normally so sweet-tempered, said sharply, 'Yes, I see that she is with child and obviously in extremely poor circumstances. That is why I want to try and help!'

'But she does not want your help! Was that not obvious by the way she reacted?'

Catherine was biting her lip and frowning. 'Surely, papa, in such circumstances, one's pride – '

'*No*, Catherine. Now drive on, Hughes.'

'Papa, please – '

'Catherine, I have said no, and I mean no. I will not have you chasing after every lame dog you see. It is unseemly, and I will thank you not to mention this young woman again.'

Catherine unfurled her parasol with so much force that one of the struts snapped, but she remained silent and refused to meet her father's eyes. Both knew that the matter of Madeleine Brett was not ended.

Madeleine never knew whether it was the shock of seeing Catherine or merely the exhausting work which brought on her labour, but for a time she tried to continue until the red-hot stabbing pains became more frequent and then she uttered a thin, high crying sound and reeled. The large, raw-boned woman next to her took one look at her sweat-soaked body and called out: 'Jem! Come quick ter thy woman afore her dap doon the babby!'

Work and singing momentarily stopped as all watched Jem run to Madeleine. He wanted to pick her up, but a woman called out, 'Nay, is be'er if her can wark.' So Jem walked beside Madeleine, silent because he did not know what to say, but with his arm timidly about her waist. By the time they reached the cottage, Madeleine was clutching her lower abdomen with both hands and staggering like a drunken woman.

The cottage door was open and Mam was seated on the step, busy with pestle and mortar. She exclaimed at the sight of her son and Madeleine and got to her feet with difficulty. 'Babby comin',' said Jem laconically as he helped Madeleine into the cottage. The interior was blessedly cool and dim and smelled deliciously of the many herbs which lay in bunches on the table.

'Get wa'er, Jem, an' set by foire,' commanded his mother calmly, 'an' den go an' doan' come back farr a long toime.'

Madeleine had sunk on to a stool. 'Oh, Mam,' she gasped, 'is it too early for the baby? Will it be all right?'

'Naow, doan' fret, my dove, everythin' will be a'roight, but get up naow an' wark about.'

So while Madeleine paced endlessly up and down the tiny room, Mam took leaves from a little covered bowl and made a tea. 'Drink all tha' an' it'll help thee.'

Obediently Madeleine drank the slightly bitter liquid, even managing a little smile for Mam. 'Lady's mantle?'

Mam nodded. 'Tha' be roight.' Madeleine had seen her gathering the large kidney-shaped leaves during the two previous months and had asked about them. 'Ah will droi

216

the leaves an' wen babby be comin' thee can drink a tea o' them ter help with pains an' thy heart.'

Madeleine never knew whether it helped her, but all through that endless day when she was gasping, or whimpering, or crying out, there was Mam holding a bowl to her lips and calmly urging her to drink more . . . When the light had faded and the velvety summer night was all around them, she was still being made to walk, even though her legs were almost buckling under her, but by then Ellen was there. Together she and Mam supported her, keeping up a constant flow of encouragement, while Ada crouched in a corner, her brilliant eyes glittering in the dim light. It was almost midnight when Mam said quietly, 'Babby be almos' yere naow, so go down on thy knees . . .' They had removed everything except her shift and now they helped her as she sank to her knees. 'Spread your legs, lovey,' Ellen instructed, her voice hoarse with constant talk, 'an' press down . . .'

'I . . . can't . . . I can't . . .' Madeleine whimpered, even as searing pain enveloped and tore at the whole of her internal body, dragging it slowly down, down. She uttered a tiny sobbing laugh. Soon only the sagging skin of her would be left, the poor, soaking frame, which would have collapsed full length were it not for Mam and Ellen holding it under each armpit, like a scarecrow . . . The laugh turned into an agonized shriek. She was bursting open . . . wide – wider. Surely the skin would rip . . . She felt rather than saw Mam catch her wrists and pull her forward until she was on all fours and squatting like a frog. From a great distance she heard Ellen say, 'Quick, Ada, get down an' take it as it come out!' Then there was a tiny mewing sound, followed by excited voices all talking at once, but Madeleine was beyond caring . . .

Thus was Sebastian's son brought forth, in circumstances not so very different from the birth of his first ancestors.

As soon as they had got her on to the straw and Mam had finished putting liquid on her skin – which at first felt cool but then was so strong that her flesh cringed – a tiny weightless object was placed on her stomach. 'Tis a boy,' Ellen said, and at once Madeleine's hands fluttered exploringly over the small mound. There was a tiny head between her breasts, with something that felt like a minute open flower beside it, and lower down little legs, one straight, the other bent at the knee and resting against the curve of her stomach, and a sweet round bottom, which fitted easily into the palm of her hand. The full realization of what this was suddenly penetrated her exhaustion: her baby! The small, unknown creature whom she had agonized over and tried so hard to shield during all the months of work and fear was now here, living, breathing and making tiny movements against her body. It seemed then that her whole being opened in a paean of the purest, most exquisite joy she had ever known, and from the depths of her very soul she yearned and cried silently for Sebastian to share it with her . . .

And far away, on a remote and completely bare plateau, Sebastian started out of a deep sleep and sat up abruptly, heart thudding unevenly. She had called; he had actually heard her voice! He knew he had, even though as he strained to hear now, all that came to him were the sounds of a sleeping army and its animals. But it was not a dream, he knew it was not, and he got to his feet, looking wildly around. All about him were other forms, huddled in their cloaks, asleep on the hard ground, while overhead the brilliant stars of a Balkan night filled the sky. Supposing something had happened to her, he thought distractedly, supposing she were in some terrible danger and had called out in desperation to him? 'Where are you?' he whispered in an agony of fear. 'If only I knew where you were, no power on earth would stop me from coming to you.' He

218

even prayed then, he who had not done so since his schooldays at Eton. 'O God, keep her safe, please keep her safe and help me to find her.'

Eventually he wrapped himself once more in his cloak and lay down, but sleep was now impossible. Gazing up at the stars, he thought deeply: should he go home? Already at Varna, the Commander-in-Chief, who lived in another age, was openly wondering why more officers who could get away chose to remain in such a filthy country. But it was not the violent changes of temperature or the discomforts of a harsh terrain which had disillusioned Sebastian and so many of his fellow officers, it was the sheer ineptitude of their commanders, beginning with the transportation of the cavalry. Instead of sending the men and their horses in fast steamships, they had been loaded on to sailing ships, which rolled and pitched and took at least ten times as long on the voyage. In the confined space of the stifling holds the horses had suffered unimaginably. Then on arrival at Varna, it was found that arrangements for landing the animals were totally unrealistic; there was even insufficient water and forage for them. The officers and men had fared little better: within a week of the British and French armies descending on the primitive town like a swarm of locusts, cholera and dysentery had broken out. Even at that stage, mused Sebastian, an efficient commander might have saved the situation, but instead chaos and lethargy prevailed. In the Light Brigade hardship was intensified by the seeming stupidity and indifference of their commander, for while they were encamped, scorched and parched by day, frozen by night and dying like flies of cholera, Lord Cardigan had comfortably installed himself in a tree-shaded house some nine miles distant. Said to be suffering from bronchitis, he remained there all day, living on a diet of fruit, while his Brigade tried to exist on salt pork, biscuits and green coffee beans.

As the stars began to fade, Sebastian got to his feet again and lit a cigar, the scraping of the lucifer sounding very loud in the stillness. Madeleine? *Of course* it had only been a dream; he was simply becoming mawkish, and if he couldn't stand a few hardships, he was a poor specimen indeed. He knew he would not go home, would not leave his troopers – good fellows, one and all – or his beloved horses.

Perhaps it was as well that on what promised to be a brilliant morning, Sebastian had no inkling of the horrors those men and their horses were about to suffer.

Madeleine slept, and did not even waken when Mam came to lift the baby gently and take him, nor did his tiny cries rouse her when he was washed and clothed and put into Ellen's tired, loving arms.

When she did waken, Madeleine at once raised herself slowly and painfully into a sitting position, and Mam came to wash her face and hands with a cooling lotion of crushed elderflowers, and to brush her hair. Then, hardly daring to breathe and wondering if she had dreamt it all, Madeleine waited for the baby to be brought to her. Surprisingly, it was Ada who came, holding him tightly against her poor travesty of a breast, her beautiful face tender. 'Ah were first ter hold him as he were born,' she told Madeleine proudly, 'an' Ah didn' le' him dap on ground!'

'Thank you, Ada dear, you did wonderfully well,' Madeleine said, holding out her arms and gazing avidly at her son.

Jem was allowed in then and came to stand at the foot of the straw 'bed', scarlet in the face with embarrassment. When he at last managed a 'Tiny, like a spring chicken, isn' he?' Ada rounded on him angrily. 'Why, 'course he be, bu' look at wha' long legs he 'as.'

'Oh, his father is a very tall man,' Madeleine said, full

of unconscious pride, while over her head Ellen folded her lips tightly.

'Wha' be his name?' Ada asked, as she stooped with difficulty to look into the baby's face.

'Thomas Henry, after his two grandfathers,' Madeleine said without hesitation. 'Thomas Henry Brett.'

Mam came forward then, smiling delightedly, and holding a large square of rabbit skins. 'Mam saved and cured all the skins from the rabbits Jem got, so tha' she could make a blanket for the baby,' Ellen said, and mam nodded, smiling again.

'Yes, farr babby at night,' she confirmed. Madeleine had often seen her stretching and treating the skins with liquid alum before putting them out to dry in the sun – always at the rear and safe from prying eyes – but the stitching together of the skins had been kept secret. The square was now double-sided, warm and very soft. Tears came to Madeleine's eyes then as she tried to thank Mam, not only for the blanket, but for looking after her so well.

'Whatever should I have done without you all?' she wondered aloud.

'Best feed babby naow,' Mam said, embarrassed as they all were by Madeleine's gratitude. They left her then, drawing the curtain across to give her some privacy, and Madeleine opened the neck of her nightgown and hesitantly held a nipple to her son's mouth. The tiny rosebud lips parted for it at once, while a minute hand came to rest, as light as a butterfly, against her breast. This, and the little sucking sensation, filled her with the utmost in sensual delight. Could anything in the world be more wonderful? she thought dazedly, and instantly remembered holding Sebastian's black head against her breast; only *that* could be more wonderful, she realized, and there was suddenly a great aching void within her: oh, how she needed his love and tenderness, the protection

221

of his strong arms about her and their baby, his reassurance that they would all be together and that their son would grow up sturdy and well. Even – even to hear his voice saying with pride that he thought his son wonderful would be sufficient, thought Madeleine wistfully.

But if Thomas's father was not there to say this, his mother was, for Madeleine was convinced that never in the history of the world had there been a more beautiful, intelligent and altogether wonderful baby. And, seeing her radiance, the whole family nodded their heads in agreement, although in the depths of Mam's eyes there was a lingering sadness.

Their entire little world began at once to revolve around Thomas: Mam insisted on doing his daily washing; Ada, as soon as she entered the cottage at night, went to look at him and, seeing her devotion, Madeleine always asked her to hold the baby, even though she could hardly bear to let him out of her own arms. Ada would then sit rocking and crooning to him in imitation of what she saw Madeleine do constantly, her beautiful face alight with tenderness. Jem's task was to fetch in the old animal drinking trough, which was all they had for Thomas's nightly bath. Then they would all gather round, silent but smiling as Mam dipped her elbow into the water to test its temperature and, at her nod, Madeleine would immerse the tiny body. Thomas loved the water and would look up at her with his great dark eyes sparkling as a wide, toothless grin slowly spread across his face. For a moment his little legs would kick in the water and his arms wave, but then, as though it was all too much for him, the tiny limbs would be still and flaccid.

'Oughtn't he to move more?' Madeleine asked Mam anxiously.

'He be too li'le an' weak farr more,' Mam said, and the first icy finger touched Madeleine's heart.

'I thought babies always cried a lot,' she said on another

222

occasion, 'but Thomas only makes the tiniest sound, more like a whimper.'

Mam turned away to stir the evening broth. 'Some doos an' some doosn't,' she replied cryptically, and another icy finger touched Madeleine.

But in the bright sunlight of day these fears retreated. Contrary to the prevailing fashion, there was no 'lying-in' period for any working woman, and Madeleine knew she must return to work the following week, no matter how she felt. Jem was already busy making a willow basket for her to carry Thomas in, for of course he would have to accompany her. Already she was worried because her wages were bound to fall when she had to stop work during the day in order to feed the baby. But for this one week I will try not to think about the future, she told herself, and every morning when she wakened she would bend over the small straw 'bed' beside her and whisper her love, very much as she had done to Sebastian on that night so long ago . . . Every day she would sit outside, with her aching back against a wall of the cottage, shaded from the sun but with all the smells and sights of high summer about her. Then she would feast her eyes upon Thomas, still only half believing that he was real and all hers. Her fingers would move with the lightest touch, tracing the thin fine line of his eyebrows and over his large dark eyes, then down to his tiny straight nose; his skin was always cool and slightly moist, and so thin that the blue veins were visible just beneath the surface. She talked to him all the time in a whisper, telling him how much she adored him and how wonderful he was. Whenever his little mouth opened and he turned it against her bodice, she would unbutton and give him the breast. His eyes, so like Sebastian's, would look up at her, wide open at first, and then sleepily, until only the slightest sliver of black was showing. Even when the curled crescent of lashes had come down on to his cheeks and he no longer

223

sucked, she would let him keep her nipple in his mouth for comfort and would remain sitting very still, grateful for the quiet and peace of the deep country.

It was on the afternoon of the fifth day that her milk dried up, and no amount of pinching, squeezing or even pummelling would make her breasts yield a drop. Thomas began to whimper nonstop, his face puckered, his mouth and hand constantly searching for her nipple. Madeleine was distraught, but Mam said she would go to the farm and beg a jug of milk.

'No, I'll go,' Madeleine said, rising as quickly as her weak legs would allow and holding Thomas out to Mam. 'I can walk more quickly.'

'It be three mile an' you be too weak,' Mam protested, but Madeleine had already snatched up a covered jug.

'I'll be all right,' she said and was gone, desperation carrying her forward at a stumbling run. She was soon gasping for breath, her legs trembling, but still she managed to go on, although reduced to a strange loping trot.

The farmer's wife was about to refuse her the milk when Madeleine gasped out that she had been one of the field workers until the previous week, then the woman reluctantly half filled the jug and Madeleine dashed away. It seemed to her frenzied mind that she had already been parted from Thomas for hours; he must be so hungry and thirsty, he must be missing her – supposing he felt she had deserted him? Panic-stricken, unable to think rationally, she could only cry out through her own parched lips, 'I'm coming, I'm coming, my darling,' and try to increase her speed. Mustn't faint, mustn't faint, was the rhythm to which she moved, her heart fluttering like a terrified bird against its cage.

She heard him crying before she entered the cottage and she burst in, eyes starting from her head. Sweat dripped into her eyes and off the tip of her nose, but she could just see that Mam was on a stool, trying to rock

Thomas, whose face was scarlet and distorted. Madeleine snatched him to her, cradling him adoringly and gasping out, 'Mama's here now, my precious, my darling, don't cry, don't cry . . .' And his cries did indeed begin to diminish until reduced to an exhausted whimper. Mam dipped a piece of flannel in the milk and then held it to his mouth: he sucked avidly and continued to do so until almost the whole of the milk had gone.

'Oh, thank God, thank God,' Madeleine murmured. She began to rock Thomas soothingly. 'Tomorrow mama will go back to work and then we shall be able to buy all the milk you need, won't we, Mam?'

But Mam's eyes were fixed on the baby, and when Madeleine looked down, she screamed. Milk and thick green mucus were pouring from his mouth. Both women were transfixed and could only gaze at the stream with horror. When at last this stopped, the little legs suddenly moved until they were drawn up against his stomach and his face became distorted once more, the mouth a wide gaping hole. Then there was a small cough, and for a few seconds the great dark eyes opened wide and looked up at Madeleine before the transparent lids slowly hid them. His face returned to normal then, rosebud mouth only slightly open, while his legs twitched briefly and fell flaccidly.

'Why, he's gone to sleep!' exclaimed Madeleine, turning to Mam with a radiant smile, but the old woman, her seamed face twisted with grief, shook her head.

'Thy babby be gone,' she said quietly.

The truth was too terrible for Madeleine to absorb. 'Why, Mam dear, what *do* you mean?' she asked, smiling still. 'Thomas hasn't gone anywhere – he's here, in my arms. Surely you can see him?'

'He be dead,' Mam said, looking at Madeleine with compassion.

Madeleine clutched the baby to her as she rose stiffly

from the low stool and began to back away across the room, her eyes staring and blank. 'Oh no, no, Mam, he's not dead, of course he's not dead – what a terrible thing to say! Thomas is just sleeping, aren't you, my precious darling?' And she raised him so that she could rest her cheek against his. Then she half turned to look at Mam with one quite wild eye. 'Sound asleep,' she said, smiling and covering the little face with kisses. 'That will do him a world of good. My papa always used to say that sleep was a great healer.'

She continued to rock and croon to the baby long after the light had faded, refusing all food or to let anyone touch him. Jem began making a little box and Mam hoped that the sight of this might reconcile Madeleine to reality; instead, she asked him not to hammer in the nails because of 'waking Thomas'.

'Ellen mus' come,' Mam said then, and poor Jem was sent off on the six-mile walk to Clifton. Now that he was able to read, he could find her address there, but when Ellen asked her mistress if she might go home, the woman told her if she went she need not come back; the choice was hers. There was no doubt in Ellen's mind as to what she should do. Madeleine was now 'family' and needed her. So she packed her few belongings and set off with Jem.

They were all still up, Madeleine on a low stool, crooning incessantly, Ada nodding beside the dying fire, and Mam sorting herbs as though her life depended upon them.

The next morning, after hours of talking to Madeleine, who gazed at her blankly throughout, Ellen said, 'Time for Thomas to be put into the box naow,' and surprisingly Madeleine let her take the baby from her, watching silently as Jem put fresh straw in the bottom and Ellen laid the little body, wrapped in the rabbit skins, on top. She even smiled as Ada strewed freshly gathered flower petals around him, but when Jem attempted to put a lid over the box, Madeleine leapt forward with the speed and silence of a wild animal. 'No!' she screamed, snatching up the coffin and backing away from them all. 'You cannot put that on top – he'll be left in the dark and terrified!'

When Jem walked forward uncertainly, she snatched up the one knife they possessed and pointed it at him. 'Don't you come any nearer,' she screamed, 'or I'll kill you! Don't you dare now! Why, you should be ashamed of yourself, wanting to box in a tiny, helpless baby!'

It was Ellen who said very quietly, 'Doan' you worry naow, lovey. Thomas will be lef' as he is, but we'd best go naow as parson be waitin'.' At that Madeleine appeared to sink into apathy again, allowing Ellen to take the knife and the coffin from her, but then, when they were all ready to leave, she insisted on going back for her bonnet and took a long time tying the ribbons. As she got to the door, she suddenly remembered her shawl and must have it, even though the morning was already hot. She then took a long time shaking the shawl, folding and refolding it aimlessly until Ellen took her arm and gently propelled her to the door. Jem had induced the farmer to let him hire one of his donkeys for the enormous sum of sixpence and Madeleine, clutching the open coffin, allowed herself to be lifted on to the little animal. She then took several more minutes to settle herself and to arrange the shawl so that it 'shielded Thomas's eyes'. They knew she was playing for time, but her mood was so uncertain that they dared not try to hustle her. Eventually Mam said, 'Sun not be good farr Thomas' and Jem began to lead the donkey forward.

So they proceeded, Mam heaving herself forward with the aid of a long stave, Ada bent and grotesque, and Ellen walking silently beside the donkey. Throughout, Madeleine kept up a strange, tuneless chant, clutching the coffin in both arms, her eyes never leaving the baby's face.

She was calm when they arrived at the churchyard, although she appeared not to notice the waiting parson, but when she saw the open grave she suddenly burst into action again. 'Thomas has not been baptized,' she screamed. 'He can't go until he has been baptized!'

The parson, who unfortunately preferred hunting to the care of his flock, looked curiously at the wild figure who resembled a scarecrow yet spoke with a beautifully modulated voice, but he was not prepared to dawdle. 'Now, look here my good woman,' he began, and then blinked as she turned on him like a fury out of hell.

'I'm not your good woman!' she screamed, spittle gathering at the corners of her mouth. 'And I'm not letting you take my son until he is baptized!' They saw then that she had somehow concealed the knife under her shawl, and when she began brandishing this wildly, the parson gave in. A bizarre ceremony was held in the church, with Thomas's stiff little body being held over the font and Ellen and Jem promising to do their duty as godparents. Madeleine remained silent, a gentle smile touching her lips, and she even allowed the baby to be put back into his coffin, but when they reached the open grave, she tried to get in, screaming that she wanted to stay with him. Jem caught her by the wrist and she spun like a top, one clog flying off. When she continued to struggle with an upsurge of extraordinary strength, he hit her lightly on the jaw, intending only to stun her. Instead, he knocked her out and she fell flat on her back, stick-like arms outflung, bonnet tilted forward over her eyes at a ludicrous angle. They all gazed at her in appalled silence until Mam said quaveringly, 'Hast thee killed her, Jem?'

But it was Mr Shuttleworth who knelt down and put his ear to Madeleine's heart. 'It's all right,' he said, rising nimbly and determined to put an end to all this drama;

after all, everyone knew that the labouring poor bred like rabbits, and he had no doubt she would be back in ten or eleven months wanting to be churched after the next child. 'She will be round in a minute,' he said, 'so get her on to that donkey, face downward, and let the family start for home. The woman is mad and dangerous, but with any luck she'll be too dazed to realize what is happening until after the child is buried.'

Madeleine did indeed appear mad, but at least she remained quiet and docile. When they reached the cottage she went silently to her portion of straw and lay down upon it, still wearing her bonnet and shawl, drawing up her knees almost to her chin, and with a finger childishly in her mouth. When Ellen tentatively approached and said, 'Won' you take orf your bonnet, lovey?' Madeleine did not even look at her, but continued to stare blankly at the wall. Ellen, seeing the bruise forming on her chin, then brought a little bowl of wormwood vinegar. 'Let me put this on tha' bruise,' she begged. 'Mam says it'll help straight away.' But without a word Madeleine raised one knee and sent bowl and contents flying. 'Oh, Madleen,' whispered Ellen brokenly, and retreated.

They did not know what to do. Centuries of hardship had bred in them a stoical acceptance of death and any other catastrophe which a harsh fate might hand out to them, but this raw, primitive grief was beyond their comprehension. 'Her mus' eat,' Mam declared, but what could they tempt her with?

'Didn' she always like your rabbit stoo an' wimmers, Mam?' asked Ellen, who felt Madeleine's plight most acutely of all.

Mam's face cleared. 'Course! The loverly smell o' thyme an' parsley mixed with celery leaves an' onion cookin' with rabbit stoo an' wimmers would surely lure Madleen ter the table.

But they could only get a rabbit if Jem went out . . .

229

The good young man, exhausted but ever willing, set off into the night to poach.

But by morning the situation was far worse. Jem had not returned; and sometime during the night Madeleine had retreated into the farthest corner of the room, where she crouched, face to the wall, entirely covered by her shawl. When Ellen timidly raised a corner of this, a huge grey eye, its pupil enormously dilated, stared back at her fiercely and Ellen withdrew, horrified and frightened.

'Jem's bin took, Ah knows he has!' Ada shouted, her voice on the verge of hysteria. If Jem, their principal breadwinner, had indeed been arrested, the grim spectre of the workhouse became much nearer to them all and this, together with Madeleine's frightening behaviour, brought the three women near the end of their tether.

'I'll go ter the gaol an' see if I can find out anythin',' Ellen said. She turned to Mam anxiously. 'I hates ter leave you alone with' – jutting her chin to indicate the dark shapeless bundle in the corner – 'bu' we mus' know about Jem, musn' we?'

The old woman managed to smile through her exhaustion and fear. 'Doan' fret, naow, Ellen. Ah be a'roight.'

But she did break down into silent weeping when Ellen returned and told her that Jem was in the Cumberland Road gaol, as he had been caught with a chicken and a rabbit. Ellen looked wearily at Madeleine, who appeared not to have moved at all. 'Wha' about her?'

'Her hasn' moved all day, even ter go ter privy. Ah made some valerian tea, but her hasn' drunk it.'

'Oh, Mam, was ever are we goin' ter do?' exclaimed Ellen in great distress.

It was Ada who provided the answer: she stumped over to Madeleine and wrenched the shawl away, shouting, 'Thee be wicked, crouping dere like an animal in thy own filth wen it be all thy fault! Jem wen' ter find a rabbit farr thee, an' Ellen got the boot cos her ask ter come an' see ter thee. Thee done no good ever since thee come yere an' us doesn' wan' thee!'

'Stop it, Ada, stop it,' begged Ellen, grabbing her half-sister by the arm and pulling her away. She turned to Madeleine, who had not moved. 'It isn't true, lovey, it isn't true tha' us doan' wan' you!' she cried, her accent broadening in her distress. 'Us all love you, true us does!'

When this brought no response, Ellen left her and went back to the table, but then they were all transfixed; the bundle in the corner was slowly moving, trying to straighten up, hands tremblingly put against the wall and then clawing their way upward. Ellen would have rushed forward, but Mam silently stopped her. When Madeleine at last forced movement into her stiff, dead limbs, all three women recoiled with gasps and cries. A death's head faced them, with bones almost bursting through ashen skin and cheeks so hollow that they appeared to have been sucked inward. But the eyes were the most pitiful: usually so luminous and gentle, often very merry in their expression, they were now dark and deeply sunk in their sockets. 'When is Jem's case going to court?' It was the merest whisper from a swollen throat and tongue.

'Why – why, tomorrer mahnin',' Ellen answered, astonished. Madeleine just managed a slight nod before shuffling from the cottage. All three women looked at each other, apprehensively wondering what to expect next from this tall black spectre. They did not have to wait long, for within minutes Madeleine was back, pail and brush in hand. She walked stiffly to the corner where she had crouched for so many hours and, after getting down on her knees with difficulty, began to scrub the floor.

Ellen rushed forward. 'Oh, le' me do tha', lovey. I'm much more used ter scrubbin' than you be!'

But Madeleine continued as though she had not heard, and when she had thoroughly swabbed and dried the floor, she rose painfully, picked up the pail and again walked outside. After a few minutes Ellen followed and found her sitting at the rear of the cottage, her back against the wall, in the favourite spot where she had loved to sit with the baby. Her arms were curved and held out from her breast as though she still cradled him, and her head was bent forward with lips moving silently. Ellen crept away, hand against her mouth to keep from crying out.

But Madeleine was in fact saying goodbye to her baby. Even though she could feel his little body in her arms and his head against her breast, she knew now that she had lost him for ever and would never again sit with him in the peace of the tiny garden. So, for the last time, she cradled him and told him his was the dearest little heart in all the world and that she would love him for ever. Then she rose and began stripping off her clothes. Ellen, returning once more, was astonished to see her stark naked in the summer night, washing herself vigorously in the tin bath, while spread all around on bushes were her newly washed clothes.

She came into the cottage only once more that night, walking unconcernedly in her nakedness, to collect shift and nightgown. The women had consulted together and decided that if they behaved quite normally, Madeleine might just respond. So at sight of her, Mam said, 'Supper be ready,' and began bustling about, but Madeleine walked straight out and eventually, broken-hearted and exhausted, they lay down to sleep.

In the early dawn they awoke to the sound of clogs on the mud floor. Madeleine was dressed in the still damp clothes of the previous night. Her hair, falling in untidy strands over her face, was put up in a large off-centre knot at her nape, with the ends, instead of being tucked in, sticking out spikily. As she put on her bonnet, Ellen asked urgently, 'Where be you goin', Madleen?'

'Must go to court to speak for Jem.'

The fact that she had at last spoken – and to utter such words – left the three women speechless themselves. Never in their wildest dreams would they have contemplated going into a court, an official place, where magistrates, lawyers and police reigned supreme. And who would ever dare to speak in such a place? Ellen was the first to recover, and scrambled off the straw, reaching for her dress and thinking only that she could not let Madeleine go alone to such a frightening place. 'I wan' ter come too – wait farr me, Madleen, wait farr me!' But Madeleine was already out in the lane and walking away.

Ellen was old and, although used to running up and down endless stairs, she soon became breathless if unable to pause frequently. So now the best she could do was to keep Madeleine in sight, since repeated calls to her had been ignored. But how could Madeleine keep up such a pace? Ellen wondered. She had not eaten for thirty-six hours and looked at death's door, yet now she continued to lope along, head bent, and seemingly oblivious of everything around her.

The truth was that Madeleine was using the very last of her physical and mental strength in an effort to help Jem. Ada's cruel words had roused her from the deepest depths of grief, and she knew she owed it to the family to make this one last gigantic effort. Jem, inarticulate and awkward as he always was, would never be able to defend himself, but she could at least tell them why he had taken the rabbit, and plead for him.

She remembered seeing the magistrate's court during the weeks when she had been rushing about the city for Dora Sharpe; she went there unerringly now, all her resources concentrated totally on the need to reach the building before it was too late. Ellen, struggling along behind, cried out several times as Madeleine was almost run over; she seemed to be walking blindly across all the roads, not even noticing the great mass of traffic or the

233

flailing hooves of horses as they were pulled up on their haunches to avoid her. She did see and hear, but her brain was too exhausted to absorb more. Nevertheless, she did reach the courthouse and entered without pause.

Ellen, feeling that she was about to enter the lions' den, followed, searching anxiously among the crowd for the battered black bonnet. At last she saw it and began to push her way towards it. She then noticed with astonishment that Madeleine had obviously asked an official a question, for the man referred to a sheaf of papers in his hand and then spoke briefly to her. At that moment Ellen heard her half-brother's name bellowed out: 'Jeremiah Shoesmith!' And there was Jem, handcuffed and walking between two policemen; they looked full of self-importance, while he had the closed, wooden expression of the peasant who knows he is in deep trouble and yet cannot quite believe it is happening to him. They disappeared into a side room, Madeleine following calmly and Ellen, frightened but determined, creeping alongside.

The room seemed enormous to Ellen and she had no idea there would be so many people everywhere. Three stern-faced gentlemen sat in an elevated position facing them, while Jem, flanked by the two policemen, was in a sort of little pen on the side. There were men in dark clothes sitting at a table directly below the stern-faced gentlemen, while at the back, in a much larger pen, there were lots of other people who appeared to be there just for the show because they were laughing and talking unconcernedly. Then there was a thump and a roar of 'Silence in court!' which brought instant quiet.

All Ellen's deep distrust of the law which was always so harsh on her class now surfaced and caused her heart to beat so loudly in her ears that she could hardly hear what was being said. She saw a policeman go into another little pen and hold up a book. 'I swear by Almighty God . . .' Fancy swearing in yere, thought Ellen, an' nobody mindin' neither! He was now saying something about having apprehended (wha' ever did tha' mean?) Jem in Mad Beth's Wood on the night of the twentieth when he was in the act of poaching a rabbit. At that time he also had a dead chicken in his hand.

The sternest of the stern-faced gentlemen turned his granite-like eyes to Jem. 'Jeremiah Shoesmith, how do you plead, guilty or not guilty?'

Wha' a funny thing ter ask, thought Ellen, when they'd caught him stealin' . . .'course they knowed he were guilty . . . Which was very similar to what Jem was thinking. He looked down and shuffled his feet in bewilderment.

'Well, man, speak up!' snapped the questioner, and Jem automatically touched his forelock and muttered, 'If you please, sir, Ah be guilty, sir.'

There was a brief whispered discussion with his two colleagues on either side, then the granite-eyed gentleman said loudly, 'Jeremiah Shoesmith, you have freely admitted your guilt, and the sentence of this court is that you be transported to Western Australia for a period of five years. That is all!'

'No!' The desperate voice rang round the room, electrifying officials and spectators alike. Madeleine had leapt to her feet and now advanced fearlessly to the well of the court, brushing past all who tried to stop her, until she was looking up into the cold eyes of Mr Llewellyn Morgan.

'Let her be,' he said, as hands tried to pull her away, and to Madeleine, 'What is it you wish to say?'

'I beg you, sir, not to send this man to Australia, for he stole the rabbit for me – because I was ill and there was no other food. He supports his elderly mother and two sisters. One is very crippled and the other past middle age and has recently been dismissed from her position as chambermaid, also because of me.'

Mr Llewellyn Morgan had seen her when she entered the courtroom and something about her seemed vaguely familiar. As soon as she spoke he remembered her as the young woman in the field whom Catherine had wanted to help. Realizing now that her appearance, so much at variance with her cultured voice, was causing a titter among the public, he spoke briefly to his fellow magistrates before facing Madeleine once more. 'Are you this man's wife?'

'No, sir!'

'Or his common-law wife?'

'Indeed not, sir!'

'Are you contesting the evidence given in this court?'

'No, but I – '

'Do you have any fresh evidence to submit?'

'Only in the circumstances which made him commit this theft.'

Mr Llewellyn Morgan banged with his gavel. 'This court will adjourn for twenty minutes. Bring the young woman to my room' – this last to the clerk of the court, who beckoned Madeleine.

As soon as she saw Madeleine being taken out by a side door, Ellen made to follow, but found her way barred. 'I be with her,' she said, but they turned her back, and she saw that Jem, too, had been taken out.

Madeleine stumbled after the magistrate into a high-ceilinged panelled room, where a manservant was just setting down a tray with a delicate porcelain cup and a silver teapot. She stared at this as though mesmerized: the delicious aroma of China tea! It brought back memories of learning to pour tea for her father, and of sitting with Catherine and Harriet on that fateful afternoon so long ago.

'You may sit.' The cold impersonal voice brought her back sharply to the present and she clenched her hands in an effort to concentrate.

'I perceive that you have no new evidence to offer,' Mr Llewellyn Morgan was saying, 'but I am prepared to hear

236

what you have to say, and have brought you here to save you the embarrassment of the whole court hearing your story.' He began to pour the tea. 'What is your interest in the man Shoesmith? Hurry, girl, I do not have all day, you know.'

So she told him how Mam and Ada and Jem had sheltered her, even though they were so desperately poor, and how hard Jem worked. If the baby had been strong, she would have continued to work herself, but instead the baby had died and Jem had gone to get a rabbit because they thought it would encourage her to eat. If he were sent away, they would be reduced to starvation level, for not only did Jem earn the most money, but it was he who was sometimes given half a sack of potatoes or a piece of salt bacon by the farmer. And it was he who rethatched the cottage after the very heavy snow the previous winter had caused some of the thatch to cave in. And then there was Ada . . . in the depths of winter when she could not make her own way to the bone works, Jem had carried her night and morning. And so, Madeleine begged, implored, that he should be given another chance. If he could be set free, she would promise most faithfully on Jem's behalf that he would never poach again.

The cold voice cut across her plea: 'Is he the father of your child?'

'No, no, of course not!'

'But how is it, that you, an educated young woman, should be living like a peasant?'

'Because I was with child, sir, and no one would employ me. As I said, the family took me in and cared for me and my baby. I owe them a great debt.'

Mr Llewellyn Morgan poured himself a second cup of tea. 'Your face is somewhat familiar. Have you been up before me on a charge?'

'Oh no, most definitely not, sir!' He knew she was

speaking the truth, for now he remembered meeting her at the ball and hearing something of her background.

Madeleine misinterpreted his silence and said passionately, 'It is the truth, sir, only the truth, I swear it. Please, what can I say to make you believe me?'

He set down the cup. 'It would not make the slightest difference, you know,' he said with a sour smile. 'I am here to uphold the law, and Shoesmith has admitted breaking it. The sentence stands!' He wondered briefly if she would now use their meeting at the ball as a last resort, but instead she went down on her knees before him, clasping her hands.

'Then please, please don't send him to Australia. It will kill his mother. Let him be imprisoned here where she can see him. Please, please, of your charity, sir.'

'Get up, girl, you are making a fool of yourself!' Mr Llewellyn Morgan snapped, and when she had slowly dragged herself to her feet, he said, 'Now listen to me. If Shoesmith goes to prison here, he will come out with nothing; if he goes to Western Australia, there is a chance that with good behaviour he will get a remission of sentence and have the chance of remaining there. The country is opening up rapidly; gold has been found and colonies are springing up everywhere. You may or may not know that convicts are now only accepted in Western Australia, so by sending him there I am giving him a chance: in this country, Shoesmith will die as he has lived – a labourer, constantly on the verge of starvation – but in Australia as a young, strong man, he could better himself considerably. Now, that is my final word, and you will oblige me by leaving quietly. If you wish to wait outside in the road, he and those others convicted this morning will be leaving in an hour's time to return to Cumberland Road. Good morning to you.'

Ellen, who was convinced that Madeleine had been taken to some dungeon to be tortured, rushed forward when she saw her clinging to the wall. 'Oh, wha' have they done ter you?' she gasped, her arm going protectively around Madeleine's waist.

'He would not change his mind, Ellen, I tried . . . I really did try, but I failed.'

'Nefer moind, lovey, it were ever so brave o' you ter try,' said Ellen, who had still not grasped what the sentence meant and was more worried about how she was going to get Madeleine home, for it was obvious that she was on the verge of total collapse.

'We must wait to see Jem leave,' Madeleine said. 'He will be passing in an hour.'

It was much longer than an hour; they saw Mr Llewellyn Morgan pass in his fine carriage; then all the spectators from the various courtrooms, closely followed by the officials, who locked the main doors of the courthouse behind them.

'Perhaps they aren' comin',' suggested Ellen, but almost at once a detachment of red-coated soldiers arrived and marched to the rear. Within seconds a crowd had gathered and an ominous murmur arose. The citizens of Bristol did not care for the military; the memory of how fiercely the riots of 1831 had been put down was surprisingly fresh still. The murmur deepened to a growl and then a roar as the prisoners appeared at last, manacled and in foot irons. As they shuffled past, the crowd surged forward, yelling, and with hands and sticks upraised to strike at the soldiers.

In the sudden mêlée, Madeleine flung herself forward until she reached Jem, and from under her shawl she thrust her Bible into his fettered hands. 'I'm so sorry, Jem,' she cried, 'so sorry . . . I tried to make him understand . . .'

He just had time to look up and, as he recognized her, the dazed look left his eyes for a moment and he nodded dumbly. Then a soldier thrust her back roughly against the wall and she slowly slid down until she lay in a crumpled heap on the pavement. To think that she had brought him to such a plight – the good, gentle young man who had always been so willing to trudge for miles, to do his own field work and hers, and whose only crime had been to try and find her something to eat – to be manacled, hand and foot, like some murderer! The cruelty of it extinguished the last tiny spark of her spirit, and Ellen, on her knees beside her, knew that Madeleine could go no further.

'You go on, Ellen, and I'll come later,' Madeleine whispered, but Ellen said fiercely, ''Course, I not be leavin' you all alone yere!' Yet Ellen herself was on the verge of hysteria: seeing Jem shuffling past in irons had made her understand what his sentence meant, and that she might never see him again. The thought of having to tell Mam made her shrink, for he had always been her favourite, and if she died of grief it would mean the final break-up of Ellen's little world. Meanwhile, here was Madeleine, totally collapsed, with passers-by either giving her a wide berth or else commenting on how drunk she was.

Unknowingly, Ellen began to moan softly as the hopelessness of their situation became more and more apparent: no one cared and no one was going to help them . . . and then, like a miracle, she suddenly saw the Reverend Mr Shuttleworth approaching on a fine bay horse. Ellen scrambled to her feet and ran forward, clutching the horse's mane.

'What the devil do you think you are doing, woman? Get away at once!' roared Mr Shuttleworth in a totally unclerical tone, but Ellen knew he was their one and only hope and she clung on even more fiercely.

'Please, sir, will you take up me friend who can't wark no more . . . you be goin' past our cottage on your way home.'

Mr Shuttleworth gave one glance at the figure slumped against the wall. He'd know that bonnet anywhere and remembered only too vividly the wild scenes at the child's burial. 'What! Take up that mad woman? Never! She should be put away before she does someone an injury!'

'No, no, sir, her isn' mad, only starvin' an exastipated.'

Mr Shuttleworth looked more closely. 'She's dead drunk!' he declared, sounding utterly shocked, and, seeing people beginning to stop and stare, urged his horse forward, beating at Ellen's hands with his crop.

Then Ellen, who had never paid much attention on all those mornings when the General had led his servants in prayer, now uttered the one phrase which Mr Shuttleworth could not ignore: 'Farr the love o' God, sir!' she screamed. And the people who minutes before had paid no heed to a collapsed woman, now began to chant, 'Farr the love o' God, Reverend! Farr the love o' God!'

Mr Shuttleworth thought briefly that he should beat the woman about the head and face to make her loose her hold, but he knew that in a second the mob could dash forward and pull him from the saddle. 'Get the creature up here,' he said curtly, and Ellen, still holding tightly to the horse's mane, turned and said to the crowd, 'Please canst someone bring her over . . .' A cheer went up, and now there was no lack of helpers. The first man who reached Madeleine scooped her up easily and came running to set her on the horse behind Mr Shuttleworth.

'I suppose she is flea-ridden,' commented that gentleman with a shudder.

'Tha' her isn',' retorted Ellen indignantly, and then to Madeleine, 'Hold on tight naow, lovey, do try an' hold on.'

Madeleine's head was drooping alarmingly, and the man who had lifted her gathered up a fistful of Mr Shuttleworth's coat tail and clamped her hands around it. 'Do yer hold on like this, missis,' he said, and somehow

Madeleine did hold on, even though Mr Shuttleworth, once free of the city's congestion, urged his horse to a smart trot, and when her head fell against his shoulder he gave her such a vicious dig in the ribs with his elbow that she almost fell. *I should have said I was not going home*, he said to himself, but then added sanctimoniously, *but of course I could not tell a lie.*

As they approached the cottage, he was astonished to see a fine open carriage drawn up outside, its horses sleek, its footmen and driver splendidly liveried. They turned to look at Mr Shuttleworth with what he deemed curiosity, no doubt because of the scarecrow creature perched up behind him. 'Get down!' he commanded in a tone he would have used to a particularly bad dog, but then as Madeleine hesitated, only half comprehending, he twisted in the saddle, put his hand between her shoulder blades and gave her a violent shove forward. Madeleine screamed as she suddenly found herself flying through the air, and it was unfortunate for Mr Shuttleworth that Catherine Llewellyn Morgan should appear at that moment. She ran forward to where Madeleine had fallen against the hedge.

'Oh, how cruel!' she exclaimed furiously, 'how callously cruel! You are a disgrace to your cloth, sir, and I promise that his Lordship shall hear of this!'

But when Mr Shuttleworth swept off his hat and would have attempted an explanation, Catherine ignored him. 'Get Miss Brett into the carriage and lay her along the seat,' she instructed her footman, and, as Mam came to the door, Catherine said, 'I must leave now and get her to bed. I fear she is in a very poor way.'

Mam nodded, the tears bright in her old eyes, and she watched silently as Catherine gently wrapped a rug around Madeleine's inert form. Catherine seated herself opposite and leaned forward, smiling. 'I shall send the pony and trap on Sunday morning to bring you and your daughters to see the cottage,' she said. 'But don't worry, I shall make sure that you are looked after, whatever your decision.'

Mam tried her best to curtsey then, but her legs were too stiff. 'Thank you, m'lady,' she whispered tremulously as the carriage moved forward.

14

So once more Madeleine drove over the moat and up to
the great oak doors of Summerleigh, but she was only
conscious that the smooth motion of the carriage had
stopped and that strong arms were lifting her. From a
great distance she heard a voice say, 'Be very gentle now
– yes, that's right – take her straight up to the blue
bedroom. Jenkins, send Jenny to me at once and then
despatch Martin to Dr Kingsley with a request that he
should attend here at his earliest convenience. I shall be
in the blue room.'

Catherine was already beginning to undress the inert
form on the bed when her maid appeared, slightly breathless. 'Lor', Miss Catherine, has somethin' terrible happened?' she asked, her long and intimate service with
Catherine allowing her to speak freely.

'I fear something very tragic might happen if we don't
hurry,' Catherine answered quietly. 'Now, run and get
one of my nightgowns and a bed shawl and, Jenny, do be
quick!'

The maid was back within minutes. 'Help me to get
these few rags off her,' Catherine ordered. 'The poor soul
is so weak and exhausted she is like a rag doll – oh, dear
Lord!' The last of the tattered underwear was off, revealing total emaciation. For a few seconds Catherine and
Jenny gazed unbelieving at the drained breasts, the flesh-
less ribcage and jutting pelvic bones, the shrunken, concave abdomen.

'Lor', miss, she isn' long for this world, is she?'

'Hush, Jenny,' commanded Catherine. 'Help me get
this nightgown on her – oh, but her arms are just sticks! –

be very gentle – yes, that's right – now the shawl – there, if you lift her legs, I will take her shoulders and I think between us we shall be able to get her into bed – oh, that's good. Now, go down and ask cook to whisk up an egg in milk and a little brandy and then bring it here, and do tell cook to hurry.'

Jenny flew, delighted to have this opportunity of imparting the dramatic and unique news that a living skeleton was in the best guest room.

Catherine bent over Madeleine's still form and gently smoothed the hair from her face. Poor little thing, she thought compassionately, poor, poor girl. How cruelly the world had used her, and yet through it all, she had struggled on and on, until literally the last drop of her strength. Mam's account, stumbling and inarticulate, had nevertheless given Catherine sufficient information to convince her that Madeleine deserved and was desperately in need of all the help money could buy. Catherine gathered up the ragged clothing, all of it darned and patched, the material so thin that it split with the smallest pressure, but everything so clean, and the poor body too. That really had surprised Catherine, who had steeled herself to face all the evidence of dire poverty. Instead, there had been only a faint aroma of herbs and of washing dried in the open air.

When Jenny returned with a tall glass of milk on a silver tray, Catherine lifted Madeleine with the utmost gentleness and put the glass to her lips. She drank thirstily, the rich smooth liquid sliding over her parched throat, but she knew it should be going to Thomas and her hands made tiny futile movements of protest. As she was lowered again she thought how soft the straw was today and how sweet the old horse blanket smelled. She longed to be able to put her hand out and feel for Thomas, but she just could not make the effort, and instead was sinking down and down . . .

Suddenly she was a little girl again and living in the Hertford Street house. Her pony, Buttercup, was there, and darling Dash, the spaniel named after the Queen's own little dog. And in her arms was a baby – or was it one of those new china dolls from France? How pretty it was! She rocked it, singing a lullaby . . . Now she was not so small, but just sixteen, and papa said that as a special treat they were going to the opera; he had chosen *Les Huguenots* because of her mother's ancestors. Of course, she was still too young to put her hair up, but she had a new dress and slippers for the occasion, and just before leaving home papa had put a string of pearls around her throat. How they had glowed against her skin – 'like little lamps,' she said excitedly. But suddenly the pretty clothes and the pearls had all gone and they were not going into the opera house after all, but trudging past, she carrying papa's heavy bag and he leaning painfully on his stick . . . Then down the steps came Sebastian in that wonderful uniform, holding out his arms to her and saying, 'Dance with me.' And oh, how joyously she ran to him and how they danced, round and round, their steps matching perfectly, and yes, that *was* a real baby in her arms, for she saw now that he had the most wonderful dark eyes and the chubbiest little arms and legs. And he was so full of life that she had to hold on tightly to him lest he bounced out of her arms. He was strong because she had such rich, good milk to give him . . .. Now he was feeding, she could feel the pull of his little mouth – oh, how sweet, he was gurgling with laughter and the milk was running down his chin. Never mind, my precious, I have plenty more . . . Oh, he wasn't a baby any more, he was a toddler playing in a field of buttercups and running in little circles, squealing with happy laughter, but whatever was he playing with? Why–why, it was a lot of baby rabbits and Thomas was chasing after their white tails. Now he had come to fling himself against her, his strong little arms

246

around her legs; he was looking up at her, eyes dancing and cheeks rosy – so strong, so fit. As she ran her fingers through his tumbled black curls, Sebastian came to stand beside her. She felt his arm around her waist, heard him whisper, 'It is you I love.' And she was happy, happy, for that was all the lonely little girl in Hertford Street had ever wanted: to love and be loved . . .

Catherine, watching the joy and the silent movements of her smiling lips, thought, at least if she dies now, she will be happy. For it was obvious that in her dreams Madeleine was living as perhaps she had seldom done in reality: with laughter and radiance.

When Jenny announced the doctor, the happiness was already fading and instead she was gazing at a stream of milk and green mucus, and knew that her baby was dying . . . Her eyes opened abruptly as she heard a voice say, 'Madeleine dear, here is Dr Kingsley, who has come to see you.'

She struggled to sit up, her face suddenly joyous again. 'Oh, a doctor! Thank God, thank God! Please will you help my baby? He is so sick; I have no milk and green slimy liquid is pouring from his mouth. You will save him won't you, for he is all I have . . . he's here, you can see him now . . .' The staccato words tumbled out nonstop, but as she turned, hands reaching for the baby and saw that he was not there, all the radiance faded for a second time and her voice was just a thread as she whispered, 'Of course, Thomas is dead . . . I killed him.'

As Catherine tiptoed from the room, she saw the doctor draw up a chair and heard him say quietly, 'Why not tell me all about it, my dear.'

Catherine was seated at her piano, playing softly, when the doctor eventually reappeared. She rose at once and came forward. 'Please come and sit down,' she said, 'and tell me if there is any hope.'

John Kingsley was young, forward-looking and keen, a forerunner of the new breed of physicians and surgeons soon to be leaving the great training centres of London, Edinburgh and Dublin. So now he answered cheerfully, 'Oh, there is always hope, Miss Llewellyn Morgan!'

'But?' invited Catherine.

'Well, she is quite severely emaciated, but surprisingly her lungs are strong. I admit to being surprised at this, very surprised. I would have expected them to be most adversely affected; her heart is – nervous, but I am hoping this is mainly, if not entirely, due to the enormous burden of grief and strain she has been under. I am hopeful that with rest and good food, she will soon begin to pick up.'

'Why, that is wonderful!' exclaimed Catherine, smiling with relief. 'I did not dare to hope for such an optimistic report.'

Dr Kingsley fiddled very briefly with the fob on his watch chain. 'Unfortunately there remains the question of her mental state,' he said quietly.

'Oh,' said Catherine, her smile fading.

'I am worried about this,' admitted the doctor, 'and I have to tell you that I fear she has less than a fifty-fifty chance. . . . Unless we are very lucky, I believe she may deteriorate into a permanent decline.'

'Oh no,' breathed Catherine. 'Is there nothing we can do? You will understand that if money can help . . . .'

'H'm. I think locating the father of her child *could* be of great value. I am sorry to ask this, Miss Llewellyn Morgan, but have you any idea who the father is?'

Catherine shook her head. 'None whatsoever,' she said with perfect truth.

'It is obvious that Miss Brett loves him greatly, and I suspect that while she had the baby she felt that she had not entirely lost the father. Now, of course, she is mourning them both and, coming after all the other hardships she has had to overcome, this is quite literally beyond her capacity to bear. She is submerged in grief, and all I have been able to do today is to try and convince her that she really was not to blame for the child's death. It was fully two months premature, and I understand extremely thin: one of the peasant family likened it to a spring chicken, and in such cases there are always great heart and respiratory difficulties. The fact that she could not continue feeding it hastened its demise, but I suspect only by a matter of hours. Perhaps it was unfortunate that the child lived at all.' Then, seeing Catherine's horrified expression, the doctor became suddenly brisk. 'Well, I will be on my way now, but I shall, of course, return tomorrow. Meanwhile, I suggest a light diet, and in frequent small quantities rather than larger meals served at conventional times.'

After he had gone, Catherine sat for a long time, thinking deeply. When at last she rose, she squared her shoulders, murmuring, 'And now for papa,' and made her way resolutely towards her father's study.

For a week Madeleine was a total invalid, waking only to eat and drink obediently before sinking back into sleep.

'We must now get her out of that bed before it becomes impossible,' Dr Kingsley said, and between them they got Madeleine on to the brocaded chaise longue, where they propped her up, covering her warmly. 'I suggest we place the chaise in the window embrasure so that she may look out over the gardens.'

But when Madeleine's eyes opened long enough to focus, the first thing she saw was the de Lacey quartering set in the old latticed pane. She frowned, trying to remember, and when the memories flooded back, so did the bitter grief.

Catherine found her doubled over, arms wrapped around her stomach, whimpering piteously. 'My dear, what is it?' she asked, coming to sit beside her and putting her hand on the trembling shoulder.

'My baby,' whispered Madeleine. 'I want my baby – he is all I have. I can't lose him, I can't . . . I can't.'

Catherine could only enfold her then in her arms and hold her tightly until the paroxysm ended.

When at last she could cry no more, Madeleine drew back from Catherine, murmuring, 'I am so sorry . . . you have been so wonderfully kind – I . . . .'

'Madeleine dear, I understand,' said Catherine gently. 'And believe me, if it were humanly possible to give you back your baby, I would do so. But I think you already know in your heart that it is too late, don't you?'

There was silence then, broken only by Madeleine's unsteady breathing and the ticking of a small enamelled clock on the mantelpiece. Outside in the gardens a peacock uttered its strange cry and, with a last convulsive shudder, Madeleine whispered, 'Yes, I know. It is just that I – I find it so impossible to accept.'

Then Catherine, remembering Dr Kingsley's words, said boldly, 'Forgive me, Madeleine, but could your baby's father not share this terrible grief with you?'

Madeleine's head was shaken emphatically. 'No, oh no, he despises me . . . thinks me a trollop.'

Catherine, her curiosity now thoroughly aroused, tried once more. 'Are you sure, Madeleine? I had thought that as you loved your baby so much, you must also love its father.'

'I do. I always have, and probably always will . . . but there is nothing to be done.'

At a loss then as to how she should proceed, Catherine decided to let the matter rest for the time being, not knowing that Madeleine would give her no further opportunity, that she dared not do so lest she inadvertently gave some clue to Sebastian's identity. It would be such a terrible thing, Madeleine thought, if Catherine were ever to know that her future husband had fathered the child. The knowledge that she herself was living in the house where Catherine would bear Sebastian's legitimate children, and where generations of past de Laceys had been born and bred, was very bitter, and from that day her resolve began to strengthen: she must recover as soon as possible. Not because she wanted to be well; not because she wanted to begin the battle of life again; but so that she could escape from the house, from Catherine, from the fear that one day Sebastian might appear and find her. So she dutifully ate all the delicious food and drank all the rich milk, but never once did she let Catherine see what an agony this was for her and never again did she break down or mention the baby.

Dr Kingsley was delighted. 'I must say, I had no idea her progress would be so rapid,' he confided to Catherine. 'I knew at once that I had some rapport with her because of having attended some of her father's lectures in my first year at Guy's. I was able to talk about him and tell her how very greatly I had admired him. Perhaps that helped – and, of course, all that you have done, Miss Llewellyn Morgan.'

Catherine brushed this aside. 'What worries me,' she said, frowning in concentration, 'is her future. A post as governess is the obvious, but I feel – I am so afraid – that looking after other people's children will bring back her own loss.'

'I do agree,' the doctor nodded. 'And this has been much in my thoughts too. She has a very tender heart and a great deal of love to give, so I feel we need a great cause – something that will engage all that tenderness, all that love, to lift her finally out of her grief and perhaps give her back some *joie de vivre*.'

'But what?' exclaimed Catherine. 'I am sure you are quite right, but what *is* such a cause and where can we find it?'

251

The answer came from out of the blue when an acquaintance, Miss Florence Nightingale, wrote saying that she was hoping to take a party of nurses to the Crimea and did Miss Llewellyn Morgan know of any sisterhood or organization from which suitable personnel could be obtained? Miss Nightingale was writing to her as she remembered her great interest in Miss Sellon's Anglican Order in Devonport, and the tremendous material aid Miss Llewellyn Morgan had given the previous year when the Sellonites had nursed the poor in the Plymouth and Devonport cholera epidemic; they had already agreed to service in the Crimea, but more were needed.

Catherine was so excited that she could not wait for Dr Kingsley, but drove to his house, letter in hand. He was equally enthusiastic. 'Just what we have been waiting for!' he exclaimed.

'Of course, Madeleine is not a nurse,' Catherine pointed out. But he shrugged and said that he very much doubted whether Miss Nightingale would find many nurses with more knowledge than he could impart to Madeleine in a month's intensive course; the general standard was extremely low, and the majority of nurses, even in the famous hospitals, were drunken and promiscuous (begging Miss Llewellyn Morgan's pardon).

Catherine and the doctor went together to Madeleine and, to their delight, she appeared to welcome the idea; she was now up and about and had put on enough weight to make her look delicate rather than emaciated. Secretly she did not think she had any chance of being chosen by Miss Nightingale, but Dr Kingsley's training course would get her out of the house and perhaps convince him and Catherine that she was ready to make her own way once more. So every day, after he had finished his rounds, Dr Kingsley would collect Madeleine and take her to Bristol Infirmary.

In the men's wards he showed her how to swab and

dress wounds, to bandage, sponge, take temperature and pulse, and to measure out medicines. He spared her nothing, allowing her to take off filthy rags and find enormous leg ulcers crawling with white maggots; to unwrap bound hands and feet, only to have fingers and toes drop off. She blanched at such times, often turning away to retch, but within seconds would press her lips firmly together and turn back to the patient. To one and all she was kind and gentle, even to the filthiest, smelliest of the poor, undressing and sponging their reeking, crawling bodies with care and patience.

What a woman! thought Dr Kingsley. Truly she is her father's daughter and a born nurse. He reported everything to Catherine, who had to tell him that a great obstacle had arisen: Miss Nightingale refused to take a girl of not yet twenty and wanted only middle-aged women. Catherine, however, was used to getting her own way and had no intention of giving up so easily. Letters flew back and forth between herself and Miss Nightingale, with Catherine emphasizing Madeleine's unique experience and upbringing: her ability to understand and communicate with the very poor and yet be able to take her place at the most decorous dinner party, and her ability to speak fluent French – surely a great advantage when she might also be nursing French wounded. To all this Miss Nightingale replied that to have so young a girl would be too great a responsibility. By return Catherine wrote at length, outlining the difficulties Madeleine had already overcome and enclosing a report by Dr Kingsley. In this he stated that, in his opinion, Miss Brett was worth two or more of the ignorant, foul-mouthed middle-aged nurses he had known. He also considered Miss Brett to be very much more mature than most girls of twenty. Eventually, Miss Nightingale, with a thousand things on her mind, made a small concession: a selection board would be sitting at 49 Belgrave Square on Wednesday, 18

October, and if insufficient numbers of suitable women appeared, *some* consideration might be given to Miss Brett's application. She should therefore attend on the afternoon of that day and, if accepted, must be prepared to sail with the rest of the party on Saturday, 21 October.

Catherine was ecstatic, Dr Kingsley jubilant and Madeleine dazed.

'Let's see, we have ten days left,' said the doctor. 'From all that I read and hear of the Crimea, there are a great number of amputations, so I think we should concentrate on stump dressings, the making of stump pads, and also on fever nursing, for cholera continues to rage, both at Balaclava and at Scutari. Tell me, Madeleine, how do you feel about going into the fever wards and nursing such cases?'

Madeleine, whose life meant nothing, shrugged and said, 'That would not worry me at all.'

But Dr Kingsley was not fooled and later said to Catherine, 'We must succeed, you know, for if we do not, I feel melancholy will overwhelm her and I would not give much for her chances of survival.'

Catherine, too, was anxious that Miss Nightingale should accept Madeleine, for she was having increasing difficulty with her father. Mr Llewellyn Morgan had been furious when told that Madeleine was under his roof, and his initial reaction was to order her removal. It was only when Catherine said quietly, 'If Madeleine goes, I go too, papa,' that he had given way, but he had remained bitterly hurt.

'I just do not understand your defence of this young woman who was never even a close friend – I believe you only met her twice before,' he said, only just managing to control his anger.

'Yet it is really not so difficult to understand, papa,' Catherine replied with the quiet firmness which in the years ahead would make her a great social reformer.

'Madeleine is a young woman, entirely alone in the world, ill and in deep distress. When you returned from court that day and told me of the Shoesmith case and her defence of the young man, it seemed obvious to me that I should see what I could do to help. After hearing from the old woman all that Madeleine had endured, I knew that I could not leave her to die of heartbreak and starvation.'

Mr Llewellyn Morgan grudgingly admired his daughter for her courage and strength, and he had no doubt that she would leave if he pressed her too hard, for she was twenty-two years old and a wealthy young woman. But aloud he said severely, 'Brett had proved herself to be a woman of unbridled passion.'

Catherine flushed deeply. The discussion of 'fallen women' and 'passion' was taboo, yet she knew she must continue to defend Madeleine. 'We do not know the circumstances, papa,' she said, trying hard to keep her composure. 'For all we know, she may have been cruelly deceived and wronged. You must remember that when you met her at the ball, you considered her most charming.'

'H'm. Clearly I was mistaken, and I want you to get her out of this house as soon as possible.' He made a last appeal: 'After all, Catherine, you must see that having her here places me in an intolerable situation.'

Catherine did see, but not by the tiniest hint did she ever let Madeleine know; she just prayed fervently that, for everyone's sake, Miss Nightingale would accept Madeleine.

Madeleine felt tearful and apprehensive on the journey to London as she remembered all that had happened since she had left the capital and, after the quiet of the country, she found the noise and traffic terrifying. Yet she arrived safely at 49 Belgrave Square and instantly some of her courage returned, for the other applicants seated in the hall appeared no better equipped for acceptance than herself: stout, middle-aged and mostly poverty-stricken, more than one reeked of gin, and from their conversation it was obvious that money rather than care of the wounded had induced them to apply. Only one admitted to having worked in a hospital, and that just for a few days, at St George's. Nevertheless, all the women were accepted and emerged beaming. Madeleine had been left until the very end, and by then desperation forced her to smooth her dress and walk calmly forward when at last her name was called.

Five ladies sat around a table at the far end of a beautiful room, with a chair for the applicant placed in front of them. From the first it was the lady in the centre who dominated the proceedings. 'Good afternoon, Miss Brett,' she said in a pretty, gentle voice. 'Please come and sit down.'

'Thank you, ma'am,' Madeleine said quietly and walked slowly forward, aware that all were scrutinizing every part of her. Catherine had insisted on kitting her out for the occasion, so she knew that her boots and gloves were of the softest leather, that her grey woollen dress, although plain, was beautifully cut and fitted perfectly, that the paisley shawl and grey velvet bonnet lined with ruched white silk were just sufficiently colourful. She sat down gracefully, not fussing with her skirts but folding her hands loosely in her lap, and then looked up into the eyes of Florence Nightingale.

Miss Nightingale, at thirty-four, retained much of the beauty of her earlier years, and with her tall slender figure, delicate colouring and slightly hesitant manner, gave the impression of delicacy and charm; it was only on closer acquaintance that the steel, the total dedication and sense of mission, showed through. She had not been present at the other interviews, but considered she should conduct this very special one herself. As Madeleine looked up, Miss Nightingale saw the tragedy in the shadowed depths of her eyes and felt a sudden sympathy for the younger woman, for she knew all about heartache, frustration and mental breakdown, and so now she smiled, showing perfect teeth. 'Perhaps you will tell us, Miss Brett, why you wish to go to the Crimea.'

Madeleine answered without hesitation, 'Because, ma'am, I understand there is a very great need for nurses. As I am without any ties, and now have knowledge of basic nursing, I feel I may be able to help, even if this means only contributing another pair of hands and feet.'

The tiniest sigh arose from the ladies, but Miss Nightingale showed no emotion as she asked, 'And how do you think you would react to the nursing of sick soldiers, who, we are told, use very objectionable language and are constantly drunk.'

'This would not bother me, ma'am, for I used to accompany my father when he had a surgery at St Giles. There was a very great deal of swearing and drunkenness among his patients, but he taught me to look beyond this and try to see the essential person behind the coarseness. Often, so very often, I found that it was the terrible harshness and tragedy of their lives which had made such people what they were . . . yet they remained so grateful for the smallest kindness.' Madeleine spoke from the heart, forgetting the titled ladies and the elegant room, and seeing instead the reeking alleys crammed with hopeless, hurting humanity whose only escape from their horrific lives was gin – and with gin came mouths that felt like sawdust, and splitting heads, and the return of reality. They gave vent to their frustration in the only way they knew how: by cursing everything and everybody, nonstop.

'Ah, yes, your father.' Miss Nightingale's voice brought Madeleine back to the present. 'I have heard of him; he must have been a most remarkable man.'

'Thank you, ma'am. I always thought him to be so.'

'Now' – Miss Nightingale's tone became just a little more brisk – 'will you please move to the side table, where you will find bandages and the plaster limb which has been severed at the patella. We should like you to show us how you would dress the stump.'

'Very well, ma'am.' Madeleine crossed the room, peeling off her gloves as she went. Then she quietly removed her shawl, turned back her cuffs and set to work.

There was complete silence as the committee watched, Miss Nightingale particularly noticing the speed and deftness of Madeleine's hands. She appeared totally absorbed, her face remote in its concentration, and Miss Nightingale deliberately broke the silence by saying in French, 'The remainder of the interview will be conducted in French, if you please.'

If she had thought to disconcert Madeleine, she was disappointed, for with a quiet, 'Comme vous voulez, mademoiselle,' Madeleine continued working. When she had finished she brought the limb to Miss Nightingale, who examined it briefly but with great expertise and then put it on the table. 'Excellent, quite excellent,' she said. 'And now will you please tell us what are the symptoms of cholera.'

'Sudden prostration – often with no other symptoms of illness or pain at first – but the patient quickly becomes powerless to move; there is extreme coldness, followed by diarrhoea and vomiting, with terrible stomach cramps, sometimes enough to rupture the muscles. There is also increasing difficulty in breathing. The blood of such patients has, I understand, been likened to treacle or tar as it is both thick and black. The skin becomes blue and wrinkled, and the stools resemble rice water.'

'And the treatment?'

Ah, thought Madeleine, I am not going to fall into this trap. 'This must be left entirely to the physician in charge of the case. There are several forms of treatment, but I understand some physicians recommend bleeding to relieve the head pains and that almost all are in favour of mustard plaster applied to the lower abdomen. The restoration of warmth and the intake of fluid, if the patient can take this, are also regarded as essential. My father always prescribed half a grain of calomel in powder form and pills of one-eighth of a grain each of opium and capsicum. He also favoured injection of salted water into veins or subcutaneous tissue.'

'And did your father also have ideas regarding the prevention of cholera, Miss Brett?'

'Yes, he very firmly agreed with Dr Snow that cholera is spread by the drinking of infected water. Therefore, all drinking water should be boiled and very great attention should be paid to keeping hands, food and cooking utensils very clean, particularly in overcrowded conditions. In such conditions it is also vital to remember that the evacuations of cholera patients are almost entirely without odour or colour.'

'I congratulate you on your French, Miss Brett. You do indeed speak the language excellently,' said Miss Nightingale. 'I have no further questions, but perhaps Lady Cranworth . . .? Miss Stanley . . .? Lady Canning. . .?'

'Yes' – this from Lady Canning – 'I do have a question: do you consider yourself to be a lady, Miss Brett?'

The second trick question, thought Madeleine, and looked down briefly at her hands. 'I suppose, your ladyship, it must depend on what one means by the word,' she said now, looking directly and calmly at Lady Canning. 'If it means being gently reared and instructed in all the social graces – why, then, I suppose I may call myself a lady. But if it means being unable to scrub floors, sponge filthy patients or dress wounds crawling with maggots . . . then I cannot be a lady, for I have done all these things.'

There was a short silence which Madeleine was unable

to interpret, then Miss Nightingale said, 'Thank you, Miss Brett. That is all. If you will now withdraw and wait in the hall, we shall give you our decision in a short while.'

I've failed, Madeleine thought miserably as she returned to the now deserted hall. But where did I go wrong? It was not over the dressing or my command of French – she praised those – but I just could not tell what she thought of my other explanations. Perhaps I was too explicit; perhaps it offended them to hear such details . . .

'You may come back now, Miss Brett.'

Madeleine started. She had not even heard the door open, but here was Miss Stanley, smiling and insisting that Madeleine should precede her into the room.

'Come and sit down, Miss Brett,' said Miss Nightingale, also smiling and relaxed now. When Madeleine was once more facing them, Miss Nightingale gave her another searching look noting the eagerness, the hardly-daring-to-hope expression in the younger woman's eyes, and then she said quietly, 'We have considered your application very carefully, Miss Brett, and have been impressed by all your answers, so I am happy to say that we have agreed to make an exception in your case. Although you are so very much younger than all the other members of the party, we are relying on your good sense to behave in a mature and reasonable fashion, and therefore we are accepting you for nursing duties in the Crimea. I take it you can be ready to sail by Saturday next, the twenty-first?'

Madeleine was speechless, not even daring to hope that she had heard correctly, and Miss Nightingale, with a hint of merriment in her eyes, continued: 'May we interpret your silence to mean you are pleased with our decision?'

Madeleine pulled herself together and tried to speak, but her throat was suddenly so dry that no sound was heard. She put a handkerchief to her lips and coughed quietly. 'I beg your pardon, ma'am,' she said at last. 'Of course I am absolutely delighted. I – I cannot believe it, but I do thank you and shall do all I can to be worthy of your trust.'

'I am sure you will,' replied Miss Nightingale, now at her most brisk. She secretly understood Madeleine's emotion, but no sentiment must be allowed to cloud judgement or wisdom. 'Now, the conditions of service: you will receive twelve shillings per week, with your board, lodging and uniform provided. After three months' satisfactory service and general good conduct, you will receive sixteen shillings, and after a year, eighteen shillings. You will be required to sign an agreement submitting unconditionally to my orders. I must warn you that discipline will be very strict; Scutari is a huge camp full of troops who are often very idle, with nothing better to do than drink and visit prostitutes – the camp abounds with these and with drink shops. Any misconduct with the troops will mean instant dismissal and a return to this country by third class and on salt rations. In no circumstances will any nurse, or any two nurses, be allowed out alone. They must always be accompanied by the housekeeper, or in a party of at least three other nurses. And, indeed, only then with permission.

'The uniform will consist of a grey tweed dress, worsted jacket and a short woollen cloak. There will also be a plain white cap, and over the right shoulder, to be worn at all times, a cotton sash with the words "Scutari Hospital" in red embroidery. You must provide your own underclothing, including four cotton nightcaps, a carpet bag and cotton umbrella. No flowers, lace or ribbons will be worn. Except for the nuns in our party, all members will wear the same clothes, share the same accommodation and eat the same food. Is all that fully understood?'

They left London Bridge for Boulogne and Paris on Saturday, 21 October as planned, a party of thirty-eight women, plus Miss Nightingale and her friends, Mr and Mrs Bracebridge. Many curious eyes were fixed upon Madeleine, who was so obviously young enough to be the daughter of most, and she returned the looks with equal curiosity. They were a heterogeneous collection: twenty-four members of religious institutions, both Roman Catholic and High Anglican, and the remainder professional nurses. Seeing them gathered together, with so many different personalities, backgrounds and aspirations, Madeleine marvelled at Miss Nightingale's courage in trying to mould them into a single, conforming unit. Her admiration for this extraordinary woman was born then and was never to falter through all the desperate times ahead. For the immediate present, she tried to make herself as useful as possible, but it was when they reached Boulogne that she was really in demand, for none of the nurses spoke French.

The town fêted the party, and the fishwives, many of whom had men serving with the French Army, snatched up the baggage and conveyed it triumphantly to the Hôtel des Bains, where the landlord refused payment for their dinner.

The burly fishwives, with their short skirts and bare legs thrust into sabots, were delighted with Madeleine's command of French, and they made much of her, patting her on the back and even hugging her. And she, more animated and excited than she had been for months, flitted about interpreting, helping to serve the food and, later, in getting the party aboard the Paris train. It was ten P.M. when they arrived at the Gare du Nord, but a crowd was waiting to cheer them on their way to the hotel, where rooms and supper had been arranged.

It was only when they had all retired for the night that Madeleine began to think back over the past three days. Catherine had tried to fill these to capacity, but even so there had to be time to visit Thomas's little grave and to say goodbye to Mam and Ellen. She had gone first to the cemetery, and seeing the little mound of earth so bare and without even the smallest of headstones had twisted the knife in the raw wound. She had fallen to her knees, stretching her arm across the mound and pressing her cheek against the dry earth. 'Forgive me,' she had whispered through her bitter tears. 'Please forgive your mama; I thought you would grow to be strong so long as you had food. I did not know that because you were so tiny you would have a struggle to live. If I had only known, my precious, there is nothing, nothing in this world I would not have done, for I loved you, my darling baby, more than anything else in this world and I only wanted us to be together. If only we could have all been together – your father, you and me. Why, I think *I* might have died of sheer joy. But now I must try to continue alone, even though all I want is to be with you. I am going far away, but I shall never, never forget you – not for a moment. You know that, don't you, my dear little darling?'

Then she had risen with difficulty, placed Summerleigh's white roses on the little grave and turned blindly away.

Going to the cottage had been easier, for Mam had come forward at once, arms outstretched and seamed old face beaming. 'Thee be here a' last!' she exclaimed delightedly. 'We be tha' glad ter see you, isn't us, El?' And there was Ellen, smiling too but just a little reticent, for Madeleine was no longer one of them but had become a 'lady' again. Madeleine's hug was to reassure her.

'I have so wanted to come before this,' Madeleine explained, 'but I've not been very well.'

Both women nodded vigorously. 'Miss Llewellyn Morgan told us,' said Ellen. 'At death's door you've bin, an' no wonder; you still be very pale.'

'Too thin,' pronounced Mam in the abbreviated language that Madeleine had almost forgotten. To steer their thoughts away from herself, she asked about Jem and watched them closely.

Their faces fell and Mam was suddenly near to tears, but Ellen said, 'We was able ter see him 'fore he lef' an' he said ter thank you for the Bible, he will keep it always.'

'It were wunnerful wha' you did,' said Mam warmly. 'An' 'cos you larned him ter wroite us'll get letters an' Ada will tell us dem.'

'An' Miss Llewellyn Morgan has bin wunnerful too,' said Ellen. 'Her wanted us ter go ter a cottage on the estate an' for Ada ter work in the dairy an' me in the house, bu' Mam, her won' go.'

'Yere be my home,' said Mam, her voice quavering. 'Ah nefer bin nowheres else since Ah were wed.'

Madeleine nodded understandingly. All Mam's life, her few joys and many sorrows had been lived through in the tiny cottage and, isolated though it was, she probably felt safe and secure within its thick wattle-and-daub walls. And the interior had been transformed: there were colourful rag rugs on the floor, a rocking chair for Mam and a high-backed gleaming oak settle for Ellen and Ada; a thick woollen curtain had replaced the ragged room-divider and, with exclamations of pride and amazement, they showed her the three beds, pushed together so that they could all sleep closely as they had always done, but now there were real sheets, blankets, a huge patchwork quilt and – most amazing of all – pillows *and* pillow cases. Madeleine exclaimed with them. It was obvious that Mam had never seen the like and she still could not quite believe any of it. Nor was that all, for in the corner was a pine chest, of which every drawer was pulled open to show Madeleine the underclothes, night and day dresses all lovingly folded within and smelling strongly of lavender. 'An',' said Ellen finally, 'every weeken' Miss Llewellyn Morgan sends over a joint an' bu'er, cheese an' milk.'

'Us soon be gettin' tha' fat!' exclaimed Mam, chuckling

at so novel a prospect, and Madeleine felt a deep surge of affection for the wealthy young woman who had done so much to make life more tolerable for them.

When it was time for her to leave, her composure faltered and she looked about her brokenly. A rug covered the spot where she had squatted like a frog to give birth and where Ada had knelt with such pride to take the newly born infant; Mam's rocking chair stood where they had placed the drinking trough to give Thomas his evening bath; and there was a bed over the little bundle of straw which had lain so close to her own. And Mam, Ellen, Jem and Ada, simple and uneducated, were the family she had never known. They had nurtured her when the rest of the world would have turned away from her in hypocritical horror; they had never chided or pried, but had shared their meagre home, food and warmth with her and, because of her, their chief bread-winner had been banished to the other side of the world.

'I can never ever repay you,' she said aloud, her voice breaking, 'and I shall never, never forget you or cease to love and thank you. I should not have survived without your help, and I am so desperately sorry about Jem . . .'

As always, they were embarrassed and silent in the face of gratitude, and Ellen began to steer her towards the door. 'We love you too, Miss Madleen,' Ellen managed at last, and Mam nodded emphatically.

'Naow life, it doos begin again farr thee, jus' like spring,' Mam said, surprising them both by such a lengthy speech.

Madeleine hugged each in turn and then, as she stepped into the carriage, Mam lifted up a large pottery bowl, its lid sealed with wax. 'Do you take this, my dove,' she said, looking deeply into Madeleine's eyes, 'an' keep it in case someone special be hurt, then do thee put dis on every two hours an' hurt will mend an' be clean – bu' keep it farr someone special, moind!'

And Madeleine had put the bowl at the bottom of her carpet bag.

Saying goodbye to Catherine had been only a little less difficult. 'I just do not know how to thank you,' she said, but Catherine shook her head.

'Please do not try, Madeleine. I know you would have done the same for me if our situations had been reversed.' She paused and took a quick turn about the room before adding, 'Promise me one thing, though, Madeleine: if you should meet someone whom you could love, do not let the past keep you from happiness.'

'I don't know, I've not even considered the possibility,' Madeleine said truthfully. 'But yes, if such a situation arises and – and if the other person concerned would be able to accept my past, then I think I would try to go forward. And – and, you, Catherine dear, will no doubt be married by the time I return to England.'

Catherine smiled a little wistfully. 'I, too, do not know,' she said, hanging her head in an uncharacteristic gesture. 'The one I should so like to marry has not declared himself, and I sometimes wonder if he ever will . . .'

It was only at the very last minute before the train pulled out that Catherine said with elaborate casualness, 'If you should meet Sebastian de Lacey in the Crimea, do please give him our very best wishes, won't you?'

Madeleine, startled and suddenly panic-stricken, gasped out, 'Is *he* there?'

'Why yes,' Catherine replied, too concerned in keeping her own emotion in check to notice Madeleine's tone. 'His regiment left in May, so he must be somewhere there, but of course he may never be even near Scutari.'

Madeleine was glad the train moved quite sharply then and there was only an instant in which to grasp Catherine's fingertips before they were separated. The two young women, each with tears in her eyes, waved their handkerchiefs until a curve in the line hid them from each other.

After an overnight stay in Paris, Miss Nightingale and her party left for Marseilles. Once they were all settled, Madeleine gave her entire attention to the passing scenery, for this was the country of her mother's ancestors; she felt excited to be seeing it for the first time and anxious not to miss any of it. But when they arrived at Marseilles all was hustle and bustle again. Miss Nightingale kept Madeleine at her side while she negotiated the purchase of stores, and many of her visitors remarked upon the two women: the older so handsome and with so much presence, the younger so pretty, personable and energetic and, of course, both of them speaking beautiful French.

It was therefore very surprising when, on the second day, it was noticed that the younger woman suddenly stood still and then, with a puzzled look on her face, put her hands over her ears. After a few minutes Miss Nightingale rose and calmly led her companion from the room. Once outside in the corridor, she gently pulled Madeleine's hands from her ears. 'What is it?' she asked quietly.

'I don't know, ma'am,' replied Madeleine. 'I can hear you perfectly, but at the same time there is a sound in my ears like – like hundreds of galloping horses, becoming louder all the time.' Her face was white and drawn as though with fear.

Miss Nightingale put her hand over Madeleine's brow; it felt cold and lightly clammy and she was beginning to tremble. 'Any other symptoms?' asked the now totally professional nurse.

'N-no, ma'am, except the feeling that someone has just – just walked over my grave,' said Madeleine, with a sudden convulsive shiver.

'I will take you to your room,' said Miss Nightingale, holding Madeleine's arm above the elbow. When they reached the dormitory-style room which Madeleine shared with five nuns, Miss Nightingale pulled back the covers of Madeleine's bed. 'I suggest you take off your dress, loosen your stays and rest on your bed,' she said, moving to the window, which she opened quite wide. 'The air is very mild this morning, but be sure and cover yourself well. I suspect you are overtired.' She softened the words with a slight smile. 'You have done very well, but there is no point in becoming exhausted before we even reach our base, so rest here until you feel quite better. I will return later on.'

'Thank you, ma'am,' said Madeleine, feeling foolish. Some twenty minutes later the sound faded as suddenly as it had begun, but then behind her closed lids was Sebastian's face, in a flash so bright that her eyes flew open and she sat bolt upright. Just for an instant she had seen him as clearly as if he were standing before her, his face very deeply tanned, but taut and exhausted. Without realizing what she was doing, she held out her arms, but there was only the empty room, with the bright sun falling in hazy golden bars upon the wooden floor and the sounds of a Marseilles morning coming up from the street below.

PART TWO
Scutari, 1854–6

15

The order to stand at their horses came before daybreak.

'I just hope to God this will mean action and not be a repeat of last time,' said Sebastian to a brother officer.

Alexander Dunn nodded and both men shivered involuntarily, for only three days previously they had remained in such a position throughout a bitterly cold night, awaiting an attack which did not materialize. Sebastian, thinking of the Lancer major who had died of exposure that night, turned to run his eye over the faultless line-up of his regiment: the months of hardship, disease and poor rations had taken their toll of men and beasts alike, and although the Eleventh were wearing their pelisses as jackets, the weather-beaten skin of most faces looked pinched with cold. Yet Lord Cardigan's iron discipline still prevailed, for every uniform, although much faded, was dust free and worn with pride, every thin, dull-coated charger was groomed, its accoutrements highly polished. 'But I suppose he's not here yet,' said Sebastian, voicing his thoughts.

Alexander Dunn laughed shortly, 'Our revered commander? Of course not! I doubt he's even awake yet.'

Sebastian's lip curled. It was a source of bitterness to the whole Light Brigade that, unlike other commanders, Lord Cardigan scorned to sleep in the cavalry camp but retired each night to his yacht anchored in Balaclava Bay, only to make a leisurely return each morning around nine-thirty. 'Thank God for Lord George – ' began Sebastian then broke off abruptly as the silence was shattered by gunfire reverberating around the hills.

Then out of the morning mist they came: two huge

columns of Russian infantry, plus thirty-eight guns, advancing inexorably on the redoubts, guarding the Army's only line of communication down to the port.

'But there's only one battalion of Turks up there,' muttered Sebastian, 'and they'll never hold the Russians. God, there must be all of eleven battalions on the march.'

'But where the hell's our infantry?' demanded a furious voice nearby and Sebastian trained his glass on the heights six hundred feet above them. 'I can't really see, but there seems to be some movement in the camp. My guess, though, is that Cathcart will not hurry to despatch them, for remember it was only three days ago that the two divisions were brought down needlessly and were said to be quite exhausted by the time they'd marched back to that damned camp.' Sebastian closed his glass and then with a quick intake of breath exclaimed, 'Good Christ! The Heavies are mounting! If they're going in, we surely must too!'

Excitement surged through them then and bodies were poised to leap into saddles as Lord George Paget galloped up. 'We are to remain in reserve while Lord Lucan attempts a feint and Maude's troop goes to the assistance of No. 1 redoubt,' he told them, and a concerted groan went up, only to be replaced minutes later by fury as they watched first the Heavy Brigade being forced to withdraw, closely followed by the decimation of Maude's troop. 'Why don't they send *us* in?' someone demanded, shouting above the continuous noise of firing, and immediately other voices joined in: 'Are we just to wait around doing nothing all day?'

An enemy gun battery in the southeast opened up, effectively drowning all voices, and the whole Division could only watch in agony as the limbs of men and horses were torn apart and flung, screaming, into the air, together with guns and equipment. After that the end came quickly, with the Russians surging over the redoubts, whose Turkish defenders fled from all but two.

'Here's Lord George again,' Alexander Dunn shouted back. '*Now* – surely, *now* – '

'The entire Cavalry Division is ordered to retire and await the Infantry's arrival,' Lord George told them sombrely, his eyes ranging over the faces massed before him: on each was all the anger, despair and stunned disbelief he was feeling himself. Then Sebastian, who had known him since boyhood, called out urgently: 'But my lord, are we to leave only the Highlanders to defend Balaclava?'

The second-in-command nodded, and a murmur of denial like a sighing wind stirred the ranks. 'We are now within range of enemy guns,' Lord George continued, and as though in confirmation the barrage of fire was suddenly increased. 'The commander-in-chief is convinced that a major infantry battle is imminent and that it is vital for the Cavalry Division to remain intact so that we can support our fellows.'

'My lord, is it known when our infantry divisions will arrive?' asked Colonel Douglas, the Eleventh's commander.

'I understand His Grace has already started to move the 1st Division and General Cathcart is expected to follow with the 4th almost immediately.' When this failed to bring any reaction, Lord George raised his voice so that all might hear: 'Gentlemen, may I remind you that Lord Raglan, from his position six hundred feet above us, is able to see the whole area in a way which is quite impossible for us; we must have complete faith in his strategy, however painful it is for us to retire.' Lord George paused and a brief smile softened his tense face. 'I am assured that vast numbers of Russian cavalry are massing at the end of the North Valley, so our time will undoubtedly come before this day is out!'

With that they had to be content, but many heads

273

turned to look briefly at where the 93rd Argyll & Sutherland Highlanders were positioned at the base of a hillock; behind them lay a ravine and the vital Balaclava Road. Yet we are leaving them alone and in bloody awful terrain – to be annihilated, thought Sebastian in savage pain.

When, simultaneously, the Russian guns began firing on them and four squadrons of enemy cavalry came into view, the Highlanders' commander ordered his tiny force of 550 men plus one hundred invalids and a handful of demoralized Turks to lie flat on their faces under the barrage. Instead, the Turks, who had already faced vast numbers of enemy infantry, rushed from the mound in total disarray towards Balaclava. The Russian squadrons, thinking the hillock now unoccupied and eager to secure the vital road, rode steadily on until in an instant it seemed that the ground opened before them and out sprang the Highlanders to the wild skirling of their pipes, their Sutherland kilts and jackets – now more purple than scarlet – bright against the dry scrubland. Incredibly, the Russians halted, thinking they had run into an ambush, and while they checked, the Argylls poured a volley of musket-fire into their ranks. Again the Russians advanced, and a second volley hit them with deadly accuracy. When they checked yet again, a third volley smashed into them, causing them to wheel and retire towards their main force.

Thus was the Balaclava Road temporarily saved and the legend born of 'the thin red line'.

The Cavalry Division had heard the volleys of musket-fire and even the sound of the pipes wafting faintly over the hills, but not the Highlanders' final hurrahs of triumph, so their mood was sombre as they took up their new position at the base of the ridge. Neither Lord Cardigan's arrival nor the deployment of two brigades of French infantry raised the Cavalry's morale, but when two regiments of the famous Chasseurs d'Afrique came into view their British counterparts scrutinized them with narrow-eyed curiosity.

But the Light Brigade were not to be left for long in critical appraisal of their allies, for to the sound of trumpets they saw squadrons of Heavy Dragoons begin to move off in the direction of Balaclava. 'Now what?' muttered Sebastian.

'Lucan is believed to be sending squadrons of the Greys and Inniskillings to help the Highlanders,' someone said.

'But surely it's too late,' began Sebastian and then stopped abruptly as on the slopes above a gigantic mass of Russian cavalry appeared and began to trot steadily towards the small force led by General Scarlett. After a moment's total silence, the ranks of the Light Brigade stirred, and low, excited voices began exclaiming: 'By Jove, what an amazing sight! There must be all of three or four thousand of them!'

'Great God! Scarlett's going in – he's ordered his fellows to wheel into line!'

'Look, there's Lucan riding hell-for-leather over to him.'

'But how *can* Scarlett be expected to attack when he's only got five hundred troopers – *and* they'd have to charge uphill!'

'Oh, Christ, the Russians are wheeling into line too.'

'They're deploying two wings from the centre – they mean to outflank Scarlett!'

'But now's the time to attack, while they're stationary. Listen, Lucan's trumpeter is sounding the charge!'

'Scarlett's drawn his sword. Surely he's not going in until all his lot are ready – Christ, he is – he's going in – that's the charge sounding again. But there are only about three hundred troopers actually with him.'

'And the Russian centre is bloody dense. They'll never get through – they'll be crushed to death within seconds.'

'No, look, they're still there, just a dot of scarlet – but

they're fighting like madmen! But – what the hell's that din?'

'It's the second squadron of the Inniskillings going in and, yes, the Dragoons too, smashing into the Russian flank.'

'Why aren't we up there helping them?'

'It's a bloody insult, that's what it is, keeping us here doing nothing!'

'Listen, for Christ's sake, listen! I thought I heard a cheer.'

'Yes, yes, *yes*! It's our fellows cheering up there because – because they've broken the Russian cavalry!'

'Yes, they're in full flight up the Heights to the north – but they must be pursued!'

'That'll be for us!'

But still the Light Brigade was ordered to remain there. Throughout the campaign they had been kept in reserve. They had been forced to either wait or retire without even drawing their swords and now were not allowed to pursue the enemy. It meant that all the hardship, all the disease, misery and death had been in vain, and they sprawled by their horses, so demoralized that some dozed or actually lit pipes. They could see that the Russian cavalry had recovered from its rout and already was regrouping. Sullenly the Light Brigade watched as at the end of the valley, over a mile away, twelve field guns were manoeuvred into position, while on each side of the surrounding hills strong forces of enemy infantry and guns began to deploy. It was only when teams of artillery horses and men approached the redoubts that anger flared again, for the Russians' intention was obvious: they were about to take away the twelve-pounder guns abandoned by the Turks – all within full sight of the British Commander-in-Chief, who apparently was going to take no action at all.

But then a lone horseman appeared, riding with the utmost speed and recklessness on a blown and lathered horse. 'It's Nolan!' exclaimed many of the officers, for Edward Nolan, the brilliant cavalry officer and ADC to Lord Raglan, was known to them all, 'and he looks demented!'

This was not far from the truth for Nolan's anger over the day's events had grown to a frenzy and he made no effort to conceal his contempt for Lord Lucan, to whom he handed an order. As the onlookers watched in silent amazement, they heard Nolan's shout of: 'Lord Raglan's orders are that the cavalry are to attack immediately!' His tone was insolent in the extreme and breath was held as all waited for Lord Lucan's reaction. But he, to whom the order made no sense, only demanded angrily, 'Attack, sir? Attack what? What guns, sir?'

And Nolan, rigid in the saddle, with head contemptuously thrown back, reacted at once. Flinging out his arm and pointing he said furiously, 'There, my lord, is your enemy, there are your guns!'

Thus, because of that one reckless gesture, was the day to be remembered with a fame that eclipsed the heroic thin red line of the Highlanders and Scarlett's charge, for Nolan had pointed not to the captured naval guns, but to the Russian artillery at the end of the North Valley.

In complete silence the Light Brigade watched Lord Lucan ride across to their own commander and heard him order that they should proceed along the North Valley, followed by the Heavy Brigade, with himself in command.

Lord Cardigan's sword arm dipped in salute as he said, 'Certainly, sir, but allow me to point out to you that the Russians have a battery in the valley on our front, and batteries and riflemen on both sides.'

His detested brother-in-law shrugged. 'I know it, but Lord Raglan will have it. We have no choice but to obey. Advance very steadily and keep your men well in hand.'

Lord Cardigan made no reply, but saluted once more in an exaggerated manner and returned to his Brigade, where he loudly told Lord George Paget that they had been ordered to attack. 'I expect your best support; mind, Lord George, your best support.' In that moment the Light Brigade thought only that the weeks of frustration were over – the Guards, the Highlanders and the Heavy Brigade had all been given their chance of glory, and bloody marvellous they had been – but now, now it was to be their own turn, now the Heavies were to support *them*, and by God they'd show them all – even those fancy Chasseurs – that the Light Brigade had the best horsemen, the best chargers, the best discipline *and* the greatest expertise of them all. If there were some, like Sebastian, who looked at the twelve brass muzzles facing them and knew they were about to be blown to pieces, they kept silent, for the light-hearted banter, the joyousness and sheer excitement of their comrades was infectious. All trace of drowsiness left them as they leapt into their saddles, forgetting that they and their horses had been waiting since four that morning and that few had eaten or drunk anything since the previous night. Every face was tense and eager now, every eye alert, and even the chargers began to toss their heads and paw the ground.

When they were drawn up in three lines, Lord Cardigan placed himself in front, raised his sword and ordered quietly, 'The Brigade will advance: walk, march, trot.'

A trumpet blew and with a concerted *s-w-i-s-h* swords were drawn, swept up, and their guards kissed; simultaneously lances were raised to glitter in the sun as the lines began to move, followed shortly afterwards by the Heavy Brigade.

It was now a beautiful autumn day of great calm; in the distance was the blue bay of Balaclava and its little rose- and vine-wreathed houses. To the watchers on the heights, the horsemen advancing with parade-ground pre- cision along the mile-wide valley were like brilliant toys, and in a momentary hush the jingle of their spurs and bits, the slap of their scabbards and sabretaches could be plainly heard. But then reality and horror returned to the watchers, for instead of wheeling to attack the redoubts, the horsemen continued straight along the valley floor. No less surprised were the Russian commanders. They had formed hollow squares around the redoubts to receive the expected charge, while on the hills their riflemen and artillerymen paused, totally unable to believe that the small, glittering force below them intended to attack the guns at the far end. Then, before the Brigade had advanced more than fifty yards, those guns roared, belching out huge tongues of flame and clouds of smoke, while a scorching fusillade came from the slopes on both sides.

Still they trotted on, as though on parade, their front line now almost non-existent, their ranks opening for the fallen and closing instantly once they had ridden past – a feat of incredible courage and discipline in itself. The toll became greater as shells, mielé balls, round and grape shot tore into them; they began to canter, leaving the Heavy Brigade far behind, and when they were more than halfway down the valley, the trumpets sounded: 'C-H-A-R-G-E!' and they responded instantly, as the fighting men of Britain have always done down the ages. With a mere touch of their long-necked cavalry spurs they sent their horses plunging forward, sword knots tightening around wrists as swords and lances were lowered to the 'engage'. Then men from the stinking alleys, the black hells of the industrial towns and mines, the country boys from the hills and valleys of Britain and their officers rose in their stirrups and galloped knee to knee, the earth shaking beneath the thunder of their horses' hooves, straight into the smoke of the Russian guns. Into death; into history. It was suicide, yet long after many other successful and *necessary* charges were to lie forgotten between the pages of dusty history books, the Charge of the Light Brigade was to live on in the hearts and minds of the British people.

Few remembered that it had all taken place on the anniversary of Agincourt.

Sebastian thought he had become inured to all the horror – after Varna and Balchik Bay, where the decomposing bodies of the dead, only sufficiently weighted to keep them upright, had risen head and shoulders out of the water to bob around the transports; after seeing the Alma turned into a river of blood which men had to wade through, and the heights above heaped with British dead, slippery with British blood; after he, and all other able-bodied officers and men had spent the night taking water to the wounded and dying who lay without cover or medical attention; after seeing men die in agony from the cramps of cholera or the equal agony of amputation without anaesthetic. But nothing, nothing could be worse than this mile-long tangle of hideously mutilated bodies of staggering, exhausted men and the dying horses, their riders refused to abandon.

He dismounted with difficulty, his limbs stiff as though from hours of hard riding, and for an instant he doubted whether his legs would function, but his horse was trembling and equally exhausted. 'Steady, Rollo old fellow,' Sebastian said to him in the rasping whisper which was all that was left of his voice. His eyes were watering in the sudden brilliant light; in the inferno, smoke had so obscured the sun that the battle had been fought in semi-darkness and now he fumbled for his watch, looking at it in disbelief: was it really possible, he wondered dazedly, that only some twenty minutes previously he had finished the last of the rum and water in his flask before the order to mount had sounded? Only twenty minutes since they had trotted off, the small brilliant force, full of confidence and excitement, knowing themselves to be the best light horsemen in the whole of Europe, chosen for their boldness and drilled to perfection; twenty minutes since he had kissed the arms engraved on his sword guard and suddenly felt the shades of his ancestors gather around him: those men of Acre, Crécy, Agincourt, Blenheim and Waterloo, and realized that *his* battle was about to join the family's roll of honour.

As he stumbled along now, holding fast to Rollo's bridle, scenes of the battle flashed, like slides from a magic lantern, before his burning eyes: of Cardigan, magnificently mounted and ramrod straight in the saddle, riding so far in advance of his Brigade, his wonderful uniform a mass of gold, royal blue and cherry red; of Edward Nolan suddenly galloping ahead and actually across the Brigadier, shouting unintelligibly and waving his sword urgently; of the shell fragment slicing open Nolan's chest a minute later and of the last sight of him, arm still upright, uttering blood-curdling shrieks which echoed all through the lines as his terrified horse galloped to the rear of the 17th Lancers disintegrating in front of him, riderless horses trying to run beside their companions, eyeballs bursting from their heads. He remembered galloping into the inferno of fire and overshooting the Russion batteries; of his sword arm wheeling, dipping and slashing from side to side: of seeing a head fly through the air on the right, a throat open like a ghastly grin after a slash on the left; of a huge hand reaching up to pull him from the saddle, and of his sword hacking the arm off at the shoulder, leaving the hand still clutching his sleeve; of meeting and joining with the last of the 4th Light Dragoons and of their tiny force – not more than seventy in all – wheeling exhaustedly once again to face the enemy cavalry; and of their final, miraculous escape in the semi-darkness.

He became conscious now of a trooper, minus left arm and leg, trying to claw his way along the ground, and with the last of his strength Sebastian lifted him, screaming, on to Rollo's back, while bullets sent up little spurts of dust all around him.

But at long last they came to safety, and as each little group staggered into view they were raggedly cheered by those who had preceded them. Men who could move went forward to greet comrades and enquire about others. To Sam, the civilian servant, who rushed from group to group asking about Sebastian, his master was at first sight unrecognizable, for his busby was gone and his red-rimmed eyes peered out from a smoke-blackened face. The entire front of his uniform was a mass of blood – and Gawd knows wha' else, thought Sam, identifying him at last. He dashed up. 'Capt'n Sebastian, sir!' he cried in distress. 'Where yer bin hit, sir?'

'No, I'm all right, Sam,' Sebastian croaked, 'but help me with this poor fellow, will you?' Together they lifted the man, but even as they did so, death rattled in his throat and his head rolled.

'He be gone, sir,' said Sam unnecessarily, and Sebastian nodded. Perhaps it is as well, he thought, for there do not seem to be any surgeons around, and with such ghastly wounds, gangrene is inevitable. So they put him down on the short, springy turf and turned away. Then Sam produced a flask and Sebastian drank as though dying of thirst. It was only afterwards, seeing Sam's horrified eyes range over him, that he looked down at himself and felt his gorge rise; when the first line of the Brigade had been blown to bits, the second line had received all the debris of men and horses, and the evidence still clung to him. He lowered his head until his forehead rested on Rollo's neck in grief for lost friends and in exhaustion. It was then that he thought of Madeleine and wanted her near-ness as he had never wanted it before – just to feel the softness of her, just to lay his head against the curve of her breasts, just to have the silken strands of her arms about him, to smell the clean sweetness of her, and silently, but from the depths of his being, he cried out for her.

Miss Nightingale and her party sailed on the twenty-seventh in the *Vectis*, an old ship notorious for her discomfort and the giant cockroaches which infested her. Most of the party, including Miss Nightingale, were soon prostrated. Madeleine and the few others less affected ministered to them as best they could. When, two days later, the ship ran into a gale, Madeleine was almost the only one left on her feet and by then she, too, was feeling distinctly unwell. Willpower alone carried her on, but as soon as the worst of the storm abated, she went up on deck and lay in a clamped-down chaise longue, where she at once fell asleep.

Small gentle movements wakened her, and when she first opened her eyes she thought she was looking at Thomas, for the face bending over her was just as she had imagined he would look as a young man: cheeks reddened by the wind, black curls tossing and large dark eyes looking down thoughtfully into her own. She stirred at once, with a tiny strangled exclamation, but then the young man spoke and she realized it was Robert Wells, who had introduced himself to the party before they left Marseilles.

'I do hope you will forgive me, Miss Brett,' he said, raising his voice above the wind, 'but I was taking the liberty of tucking a rug around you. I found you asleep and was afraid you would wake feeling chilled.'

'Why, how kind,' exclaimed Madeleine, smiling up at him gratefully. 'You are not troubled by seasickness then?'

He was standing with legs apart, braced against the still quite violent movement of the ship. He shook his head. 'Fortunately not. I spend much of my time in Dorset, where I sail a great deal, so I am used to quite rough seas.' He smiled, showing perfect teeth in a wide, artless grin. 'If you do not wish to sleep again, may I perhaps join you for a little while?'

'Oh, please do,' said Madeleine, continuing to watch him through her lashes. He held a kind of fascination for her because of the imagined likeness to Thomas and, as he was the nearest to herself in age, they had met and talked on several occasions during the voyage.

'He must be a TG,' said Mrs Bracebridge soon after they had first noticed him.

'A TG?' queried Madeleine, not understanding.

'Yes, a Travelling Gentleman, going to watch the war,' Mrs Bracebridge had replied.

'Going to *watch* the war!' Madeleine repeated, amazed at such action.

'Why yes.' Selina Bracebridge turned to smile at the young woman who, despite her reserve and self-assurance, had such a look of naïveté and innocence about her. 'There are quite a large number of people who have gone out from home to watch the battles, you know.'

But she was wrong about young Mr Wells, for on their second meeting he had shyly told Madeleine that he had obtained a commission in the Grenadier Guards and was hastening to join them. 'I do hope the war will not be over before I have a chance of action,' he said seriously, and Madeleine thought how heartbreaking it must be for a mother to see her son going off to war.

'May I ask what your mama feels about your joining the Army?' she asked now, and Mr Wells turned at once to look at her in surprise.

'Oh, I do not have parents,' he said quietly. 'My mother was killed in a hunting accident when I was a small boy and my father died last year – but,' he added manfully, 'I have two sisters and many cousins, so I am not alone.' He was silent for a moment, a small frown appearing between his eyes. When he spoke again his voice was more decisive: 'Perhaps my sisters felt it was rather my duty to remain at home for – for various reasons, but of course I could not do so while such a scrap was on – after all, I might not get another chance to go to war during my lifetime.'

When they reached Malta, Mr Wells asked if he might escort Madeleine around the island, but Miss Nightingale's rule forbade this and Madeleine did not wish to go with the official party, who were lined up in military formation. Since the strange incident in Marseilles she had felt depressed; the sudden vision of Sebastian and her own instinctive gesture of holding out her arms had shattered her precarious peace and left a nagging worry. She could not shake off the fear that something terrible had happened to him, and whereas before she had been afraid of hearing about him, now she could hardly wait to reach Scutari and enquire. Surely there would be someone whom she could casually question about his regiment.

The party were all up on deck on 3 November when the *Vectis* ploughed her way up the Bosphorus in raging wind and rain to anchor off Seraglio Point. The Constantinople skyline, so fascinating in clear weather, was reduced to dreariness. But all eyes were turned to the opposite shore, where the huge building of the Barrack Hospital was just visible through a curtain of rain. The women had been told that they must proceed to the hospital without delay as casualties were expected from a great battle that had raged at a place called Balaclava. So when the slim, exotic-looking caïques arrived alongside, all the party were eager to be lowered into them, four to a boat, and rowed across to Scutari.

Nor was their enthusiasm dampened when they approached the rickety landing stage and saw the stinking, bloated carcases of horses moving with the tide and being pursued and fought over by packs of dogs. Then they realized that the one and only track leading up to the hospital was steep, refuse-laden and slimy with mud from the deluge; it was also a drain and smelled accordingly. But, following Miss Nightingale's example, the women grasped their skirts firmly above their ankles and, loaded with their carpetbags and umbrellas, began the ascent.

The third shock was the building itself. They might have expected that, having braved the filth of the track, they would arrive at a clean, well-ordered hospital. Instead they faced a huge, three-storey mass built around a hollow square, with towers at each corner. Even before they had passed through the great gateway the stench hit them; it was soon only too apparent that here was an enormous shell, dilapidated and filthy, the walls of its endless corridors streaming, its wards devoid of furniture, even beds, or any other amenities. Nor were their own quarters any better; they had been allocated six rooms, including a kitchen and a closet. All were filthy, damp and empty except for a few chairs. In a further upstairs room the body of a Russian general was discovered and only removed after some difficulty. There was nothing to clean that or any of the other rooms; no food, no cooking utensils, not even beds or bed linen. But thanks to Miss Nightingale's marble calm, no one succumbed to hysterics and instead they began cramming themselves into the small rooms and started unpacking.

Miss Nightingale departed, only to return later with basins of black tea and told the women that these utensils must be used for washing, eating and drinking. As there was a shortage of water, this was rationed to one pint per person per day for washing and drinking; to obtain their ration they must queue in one of the corridors where there was a fountain. Meanwhile, the women must sleep on the wooden platforms lining the walls of their rooms and, as candles and lamps were almost nonexistent, they would have to undress in darkness. Few, if any, of the party slept that night, for rats raced endlessly beneath the low platforms. To add to their misery, the rooms were infested with fleas.

If they consoled themselves with the thought that the

286

next morning they would begin nursing, they were to be disappointed for, after the official welcome by the doctors on their arrival, they were ignored by the medical staff. All Miss Nightingale's offers of nurses and supplies were refused, even though there were only twelve orderlies and a single clerk to deal with stores. In the solitary kitchen stood thirteen coppers in which meat and tea were boiled, and that was all.

The women caught glimpses of patients still dressed in ragged, filthy uniforms, but no other protection against the damp cold, and of others wrapped in rain- and blood-soaked blankets, all totally without attention. Those who were not screaming or moaning in agony lay in apathetic silence. A few – a very few – of the less seriously ill tore with their fingers at the half-raw meat which was their food. It was hard to stand by and ignore the piteous scenes, but until the doctors requested their help, Miss Nightingale would allow no nurse to enter a ward.

Even when the first casualties from Balaclava began to arrive, the women – many muttering rebellion – were employed making stump-pads, pillows, shirts and slings. Miss Nightingale, however, maintained her implacable calm and eagle eye. She had seen the terrible agony the hospital diet produced in men already tortured by cholera and dysentery. The day following her arrival she began to use the kitchen in her quarters to prepare the supplies she had purchased in Marseilles, and Madeleine was to marvel at the older woman's foresight in obtaining portable cooking stoves at the same time. As the Balaclava survivors poured in they were met with port wine and buckets of hot arrowroot, and within a week Miss Nightingale's kitchen was providing invalid diets for the whole hospital.

Then news began to filter through of a grim battle fought at Inkerman, but while emphasis was laid on the great British victory, no mention was made of the Army's exhausted state. Stranded on the heights above Sebastopol, it was without fuel, winter clothing or shelter, drenched by incessant rain, frozen by roaring wind, and with only icy mud to sleep in and salt pork with dried peas to eat. Sickness soared. Many did not survive the terrible hazards of the journey, but those who did poured into Scutari.

In the complete confusion that this caused, the prejudices against Miss Nightingale and her party were left in abeyance and help was required of everyone: a Church of England minister who had volunteered to be a hospital chaplain was pressed into assisting at operations; an MP who had come privately to investigate the hospital system found himself down at the landing stage, saucepan in hand, trying to get some warm liquid into the frozen, agonized men.

As for the Nightingale women, they ran from their quarters and began feverishly to fill huge bags with straw to lay in the wards and along both sides of the corridors. But no one could cope with the numbers who continued to pour in daily. Soon there were no more bags to fill, and men lay on bare, rotten boards which were crawling with lice and vermin; pillows and blankets were unknown and patients lay with heads resting on their dirty boots and covered only with whatever they had found before leaving Sebastopol. Amputations were performed without anaesthetics, operating tables or screens. As the lavatories in the towers had become useless without water to flush them, liquid filth covered the floor and overflowed into the anteroom, so huge wooden tubs were left in the corridors and wards for the thousand dysentery patients to use, but because the orderlies did not like emptying these tubs, they were often left for twenty-four hours, and by the middle of November the atmosphere in the hospital was so thick and stench-laden that it could be smelled for a considerable distance outside the building.

To add to such misery, a hurricane of greater force than ever before known raged over the Crimea, destroying

288

every ship in Balaclava Bay, including one just arrived which was laden with warm clothing and stores. The canvas covering the field hospital was blown completely away, as were horses and the few trees not already cut down for fuel. If Scutari had been inundated before, it was now completely overwhelmed, and the ragged, often barefoot casualties begged the nurses not to come near them because they were so verminous.

And then, out of the total chaos, the total breakdown in organization, were sown the first seeds of Miss Nightingale's immortality, for it was she who obtained the first two hundred scrubbing brushes with which to wash the floors; she who insisted on the regular and frequent emptying of the lavatory tubs; she who organized the washing of patients' clothing and installation of giant boilers; she who purchased thousands of shirts, socks and trousers, cooking and eating utensils, towels and soap, operating tables and screens, tin baths and bedpans. When it was no longer possible to cram more patients into the corridors and wards, Miss Nightingale engaged Turkish workmen to repair that part of the hospital damaged by fire. It was ready for the last eight hundred patients, who were received by the nurses with warm food and clean beds, and Miss Nightingale's fame spread through the Crimea.

During all this time Madeleine, like most of the nurses, had been working round the clock, so desperate to try and relieve her patients' suffering that she was completely unconscious of her own exhaustion. The ward orderlies were either elderly pensioners or mere boys, all of whom were uncaring and ignorant, so nothing could be safely entrusted to them. At first they deeply resented Madeleine's supervision, but slowly her quiet determination instilled some sense of duty, some feeling of compassion in them. She had quickly become devoted to her patients and never ceased to marvel at their quiet acceptance of terrible wounds, pain and hardship; to her

289

surprise, she had found that almost without exception they were polite and well mannered in her presence, and all were pathetically grateful to her. So she spent every available moment washing, bandaging and feeding them. She also pleaded with the doctors to sign chits for clean shirts, linen and invalid diets. If she could do nothing else for the patients, she would spend time rubbing oil into stiff, aching limbs, and when she discovered that dying men of all ages invariably called for their mothers, she tried her best to act as surrogate mother to each in turn.

On two occasions when she was scrubbing a vast area of floor, she had looked up to see Mr Wells, resplendent in the uniform of the Grenadier Guards, gazing at her in amazement. She never knew why he was still at the depot, nor that he had come especially to see her, because she could not spare the time to talk to him. After greeting him and telling him that he looked splendid, she had asked him to excuse her and continued with her scrubbing.

The one question uppermost in her mind was to find out about Sebastian, but such was the magnitude of the work and the desperate state of the incoming patients that she was never able to ask. A further four thousand wounded arrived in seventeen days, followed by a short lull, and it was during this time that Madeleine began to ask timidly for news of Sebastian. She still knew nothing of the Army in general, so when the first patient she asked replied, 'Wot is Cap'n de Lacey's regiment, ma'am?' she said, 'The Cavalry,' and continued dressing his shattered arm without looking up.

The patient, an old soldier, smiled gently at the bent head and telltale blush just beginning to stain the thin cheeks, before he said: 'But which regiment of Cavalry, ma'am? An' is it Light or Heavy Brigade?'

'Oh, I don't know,' said Madeleine, beginning to wish she had never put the question.

Her patient held up his one remaining hand and began naming the various regiments, bending a finger each time she shook her head. 'Well, the Cap'n ain't in the Heavies, tha's fer sure,' he said at last. By this time other patients nearby were taking an interest and started to call out: 'Hussars? Lancers? Light Dragoons?' until Madeleine, now thoroughly embarrassed and wishing the floor would open beneath her, could not remember at all, but said desperately, 'Perhaps it is the Lancers.'

An instant hush fell over the little group until Madeleine, looking up, turned from face to face, her eyes huge and dark. 'What is it?' she asked finally, and one patient, braver than the others, said softly, 'I heard only thirty-seven troopers of the 17th come back from the Charge, Ma'am, I dunnow about any officers . . .'

Madeleine's blood ran cold then and suddenly she felt completely worn out. 'Thank you,' she whispered, turning away, and the patients watched her with pity, every man wishing he could do something to help her. Perhaps it was the thought of Sebastian being already long dead which was too terrible for her to believe, for as she progressed down the ward, she kept trying to remember; so much had happened since that first evening in Bath when Harriet and the General had been explaining the regiment to her . . . what had they said . . . oh, what, what, was it? Something unusual – she whirled and dashed back to the group.

'It was something about their trousers!' she exclaimed, and no one guffawed or even sniggered, but all looked back with straight faces at the distraught young girl. 'Something unusual about the trousers of that particular regiment,' she said again, and one patient, more alert than the others shouted: 'Were it the colour, ma'am?'

'Why – why yes, that was it! They wear Prince Albert's colour because – because they escorted him when he came to England for his wedding.'

A single voice shouted, 'Them be the Cherry Bums – aw, beg pardin, ma'am!' followed by a delighted concerted shout of: 'It's the Eleventh – the Eleventh Hussars, ma'am!' But beyond that, no one knew anything further and all their faces fell until a man across the ward raised himself painfully on an elbow and shouted: 'There's a Cap'n Winstanley yere somewhere, ma'am, an' he's from Fourth Light Dragoons – they were in the second line wif the Eleventh, so he might know abaout this yere Cap'n dee Lacey.'

It was like looking for a needle in a haystack to find a particular patient in those numerous wards and four miles of corridor, all crammed with wounded; but slowly, by persevering and asking countless times, she began to track down Captain Winstanley until at last she knew where he was. It then took her some time before she found the courage to approach him, but eventually desperation made her do so.

Captain Winstanley had received extensive sword and gunshot wounds at Balaclava, but had been extraordinarily lucky in obtaining early medical attention. He had been at Scutari for many weeks when Madeleine, to his delight, approached him.

'Sebastian de Lacey of the Eleventh?' he queried in answer to her timid question. 'Why yes, I knew him quite well.'

Once again Madeleine's blood ran cold. 'You *knew* . . .?' she whispered.

What an absolutely beautiful girl, Captain Winstanley was thinking appreciatively, such wonderful eyes, and that mouth . . . He pulled himself together and tried to concentrate on telling her gently, 'Well, I have no up-to-date news of him,' he said, hoping she would not ask for more. But of course she did.

'Please tell me what you do know about him,' she said quietly.

'If you wish. It was as we were approaching the guns that the Eleventh pulled a little ahead of us and overshot the battery; my last sight of Sebastian was of him standing in his stirrups, yelling at the top of his voice and whirling his sword to great effect. I particularly noticed him because of his height and also because he had lost his busby, and I just had time to think how vulnerable he was without it before we, too, leapt over the guns . . .'

'I see,' said Madeleine untruthfully. 'But – if he had been wounded . . . or – or killed, would you have heard?'

Captain Winstanley groaned inwardly; if Sebastian had not written to her by now he must be dead, for surely no man in his right mind would leave such a delicious girl without news. 'Well, not necessarily,' he answered reluctantly. 'You see, I was wounded almost at once and was carried back semiconscious through the lines by my horse, and this meant that I received medical attention pretty quickly.'

'Do you think that if Sebastian had been wounded, his horse might have carried him back, as yours did with you?'

Captain Winstanley realized that she was clinging to every small hope and paused, uncertain whether to be frank or not. Madeleine solved the dilemma for him. 'Please tell me honestly what you think,' she said, forcing her voice to be calm and steady.

The young man looked at her with admiration and pity. 'I can only say that in that last glimpse I had of him, Sebastian was surrounded by huge Russian gunners who were trying to pull him from his horse . . . and out of six hundred and seventy-three men, only one hundred and ninety-five of us returned alive.' He paused again and then added sadly, 'And five hundred of our horses died too.'

Madeleine shuddered convulsively, but then she rose to stand very quietly, with only the tight clasping of her rough red hands to betray her. 'Thank you very much, Captain Winstanley,' she said steadily. 'It must have been very painful for you to tell me all this, but I am grateful.'

Oh, what a girl, thought Captain Winstanley lyrically, what I wouldn't give to have someone like her care for me . . . He had always heard that Sebastian de Lacey had a devastating effect upon women of all ages, and he found himself hoping fervently that Sebastian had treated this lovely girl with care. As she turned away, he said, 'Why not write to the regiment and ask? I'm not sure about their adjutant, but I know their CO, Colonel Douglas, came through – he'll be able to tell you at once.'

Madeleine nodded. 'Yes, of course. Thank you again.' But there was no further hope in her heart. Sebastian must be dead, Thomas's father must be dead, and she felt as though she had been poleaxed. Yet giving way to grief was a luxury which could not be afforded, not when there were so many living in need of all her energy and thoughts. So she mourned silently, forcing herself to eat and to work, and only gave way to tears in the darkness of night.

It was some weeks later when Mr Wells appeared yet again, and this time he would not let Madeleine scurry away. 'Miss Brett,' he said earnestly, 'do you have just a minute? I have come especially to ask if you will do me the honour of accompanying me to the Ambassador's reception next Thursday.'

Madeleine looked at him blankly; what could he be thinking of – Miss Nightingale would never approve and, besides, there was no time for socializing, especially as Sir Stratford and his lady had been less than helpful to Miss Nightingale. 'Oh, that is most kind of you,' said Madeleine, 'but of course it is out of the question. There is no time and Miss Nightingale would never permit it.' But by merest chance the lady herself appeared at that moment and greeted the young officer in her usual quiet way. Then, as Madeleine was on the point of leaving them, Mr Wells suddenly reddened and spoke up.

'I was just trying to persuade Miss Brett to accompany me to the Ambassador's reception next Thursday,' he said, his voice trailing off very slightly in the face of Miss Nightingale's stupendous calm.

'Oh?' she said, with only the slightest lifting of her brows. 'And what was Nurse Brett's response to that?'

'Why, ma'am, that you would never permit her to accept!'

Miss Nightingale smiled then, with a hint of merriment. 'On the contrary,' she said smoothly, 'I think it an excellent idea, and as I shall also be going, with Dr Menzies, there is no question of any rule being broken.' She turned to the stupefied Madeleine. 'You will, of course, wear your uniform, Nurse Brett, together with your cap and sash.' Then, as Madeleine continued to look utterly astonished, Miss Nightingale continued, 'I think it about time that we realized there is a world outside this hospital – and for people in that world to know we are here.' She turned to the equally astonished young man. 'I bid you good day, Mr Wells, and I shall look forward to seeing you next Thursday.' She laughed inwardly as she left them – they both looked so dumbfounded – and well they might, she thought, but the fact was that she had been concerned lately about her youngest nurse. The girl was obviously grieving, although making every effort to conceal it, and to have an evening out might help her; there had been so many difficulties with the other nurses, but with the youngest there had always been instant obedience and very great devotion to duty. She deserved a little light relief now.

And Madeleine found to her surprise that she was actually looking forward to the evening. It also seemed to her quite wonderful that other people were happy for her and anxious to help. The laundry by then was being done

by some of the two hundred-odd wives and camp follow-
ers who had been discovered living in filthy conditions in
the basement of the hospital. To one of them, Madeleine
gave her spare uniform to be washed, adding artlessly
that it had to be particularly well laundered for a special
occasion, and because Madeleine was always friendly and
kind to the outcasts in the basement, the woman washed
and ironed the dress with great care. Also, from one of
the many trading booths around the barracks, she bought
starch for the cap and sash and even a small piece of
scented soap, which she handed diffidently to Madeleine.
Nor was that all, for the Roman Catholic nuns with whom
Madeleine shared a room twittered amongst themselves
when they heard about the reception and willingly gave
up their ration of washing water so that she could sham-
poo her hair and have a real bath. When she was ready,
they all stood back, smiling and murmuring admiringly.
Madeleine, her heart lighter than for months past, kissed
each of the nuns in turn and then almost danced down the
stairs to where her escort was waiting, very proud if a
little self-conscious of his brilliant uniform and the lovely
girl he was to accompany.

'I am sorry I cannot wear a pretty gown,' Madeleine
said shyly, 'and my hands are a disgrace.' They were
indeed red and swollen, with the skin calloused and
rough, but the young officer shook his head, his dark eyes
admiring.

'I think you look splendid as you are, Miss Brett,' he
said gallantly. 'And everyone will know that your hands
have only become rough in the care of others.'

Sir Stratford de Redcliffe and his Ambassadress lived
luxuriously in a gleaming neo-classical mansion with spacious gardens overlooking the Bosphorus. Soldiers in
pristine uniforms stood in red and white sentry boxes at
the entrance. The interior of the house was no less
magnificent. As she entered, Madeleine was literally

dazzled by the light from hundreds of candles and found herself taking deep breaths of the perfume emanating from the banks of flowers. With the highly polished furniture, splendid paintings and gleaming silverware, it was another world from Scutari, and one which she had forgotten existed.

Mr Wells stood courteously aside to allow Miss Nightingale and Dr Menzies to be announced first, and Madeleine was still in a daze as she heard a stentorian voice call out their names. Then it was the turn of Mr Wells and herself; she saw him hand over a piece of pasteboard and felt his fingers very lightly touch her elbow to propel her forward as the voice bellowed: 'Lieutenant the Earl of Wells, Grenadier Guards, and Miss Madeleine Brett!'

Madeleine came to an abrupt halt. *The Earl of Wells!* In her head there was the echo of a cold voice saying, '. . . he gave the earldom of Wells to us' – and the shattering realization that she was with Sebastian's cousin. Speechless, she turned to him as he said urgently, 'Miss Brett, please. We are holding up the line,' and allowed herself to be propelled forward once more to where the handsome Ambassador stood, smiling indulgently and waiting to take her hand. It was the sight of Lady Stratford that made Madeleine pull herself together, for the Ambassadress was obviously hard put to disguise her displeasure at this gauche girl in the hideous gown who plainly did not know how to behave.

As soon as they were out of the receiving line, Madeleine turned, white-faced to her escort. 'Is it true,' she whispered incredulously, 'that you really are the Earl of Wells?'

He nodded, thinking she was overawed by the title and feeling just a little disappointed at her reaction. 'I am sorry to cause you such surprise,' he said with the faintest hint of stiffness in his voice, 'but I purposely did not tell anyone because I did not want any special treatment.' He quickly lifted two glasses of champagne from a hovering waiter and held out one to her. 'Do please drink a little champagne, Miss Brett,' he said, alarmed now at the whiteness of her face, 'I am sure it will help you to recover.'

But she continued to look at him with wide, blank eyes, her thoughts whirling. Thomas – of course, the likeness – and the name, why hadn't she remembered and guessed. And all the time he could have told her about Sebastian . . . but dared she ask now?

'Well, well, well,' said a drawling icy voice, 'if it isn't my beautiful stepmother! *Really*, Rob, it is most flattering the preference she shows for us de Lacey men. My father provided the wedding ring, I the caresses, and now I find *you* are the escort!'

There could only be one voice in the world like that, and even as she turned towards it, she reeled back, her lips silently forming his name. He seemed taller than ever and much thinner, with weather-beaten skin tightly stretched over cheekbones and temple. The once brilliant uniform was now faded and the gold braid tarnished, almost black in places. But he stood confidently enough, one hand holding a glass, the other resting negligently on the hilt of his dress sabre.

It should have been the most joyful reunion after all the months of anguish and yearning – a yearning which had been great enough to reach across hundreds of miles and make each aware of the other's needs.

But instead instant jealousy made all his old mistrust of her flare to obliterate all other feeling. And for her it was a moment of supreme disillusionment: instead of the Prince Charming which her starved heart had turned him into, here was the hateful voice, the curled-back lips of the man who had flung her nightgown at her as he uttered a last insult.

Vaguely they both heard the young Earl exclaim: 'Oh, I say, steady on, Sebastian, this is Miss Madeleine Brett.'

The heavy black brows rose in supercilious exaggeration. 'What! Does this mean that you do not use our name – the name you were so anxious to acquire? But then, perhaps you feel that a certain amount of anonymity is preferable while you are here, in the midst of the British Army?' A slight, insolent smile began to touch his mouth as his eyes ranged over her in a look which plainly indicated that he had full knowledge of her body.

Madeleine, who had felt like ice, now seemed to burst into flame. She flushed deeply as hot blood poured through every vein and she realized the full implication of his words. Without conscious thought or hesitation, the wrist which had been so adept at tossing beets and turnips into a farm cart now turned in the merest flick and tossed the glass of champagne into his face. 'How dare you?' she whispered through lips suddenly as thin as his own. 'How dare you look at me like that and insinuate that I am some kind of camp follower.'

For a few seconds Sebastian remained totally immobile while the champagne trickled slowly down his face. Then a dark red flush crept up his thin neck as with the utmost calmness he drew a handkerchief from his cuff and unhurriedly wiped away the liquid. 'Observe, Rob,' he said evenly, 'that we have here a lady of spirit as well as all her other attributes.'

'Nurse Brett, you will withdraw at once!' It was a new voice, speaking with controlled quietness, and all three turned to the speaker. Miss Nightingale stood just behind them, coldly furious. 'Go to the aide-de-camp on duty and request transportation back to the hospital,' she said, not raising her voice. 'I will make your apologies to the Ambassador and explain that you had a sudden indisposition. I shall expect you outside my office at six-thirty tomorrow morning, but meanwhile pack your bag. You will be leaving on the first ship for England, and until then are suspended from duty.'

It seemed to the onlookers that the four figures in the drama were frozen as though in a tableau, but then Madeleine seemed to shrink before their eyes and to blanch to such an extent that the delicate blue veins were clearly visible beneath her skin's surface. Her mouth opened to protest that so many patients were expecting her first thing in the morning, but instead she breathed: 'Very well, ma'am,' and began to turn away, when she realized that the young Earl was looking completely bewildered and distraught. She made a supreme effort: 'I am so sorry, my lord,' she said, her voice coming from a closed throat, 'that the evening should end like this before it has even begun . . . it was most kind of you to bring me, but if I had known your true identity, I could have spared you this embarrassment.'

Lord Wells jerked back into life. 'I will, of course, escort you back,' he said, but Madeleine shook her head.

'Please, I would prefer to go alone,' she said, already moving away.

The young man turned back to Miss Nightingale distractedly. 'But what about your rule that no nurse should travel alone?' he demanded.

Miss Nightingale, still maintaining her calm, said coldly, 'That hardly applies now that Nurse Brett has been suspended from duty and will be returning to England within the next few days.'

Sebastian, who had begun to see that he had made the most terrible mistake, now said urgently to his cousin, 'Rob, I beg that you will present me to Miss Nightingale,' and Lord Wells, now more agitated than ever, stammered, 'Oh, I do apologize, Miss Nightingale. But may I now present my cousin, Major Sebastian de Lacey of the Eleventh Hussars.'

Miss Nightingale held out her hand and allowed herself

to smile, if somewhat bleakly. A magnificent specimen, she thought objectively, but what an extremely strong and passionate nature!

Sebastian was saying, 'Miss Nightingale, I beg that you will not punish Miss Brett for this most unfortunate incident. It was entirely my fault, and, if you can, I ask you to forgive my behaviour and overlook Miss Brett's reaction to it.'

How very surprising, thought Miss Nightingale, before she replied, 'I do not know what caused your behaviour, Major de Lacey, and it is not my concern, but I am afraid I cannot overlook Nurse Brett's part.'

'But to send her home!' protested Sebastian, who realized that having found Madeleine at last, he was about to lose her again, perhaps for ever. His face twisted as though in pain and his eyes, which a few minutes before had been full of bitter mockery, were now focused upon Miss Nightingale in velvety earnestness.

He must be almost impossible to resist when he really tries, she thought even as she shrugged slightly. 'Nurse Brett has always been fully aware that gross misconduct means instant repatriation to England,' she said coldly.

Sebastian was by no means vanquished yet. 'But "gross misconduct",' he echoed, 'that is surely a very strong term. Do you really consider that throwing a glass of champagne over me comes within such a category?'

Miss Nightingale continued to stand absolutely still and looked fully at Sebastian, showing all the hidden steel in her nature. 'To throw wine over an officer holding the Queen's Commission in public *and* in the home of the Queen's representative? Why yes, I most certainly do consider that gross misconduct,' she said, still not raising her voice.

'But under extreme provocation?' he persisted, his voice as even as her own, but the hand holding his sword hilt was now clenched around it so tightly that the

301

knuckles were white. 'I suggest that any woman of spirit would have reacted in exactly the same way.'

'Yes, and it must be remembered that Nurse Brett must have been pretty tired after a long day's work,' interposed Lord Wells eagerly.

Miss Nightingale suddenly smiled enchantingly at them both. 'I cannot agree with you, gentlemen, but I do feel that Nurse Brett is lucky to have you both champion her cause. And now, if you will excuse me . . .' She had already turned away and there was nothing the two men could do except bow deeply to her retreating back.

As they straightened, Lord Wells said hurriedly, 'I think I'd better see – '

'Do that,' answered Sebastian curtly, while he tried to sort out his chaotic thoughts.

In a moment his cousin was back. 'She did not go to the duty ADC,' he said worriedly, 'but all the same, she appears to have vanished!'

The tiniest smile lit Sebastian's eyes. 'Yes,' he said, 'she's good at that.'

'I say,' began the Earl, 'did Uncle Henry really – '

'Yes, on his deathbed. He did it in the hope that we, as a family, would see to her future.'

Lord Wells began to feel that he would never get to the bottom of this tangle. He frowned, trying to look as fierce as his cousin. 'But did we?'

'No, she left us while Aunt Thea and Harriet were still with you after father's funeral. I had returned earlier to Bath, if you remember.' And inwardly he added bitterly, with the sole object of seducing the adventuress, but instead she enslaved me and I can't, I won't lose her again! 'I'm going after her, Rob,' he said aloud.

'Yes, let's,' replied his cousin, brightening instantly. 'I'll come with you, of course!'

'No!' It was barked out, like an order. 'We cannot both go – remember the C-in-C is here, and for one of us to

302

leave before him is damned bad form, but for us both to do so would be unforgivable. You, as head of the family, must stay. And besides,' he added grimly, 'it is I who have to beg Madeleine's forgiveness.'

Lord Wells, who had been brought up as the only boy among adoring sisters and who was entirely without Sebastian's sophistication, now asked of him urgently, 'But what shall I say to the Ambassador?'

'Oh, to hell with the pompous old ass!' retorted his cousin. 'Tell him anything.' And then left the young man to reflect that life with Sebastian must certainly be exciting, if somewhat nerve-racking.

Madeleine had rushed blindly from the Embassy, only pausing beneath one of the two lamps at the gateway. Her brain was quite numb and she had no idea how she was going to get back to the hospital, or even which direction she should take. But as she stood within the circle of light, four approaching artillerymen saw her and began to whistle appreciatively. Then, as they drew abreast of her, they all stopped and one boldly called out: 'Can we 'elp yer, miss?'

'Oh, yes please,' said Madeleine, moving forward to them, 'I must return to the Barrack Hospital, but I don't know the way.'

They recognized her uniform then, and the wide grins and telling glances ceased immediately. 'Ain't yer one of the Nightingale women?' asked one, and when Madeleine nodded, they said unanimously, 'Yer come wif us, miss. We'll git yer there safely!' And they did, too, right to the hospital entrance.

By then the ice encasing her brain had melted, and as she went slowly up the stairs to the nurses' quarters, little whimpering sobs escaped her. The artillerymen's respect had made her realize that she loved the rough, ill-used men of the Army, who were too often labelled as brutes

303

by their so-called betters and yet who were so stoical in the face of agony and unendurable hardship. And now she was to be sent away in disgrace! She thought of all the patients who would be waiting for her in the morning; of Catherine, who had done so much for her and to whom she could never explain; of Dr Kingsley, who had given her so much of his time – what would they all think of her? 'Yet I have done nothing really wrong,' she whispered to herself, 'only to toss the champagne at him, and that was because he was looking at me as though I did not have my clothes on. Why should I have had to endure his insults, which were not even true?'

In that moment her feelings for Sebastian changed completely. From the first she had been dazzled by his looks, his magnetism and his kisses; she had adored their baby, not only for himself, but because in some strange way he was also Sebastian, and she had lavished upon him all the tenderness of her nature. When Thomas died, the rosy dream in which she had enveloped his father continued, but now she saw him as he really was: a ruthless womanizer, a rakehell who cared for no one but himself. He had pursued her mercilessly, only to trick and use her. Because of him, her life had been shattered. Every time a pattern began to form, it broke, and now she was broken too. She would get on the ship, but she would never reach England, never again be at the mercy of people like the Sharpes, never again have to toil until she dropped for a mere pittance – no, it would be easier just to climb on to the ship's rail and then let herself fall forward. Her father and the General would never have believed it of her, but she could not go on. She whispered aloud, 'You must understand that I just *cannot* go on.'

The communal bedroom was in darkness, for which she was grateful, but instantly there were rustles from the various beds and then a gentle voice said, 'You are back early, dear child, did you not enjoy your evening?'

'Oh, sister, it was terrible,' Madeleine whispered, her voice breaking. 'And now Miss Nightingale has suspended me from duty and I am to be sent home.'

There was immediate consternation in the darkness. 'But why? How can it be so? What has happened?' they all demanded. She was a favourite with them and they had been happy to see her so excited when she set off. She tried to explain, but at that moment a series of thumps sounded on the door.

'Who is there?' called the eldest of the nuns.

'A 'ussar officer is downstairs wantin' ter see Nurse Brett,' came the loud response.

'We have retired; tell the officer to come back in the morning,' Sister Benedicta replied authoritatively.

'I can't do tha', ma'am. 'E's a major an' says 'e ain't goin' till 'e's seen Nurse Brett.'

'I will go down,' said Madeleine quietly. It was obvious that Sebastian had followed her and she knew with absolute certainty that he meant what he said.

'We will pray to Our Lady for you, dear child,' said Sister Benedicta, and as she left the room Madeleine once more heard a concerted rustle as the good sisters rose from their beds to kneel and pray for her. It was a wonderfully warm and comforting gesture to make and it helped to calm her as she walked soundlessly down the stairs, a lighted candle from the landing now in her hand.

The stairs led immediately into the room. She remained standing on the third step from the bottom, some instinct telling her that she might be less overwhelmed by Sebastian's presence if she were more his equal in height.

He was standing with his back to the room, looking out at the brilliant lights across the water at Constantinople. In the room's semi-darkness his caped figure looked enormously tall, even menacing, with the candlelight touching only the long-necked cavalry spurs and gold engraving on the scabbard protruding from the hem of his full-length cape.

Madeleine spoke at last. 'What is it that you want now, Major de Lacey?' she asked curtly.

He whirled instantly, with a jingle of spurs. His eyes, which had lit up the moment he heard her voice, now became opaque in his dark, tired face.

'I – I – I don't want anything,' he began quietly, and swore inwardly, God dammit, he was stammering like a schoolboy and all because she was standing there with her hair down her back, candle in hand, as she had been when she stepped into the library that night so long ago, just as he had dreamt of her so many, many times, except that now, although obviously in her nightgown, she was wearing a quilted robe buttoned from neck to hem.

'Then why have you come?' she asked coldly. Although she spoke very quietly, her anger was only too apparent, and instead of reacting in his normal arrogant way, he said almost humbly, 'Because I wanted to make sure that you had returned safely, and also to – '

She cut him short with a little tinkling laugh that was completely contemptuous. 'So kind of you,' she said, lips thinning to hardness, 'after you had humiliated and tormented me before a roomful of people.'

'Madeleine, listen – ' he began pleadingly, but again she interrupted.

'No, *you* listen! Ever since I had the misfortune to set eyes on you, you've treated me abominably – saying that I was some sort of – of harlot when there was not the slightest reason for this. The last thing in this world that I wanted to do was marry your father, and I only did so because he kept on insisting. I have never used your name and never ever will do so! I did not know of your cousin's identity before this evening, but if I had I certainly would not have accepted his invitation for, you see, I just cannot *stand* any of you de Laceys – not your poor young cousin, nor your sister, nor even the memory of your good, kind father – and it is all because of *you*, because *you've* spoilt everything for me: my first ball; this evening; and now I'm being sent home in disgrace from this work which I love, where I am useful, where I can help – and it is all *your* fault. Even – even another occasion when, because I had never known a man, I – thought people shared the deepest secrets of themselves because they loved each other, you lost no time in disillusioning me, did you? And just as brutally as only you could make it!' In spite of herself, she could not suppress a little sob, and his head, which had been bent under the furious torrent of accusations, was quickly raised.

'Madeleine, I *beg* of you – '

Her lip curled as his had so often done. 'Surely you were not about to ask my forgiveness, Major de Lacey? Please don't bother, but perhaps instead you will do me one great favour?'

He answered eagerly and at once. 'Anything,' he said, stepping forward.

If she had made one move, one gesture of forgiveness at that moment he would have knelt and kissed her feet, so deep and abject was his remorse. But instead she stepped back. 'Then get out of my life and stay out for ever!' she said, with her voice as near a snarl as it had ever been or would ever be again.

Women had been furious with Sebastian many times before. One had regularly hurled the nearest available object at him, and another was in the habit of raging for fifteen minutes or more in a nonstop flow of French that was far too idiomatic for him to follow. But always before he had emerged victorious, for his technique was infallible and never varied: when the woman was finally forced to pause for breath, he would scoop her up in his arms, silence her with kisses and take her to a bed from which they would emerge only after several hours. But

Madeleine's cold, utterly controlled contempt was something new, and for the first time in his life he did not know what to do. He stood before her, arms at his sides and head still half bent; in the dim light his face was carved in deep lines of grief, his eyes black with hurt. 'Is there nothing I can say or do to make you believe how deeply I regret everything that has happened?' he asked very quietly.

'Nothing.'

'Then I will, of course, accede to your – your demand, and try to see that we do not meet again.' He paused fractionally, and in a last unconscious appeal added, 'The way things are going, there is every chance that the Russian army will give you your wish.'

But it seemed too obvious a plea and she shrugged indifferently. 'That is a risk you must have known you would have to take,' she replied. 'Or did you hope that you would merely have to parade about in a brilliant uniform?'

That touched his honour and was something he would not accept. He drew himself upright and his head lifted proudly; he was, after all, the scion of a great warrior family and the fierce blood of his Norman ancestors still ran in his veins. 'You go too far, madam,' he said, his voice now as icy as hers. 'May I remind you that I hold the Queen's Commission? I should be honoured to die on any battlefield for my Queen, my country and my regiment.'

In an instant their roles were reversed, for with the resumption of his normal voice and manner, her façade of hate and bitterness disintegrated.

'Have I your permission to withdraw?' he asked, icily formal.

Madeleine put a trembling hand to her forehead. She felt completely disorientated, neither knowing what she had been saying nor whether any of it had been real.

'Yes, please go,' she whispered unsteadily, and he snapped to immediate attention, heels clicking, spurs jingling, sword upright against his leg and hand sweeping up in a parade-ground salute.

'Then I bid you goodbye, madam,' he said, and left her standing there, exhausted, bewildered and only conscious of a voice screaming within her head: Don't let him go! Not like this! Not in anger, when he is about to face terrible injuries, terrible mutilation, even death! Go after him, tell him you didn't mean it – that you wish him well.

She fought a short losing battle with her pride before beginning to run along the corridor, heedless of the now almost total darkness and not knowing what she would say, but only wanting to reach him before he left. If she had managed to catch up with him, there is little doubt that within seconds she would have been in his arms, held in his adoring embrace, with everything immediately forgiven and forgotten.

But she had left it too late, forgetting how quickly he could move, and when she reached the outer door there was nothing but the fading sound of Rollo's hoofbeats.

16

Like most cavalrymen, Sebastian was devoted to his horses and, since Balaclava, particularly to Rollo. Being detached from his regiment for special duty at the Scutari base two months previously had undoubtedly saved the horse's life, for during that time the other equine survivors of the charge had slowly died of starvation, while Rollo remained powerful and almost sleek.

At the best of times Sebastian saw nothing untoward in talking aloud to his horse and now, in a mixture of furious anger and desperate grief, he was not even aware of doing so. 'I've been a stupid, bloody fool,' he muttered as he untied Rollo's bridle and vaulted lightly into the saddle, 'bringing us both up here on this damned awful night, only to find that she's turned into a termagant – an absolute termagant – and to think I've been mooning over her all these months! I tell you, old boy, I've had a damned lucky escape.'

Yet by the time he was halfway down the hill his anger had cooled and he was muttering, 'It's true, everything she said is true, and I've behaved like the blackest of blackguards; what the devil was I thinking of – even tonight . . .'

When he had heard her name announced his head had jerked up and his heart suddenly pounded. Then he had seen his cousin, and within seconds he was slicing his way through the crowd, moving with all the speed and purpose of a panther stalking its prey. Mrs Doubley, who could never resist the exchange of a flirtatious smile, had pouted as Sebastian looked through her and even brushed past as though oblivious of her presence. But he had seen

Madeleine, seen that she was gazing up into the Earl's eyes as though mesmerized – yes, at his cousin! His own cousin, who was a mere boy! And what in hell could she be doing in Turkey if she were not under someone's protection, or seeking to be?

If he had paused to think for a moment, perhaps reason would have prevailed, but instead he had gone straight to her, jealousy and hurt blinding him. Yes, it was true he had spoilt it for her, just as he had spoilt her first ball; he remembered her as she had come tripping down the stairs in her home-made gown and his aunt's old pink velvet cloak, her cheeks delicately flushed and her eyes reflecting all the lights of the chandelier. She had blushed even more when he had handed her his bouquet of white roses for 'the heart that has never known love' he had said mockingly, determined not to believe that it was true. He remembered how, as they waltzed together, their steps had matched perfectly, and she had come softly, radiantly to life – until he had swung her out of the ballroom and begun kissing her brutally and crushing her breasts as he would a little street girl in some dark doorway. And the night in the library: it was true that he had returned early with one purpose in mind; that if she had not appeared he would have gone to her room; that he had plied her with brandy in order to lower her resistance and then, feeling suddenly trapped by her whispered declaration of love, had reacted with cruelty. What a bastard, he thought now, consumed by self-hate, what a total, bloody bastard . . . if anyone behaved like that to Harriet, I would have killed him; and yet I have done it to Madeleine, the gentlest, most tender, most adorable girl in the world. I should be horse-whipped, he told himself through gritted teeth, horse-whipped to within an inch of my miserable life!

It was fortunate that the camp was not nearer and that Rollo, left to his own devices, was only ambling slowly along, for by the time they did arrive, such highly coloured thoughts had faded and Sebastian was concentrating on how he could repair some of the damage he had inflicted on Madeleine. Good, faithful Sam was waiting patiently for him, and as he handed over his horse, Sebastian said tautly: 'At first light, Sam, I shall require you to take a letter to Miss Nightingale at the Barrack Hospital. Hand it to her personally and wait for her reply.' Then he retired to his tent, took a long swig of brandy and began to write in his bold hand:

Dear Miss Nightingale,

I am to return to Sebastopol in the morning, but I cannot depart before once more begging – no, imploring – you to reconsider your decision regarding Madeleine Brett.

Relations between Miss Brett and myself have always been difficult. I will not bore you with the details, but only say that everything has been due entirely to my own intransigence and misunderstanding of her character. This evening was a typical example of my execrable behaviour, and I feel sure that my sister and my cousins would have reacted in much the same way as Miss Brett, were they to be faced with unwarranted provocation. Furthermore, whether Miss Brett chooses to use my name or not, she remains my kinswoman by marriage, and, as you will perhaps know, we are a family with a history of almost eight hundred years of service to our country. During the whole of that time, I cannot recall any de Lacey being sent from any battlefield or campaign in disgrace and, therefore, for the sake not only of Miss Brett but of the honour of my house, I beg you to allow her to remain here.

In addition, as a veteran of the Alma, Balaclava and Inkerman, I know that the one thing a soldier longs for when he leaves the battlefield is the sight and smile of a pretty, gentle young woman. I know, too, that you are few in number here and of the heroic work you have all done; I now venture to ask if it is really fair to withdraw even one of your nurses in the present circumstances, especially as Madeleine Brett must surely be one of the gentlest, most tender-hearted and, I am persuaded, the most excellent of nurses.

I am sending this note by my servant, Samuel Wilkes, and I

would esteem it the very greatest favour if you would allow him to return with your decision.

I have the honour to be, dear Miss Nightingale,

Your most obedient servant,

Sebastian de Lacey

Miss Nightingale knew all about relationships between men and women: she had adored dancing and socializing in her extreme youth and had always acquired more than her fair share of admirers. She therefore recognized at once from Sebastian's letter that he was in love with Madeleine and she was smiling faintly when she called the younger woman into her office.

'Good morning, Nurse Brett,' she said quietly. 'You may sit down.'

'Thank you, ma'am,' Madeleine answered, her voice low and steady.

'Now,' continued Miss Nightingale in a slightly more brisk tone, 'I believe you owe me an explanation.' Silently she observed that the girl looked wraith-like in the cold early morning light, but when she raised her eyes their gaze was calm and level.

'An explanation, ma'am?' she queried, trying to focus her tired brain.

'Yes. I am surprised that neither you nor Miss Llewellyn Morgan thought fit to tell me that you had been married.'

Madeleine's brow cleared and some life returned to her white face. 'Oh, Miss Llewellyn Morgan knew nothing about it, ma'am, and I – I keep forgetting that it ever happened! You see, it was not a real marriage, and I only agreed to it because General de Lacey was dying and was so anxious about my future. My father had left me in the General's care and he thought if I became one of the family I should be looked after.'

313

'Yet you have never used their name?'

'No, ma'am,' said Madeleine, and Miss Nightingale, watching her closely, saw her soft lips close with unusual firmness.

'May I ask why you do not?' she queried. Again the level gaze, which she had always found so attractive, held her own.

'Because my father's is a perfectly good and honourable name and I prefer to make my way alone.'

H'm, thought Miss Nightingale, only half an explanation, but I doubt whether I shall get more out of her. Aloud, she said, 'I have this morning received a letter from Major de Lacey in which he accepts full responsibility for yesterday evening's most unfortunate incident and begs me not to send you home.'

The grey eyes lit up then. 'A letter, ma'am?' It was just breathed, as though her throat had suddenly become very dry.

'Yes, you may read it if you wish,' said Miss Nightingale, taking pity on her and handing over the letter. She saw Madeleine take it in trembling hands and begin avidly to read. Then, as though not able to concentrate or believe what was written, she began silently to mouth the words, while a delicate flush crept slowly up her thin cheeks. She took a long time to read the letter through and then immediately began again. Miss Nightingale sighed inwardly: she had a thousand things to attend to and enough writing to keep her sitting at the plain deal table until the early hours of the following morning, but she remained absolutely still, her hands lightly clasped and resting on the table.

When at last Madeleine had read through the whole letter twice, she looked up, suddenly radiant. So she *is* in love with him, thought Miss Nightingale, but in the eyes of the law she is his stepmother and therefore marriage between them would be out of the question. Keeping her voice quiet and impersonal, she said, 'In view of Major de Lacey's plea, I have decided to overlook your part in the incident and therefore your return to England is cancelled.'

'Oh thank you, ma'am, thank you,' Madeleine stammered, blinking rapidly to keep the tears in check.

'However, should there be another such incident, I must warn you that no persuasion in the world would make me alter my mind a second time,' Miss Nightingale said, allowing some of the steel to show. But then, before Madeleine could answer, she softened and her tone became almost conversational. 'The de Laceys are an interesting family, are they not? I am very well acquainted with the Earl's elder sister who is married to the Duke of Wessex, for I was presented at Court at the same time, but I know nothing about Major de Lacey's side of the family – is it a large one?'

'Why no, ma'am. There is only his sister Harriet, who married earlier this year and, I believe, is now in India, and an aged aunt, Lady Frensham.'

'The Major is not married then?' The tone was very casual now.

'No – not yet, but I – I understand he is expected to marry Miss Llewellyn Morgan,' said Madeleine, lured into a rare confidence.

Miss Nightingale's delicate brows rose very slightly. 'Indeed? How very interesting.' Her tone reverted to briskness: 'And now, I suggest you return to duty, Nurse Brett.'

'Yes, ma'am. And – thank you, I am very grateful,' Madeleine said shyly, and was rewarded by Miss Nightingale's full and most charming smile. But when she was once more alone, Miss Nightingale sat silently for a few moments. Then she sighed and picked up Sebastian's letter.

'A pity,' she murmured, 'such a pity,' and deliberately

tore the letter twice before letting it fall into the box at her feet.

Sebastian was watching Rollo being lifted on board ship when he heard his name called, and turned to see a figure limping painfully but hurriedly towards him. 'Winstanley!' he exclaimed, striding forward, hand outstretched. 'How are you? I had no idea you were down here!'

Captain Winstanley appeared reluctant to let go of Sebastian's hand. 'I am so glad you are alive!' he said impulsively, his thin face creasing in a boyish smile.

Sebastian withdrew his hand. 'Decent of you,' he said, his voice suddenly very clipped.

The younger man shot him a keen glance from beneath fair brows. 'Oh, not so much for your own sake, old boy, but for that beautiful girl who has been grieving for you. She asked me for news of you, you know, and I – I had to tell her that I thought you'd not survived Balaclava. She was so wonderful – didn't have the vapours or hysterics, but just thanked me very quietly for telling her, yet I could see that she was absolutely stricken, and she's looked heartbroken ever since. She must have been overjoyed to see you, you lucky dog!'

'What the devil are you talking about?' demanded Sebastian, and Captain Winstanley looked at him in amazement.

'Dammit, man, there's no need to be so bloody coy about her – you must know that there's not a fellow in the Army who would not envy you! But now, we'd better get on board; I take it you are for England, Home and Beauty, too?'

Sebastian shook his head. 'No, I'm going in the other direction, back to Balaclava.'

'*Back* to Balaclava?' echoed his friend. 'Where the hell have you been up till now then?'

'Here, for the past two months,' said Sebastian, and watched instant anger suffuse the other man's face.

'You've been here two months and you've not contacted her, seen her or written to her?' demanded Captain Winstanley incredulously.

'I am not prepared to undergo an inquisition and I'll thank you to restrain your curiosity in my affairs!' retorted Sebastian icily, but the lines of stress deepened around his eyes and mouth.

Well, of all the damnable fellows, thought Richard Winstanley. He just does not deserve her. He would have been amazed if he had known that Sebastian was thinking much the same about himself. Richard Winstanley drew himself up. 'I beg your pardon, de Lacey,' he said stiffly, and turned away. But after a few steps he paused and then came painfully back to Sebastian. 'Perhaps you do not realize what a wonderful job she is doing and how remarkable it is that she, a gentlewoman, *can* do it – I tell you, I've seen her rise from scrubbing a floor only to find the whole of her sack-cloth apron covered with lice; I've seen troops beg her not to come near them because they were not only verminous, but awash in their own filth, and yet she has knelt beside them, removed their filthy rags and cleaned the most revolting, most horrific of wounds, while maintaining the most gentle, most sweet manner.'

'I see that you are more than a little infatuated with the lady,' said Sebastian, his voice only slightly less icy, while Richard Winstanley now looked at him with positive dislike.

It is true then, he thought, that de Lacey is kinder to his horses than to his women. Aloud he said, 'I assure you, de Lacey, that there is not a man in the hospital – patient or staff – who does not admire Nurse Brett. Of course, Miss Nightingale is magnificent and an example to all, but while she is known as "The Angel", Nurse

317

Brett is called "The Little Angel", and no one could be more deserving of such a tribute.'

A sergeant bustled up and saluted Captain Winstanley. 'Will you board now, please, sir,' he said officiously, and as the young officer nodded and prepared to leave, he was astonished to find Sebastian holding out his hand and saying affably, 'Thanks very much for trying to help Madeleine; I did not know she was here, and if I had, I would not have believed her to be upset over my fate.'

It was only when he was on board the ship bound for Balaclava and standing at the rail that the full impact of Richard Winstanley's words hit him. Madeleine had grieved for him, been 'stricken' and 'heartbroken' to believe him dead. His own heart lifted then; she had not meant what she said the previous night! Of course not! She was as hurt as he had been and it was because – it was because she loved him as much as he did her. The knowledge, which had lain in his subconscious for so long, was at last admitted: they loved each other.

We shall be together; nothing will keep us apart, he vowed silently, eyes never leaving the great square mass of the Barrack Hospital as the ship slowly glided past beneath it. Of course it was damnable that, having spent the last two months at the base agitating to get back to the Brigade, he should be doing so on the very morning after he had found her. His clenched fist thumped the rail in angry frustration: to think he had been within a couple of miles of her for two whole months and had not known! But I'll get back, he thought determinedly. Somehow, I'll get back.

But in this he was mistaken. He returned to a Balaclava which had become a hell of filth and cholera, its bay a nightmare of amputated arms and legs still clad in their uniforms, of bodies suddenly rising from the sea bed, and of ships' cables and anchors entangled with limbs.

As he disembarked, a never-ending procession of starving mules was slipping and sliding in the mud towards the harbour, bearing on their backs skeletal figures, dressed or half dressed in rags, with hideous wounds and bloodless faces, their only sign of life the thin stream of breath emanating from their gaping mouths and rising in the still, icy air. As each living skeleton was strapped to its animal, there was no possibility of attention to natural functions, and it was all too obvious that many were suffering from dysentery. The stench arising from so much suffering humanity, combined with that from the loathsome bay, was utterly appalling. Sebastian felt nausea rise in his throat, and it needed all his willpower not to cover his nose. But, horrified beyond words though he was, his first coherent thought was for Madeleine. Those who survived the sea crossing would be in an even more terrible state than now, so how could any woman – no matter how angelic – bear to go near them? Yet he knew that she would do everything humanly possible for these men and, in fact, had been doing so ever since her arrival.

It was this knowledge which brought Sebastian's love for her to its full flowering. At first he had merely desired her, then he had admitted that he loved her, but now he realized that he *cared* about her – desperately, passionately – and was almost distraught at the thought of what effect so much suffering would have upon her. Besides, she was a delicate woman; how could her physical health bear up in such a situation, day after day? Of course, in his almost frenzied anxiety he gave no thought to Miss Nightingale or the other nurses, but pictured Madeleine, his slender, gentle angel, as having to bear the whole burden. I should be there, he raged inwardly, I should be there so that I could watch over her, try to shield her. But how could he, with all his love and strength, keep her from the many fevers for which the Barrack Hospital was now infamous? The realization that she could so easily

319

succumb to one of these was yet another reason for driving him very nearly frantic.

To add to his misery, when he rode into the Cavalry camp it was to find that the survivors were enduring unimaginable hardships. Without fuel, almost without food, they had only tents to protect them against the roaring gales and great storms of sleet and snow sweeping down on them from the Ukraine. Their horses had even less: they stood knee-deep in mud, without shelter of any kind, and their ration for a day was one handful of barley per horse. They ate everything else – saddle-flaps, straps, and each other's tails until these were down to stumps. All Sebastian's ingenuity was to be engaged in the fight for survival, not only for himself, but for Sam and Rollo. He just managed because Sam, being a civilian servant, was free to ride the six miles to Balaclava and bring up forage and some scanty supplies, but even though all three got through the terrible winter they, like all the others who survived, were reduced to emaciated shadows of their former selves.

By January there were more men in hospital than those encamped outside Sebastopol, while at the Barrack Hospital an epidemic of fever had broken out. Four surgeons died in three weeks, together with three of the nurses. But Madeleine, the slenderest, most delicate, was not among them. She had gone through the whole gamut of emotions since Sebastian's departure, alternating between depths of despair over her cruel words to him and the heights of happiness when she recalled what he had written about her. Every day when a new batch of casualties arrived, she would go to the reception area and scrutinize the gaunt, bearded faces. Every time she left without having found him, she breathed a prayer of relief and thankfulness.

Then, quite suddenly, things began to improve. At

Sebastopol the snowstorms ended and the faintest hint of warmth came to that bleakest of plateaux; while at Scutari, the Sanitary Commission, which had arrived from England early in March, was doing tremendous work. They had found that the entire building stood on open sewers which were choked and overflowing, hence the stench which emanated through the porous plaster of the walls and was wafted on the slightest breeze through wards and corridors filled with patients. The Commission also found that the water supply was not only totally inadequate but horrifically contaminated, with most of it filtering through the carcase of a dead horse. Immediately orders were given for the clearing and cleansing of the sewers, for all interior walls to be lime-washed, and for the removal of the wooden planks – the so-called divans – on which many patients had to sleep. With the planks went the notorious vermin.

Nor was this all, for early in March came Alexis Soyer, the Reform Club's famous chef. He at once set about devising splendid stews, broths and soups from Army rations. He campaigned for soldiers to be trained as cooks, perfected ovens to bake bread and had a teapot which kept tea hot for fifty men.

All this, together with the crisp air of early morning and the sun-filled days of spring, had an instant effect upon the morale of patients and staff alike. But not even this lessening of the horrors could ease the total exhaustion felt by the doctors and nurses. They had all worked heroically – 'like lions', in Miss Nightingale's words, but now they had nothing more to give.

Dr Fraser, the young medical officer with whom Madeleine had worked closely throughout, had been watching her anxiously for weeks. He now told her that she must take more time off and go out into the fresh air. When she wanted to know where she should go, since the hospital was surrounded by a huge Turkish cemetery and the depot filled with booths and stalls, he asked her if she rode. Her assent and the involuntary brightening of her face were enough to send him straight to Miss Nightingale: would she permit him to escort Nurse Brett on a daily ride?

Surprisingly, she did agree, but Madeleine remained strangely reluctant, putting forward the excuse that she had no riding habit. Within an hour Miss Nightingale had written to the Ambassadress with a plea for the loan or donation of a habit to fit an extremely slender girl. Later that day a selection arrived, and so Madeleine was kitted out with cloth trousers, which were strapped under her boots and worn beneath a long, almost ground-length skirt. A tight-fitting jacket and a pert little cavalier hat with a dark green plume completed the outfit. Alastair Fraser, seeing her for the first time without the hideous uniform, could hardly take his eyes off her. His admiration increased when he saw how well she rode, although she protested it was years since she had ridden.

From the first, the expeditions were a success. Dr Fraser, already more than half in love with her, did everything he could to entertain and amuse her, and she responded without realizing what it all meant. She just knew that she was happy to be out in the wonderful sparkling air and away from all the responsibility and sadness.

The doctor next suggested an expedition to explore Constantinople; again Miss Nightingale gave permission, and again Madeleine appeared reluctant.

'I am afraid,' she finally whispered to Miss Nightingale, who immediately understood, but chose deliberately not to let her youngest nurse know this.

'I cannot see why,' she said crisply. 'Dr Fraser is a civilized young man and I am sure will take great care of you.'

'Oh, it is not that at all,' Madeleine said in distress. She longed to confide in the older woman, but dared not overstep the bounds of their professional relationship.

'Well,' said Miss Nightingale, 'it has to be your decision.' As she watched Madeleine walk slowly to the door she thought, of course she is afraid that the magnificent de Lacey will suddenly rise up in front of her and cause another drama. But although she loves him, obviously nothing can come of it, so the friendship with Alastair Fraser should be encouraged. Madeleine was almost out of the room when Miss Nightingale suddenly said, 'Oh, by the way, I have it on the very best authority that Major de Lacey and his cousin are both encamped with their regiments before Sebastopol and, barring wounds or sickness, neither is expected here in the immediate future.' The eyes of the two young women met then and they smiled, understanding each other perfectly.

'Thank you, ma'am,' breathed Madeleine.

So she and Alastair set off to explore the ancient, exotic city, and both were in high spirits. Just like a couple of bairns let off from school, Alastair thought, and no wonder, for the burden of suffering and tragedy had been intolerable. But looking down at Madeleine now, he knew he would not have missed a moment of it, for then he would not have met this delightful girl who had fascinated him from the very beginning. She was now wearing the awful gown, but at least Miss Nightingale had let her wear her grey and white bonnet instead of the cap, and Alastair thought that her small face, thin and exhausted though it was, still managed to look enchanting. He offered her his arm and unconsciously began to walk proudly when he felt her hand slide into the crook of his elbow.

Madeleine stole a shy glance at him: at six feet he was three inches shorter than Sebastian and built on far less massive lines, but his broad-shouldered figure looked elegant and strong in the medical service uniform of dark blue frock-coat with brass buttons and small peaked cap.

Madeleine considered that, with his dark red hair, deep blue eyes and ruddy complexion, he wore the uniform exceedingly well and made a handsome figure. His face, too, with its strong, straight features, gave the impression of calmness and resolution. Having now worked with him a great deal, she knew that he was a brilliant surgeon who regarded his patients with great compassion and care.

She realized that he admired her greatly, but she shied away from the thought of anything deeper and tried to keep their friendship on a casual basis. Nevertheless, it was a time for exchanging confidences, and she learned that he came of a large family in which there was always much laughter, with leisure spent in songs around the piano and games of sardines, charades and theatricals in which everyone joined. Like so many Scots, all the sons were eager to explore the world: there was one brother in Canada, another in South Africa.

'But,' said Alastair, 'it is India which fascinates me, and I mean to go there as soon as this campaign is over.' He smiled at Madeleine, eyes crinkling. 'That's one of the good things about being a doctor: we are always in demand, and I am told that if I apply to John Company for a medical post, I might even be sent to India straight from here, even though the normal procedure is for an applicant to go before a board in London.' He paused for a moment, then said very casually, 'Have you ever wanted to travel the world, Miss Madeleine?'

'Oh – I don't believe I've ever thought about it,' Madeleine replied.

Skilfully, he began to draw her out about her own background and was astonished to find how solitary, how devoid of fun and laughter her life had been. She had never been to any kind of family party and only ever to one ball. He thought how delightfully she would blossom in the warm kindliness of his parents and sisters – and did not see how shadowed her eyes became when she mentioned her stay at Bath.

Early in May Miss Nightingale left to visit the two hospitals at Balaclava, of which she had received disturbing reports. At the last minute Madeleine, after much inner debating, could not refrain from saying, 'If you should meet any ex-patients or – or acquaintances of mine near Sebastopol, ma'am, would you please give them my very best wishes?'

'Naturally,' Miss Nightingale said crisply. So she has not forgotten him, she thought, but then it would be extremely difficult to forget such a man. Aloud she said to Alastair, 'Nurse Brett looks much improved since you have been taking her on these little expeditions, so you have my permission to continue, as I have no doubt that you will care for her and be ever mindful of her reputation.'

'Absolutely, Miss Nightingale, you have my most solemn word on that,' replied the delighted young man, looking her straight in the eye.

In the Cavalry camp, Sebastian thought, thank God, now I shall be able to get first-hand news of Madeleine.

But once again he was to be mistaken, for although Miss Nightingale came to Sebastopol, she was surrounded by a large company of staff. Like other officers and men, Sebastian went forward to cheer her and was just able to catch a glimpse of her, but that was sufficient to send his fears soaring, for he would not have recognized her as the handsome woman he had met at the Embassy barely five months previously. And if she could look so desperately ill, what about Madeleine? Two days later Miss Nightingale collapsed with Crimean fever and hovered between life and death. At Balaclava the Army appeared to be already in mourning, and at the Barrack Hospital patients were seen to cry openly.

* * *

Madeleine was more than ever grateful for Alastair Fraser's company, especially as the nuns had returned home. On leaving they had all been in tears and had hugged her in turn. At the last moment Sister Benedicta had given her a small coloured print of the Sacred Heart, to whom, she said, they were commending Madeleine for protection, worship and imitation. 'And remember, dearest child,' added the Sister earnestly, 'that at all times and especially in crises, pray to Our Lady, the Mother of God. She *always* hears and Her help is *always* given.' Sister Benedicta looked deeply into the younger woman's shadowed eyes and then went on: 'Sometimes God demands sacrifices of us which we do not understand, but if we believe that we are in His loving hands and accept His will, nothing can harm us . . .'

Madeleine was to remember these words in the very near future, for on 18 June the allies launched an unsuccessful assault on Sebastopol and once again the casualties began to arrive. 'Were the Cavalry involved?' she asked at once, and felt an immediate lightening of spirit when the reply came, 'No, ma'am, they were only on stand-to.'

But five days later when she was in the reception area and surrounded by stretchers of newly arrived wounded, she suddenly heard her name called. Puzzled, she turned in the direction of the voice and saw someone beckon from across the room. As she approached and recognized him, her heart and brain seemed to freeze, for it was Sam, standing sentinel-like over a stretcher at his feet. He was looking at her with imploring, panic-stricken eyes. 'Miss Brett – aw, thank God, us have found you, farr the Major, he be hurt reel bad. Can you help 'im?'

Madeleine dropped to her knees beside the still figure and forced herself to look at him. The sunken, stubble-covered cheeks, large nose and matted black hair bore no resemblance to the strong, handsome features she remembered so well. But then she saw how tightly the black lashes curled against the bloodless skin and she began to scream inwardly, for this was just how Thomas had looked as he lay dead in her arms. Hardly aware of what she was doing, she undid the dirty blood-stained cape to take his hand and put her fingers against the thin wrist, but she could find no pulse. He's dead! Sebastian's dead! the voice screamed within her, and she clasped his hand in both of hers and held it unknowingly against her breast as she bent over him in total grief. Afterwards she was never completely sure whether she had imagined it or not, but at that moment she thought she saw his mouth, which was drawn into one long line of pain, move very slightly so that the lips just parted to let the faintest sigh escape them.

It was enough to galvanize her into action. She saw that he wore no jacket or shirt beneath the cape and that a rough bandage of the new, recently issued field dressing had been inexpertly wound across his lower chest where, on the left side, the bandage was soaked in blood. Nor was that all, for the left trouser leg of his uniform had been slit because of another blood-soaked bandage around the knee joint, while lower down his leg the sharp pointed end of the broken shinbone protruded through the skin. With her brain still encased in ice, she unwound the bandage around his knee to expose the bullet hole on the inner side. The wound was oozing, with the skin around it fiery red, but when Madeleine bent still further, she could detect no whiff of the deadly gangrenous odour. Yet she knew that within a few hours the wound could become terribly infected, and meanwhile Sebastian had obviously lost a great deal of blood. She jumped to her feet and began searching the huge room for Alastair, but unfortunately it was Dr Lawson who approached and Madeleine's heart sank.

Dr Lawson had been principal medical officer at Bala-clava until Lord Raglan recommended he be relieved of his duties because of his neglect in the care and welfare of the wounded – with the result that he was promptly appointed senior medical officer at the Barrack Hospital! In addition to his apathy as a doctor, he was a harsh man and no friend of Miss Nightingale. He took one brief look at Sebastian's leg wound and said as he moved to pass on, 'Prepare for amputation above the patella.'

'No!' It was one of those rare moments when speech is involuntary and without conscious thought. Yet her voice rang out clearly and decisively.

Dr Lawson turned very slowly, hands behind his back, and his eyes swept over her contemptuously from head to foot. 'No?' he queried silkily. 'Am I to understand from that remark that you are daring to question my judgement?'

'Why no, sir, of course not,' stammered Madeleine desperately. 'But I – I just thought that as there appears to be no gangrene at present, we could wait.'

'*You* "just thought that *we* could wait" – you, a glorified ward servant.' He was coldly furious, yet she felt that at the same time delighted to be given this opportunity of getting at Miss Nightingale through herself. 'I shall report you to that woman who is deputizing for Miss Nightingale,' he said, 'and demand that you be suspended from duty!'

As Madeleine gazed at him, silent and agonized, another voice spoke from the other side of the stretcher. 'Sir,' said Alastair Fraser calmly, 'I see that there is no splintering of the bone and I would be prepared to delay amputation, for if gangrene does not develop, I consider there may be a chance of the bone uniting.'

'How dare you, sir?' demanded Dr Lawson furiously. He looked from one to the other. 'I can see that I am surrounded by a crowd of fools and incompetents. And I will not have my professional judgement queried in this disgraceful manner.' He turned and bellowed: 'Orderly!'

and as an elderly, scared-looking man approached, Dr Lawson said curtly, 'Prepare this man for amputation of the left leg above the patella!'

Mother of God, implored Madeleine, Mother of God . . . and heard her own voice say quietly, 'You will do no such thing, for I am Major de Lacey's kinswoman and I do not give my permission for the operation.'

All three men stared at her in amazement and then Dr Lawson said sneeringly, '*You* his kinswoman! And who is this major, anyway?'

Madeleine's chin lifted in the old proud way. 'He is a cousin of the Earl of Wells, who is serving with the Grenadier Guards at Sebastopol,' she said, looking straight into the doctor's eyes. 'It should not be too difficult to obtain his confirmation of all this. Or, if you prefer, from Lord Raglan himself, for as a son of the Duke of Beaufort, he must be very well acquainted with the de Lacey family!'

Dr Lawson, although clearly astonished, made an effort to salvage his dignity. 'Very well,' he said, drawing himself up and speaking with what he considered impressive professional calm, 'I shall leave this patient to your – er – devices, but when he dies a full report will be sent to the chief of medical staff, with copies to Lord Raglan and Miss Nightingale!'

'Is it really true?' whispered Alastair when his senior was out of earshot.

'Yes, quite true,' Madeleine said, beginning to tremble now. 'Oh, Dr Fraser, has he a chance, do you think?'

'A chance, yes. But that's all. Let's get him into a ward where we can have a good look at all the wounds.'

The bullet which had inflicted the knee injury was found to have passed through the outside of the joint, but the other bullet in Sebastian's chest, although its passage had been stopped by a rib bone, needed to be extracted. Alastair Fraser, using a long, ivory-tipped extractor, gently probed until he found the bullet, and Sebastian moaned softly as the pincers closed around bullet and tissue alike.

'Must get it out before he really comes to,' murmured Alastair. 'The rib bone is broken and he'll always have pain from it, but my guess is that it will be the least of his troubles. Ah, it's coming now, I think.' A moment later and the bullet was out. Alastair looked carefully at the wound, his face closed in frowning concentration. 'Yes,' he said at last, 'that's all I can do to that one. Clean it, nurse, and bandage it. Now, the other bullet passed the condyle of the femur and out close to the head of the fibula. *If* the infection remains localized, this could heal well and not affect the joint too adversely, but this fracture . . .'

Later that day Sebastian's chances appeared to be diminishing for his temperature soared and by nightfall he was in a high fever and delirious. Frantically Madeleine kept sponging his body, which for a few seconds made his skin cool to her touch, but then with terrifying rapidity it would once more become burning and dry. Towards midnight, when she undid the bandages, she saw that the skin around both wounds was a deeper shade of red and was also puffy at the edges. As she reached for the charpie – the teased grey threads which were used for both packing and cleaning wounds – Sister Benedicta's words seemed to echo in her head: '. . . *especially in crises, pray* . . .', and without fully realizing what she was doing, Madeleine clasped her hands together and, oblivious of Sam standing faithfully beside her, murmured softly, 'Mother of God, I beg, I implore you to save him. You know what he means to me and how I loved our son. Please let the sacrifice of *him* be sufficient – please, please, I won't ask for anything else, if you'll just let Sebastian live and if you'll help me to do the right thing. Please, please, *please*. Take my life in exchange for his if you wish, but help me, for I have no one else but you.' The tears fell, but she was not aware of them until she heard Sam's small, smothered sob, and she turned to him apologetically. 'I don't know what else to do, Sam,' she said brokenly.

'You has done your best, miss. Can't do more,' replied Sam, already quite resigned. But it was the sound of his soft West Country accent which instantly triggered a memory: Mam's pot of herbs and the earnest look in her blue eyes as she said, '*Keep it in case someone special be hurt.*'

Madeleine leapt to her feet. 'Stay here, Sam,' she said urgently. 'If the orderly wakes, tell him I'll be back in a few minutes.' Hope lent speed to her tired limbs as she rushed along the endless corridors and up the stairs to the nurses' quarters. Her new companions were asleep and the room was in total darkness, but Madeleine found her carpetbag at once and her hands delved down, tossing aside underwear in frantic haste – ah, there it was, still covered, still upright. Her hands closed tightly around the pottery bowl and once more she was running, just as she had run with the jug of milk for Thomas so long ago . . . It seemed to take ages to prise off the lid, which had been sealed with hot wax, and then when she looked at the thick greyish mass within, she had a moment of terrifying doubt: supposing it had turned 'bad' – supposing she was about to do irrevocable harm by applying it, supposing . . . Sebastian's arms suddenly began to thrash and his body to move in an effort to toss and turn, while his nonstop muttering took on a deeper tone. Madeleine began to apply the soft thick cream, which smelled of everything and of nothing.

Thank God, she thought as she rebandaged the wounds, that at long last there was no shortage of bandages; thank God, too, that she had sent Sam earlier in the day to buy a huge bag of oranges and lemons; he

331

had spent much time squeezing these into a pottery jug. Now she and Sam settled down to their long night vigil: he sleepless and silent, but watching intently as she frequently sponged Sebastian's ever moving body or raised his head in the crook of her arm to pour juice between his cracked lips. He drank avidly, and it was the only time his muttering ceased.

But dawn brought no change in his condition. As Madeleine undid the dressings she realized that she was hoping, even expecting, a miracle, but the skin around the wounds remained the same. She could only smooth on more of Mam's concoction and apply a fresh dressing. It was a routine which she was to continue throughout that day. Between her other duties she would rush back to Sebastian, and all the while Sam remained seated on the three-legged stool she had found for him. He told her that Sebastian had volunteered for a dangerous secret mission and had returned to the Cavalry camp wounded, lying across Rollo's back. 'Get me to Scutari,' he had whispered to Sam before losing consciousness, and the faithful servant had rushed about, demanding a place for his master in one of the new ambulance wagons which had recently appeared in the Crimea. Eventually Sebastian had been put into the rear compartment of an ambulance and conveyed to Balaclava, Sam mounted on Rollo and riding beside the six mules drawing the wagon. ''Twere the speed wha' saved him,' Sam told Madeleine, and they both looked silently at the prone body, wondering if all the effort was to be in vain.

As the second night's vigil began, Madeleine, who had been on duty nonstop and with only a few cups of broth for sustenance, felt only despair. The following morning the ward was to be inspected by Dr Lawson, who, she was sure, would then demand amputation and could she, in all conscience, delay it any longer? There was no doubt that both the leg wounds were locally infected and that

Sebastian's strength was being drained; even now surgery might be too late, but if it were not, would he ever accept permanent disability? He was a brilliant horseman, a consummate dancer, and at all times he was used to moving with tremendous speed and lightness. She remembered how he had leapt up the stairs, carrying her in his arms, on that first evening in Bath; how would he feel if he could only ever take one stair at a time, never dance or ride again, and not even stay in the Army? The answer came at once: he would hate it, would find life a misery, and therefore perhaps it would be best . . .? She shook her head, swallowing her tears. How stupid to think like that! Life could always be worth living, and this war had caused thousands of men to suffer even greater handicaps than the loss of a leg.

Throughout that night she continued sponging him, giving him liquid and renewing Mam's cream. For the first time since Miss Nightingale's illness, she was glad her chief was not in the hospital for if, on her nightly rounds, she had seen Madeleine was still on duty, she would undoubtedly have ordered her to bed. But Miss Nightingale was still away convalescing and her deputy, not possessing her chief's superhuman energy or willpower, had no strength left for nightly rounds.

The orderly, who had his own bed on the ward, was snoring, as were many of the other patients, when just before dawn Madeleine slid off the stool on to the floor and, with her head resting on her arm against the side of the bed, slept.

She awoke with a start, stiff in every limb and wondering dazedly where she was. Early morning light was filtering through the long windows, while outside the birds were in full song. But there was no sound from Sebastian, no muttering or movement, and with a rush of terror Madeleine raised her head to look straight into his eyes. He blinked, and the terror receded. On her knees she

333

moved closer to him, her hand going to his forehead. His skin felt cool and slightly damp, but she touched his throat, chest and hand before daring to believe that all trace of fever had left him.

'Sebastian,' she whispered, breathless joy suddenly overwhelming her. His own lips moved then, but no sound came, and she reached quickly for the cup, raised his head and put the rim to his lips. Sebastian, light-headed and in great pain, only knew that the most exquisite nectar was pouring down his throat and that his head was being pillowed on softness. When at last his thirst was quenched he felt the butterfly touch of her hands and knew that it was Madeleine who was with him. As the heavy lids closed over his eyes, he sighed content-edly and, like his son before him, turned his head into the curve of her breast and slept.

Dr Lawson made no comment and hardly glanced at the wounds which Madeleine had exposed for him, but Alastair Fraser could not restrain his enthusiasm. 'I think this is quite remarkable,' he exclaimed as he followed in Dr Lawson's wake. 'Well done, Nurse Brett!' He glanced up quickly to smile at her, then immediately looked at her again, searchingly, 'How long is it since you slept?' he asked quietly.

'Why, last night, sir,' said Madeleine. It was not entirely untrue, she told herself, for she had slept beside Sebastian's bed for almost an hour.

But Alastair was a man in love and not to be fooled. 'As soon as your duty ends, nurse, you must have proper rest. Your patient is out of immediate danger now, and if you exhaust yourself completely you may miss some vital symptom, either in Major de Lacey or one of the other patients. Remember now, this is an order!'

'Yes, sir, thank you, sir,' Madeleine said demurely, but could not suppress the tiniest smile touching her eyes. Alastair grinned back, fondness making him forget momentarily that they were both on duty. The look was instantly noted by watching patients, and within minutes the word had been passed around that Dr Fraser was 'sweet' on the Little Angel.

Madeleine only partially obeyed Alastair's order: she remained with Sebastian until midnight then retired to rest, fully clothed, on her bed until dawn, when she returned to him. She could hardly believe that his improvement was real. The fever had not returned and the skin around both wounds was pale and without any puffiness. 'Thank you, dear Mother of God, thank you, thank you,' she whispered again and again as she dressed the wounds, tears of gratitude stinging her eyes.

17

Sebastian slept for most of the first week, but then Madeleine asked Alexis Soyer to provide especially nourishing invalid food, and Sebastian's improvement became dramatic. Within days he was more alert, slept less, and was able to sit up in his bed for short periods.

Sam lost no time in telling him how Madeleine had saved his leg. 'Her were a bleedin' marvel, Major Sebastian, sir. When the big doctor come up an' say, very curt-like, "Tha' leg mus' come orff" miss says "No," ever so cool, an' then the doctor, he say he will have her took orf dooty an' tells an orderly ter git you ready, bu' miss says, "You will do no such thing farr I be the Major's kin an' don' give no permission," an' – an' then her add, "If he wan' he can ask the Earl or Lor' Raglan hisself," cos you see, the doctor, he don' believe her be your kith an' kin. The miss stays with you two nights washin' you daown – '

'Washing me down!' echoed Sebastian weakly. 'Why couldn't you have done that?'

'Aw, miss, her don' let no' un touch you, her say them dressin's mus' be kep' dry.' Sam thought for a moment, then added slyly, ''Course, her kep' you covered all the toime her was washin' you.'

'Did she now?' queried Sebastian dreamily, while one corner of his mouth lifted in the merest trace of amusement. He was beginning to drift off to sleep again, but Sam had not finished. 'An' I heared her prayin'. I couldn' hear everthin' her say, only summit abaout Mother o' Gawd an' sac'fice an' offer her life farr yourn.'

Sebastian's eyes snapped open. 'She said that?' he asked, now fully awake and alert.

'Ho aye, tha' her did,' said Sam, nodding his shaggy head emphatically, and was astonished to see a beatific smile transform his master's face. She loves me, Sebastian thought joyfully, she loves me, despite everything, and we'll be together always. He sighed with something very like contentment. The weary months of frustration were over, she was here and he was here and, judging by the bloody awful pain in his side and leg, he would be here *months*. As he drifted into sleep he murmured, 'Look after her for me, Sam, until I am on my feet again, for she means everything in the world to me.'

Yet when he was alert long enough to really look at her, he was shocked: the once slender, deliciously feminine figure looked straight and shapeless in the baggy dress, and even the beautiful carriage was gone, for her shoulders were bowed a little as though under a gigantic burden. As she turned to him he saw that the huge grey eyes were sunken and circled by bruise-like shadows. The delicately pretty young girl who had shown promise of radiant beauty was now almost plain, except for the sweetness of her expression.

Seeing the horror in his eyes, Madeleine thought that it was because he had realized she was nursing him, and the tears – ever too ready to flow these days – pricked her lids. She blinked them impatiently away and her manner became quietly professional, but Sebastian, made newly perceptive by love, partly understood and reached for her hand.

'Darling Madeleine,' he whispered, letting all his devotion show in his eyes, 'thank you for saving my leg and for all you have done for me – Sam told me.' Their fingers had entwined at once, but now as she was suddenly called away, he just had time to see the blush and the wonderful radiance in her eyes before she left him. I must go carefully, he thought, brow furrowed in deep concentration. Must win her confidence. I've hurt her grievously

337

in the past and she's obviously afraid still, but oh, my darling angel girl, if only you knew how much I long to make it all up to you. Just to be able to hold you, that's all I would ask for now because I couldn't do anything else – I know I'm as weak as a kitten, God dammit!

His days began to rotate around her appearances. When she was absent the hours were long and pain-filled, but when she was on the ward he felt nothing but happiness and his eyes would follow her every movement. Every morning he would awake feeling alert and full of anticipation, his eyes glued upon the doorway. When she appeared she would immediately turn her head and look at him, but when their eyes met she would quickly glance away. Then he discovered that if he pretended to be asleep, she would continue to look at him, her small face tender, and so he endeavoured to keep his eyes almost closed and to watch her through his lashes.

It was the same at night. Because she was so afraid he might have a relapse, she had begun a round of the ward when the orderly and most of the patients were asleep. She would shine her lantern very briefly on each in turn, except when she reached Sebastian, and then she always went to stand beside his bed. Keeping his eyes firmly closed and trying to breathe very evenly, he would listen for the soft rustle of her dress, and when the light shone behind his closed lids he would know she was there, looking down at him. He often wondered why she paused so long and of course never knew that in sleep he reminded her so much of their son. And always she touched him; her hands were permanently red and rough, the fingers often swollen, but because to touch him was her only means of expressing her love, the featherlight movement of her hand against his cheek or on his brow was full of tenderness. She never knew the torture this was to him because he so desperately wanted to turn his head and kiss her palm, to press it against his cheek, and

338

yet was afraid to do so lest in some way it shattered the fragile understanding between them. Once when he involuntarily groaned with the effort of keeping still, he heard her quick gasp. The lantern was set down and her hand immediately sought and held his pulse; then the bedclothes were very gently lifted so that she could see from the dressings that he was not bleeding. He heard her quivering sigh of relief as she tucked the sheets around him again, and then the light receded. Through his lashes he watched her almost completely silent progress to the door. She turned there and gave him a last lingering look and his heart sang. That she loved him, cared deeply and tenderly for him, was perfectly obvious, but this placed him in a dilemma: he wanted to be fit so that he could spend every available moment with her, yet he knew that as soon as he was ready for convalescence he would be moved away, probably to the General Hospital, but so long as he remained a patient, he would be able to see her, if only for such maddeningly short times, and then never alone.

Then one morning his problem was brought to a head. It was Dr Fraser's round and all the patients were silent and watching with interest as Alastair, accompanied by a young assistant surgeon, the orderly and Madeleine, went from bed to bed. Because everything a doctor ordered or remarked upon had to be written down, Madeleine carried a very large book, a pen and portable inkpot, and after each examination Alastair gave her his instructions, speaking very quietly and sometimes looking over her shoulder at what she had written or bending down to glance at her totally absorbed little face. As the group came to the other side of the ward opposite Sebastian, his neighbour said softly to him, 'It's clearly love, isn't it? They go riding together frequently, you know, and I've heard they've been seen arm-in-arm in Constantinople.'

'I don't follow you,' said Sebastian curtly, even though his black brows drew together ominously.

'Why, Doc Fraser and the Little Angel, it's obvious that he's totally besotted with her.'

'What!' It was barked out furiously and every head turned to look at him in surprise. Then Madeleine, with a little smile, put her finger to her lips, and Sebastian muttered, 'I beg your pardon,' while continuing to glare at Alastair. When they came to his bed and Alastair said pleasantly, 'How are you today, sir?' Sebastian snapped, 'I'm perfectly fit and I want to get up!'

Once more they all looked at him in surprise. He had been so quiet, so uncomplaining before – a model patient, Alastair had called him – but now he appeared to be extremely angry, his thin face taut and white, his black eyes blazing.

'I'm afraid that's out of the question, sir,' said Alastair mildly. He bent over the bed, anxious to explain. 'You see, you had a compound fracture of the leg and this will need to remain splinted for some weeks yet. Because the bone had protruded through the skin, we were not able to splint it properly immediately after we'd realigned the bone; it was necessary to wait until the skin had healed, which I'm happy to say it has done.'

Sebastian, who had not listened to a word, was thinking: perhaps the fellow is married already and just amusing himself, and he barked out, 'Are you married, doctor?'

Alastair looked at him closely. Had the poor chap gone off his head? 'No, sir,' he replied, and then could not resist a quick upward look at Madeleine before adding with a merry smile, 'but I live in hopes of being in that happy state before too long!' Madeleine smiled back, too worried about Sebastian's sudden change of demeanour to be paying much attention. Alastair was saying soothingly, 'You may be sure, sir, that we shall get you up as soon as ever possible. I expect you are anxious to return to your regiment.'

Well then, you expect quite wrongly, you damned young idiot! thought the furious Sebastian. Alastair, receiving only a glare in reply, decided to move on, but outside he said to Madeleine, 'What's got into de Lacey? He looked at me quite murderously and I don't think he heard a word I was saying about his leg! Better keep a close eye on him, nurse, and report at once to me if he continues to behave in this way.'

Madeleine dashed back to Sebastian as soon as she was able, and some instinct made her put screens around his bed. 'What is it?' she whispered, gently sinking down beside the bed. 'What has upset you so much?'

Sebastian twisted his head on the pillow in angry frustration and gave her one of the intense looks which in the past had unnerved her so completely. She sat back rather suddenly on her heels, but then a little ripple of laughter escaped her. 'You look like a thundercloud,' she said, smiling, 'but I'm sure there's a very good reason for it. Can't you tell me what it is?'

'You,' he said bluntly, and then cursed himself as he saw the smile abruptly wiped off her face to be replaced by an utterly stricken look. 'Ah, dear God,' he whispered in desperation, 'I don't mean *you* in that sense. I mean – is it true that you've been riding and sightseeing with that fellow?'

'What – oh, you mean Dr Fraser?' she queried, astonishment and relief making her round-eyed. 'Why yes, he has asked me to accompany him sometimes. But *that* cannot be why you are so angry!'

'Well, of course it can – and it is!' Sebastian retorted. 'How do you think I feel, cooped up here, when I hear that you have been gallivanting with that – that fellow!'

The words were so astonishing, so wonderful, that she put her hand to her mouth to stop the joyous laughter,

341

and just gazed at him in disbelief, while inside Sebastian there was a small boy who desperately wanted to throw a temper tantrum, to bawl, thump and throw things in sheer and utter frustration.

'I've not been out with Dr Fraser since you've been here,' said Madeleine at last. 'And I only went because he thought I should get out into the fresh air and Miss Nightingale approved.'

Instantly the black eyes, which had been blazing seconds before, softened to a velvety tenderness. 'Had you been ill, Madeleine?' he asked, all concern now.

A more worldly woman might have concurred and made capital out of it, but Madeleine answered at once, 'Oh no, of course not! It was just – just that we had been indoors all winter and with a great deal to do, so when – when spring came, it was felt we should take advantage of it.' She paused before adding hesitantly, 'I shall not be going out again with Dr Fraser.'

With this Sebastian had to be content, but as his strength returned, the enforced immobility became more and more difficult to bear. He had always been a splendidly healthy and strong man, his longest sojourns in bed being those times when he was in the throes of a new passion or intent on quelling the jealous fury of an old. Now, to add to his frustration, was bitter guilt. He knew only too well how badly he had treated Madeleine in Bath and he longed to make up for his cruelty. Because, he thought constantly, I always knew what she was really like – in my innermost heart – and I also knew that I would love her as I have loved no other woman. It was this I was fighting against all the time, because I did not want to be hurt again. And perhaps by hurting Madeleine I was repaying Sophie, simply because they are both women. My God, I was a child – a mindless, dangerous idiot of a child at that. I must talk to Madeleine . . . I must, I must.

Eventually one morning he said to Sam, 'Will you please get me a shirt, trousers and some leather slippers from somewhere.'

'But, Major Sebastian, sir – '

'Do it, there's a good fellow, Sam. And hurry, please hurry.' Sebastian was now in a fever of impatience, and when the old servant returned with the clothes, he announced, 'I'm getting up!' As Sam stood speechless with dismay, Sebastian gave him a quick look and said curtly, 'Don't try and stop me, but set to and help me, for God's sake, man!'

It took all his considerable willpower to get into the trousers because he was extremely weak and his left leg was still splinted. By the time he had finished dressing, the sweat was pouring off him and he was breathing hard. 'Now help me to stand,' he commanded, quite oblivious of the concerned attention he was getting from every other patient. But of course after so many weeks in bed his right leg was like jelly, and even just putting the heel of his splinted left leg to the ground caused excruciating pain. Nevertheless, using his sword as a crutch and with Sam clinging on desperately to him, he just managed to stagger upright, where he stood swaying dangerously. With teeth clamped together, exerting the last ounces of his strength and willpower, he tried to hobble forward, but immediately the room began to whirl around him and his right leg to buckle. Within seconds he would have fallen had Madeleine not entered the ward and rushed forward.

'Don't let his leg touch the floor!' she shouted at Sam as her arms went around Sebastian's waist from behind and she leant against the wall, holding his body against her own. 'Orderly! Orderly!' she screamed, and by chance one was passing in the corridor. He rushed to her aid and, together with Sam, they got Sebastian back on his bed, where he lay with eyes closed, his face a mask of pain.

Madeleine drew the screens around him, but sensing his deep humiliation, she stood outside while the two men undressed him. 'Please be very careful of his leg,' she called to them in an agony of apprehension, for the ward orderlies were not renowned for their gentle handling of patients. When a low 'a-aa-ah' escaped Sebastian, she could no longer remain apart but slipped behind the screens. They had got his trousers off and were trying to pull him into a sitting position. 'Thank you,' Madeleine said to them. 'I can manage now.' She bent anxiously to examine the splint. Thank God that seemed all right, but what a terrible risk he had taken, and for what reason?

As soon as they were alone, with the screens still around them, she knelt beside him. 'Why?' she whispered urgently. 'Why did you do it?'

His eyes were open now and full of despair. 'I just wanted to be with you, talk to you, hold you, tell you how much I love you,' he said miserably, all his defences down. And instinctively she responded, leaning forward until she lay lightly against his chest, her arms going around his shoulders, her face just above his own.

'Then hold me now,' she whispered, her eyes full of tenderness.

With the tiniest sound of amazement and joy, his arms enfolded her, strongly and urgently, all his frustrated tenderness in the touch of his hands. Then, as she felt his fingers on her nape, she bent her head to kiss him full on the lips, not very expertly, but with all the love in her heart, and instantly his mouth drew her down into the bottomless depths of his own love and hunger. It was a kiss which sent both their minds reeling, and when at last Madeleine tried to pull away, their lips still clung. She kissed him lingeringly once more, feeling his body shake beneath her own, and knowing instinctively that he was completely hers at that moment. Fortunately, she also realized that she must be the strong one. They were in a

344

ward full of men, with only the thin screen to protect their privacy; if discovered in each other's arms, she would be instantly dismissed. Fear of this now made her pull away with determination, but she whispered into his ear, 'You must let me go now. If anyone should see or hear, I would be sent away.' He nodded, unable to speak, but his eyes told her everything she wanted to know.

'There now, Major de Lacey,' she said aloud, hoping her voice sounded more or less normal. 'Are you fairly comfortable?'

The old mischievous grin spread delightedly across his face. 'Very comfortable, thank you, Nurse Brett.' And just before she began to fold the screens, he grasped her hand and pressed it yearningly against his lips. 'Thank you,' he whispered humbly.

These snatched moments became their joy and their torment, particularly for Madeleine, who had to try and be sensible and ration them strictly, an almost insuperable task when every time he looked at her, Sebastian's eyes begged, and she felt almost totally unable to prevent herself from melting into his arms, regardless of everything and everyone.

Then at long last the day came when Alastair Fraser said, 'I think we might try that leg on the ground,' and was not prepared for the speed with which Sebastian got himself to the side of the bed, legs already over the edge. It needed four strong orderlies to hold up his massive frame, but when Alastair asked, 'Do you feel any pain in that leg now there is some pressure on it?' he answered at once, 'None at all.'

'Right, let's try it without the splint,' suggested Alastair, and again Sebastian was able to reply truthfully that there was no pain, 'but it feels like a board, while my right leg has no strength at all.'

Alastair nodded. 'That is normal and, of course, you will need to learn to walk again, but it is all very satisfactory.' He turned to Madeleine. 'Major de Lacey is a great tribute to your devoted nursing,' he told her smilingly, and was surprised that she should blush so very vividly.

'Yes, aren't I?' quipped the delighted Sebastian, who knew he must be grinning fatuously, but did not care. 'I'll begin walking right away!'

'Now, steady on, sir,' began Alastair hurriedly. 'You must only take two or three steps at a time to begin with, and only when you are fully supported.' He thought for a moment and then added seriously, 'It would be a tragedy to undo all the good work now, wouldn't it?'

'Of course,' agreed Sebastian, thinking only of the time when he would be able to meet Madeleine and be alone with her.

It was to be a long, slow business, and even when at last he could walk out of the ward there was little advantage, for the corridors were endless and totally beyond his strength. As soon as I'm discharged, he thought, I shall apply for a posting to the depot here and then we shall be able to meet when we're off duty. My God, though, I'll have to control myself. Now, with his new-found tenderness for Madeleine, he was also fiercely protective and very aware that he must do nothing to harm her or her reputation. But somehow I shall manage to behave, he told himself, and then grinned when he realized what a novel situation that would be.

But that was not what destiny had in store for him.

On a fine autumn morning he was suddenly summoned to the principal medical officer's room, only to find the new Commander-in-Chief, Sir William Codrington, awaiting him.

'Ah, good to see you, de Lacey, knew your father very well,' said the C-in-C heartily. 'Got good news for you too!'

'Really, sir?' said Sebastian politely.

'Yes. Her Majesty has been graciously pleased to honour you with her new medal for your valour at Sebastopol and particularly wishes to present this herself – no doubt because of your family and the fact that you belong to the Prince Consort's Regiment. Arrangements have therefore been made for your immediate transportation to England.'

Sebastian was transfixed with shock. Immediate transportation – immediate separation from Madeleine! 'Sir,' he broke in desperately, 'I am truly honoured, but I should so like to remain here until the war finally ends. Now that Sebastopol has fallen, it cannot be long before – '

Sir William's expression hardened. 'I hope, sir, that you are not trying to make me believe you wish to disobey your Sovereign's wishes,' he said, his voice raised.

Sebastian instinctively drew himself up between his two sticks. 'Of course not, sir,' he replied quietly. 'It is just that I would wish to be more mobile when I am in Her Majesty's presence.'

'Ah, no need to feel like that, my boy,' said Sir William, mollified. 'You will go from here to the hospital at Fort Pitt, Chatham, which Her Majesty plans to visit before Christmas to make several awards, yours among them. Now, the *Jura* sails within the hour, and the best transport we have been able to arrange to get you down to the quay is an araba – one of those tumbril-type carts used by the Turks – bloody uncomfortable, but the doctor fellahs here did not consider you fit enough to ride.'

Ah now, thought Sebastian, not within the hour! That is too cruel. 'Sir,' he said, trying to force his voice to calmness, 'may I request permission to wait until the next transport is leaving for England? That surely would be in sufficient time.'

'You may not!' barked the C-in-C. "Pon my word, sir,

347

you amaze me with your reluctance. I would have expected that as a regular serving officer – and of field rank too – you would be instantly ready for transportation anywhere.'

Once more Sebastian drew himself up. 'I believe I am so ready, sir, but I have been a patient here for many months and there are people I wish to thank and say – goodbye to.'

'Then get on with it now,' commanded Sir William, moving to the door. 'You've got half an hour.' At the door he quickly turned and came back, hand outstretched. 'Congratulations, m' boy,' he boomed, 'and good luck to you!'

Sebastian bowed. 'Thank you, sir.'

As the General left, Dr Lawson returned. 'Dr Lawson,' said Sebastian, again trying to hide his desperation, 'I beg that you will allow me a few minutes alone with Nurse Brett.'

Dr Lawson had never forgotten the scene on this man's arrival, and it pleased him greatly to say now, 'Out of the question. Nurse Brett is on duty.'

'Dr Lawson,' said Sebastian again, his voice dangerously quiet, 'I am being shipped out within the hour at the express wish of Her Majesty, but I refuse to leave until I have seen Nurse Brett. It is immaterial to me what the consequences of such action might be, but I should not hesitate to explain why I refused to leave.'

Once more Dr Lawson was beaten and he knew it. 'Very well,' he said coldly, 'but a report will be made to higher authority that Nurse Brett was withdrawn from duty for personal reasons.'

Sebastian bowed slightly, unable to trust himself to speak. Bloody old hypocrite, he thought savagely, trying to make out he thinks it terrible for her to leave for a few minutes when in reality he'd do anything to get all the nurses permanently off the wards.

When she came, he saw at once that she knew, for her small face was stricken, the great eyes bright with tears. He hobbled forward and, putting his two sticks together, swept his free arm around her, drawing her close. 'My beloved girl,' he whispered hoarsely, 'I'd give anything not to leave you like this, but there's nothing I can do.'

She was very calm, even managing to look up at him with the ghost of a smile. 'Of course,' she said, trying hard to keep the quiver from her voice. 'I understand.'

'Madeleine, we must talk,' he said with desperate urgency. 'There's so little time!'

'Let's sit down,' she suggested, even at that moment mindful of his weakness.

He eased himself down beside her with a slight grimace, and she saw there was a fine film of perspiration along his hairline and upper lip. How weak he is still, she thought, totally anxious for him. Yet there was great strength in his fingers as he took and held her hands.

'Madeleine, my dearest love,' he began, his face tense with strain, 'I have so little to offer you except my love, but I want us to be together always. Will you – will you follow me home and be my mistress? I can set you up in a little house and, after all, we really should be like Mr and Mrs de Lacey. I know it is not much and if I had money I would give you the earth, but – but as it is, we shall be together and have each other always . . .' His voice trailed away into silence. He had put it clumsily, could not think clearly, and silently begged her to understand.

At last she said very quietly, 'But wouldn't you have to marry one day, for family reasons?'

Sebastian shrugged. 'I suppose so – one day. But that need not make any difference to us, for it would only be a marriage of convenience and I would be with you every available moment, I promise you.'

'Your aunt and Harriet expect you to marry Catherine

349

Llewellyn Morgan,' said Madeleine, looking down at her hands, which he still held.

'Yes, well, perhaps I could do worse,' Sebastian replied, vainly trying to think how he could get her thoughts away from his future marriage.

Gently Madeleine withdrew her hands and went to stand looking out of the window. 'If there were no legal bar, would you marry me?' she asked, her voice a mere thread.

It was a question which took him completely by surprise. He had always thought of marriage as a necessary evil to be put off for as long as possible, and the idea of ever actually *wanting* to enter into such a state was still so novel that he paused, totally nonplussed for a few seconds.

And Madeleine completely misunderstood his silence. Sadly she turned to face him. 'It is all right,' she said gently, but with finality. 'I do realize that marriage to a penniless doctor's daughter would be a shocking mésalliance for a de Lacey, and if it were only the law preventing our marriage, I would be your mistress and follow you to the ends of the earth, if necessary. But I cannot share you with someone else – and especially not with Catherine, who took me in when I was starving and near death, who cared for me, fed me, clothed me and overcame all opposition to get me here. No, I could never do that to her!'

Sebastian got clumsily but hurriedly to his feet. 'Then I'll not marry her or anyone else!' he said decisively. 'I only want you, my darling – you must know that.' His voice and his eyes told her that it was true and she longed to rush into his arms, but instead she was back at the ball, sitting beside Lady Frensham and hearing her say, 'Sebastian could never have lived on love in a cottage.' So now Madeleine whispered, 'I do believe you, but – but in time

you would feel differently, the pressure of your obligations to your family would make me like a millstone
around your neck. And you have never known poverty as
I have; you would so hate it – and me for having brought
you to it.'

'No, no,' said Sebastian, beginning to feel real fear
now. 'It won't be like that, I promise you! I'll find some
way of making money.'

'But how?' persisted Madeleine, feeling that her heart
was being torn from her. 'Don't you realize that you may
not even be allowed to remain in the Army because of
your leg?'

Sebastian ran his hand distractedly through his hair.
'Well then, perhaps I could manage a large estate, or
teach riding.'

'Oh, my dear,' said Madeleine pityingly. 'A de Lacey
reduced to that, and all because of me! I should never
forgive myself.'

The door burst open. 'Time's up!' shouted Dr Lawson.

'Get out!' roared Sebastian, and looked so menacing
that the doctor's face disappeared at once. Sebastian
turned back to Madeleine, suddenly much calmer and
more decisive. 'Whatever you say, Madeleine, I will never
give you up. I love you and need you too much.'

Madeleine began to move towards the door. 'Thank
you,' she whispered. 'But I promise you, you will feel
differently when you get back to your familiar surroundings and to your friends.'

'I thought you loved me,' he began harshly.

'I do,' Madeleine said, without hesitation. 'I love you
enough to let you go because it is the only thing to do.'

'But is this to be the end – are we just to say goodbye
and never meet again?' he demanded incredulously.

'Yes,' she said, her hands now tightly clenched in the
folds of her dress.

'No!' shouted Sebastian. 'This cannot be!'

But time and her composure were almost gone. 'Forget me,' she whispered. 'Go home and be happy and – and God go with you always.'

'Madeleine, wait! Don't leave me!' he shouted in despair, but she had already disappeared and there was only patient Sam waiting outside.

'Come quick, sir,' the old servant urged, hurrying forward to drape Sebastian's blood-stained and torn campaign cloak about his shoulders. 'Us'll be lef' behind if you don' hurry.'

'God dammit!' shouted Sebastian. 'Was ever a man so tormented?' Sam held out his sealskin busby and, hardly knowing what he was doing, Sebastian put it on, automatically easing the chain at his chin.

'Doan' furgit 'tis the Queen as wants you!' Sam urged, and Sebastian began to hobble painfully along, his thoughts entirely chaotic. The araba was drawn up at the entrance and he allowed himself to be half helped, half lifted into it, then immediately turned his head to look back longingly. Surely this cannot really be happening, he thought in a panic, surely I'm not to leave her like this? But then the cold, salt-laden air was on his face and the troops drawn up on the quay were only too real. They hauled him out of the cart and, as he stood, his legs trembling with weakness, he became aware of a female figure standing before him. Her kind face under its large black hat was of West Indian darkness, but her ample form was clad in a tartan riding habit. She was looking at him with extraordinarily deep penetrating eyes, and she said at last, 'I have a message for you, sir,' causing his heart to leap with irrational hope.

He spoke hurriedly to Sam: 'You get yourself and Rollo on board and I'll follow in a minute.' Sam wavered until he saw Sebastian's expression and then he hurried away.

'What message?' Sebastian asked impatiently.

'A message from the Other Side,' said the woman, continuing to stare very deeply into his eyes.

'I'm afraid I don't understand you,' said Sebastian.

'Why, from the spirit world, sir.'

'Oh, for God's sake!' he muttered, turning away in disgust.

'Please don't go, sir. It concerns the woman you love.'

That brought him instantly back to her. 'Yes?' he said eagerly.

'The woman who bore your son, sir.'

Once more Sebastian turned away. 'I have no son,' he replied curtly, and began to hobble towards the ship, but the woman fell easily into step beside him.

'This is true, sir, for your son is dead, and the woman you love will die too, unless you save her. You think now that you have lost her, and she will go with another to a burning land far, far away, but you must follow her and watch over her, sir, for if you do not, your long life will be a desert. Even though you will be one of the great ones of the earth, with great riches.'

A bark of derisive laughter escaped him at that. 'I'm afraid you've got the wrong man,' he told her bitterly. 'I have no money and I'm certainly not a "great one"!'

'It awaits you, sir, in England,' she persisted. Sebastian stopped and fumbled in his trouser pocket for a few coins, but at once she forestalled him. 'The information is a gift, sir,' she said calmly. 'My mother was a West Indian doctoress and my father a Scot. I am fey, and I just pass on the messages.'

Leaning heavily on his sticks, Sebastian took a good look at her. She appeared to be completely serious and sincere. 'Why me?' he demanded. 'There must be a lot of messages waiting for a lot of men here, so why me?'

She answered without hesitation. 'Because, sir, you and the woman you love are to be offered a second chance; it is something very rare and it is being offered you because your love for each other is also very rare and very deep. Please remember what I have told you, sir, for great happiness awaits you and the lady. There will be four more children to bless your union.'

At that he laughed outright. Assuming Madeleine did eventually become his mistress, they might well have a child – but four! It was ludicrous, and surely even he, though not renowned for his control, would be able to manage things better. 'Well, thank you for telling me,' he said, and then, with a slight bow, he turned and began painfully to ascend the gangway.

Still she persisted, standing close to the rail and looking up at him. 'I beg you to remember, sir,' she said earnestly.

'Yes, yes,' Sebastian replied, endeavouring to keep his feet on the steep incline. Once on deck he turned, breathing hard, to see if the strange woman had approached anyone else, but she was walking determinedly away.

'I see you've made the acquaintance of Mother Seacole,' said a Rifle Brigade officer who was leaning over the rail.

'Who the devil is she?' demanded Sebastian.

'You mean to say you don't know?' queried the other in genuine surprise. 'Mrs Seacole – fondly known as Mother Seacole to the troops – is a wonderful old gal who has been running an hotel and canteens up at Sebastopol, all for the Army. She's a wise old bird, very kind and amazingly knowledgeable about a lot of things, and she's done a very great deal for the private soldier. I hope, when the history of this campaign comes to be written, that Mrs Seacole will be mentioned with Miss Nightingale.' The rifleman turned to look more closely at Sebastian. 'She certainly had a lot to say to you, didn't she?'

'Yes, she was full of strange predictions which were completely inappropriate and haven't a cat in hell's chance of coming true. But then, I suppose such sayings are part of her stock in trade.'

'No,' said his companion thoughtfully, 'you are quite wrong there; I cannot remember ever seeing her behave like that with anyone else.'

'Then I am indeed honoured,' said Sebastian, smiling cynically as he turned away. He went to stand alone at the rail, his eyes fixed on the great bulk of the Barrack Hospital. Once before he had stood thus after his first parting from Madeleine, but then he had been full of confidence in the future and now . . .? I won't let her go, he thought savagely, and then more humbly, I *can't* let her go.

He became aware of Sam standing beside him, also looking up at the hospital.

'Hurr kisst oi,' Sam was saying, a wide, delighted grin spreading across his lined face. 'The Li'le Angel give oi a kiss, jus' yere.' He stabbed his cheek with a gnarled finger.

'Did she indeed,' Sebastian said wryly. 'It was more than she gave me.'

'An' hurr says, Gawd bless you, Sam, do you take care o' the Major an' yerself an' see he looks after tha' leg.'

Sebastian sighed. The loving heart, he thought, grief-stricken now, always caring, always putting me first. He looked again at the hospital. I never knew a woman like you existed, he told her within his heart, and now that I've found you, I cannot live without you. I'll think of some solution for us, I will, I will, for it's absurd that we should live our lives apart just through some stupid legality, when we belong to each other, and nothing, nothing is going to keep us apart! He remembered her whispered words, '*I would follow you to the ends of the earth, if necessary*', and his hand clenched on the rail. Perhaps that was the answer; to go to the ends of the earth together. After all, the world was opening up everywhere: Africa, Australia, New Zealand, America,

Canada, surely there would be something he could do in one of those countries. They could go as Mr and Mrs de Lacey and no one need ever know that they were not married to each other. That's it! he thought in sudden jubilation, that's the answer! Perhaps I could buy a ranch or a sheep farm – Rob would have to lend me the money, but with all his estates he wouldn't miss it and I'd pay it back eventually. Yes, Rob will be the one; he thinks Madeleine wonderful and he already knows our story, so there won't be any need for a lot of awkward explanations. I'll write to him tonight and send the letter back from Malta.

With a great lightening of spirit, Sebastian relaxed against the rail and allowed his eyes to wander over the dock until they fell upon the figure of Mrs Seacole. She was far back, standing quite still, and even across the distance he realized that she was staring at him with great intensity. Extraordinary woman! he thought, and then automatically straightened under her scrutiny. '*Please remember, sir,*' she had kept saying, sounding so earnest, but what *had* she said? Something about 'the woman you love . . . who bore your son . . .' Could Madeleine . . .? Was it possible? Of course, it was only too possible after the ecstasy of that night in the library . . . But how would she have cared for herself and the unborn child when she had no family or money? No, thought Sebastian decisively, that certainly cannot be true, for she would have had to tell me, or Aunt Thea at least; she could not have done otherwise. What else had the old gal said? '*One of the great ones of the earth . . .*' What a lot of rot that was too, for there was no chance of him becoming a great one now, and it would be totally impossible if he went to some remote country. '*There will be four more children to bless your union*' – Madeleine, the slender, the delicate, giving birth *four* times in some wilderness? Again impossible. I should never allow it, he thought, but of course one child at least was almost inevitable, and what a strange legal situation the poor little devil would be in: entitled to the family name and yet a bastard! Well, there'd been other skeletons in the cupboard, other bastards in the family before – but father would turn in his grave, Sebastian thought sadly, and it would be confirmation of all his fears that I was simply no good. The family and its continuation had meant so much to him and he'd always hoped that I would settle down and produce a large brood.

It would be up to Rob to do that for, when Sebastian came to think of it, the family had bred an awful lot of girls and mighty few boys over the last fifty years. Rob would never be a rake-hell as he himself had been – no, he could see Rob finding some broad-hipped, rosy-cheeked girl from deep within the west and marrying her very soon after his return home. And with the war all but over, the danger of Rob not returning was almost nil. Meanwhile, until he had a son, his heir was his great-nephew, born to his uncle by his sprightly young French wife. A smile flitted briefly across Sebastian's face as he thought of that surprising birth. Sir Arthur de Lacey's first marriage had been childless and the family had heard with astonishment of his subsequent marriage to an unknown Frenchwoman, but it had obviously all been too much for the old boy because within a year he was dead, leaving a month-old son. Sebastian remembered his own father returning from Paris after the christening and saying that the wife was 'charming' and the baby 'sturdy'; he had been named Marc, after the Norman founder of the family.

Sebastian's teeth suddenly bit deeply into his lower lip. What a miserable twist of fate to deny his birthright to any child of *his* and Madeleine – a child who would be conceived in deep love, who would be treasured and adored by them both as the living, visible proof of that love . . . Sebastian, who had so often laughed and derided

357

his own father's pride in their family, now realized how much he would like to tell a son of his about the many different men and women who had borne their name down the centuries. And there was no denying the nagging feeling of betrayal in the thought of going across the world, of cutting himself off from all kith and kin.

Sam said, 'Will her be followin' us home, sir?'

'I don't know, Sam, I just don't know,' Sebastian said with great sadness, but as the ship began to slowly pull away, he kept his eyes glued upon the vast building on the hill above.

And in one of that building's long windows a small, solitary figure stood watching the ship through a veil of tears.

It was there that Alastair Fraser finally found her.

18

When Lord Cardigan returned to England he was given a hero's welcome and fêted everywhere, but a year later his reputation had become somewhat tarnished. Too many returning veterans had spoken of his callousness towards those under his command, and with his controversial behaviour at Balaclava, there were rumours that he had never really led the Charge.

The sight of his peacock-like figure at the presentation of Sebastian's Victoria Cross had therefore attracted great publicity, and in all the newspapers there were line drawings of the two officers shaking hands. There were also dramatic illustrations of the tiny Queen, standing upon a dais and still needing to reach up in order to pin the medal on Sebastian's chest; the artists had of course slightly caricatured the Queen's features, depicting her with sharp nose pointing upwards and emphasizing her slightly protruding eyes and adenoidal mouth. There was, however, no exaggeration in the portrayal of the now famous Major de Lacey, for Sebastian, although disappointed in the tiny, rotund figure, had nevertheless regarded her with almost reverent eyes. She was without doubt the greatest Queen in the world, ruling the greatest Empire yet known, and he was her liege man, whom she was honouring. He had therefore stood absolutely straight and the Queen, who admired a handsome man as much as anyone, had later been heard to remark on his 'fine, soldierly bearing'.

Nor had she subsequently forgotten him, and upon hearing that he was unmarried had at once thought of the Duke of Rockingham's daughter, Lady Henrietta; what a truly wonderful couple they would make! When discreet enquiries revealed that they were not acquainted, an invitation to dine was sent to them both. Sebastian, who had half suspected some matchmaking plan when he was so quickly introduced to Lady Henrietta, had to admit that she was very beautiful. She was also a vivacious girl with a lively, intelligent mind and an amusing turn of conversation. Sebastian's eyes lingered appreciatively on her pure Grecian profile, so often turned for his notice, and on her fashionably sloping shoulders, which were very white and covered with just the right amount of flesh. In addition, she was very blonde, with large hazel eyes which sparkled and laughed into his own. When he stood and offered his arm to lead her into dinner, they were both aware of the tiny murmur rippling through the guests in all that glittering assembly. For there was no doubt that Sebastian, with his splendid looks, his height and new, brilliant uniform was the handsomest man present; equally without doubt he had on his arm the loveliest girl: tall, willowy and slender, her extreme blondeness contrasted perfectly with his darkness, and even her magnificent white gown with its edging of gold lace complemented the gold on his uniform. Yet, as he continued to smile down at her, there was a weariness in his eyes; he had known and carelessly accepted since early manhood that his mere presence had a devastating effect upon women and that with a minimum amount of effort he could make himself completely irresistible to them; he had been making such efforts constantly over the years and no doubt would continue to do so, for he freely acknowledged that he adored women and everything about them, but never before had he known a feeling of total commitment to one woman – a feeling which allowed him to admire and even flirt as he had always done, and yet remain completely unmoved by all their charms.

So when Lady Henrietta gave him a glance of total

coquetry from behind her fan, he smiled back delightedly and, looking into his dancing eyes, she thought triumphantly, I believe I have got him – he has not taken his eyes off me all evening. A delicious little frisson caused her slender frame to sway for a second, but her confidence would have been lost for ever had she known that he was only thinking, I wonder if she uses mule's piss to lighten her hair, like Sal.

At the end of the evening, when the Duchess of Rockingham said, 'I do hope you will call upon us very soon, Major de Lacey,' he bowed over her hand, saying how delightful that would be, even as he realized that he had no intention of doing so. For Rob had written agreeing to any loan, and soon, very soon, Sebastian hoped that he would be writing to Madeleine with an outline of his future plans for them both.

Meanwhile, the first thing he had done on leaving hospital was to go to Garrard's. Trays of magnificent pieces had been brought out for him, but those of diamonds were beyond his means, and others of enamel were, he considered, too heavy. 'It is for a very beautiful, very ethereal lady,' he explained, unaware of the pride in his voice. 'She is so slender and delicate that something of the finest workmanship is needed to complement her.' In the end a brooch was to be specifically designed: a long-stemmed rosebud, the flower a pear-shaped pearl just peeping from its tight leaves of gold, which were to be reduced to near transparency so that a filigree look was achieved, and on the top of the largest leaf a tiny trembling dewdrop of a diamond was to be placed. 'Perfect,' said Sebastian, feeling happier than for weeks and delighted at the thought of giving Madeleine something that she would exclaim over. She had nothing, his beautiful, his precious white rose who deserved so much, and if he could he would give her everything and more than she could ever want.

If he had not appreciated her before, the weary weeks at Fort Pitt would have convinced him of her devotion. There were no female nurses at the hospital, where the care was minimal and rough. All his waking hours – and many of his sleeping – had been filled with memories of Madeleine: her exquisitely gentle touch, the look of complete concentration on her small face when she dressed a wound, the smile always ready to touch her eyes, and most of all the stolen moments when the screens were around his bed and she knelt beside him. How wonderful it had been to feel her soft breasts pressed against his chest, her fingers touching his face and threading their way through his hair. Her kisses had been so shy, but he had hungered for them and their lips had clung in mutual need. I hunger for her now, he told himself, getting up and pacing about the room like a caged animal. I hunger and yearn for her as I never thought even remotely possible, but soon we shall be together.

Rob's ship was due at Portsmouth in two days' time and he had said he would come at once to London to meet his cousin. Then, thought Sebastian, as soon as the loan is agreed upon, I will find out from the War Office when Madeleine is expected to leave Scutari and if there is time, I shall journey out to her; if not, then perhaps to Malta . . . We shall spend every available moment together, make our plans, and I will resign my commission, book our passages to whichever country seems best, and we shall be away, as Mr and Mrs de Lacey, as man and wife, never to be parted again.

But of course everything was changed when the telegram arrived – the telegram announcing with regret that Lieutenant the Earl of Wells had died at sea. As the ship was so near her home port, the body was being brought to England, even though cholera was suspected. It was very nearly a knock-out blow for Sebastian, not only because he had been very fond of his young cousin, but because it meant the end of all his hopes and plans.

There was more to come, for when Mr Lethbridge waited upon him, it was with the incredible news that the baby in Paris, Rob's heir, had died of scarlet fever. 'And within some five hours of each other,' said the precise Mr Lethbridge, removing his pince-nez with care. 'Therefore, my dear sir, as I am sure you already realize, the earldom passes to yourself. May I be the first to offer my felicitations, even in such tragic circumstances?'

'No, you may not,' said Sebastian curtly, as he sank hurriedly on to the nearest chair, 'for there must be some mistake. What about my uncle in Vienna? Surely the title goes to him.'

'No, indeed not, my lord,' replied Mr Lethbridge with great dignity. 'If your father were still alive, the earldom would naturally be his. As he is unfortunately no longer with us, you, as his only son, inherit.' Mr Lethbridge paused and looked quite anxiously at Sebastian: his lordship was totally silent and white to the lips.

When Mr Lethbridge delicately cleared his throat and went on, 'I so hate to intrude on your grief, my lord, but there are all the funeral arrangements . . .'

Sebastian looked up at him with stricken eyes, 'What?' he asked blankly.

Dear me, thought Mr Lethbridge, how very surprising; one would have thought he might be overjoyed to have the world so suddenly placed at his feet. 'The funeral arrangements, my lord,' he said again.

Sebastian roused himself. 'Yes, of course. Please forgive me, Mr Lethbridge. I am sure you will understand that this has been the very greatest shock; that one of them should die might perhaps have been feasible, but both, and within a few hours of each other . . .' His voice trailed away and he shook his head, still not able to believe any of it.

He continued to disbelieve it, even when ordering the special train, the carriage, the mourning clothes; even when he went first to Dover to meet the unknown aunt from Paris, and then to Portsmouth to receive Rob's coffin; even when he saw the great array of black-clad servants lined up outside to meet him at Royston Lacey and all the cousins and in-laws lined up inside. So many hands to shake, so many carriages coming and going as all the local gentry arrived to offer their condolences, so many letters and cards, all with thick black borders, so many people to invite to the funeral and for the meal afterwards. Luckily, Rob's eldest sister, the Duchess of Wessex, took over almost everything; she always had been a bossy piece, thought Sebastian, even as he added, and thank God for it.

The actual funeral seemed interminable too, but there was pathos in the sight of the two coffins, side by side in the family chapel, beneath the tattered, threadbare banners of their ancestors.

Then at long last it was all over. The house was silent, the myriad servants invisible, and he was alone. His leg ached abominably with so much standing, his head ached and his ears rang with all the talk, but most of all his heart ached, for he knew now that he would not go to meet Madeleine, nor travel across the world with her, nor even see her again. He was tied with silken ropes to his new, great destiny. The moment he stepped into the huge flagged hall with its magnificent hammer-beam roof he had realized it. It was there in the uncompromising eyes which looked out from all the family portraits; in the coat of mail worn by Hugh at the crusades; the suits of armour made for William at Crécy and Richard at Agincourt; in the silk banner carried by John's page at Malplaquet and Blenheim; in the arms of the de Laceys which met his eyes everywhere. And, incredibly, he was the last of the direct line, for wars and high living had decimated the once numerous males; if the line were to continue, he must marry and breed sons. He thought then of Lady Henrietta, pictured her seated at the end of the great dining table, intelligent, and as sparkling as the jewels with which he could deck her . . . Yes, Henrietta would bring good new blood into the family and produce children who would go forward into the twentieth century.

But it should be Madeleine, he thought with fresh grief. Madeleine should be my wife and the mother of my children. Without her I might not even be here at all, and she is the one I want. And she was the one he could not have. He took out the velvet case containing the brooch. It was beautiful and so appropriate for her. He ran his finger lightly over it as her words echoed in his head: *'the pressure of your family obligations . . . I love you enough to let you go . . .'* Where had she learned such wisdom? But you will always be my beautiful, my beloved white rose, he thought, and suddenly covered his face with his hands.

Later, much later, he composed himself and drew a small piece of pasteboard towards him. He had planned to write 'I shall love you forever and will never give you up', but now he took up his pen and wrote simply 'Thank you for my life. S. de. L.' It was so cold, so formal, and she would think that it had only taken him a few months to cease loving her. He knew exactly how she would look: white-faced, with those great eyes very bright and her soft lips tightly folded together. His own mouth twisted at the thought of causing her such pain, but he continued to wrap up the little parcel, sealing it with hot wax into which he pressed his signet ring. Thus, he thought, I say goodbye to my one and only love – with a solitary pearl and a few ounces of gold – when I should be giving her the family jewels.

* * *

Sebastian remained for two months at Royston Lacey, but eventually he was driven back to London by loneliness. Although he hunted five days a week and spent every evening poring over estate papers, he could not stand the solitude and silence of the great house. There was an army of servants just a bell-pull away, ready and willing to serve his every need, but until he summoned them they were entirely invisible. Local families had begun to invite him to their dinner parties, but bearing in mind that he was still in mourning, these were kept to small, quiet gatherings which Sebastian found extremely boring. All the people he met were immersed in country matters and the running of their estates, whereas he had been used to company at the highest and lowest of social levels, where laughter, bright lights and music prevailed.

He returned to London and almost at once went to find Sal, telling himself it was only to see if she were still at the shop. She was serving a stout matron in a hideous bonnet when she suddenly looked up and saw him; shock made her speechless and immobile until the customer said shrilly, 'Pay attention to me, girl, or I shall report you to the manager,' and then the quick-witted Sal answered hastily, 'I beg pardin, ma'am, but I just thought I saw a pickpocket!'

'Oh, where? Where?' exclaimed the woman anxiously as she turned to look about her. The shop was crowded in the middle distance, but nearby there was only a very elegant man who appeared incapacitated by a fit of silent coughing, for a large handkerchief covered his nose and mouth and he was half turned away, massive shoulders shaking. 'I see no one,' began the customer querulously, and Sal said quickly, 'No, it's all right, ma'am, I think I just saw 'im dart out the door – never catch 'im naow, with all the craowds outside.'

As soon as the woman had gone, Sal turned to Sebastian, smiling excitedly. She saw at once that he was much changed, for the selfish, rather raffish young swell had turned into a thoughtful, perceptive man with weather-beaten skin deeply lined around the eyes and mouth. So although the old grin immediately scored his face and his eyes looked smilingly and intimately into her own, she saw there was both sadness and weariness in their depths. As he stepped forward she noticed the limp and exclaimed, 'You're hurt!'

'But intact,' he assured her, and saw delight in her eyes. Why not? he thought grimly. If I were about to go to Madeleine I certainly should not be loitering here, but I shall never see her again and celibacy is not for me. 'Could you spare a night of comfort for a poor, wounded soldier who has been very lonely?' he asked Sal, without any further preamble.

'Oh yes, please, Capt'ing dear,' she replied brightly. 'Tonight?'

'Tonight,' he affirmed decisively.

He arrived as always in full evening dress and clutching a magnum of champagne. Sal ran to him at once, first to hug him about the waist and then to fiddle at his shirt front. 'Hey,' he protested laughingly, 'what are you doing to me, sweetheart?'

'Wot does it look like?' she countered saucily.

'I think you're undressing me!'

'That's right, Capt'ing dear, but these pearl studs ain't 'alf difficult to undo!'

Sebastian uttered a whoop of delight and, with one arm, lifted her bodily to circle the room before setting her down. 'Sal, you darling! I thought you'd want to go out first.'

The round brown eyes were already heavy lidded as she raised them to his. 'You ain't the only one who's bin very lonely,' she said softly.

Sebastian put down the champagne with a thump and began pulling off his gloves. 'Then let's not waste a minute more,' he said, grinning happily as his eyes swept over her. 'This, I believe, will be a night to remember!'

It was, but not in quite the way he anticipated, for when at last he moved away from her, he lay on his back, breathing deeply and with an arm flung across his eyes; both his hands were clenched so tightly that the knuckles were white. Eventually he realized that Sal was completely silent, and he turned his head to look at her sombrely. She was on her side, head resting on her own closed fist, and looking at him thoughtfully. 'You're very quiet, Sal. Are you all right?'

'I think I've jus' bin run over by an express train and a steam roller at the same time,' she said, straight-faced, 'but other than that, I'm fine!'

He uttered a harsh bark of laughter and stretched out his hand to curl his fingers around her wrist. 'I'm sorry, love,' he said, his tone gentle but almost absent-minded.

Sal noticed at once. 'You've changed, Capt'ing dear.'

Sebastian shrugged. 'War always changes a man, Sal.'

'Bin a long, long time alone, 'aven't you?' she persisted. ''Asn't there bin any – '

He shuddered involuntarily as he remembered the horde of screaming women on the quay at Varna; most of them had been soldiers' wives, but being stranded without money or food soon made them forget whatever scruples they had. And there was the troops' own well-known slogan that in Constantinople a man could get drunk for sixpence and syphilis for a shilling. 'Yes,' Sebastian said aloud, 'but I was saving myself for you.' It was a lie, carelessly uttered and not to be taken seriously.

'How strange,' Sal said softly, 'when all the time you was makin' love ter me, I felt you was thinkin' of someone else.'

He caught his breath at that, astonished that she should have realized his misery. Sal's heart sank and tears rushed to her eyes as he made no reply. I knewed it all the time,

368

she thought sadly. She waited, but the silence was only broken by the raucous ticking of her cheap clock. At last she said very softly, 'Why don' you tell me about her, Capt'ing,' then felt every bone in her body jerk as he roared, '*What!*' Sal cringed and a tear began slowly to fall. She had only meant to help him, and instead his instant reaction was horror that he should discuss this other woman with the likes of her! He finks 'er so wunnerful that I ain't even good enough ter mention 'er, Sal thought in terrible hurt.

But Sebastian, turning a cold eye to her, noticed the tear and, like many large men, he could not bear to see a woman cry. 'Why, Sal, poor little girl, you're crying!' he exclaimed, and then added contritely, 'Was I such a brute – did I hurt you?' When the blonde curls were shaken vigorously, he pulled her gently by the arm. 'Well then, come and have a cuddle and tell me what is the matter.'

As she sank against his chest, he put his arms warmly about her. 'Now, surely you can tell me, love?' he insisted, softening his voice.

Tears were a luxury which Sal had learned at a very early age to suppress, for they had invariably brought a sharp cuff to the side of her head and a harsh order to 'stop tha' snivellin'.' Sebastian's entirely different reaction now made her cry all the more, and her tears literally rained down on his bare chest. Eventually, as he continued to question her, she raised swollen, half-closed eyes and said between little sobbing breaths, 'I only wanted to 'elp you, Capt'ing, an' – an' I didn't know you would get angry when I jus' spoke of 'er. I know I ain't anybody, but – '

Sebastian suppressed a laugh with difficulty. Well, by God, his father had been quite right: 'Never imagine that by loving and bedding them you will ever understand women,' he had said, 'for they are a breed apart.' Only too true, Sebastian thought, for there had been

Madeleine, all love and tenderness when he had expected anger after he had tried to leave his hospital bed, and now here was Sal, usually as chirpy as a London sparrow, shedding tears like a waterfall. 'Why, of course I didn't mean to give such an impression!' he exclaimed now, and because this was a complete lie he took great care to sound absolutely convincing. 'I thought you might feel unhappy to know about Madeleine, but we can speak of her, if you wish.'

Madeleine! It was the name he had muttered over and over in his sleep, and confirmation of her existence drove a dagger into Sal's heart. Yet at the same time she felt overwhelmingly curious, and so she sat up, gave a huge sigh and rubbed the back of her hand across her mouth.

Sebastian, remembering his jacket had been hastily flung down beside the bed, stretched out an arm until he found the handkerchief in the breast pocket. 'Here, love,' he said, handing it to her. 'Now, what is it you want to know?'

The handkerchief was silk, incredibly soft, and with a coronet above the monogram. Sal buried her face luxuriously in its folds and her voice was muffled as she asked the eternal question, 'Wot's she like?'

'The most beautiful woman I have ever seen,' Sebastian answered at once, now meaning every word. 'Her face is a perfect oval, with high cheekbones and the loveliest skin – like a white rose – her hair is chestnut brown and she has the most wonderful eyes: absolutely huge, fringed with thick dark lashes, and although they are grey they reflect every shade of light. When she is sad the grey turns to a shadowed darkness, but when she is happy – and especially in candlelight – they shine brilliantly, and always, always, they have the most tender, gentle expression.' Sebastian, having been launched on his favourite subject, now found that he could not stop. 'And her

370

mouth is wonderful too – very soft and sweetly curving – and her smile transforms her.'

Sal was now as fascinated as he was enraptured; when he paused, remembering the pressure of Madeleine's lips, Sal said, 'An' 'er figure?'

'Oh, she's tall for a woman, but is very slender and with the most delicate bones; holding her is like holding a tiny, fragile bird, and I'm always afraid of crushing her. Even her wrists are the smallest I've ever seen and they look positively brittle.' Sebastian was now totally oblivious of Sal as a woman and she, while all the time feeling the dagger twist in her heart, could not stop. 'I s'pose she's always bewfully dressed,' she said wistfully.

'Well, she has exquisite taste, but she went to her first ball in a dress she'd made herself and wearing an old cloak belonging to my aunt.'

'G' on!' exclaimed Sal in disbelief.

'Oh yes,' Sebastian said seriously. 'You see, she's known great poverty, and I was told once that she'd had to borrow a handcart so that she could take the last of her furniture to be sold.'

'Nefer!' Sal was round-eyed with amazement. A new thought struck her and she asked: 'Ain't she a lydy then?'

'The most perfect, most gentle lady imaginable,' answered Sebastian dreamily, 'but her father lost all his money and was very poor when he died.'

Sal, who had been picturing a huge-eyed bird with a diamond tiara on its head and a luxurious life style, now began to see the unknown Madeleine as a fellow woman; the fact that she had been so poor was something which Sal could immediately understand, and she even began to think if the Capt'ing had to marry, Madeleine was the right person for him. 'Wen you goin' ter marry 'er then, Capt'ing?' she asked, dreading the answer but unable to stop herself.

There was a short pause while Sebastian came out of

his dream world, then he said tonelessly, 'I can't marry her.'

'You don' mean ter say she's got a 'usband already!' exclaimed Sal, feeling slightly let down. Because she had lost her own virginity at an extremely early age, the heroine of all her fantasies was always spotless and untouched.

'No, there's no husband.' The words were uttered with a sigh and a great weariness of spirit, but Sal persisted boldly, 'Wot then?'

Afterwards he never knew why he answered and gave the secret to a woman who did not even know his full name, but the words were spoken in grief and without thought. 'Because my father married her on his deathbed, and therefore the law forbids me to marry her, or her me,' he said, and suddenly he was choked and had to put his hand over his eyes.

For the second time that night Sal was shocked into complete silence. 'is old man! 'oo'd 'ave thought it? she kept asking herself, and then frowned, for there was another thought niggling at the back of her mind, but before she could clarify it, Sebastian had leapt off the bed.

'We need a drink!' he exclaimed in a harsh, brittle voice. 'Can you find a couple of glasses, Sal?'

She scrambled up, and for the first time in their long relationship felt embarrassed at her nakedness. Hastily she pulled on her shift and took two ancient glasses from a cupboard. Sebastian filled them, then handed one to her and touched it with his own. 'Here's to you, sweet Sal,' he said, managing to smile down at her. He tossed off his glassful. 'Drink up!' he urged, as he gave himself a refill.

Sal took a brief sip but continued to frown at the floor, until Sebastian gently tweaked a curl dangling over her ear. 'Penny for them, love.'

She looked up, still frowning in concentration. 'Wot I

can't understand . . .' she began, and then stopped in uncertainty.

'Yes?' prompted Sebastian. 'Stop frowning and tell me what's bothering you.'

'Well,' she began again, 'if it was on 'is deathbed, it nefer was a proper marriage, was it?'

'No, of course not,' Sebastian said, filling up his glass again. 'And my father never intended it to be – he just wanted to give Madeleine his name.'

'So why can't it be unmade?'

Now it was his turn to frown. 'Unmade?'

'Yes, if there wasn't no reel marriage . . .'

It was like a great thunderclap in his brain, and for a few seconds he seemed turned to stone. Then with a loud shout of joy, he exclaimed, 'Annulled! Annulled! Of course, *of course* – oh, my God, Sal, you don't know what you've just said!'

'Yes, I do,' she replied soberly, but he was like a man transported to the very pinnacle of happiness.

'You wonderful, wonderful girl!' he shouted, picking her up and waltzing around the tiny room with her, his face suffused with such joy that Sal's heart lurched. Blimey, she thought, 'e don' jus' love 'er, 'e adores 'er!

Sebastian, having put her down, was now galvanized into frantic action, pulling on first his trousers and then his elastic-sided patent-leather evening boots as though there was not a second to be lost, while all the time he kept saying, 'I can't believe it – I can't – to think it was staring me in the face all the time! Why didn't it occur to me at once? I've always known I was a blackguard, but I didn't realize I was a cretinous one as well!'

'I expec' you couldn't see the wood for the branches,' Sal said comfortingly.

'Trees,' he corrected automatically, and she nodded. 'Tha's wot I said.'

She went to perch on the edge of the bed. 'I don' reckon I'll be seein' you agin, Capt'ing,' she said sadly.

Sebastian paused in the act of securing his cuff links and looked at her. She was hunched into a small, forlorn bundle, head bent, and he realized at that moment that she loved him. Formerly he would have exclaimed impatiently and got out of the room as quickly as possible, but now he came to sit beside her. 'I think perhaps not, Sal,' he said gently, and covered her clasped hands with one of his own. 'Certainly, if I do marry Madeleine, I shall never want anyone else.' And then, as her head drooped even more, he added, 'I'm so sorry, but you do understand, sweet, don't you?'

Yes, she understood only too well what he was trying to say: that there never could be any other solution, nor had he ever contemplated one, for he was a great toff and she a semi-literate little shopgirl who was only good enough for a night of boisterous lovemaking, with perhaps a visit to a music hall as an added treat. ''Course I understand,' she said, getting up. 'An' naow I could do with a bit more bubbly, please.'

He jumped up to fill her glass, eager to do something for her, and then suddenly remembered that he was now one of the richest men in England. 'Sal,' he said quickly, 'let me set you up – buy you a nice little house somewhere so that you are independent, or perhaps a business of your own. How about a cigar shop? They're springing up everywhere and they always have pretty girls serving in them. Think what a lot of men you'd meet if you had your own.'

She smiled into her glass; he still had not realized that she wanted only him, but she said, 'Tha's reel loverly of you, Capt'ing, but I expec' I'll go ter Fred.'

'Fred?' demanded Sebastian, stiffening slightly. 'Who the devil is he?'

Cor, Sal thought, talk abaut wantin' ter 'ave yer cake

an' eat it! 'Why, Fred is someone I growed up wif,' she said. ''E went ter America three years ago, diggin' fur gold out West, an' 'e's done ever so well, an' 'e 'as kep' on writin', askin' me ter go out an' marry 'im.'

This was something entirely new and Sebastian felt he should give it some thought. 'But has he found gold?'

'No,' Sal admitted reluctantly. 'But meanwhile 'e's got hisself a store an' supplies all the other diggers wif tools an' everyfing they needs.'

'Well, Sal dear,' Sebastian said gravely, 'I do think you should give careful consideration to it all before you decide. I believe life in the American West is very hard.'

She managed some semblance of her usual chirpy smile. 'I'm sure I could manage.'

'Then let me stock you up with some pretty clothes and pay your passage so that you can travel in comfort. I should so like to do that,' Sebastian said, meaning every word.

But again she shook her head. 'I don' expec' 'e'd wan' tha'.'

Sebastian swung his cloak around his shoulders and then stood looking down at her gravely. 'Isn't there anything, Sal?'

'No, bu' thanks ever so, Capt'ing dear.' She just managed to look bright and happy.

'Then, thank *you*, love, thank you for everything,' Sebastian said, putting his arm around her shoulders.

'Tha's all righ', it was always loverly, an' per'aps you'll sometimes remember me . . .'

'Always, when I pass the Burlington Arcade, I'll remember the short skirt and those little slim legs in their pink stockings.'

She giggled a little shakily. 'Me first an' last customer.'

'Have I really been the one and only?' Sebastian asked, knowing that he was being unfair, but Sal answered at once, 'Oh, yes.' He hugged her then and kissed her lingeringly on the temple. 'You've given me a great deal,' he said, and thought: I've never given her anything; I hardly thought of her unless I wanted a night of cheap whoring, and the moment I left her, I completely forgot her.

And she had made it so easy for him. Almost from the first, money had been out of the question, so he had always offered to take her out, but the theatre was taboo in case they should be seen and the music halls, which she loved, bored him exceedingly. She was fond of champagne, so he had always brought that, and occasionally, very occasionally, he had sent her a hamper from Fortnum's, but although she always thanked him profusely, he often wondered if she really enjoyed the contents, for her favourites were jellied eels, cockles, chitterlings, pigs' trotters and tripe – food which he had never tasted before he met her and which revolted him.

It was time to go but, acting on a sudden impulse, he drew out his silver card case and handed a piece of pasteboard to her. 'If you should ever need anything – anything at all – this address will find me,' he said. Then he was at the door, eager to be gone. 'So goodbye, sweet Sal, I hope you'll be very happy with Fred.'

'Oh, an' I – I 'ope you'll be wif your Madleen,' Sal managed to say, but he was already halfway down the stairs. She rushed to the small window and looked out into the early morning light. Of course he had got a hansom straight away; for him they seemed to materialize from the shadows. With his foot on the step, he looked up and raised his hat to her, his smile joyous. Sal flapped her hand energetically up and down, but she knew then that he would not return, for always before he had bounded into the cab without a backward glance. She remained at the window until the cab turned the corner, then she sank down on to the bed. There was a great lump in her throat, but somehow she could not cry now.

She looked down at his card and then whistled softly through her teeth as she laboriously spelled out: *Major the Earl of Wells, VC*, and in small script just beneath, *11th Hussars*, and in the corner, *Royston Lacey, Near Wells, Somerset*. Cor, she thought, he reely was a toff, but 'e'd nefer tried ter put me down – in fac' 'e always treated me like a lydy an' all, wasn' 'e a wunnerful lover! There won't nefer be another like 'im, the beaut'ful black stallion. Bu' I'll nefer see 'im agin.

In this, however, she was wrong, for they were to meet again some twenty-five years later, soon after he had been given the Garter by a grateful Sovereign and Sal was the fourth richest woman in America.

Sebastian remained at his club only long enough to shave, take a bath and change. Breakfast, he decided, was something he could easily forgo, for now he was in an absolute fever of impatience to see Mr Lethbridge, who could surely tell him at once whether Madeleine's marriage could be annulled.

Bowling along to Lincoln's Inn, Sebastian's heart was lighter than it had been for months. To think that the possibility of annulment had been there, staring him in the face all the time, and he had never realized it.

But the offices of Lethbridge, Lethbridge & Masters were closed. 'It's Whitsun, guv,' the cabby told him. Good God, he'd even forgotten that! He leapt back into the cab and drove to Kensington, only to be told by the Lethbridge maidservant that the family were in Yorkshire and not expected back until the following Tuesday.

'What about Masters?' demanded Sebastian. The maid said primly that Mr Masters had gone to Paris. Sebastian groaned inwardly: to have to wait another two full days! Surely there must be someone who could tell him! But the City appeared to have come to a standstill, and it was the ringing of a distant church bell that made him remember the Reverend Mr Johnson; it was his curate who had conducted the marriage service. Mr Johnson had known all the General's family very well and he had been Sebastian's first tutor. Surely, as a minister of the Established Church, he would know the law on annulment.

Within the hour Sebastian was on his way to Bath, where he drove straight to the vicarage.

Mr Johnson rose with a smile of real pleasure when Sebastian almost ran into his study. 'Sebastian – may I still call you that, now that you are so elevated? – this is a most pleasant surprise! Come and sit down, my dear boy, and tell me how you are.'

It was with the very greatest difficulty that Sebastian curbed his impatience and complied. The old boy was genuinely fond of him, he knew, and even he could not hurt the clergyman by cutting across his questions. But finally, after what seemed to him hours, he leaned forward and said urgently, 'Sir, I have come for your advice on a matter of the utmost importance to me.'

'Why, my boy, you know that if there is anything I can do, I shall be only too pleased,' began the old man courteously.

'Thank you,' Sebastian said, and drew a deep breath. 'It concerns the marriage of my father to Miss Brett; I want to know if it can be annulled.' He stopped abruptly, staring at the clergyman. Mr Johnson had been leaning back, smiling benevolently, hands clasped over his stomach, but then in an instant the smile was wiped off his face and his hands had moved to clutch at the arms of his chair.

'Oh, I cannot tell you about that,' he said agitatedly. 'I cannot tell you anything at all!'

'But why not?' demanded Sebastian, brows drawing together. 'You must know what the law is.'

'Yes, yes, my boy. But, you see, this is a matter of honour.'

Sebastian stood up, his huge frame filling the low-ceilinged room. 'I am afraid I do not understand,' he said, trying hard to keep his voice low and calm. 'Please oblige me by explaining.'

The trembling hands, with their rheumatic fingers and brown-spotted skin, came together, only to twist and fly apart again. 'I cannot,' Mr Johnson said, now obviously distressed. 'I truly cannot; you must ask Lady Frensham.'

'Lady Frensham!' echoed Sebastian in total astonishment. 'What the devil has she got to do with it?'

'Everything,' breathed the old man. 'And I gave her my word – you must not, you really must not press me on this!'

'All right,' Sebastian said. 'But at least you can tell me whether a marriage which is not consummated and has one partner dying within two hours qualifies for annulment.'

To his further astonishment, this appeared to increase the clergyman's agitation, for he shook his head and said, 'Yes – no, no, the law does not apply in this case; it is quite different.'

'You are talking in riddles, sir.' Sebastian was now coldly furious and standing over Mr Johnson, unaware of how menacing he appeared. 'I have asked you a question in what I hope was a civil manner, and I believe you owe me the courtesy of an explanation.'

The coldness of Sebastian's words suddenly calmed the old man. His hands became still and his voice quiet as he looked up into Sebastian's eyes. 'Believe me, my lord, I should dearly like to help you, but as I have said, this is a matter of honour and I am sure you will understand that, having given my word to Lady Frensham, I have to remain silent. If she gives her permission for me to do otherwise, I shall be most happy to comply.' As Sebastian continued

379

to stare at him, he added, 'I beg you to forgive my seeming unhelpfulness.'

It was obviously no use trying to force him further, and with a 'goodbye to you, sir!' Sebastian dashed away. At the White Hart he hired a racing curricle and drove at top speed to Norton St Philip, only to be told that Lady Frensham was not due back from Warwickshire until late in the afternoon. Would his lordship care to leave a message? No, he would not, but he would return later. As he gathered up the reins, Sebastian sighed, suddenly feeling tired and dispirited. He had been on the move since daybreak, trying to get a simple answer to a simple question, but there seemed no end to the frustration. And what the devil was he to do until late afternoon?

When the distant towers of Summerleigh came into view, he turned the horse at once in the direction of the Manor. Catherine and her father had attended Rob's funeral, but there had been no opportunity to talk and he wanted so much to know how she had come to look after Madeleine.

Catherine received him at once, rising and coming forward with hand outstretched. She was a little plumper than he remembered, but the wild-rose blush staining her cheeks made her very pretty and her smile held real warmth. 'My lord, what a very happy surprise,' she said, as he bent over her hand. 'And just in time for luncheon. I do hope you will join us.'

Sebastian started guiltily. How awful, arriving at such a time without an invitation, but he'd had no idea – and now he felt extremely hungry. 'Thank you,' he said. 'I should very much like to do so.'

Catherine turned her graceful head towards the door. 'Jenkins, please lay another place and tell my father that his lordship is here.'

'I do apologize for arriving out of the blue like this,'

380

Sebastian said, 'but I left London very early this morning and seem to have lost all idea of time.'

'Oh, but my father and I have been so hoping to see you, my lord, and we have spoken of you very often.'

Catherine's father, whom Sebastian had always disliked and labelled as a cold man, was equally welcoming, almost effusive, and the meal passed very pleasantly. Both Llewellyn Morgan and Catherine were informed people and good conversationalists; also, they were eager to hear about the war, which made Sebastian even more anxious to ask about Catherine's part in getting Madeleine to Turkey. So when they rose from the table he said at once, 'Miss Llewellyn Morgan, before I take my leave, will you do me the honour of walking on the terrace with me?'

Catherine's heart gave a great leap. Was this to be the moment when he declared himself? She blushed very prettily and said, 'I shall be only too pleased, my lord, if you will excuse me while I fetch a bonnet.' Upstairs she said to her maid, 'Jenny, I believe I may be about to face the most important moment of my life. Which bonnet shall I put on?'

Lordy, thought Jenny, hurr mus' be all a-flutter not to choose hurrself. For Catherine, usually so calm and collected, had never resorted to such help before. 'Why, this one, Miss Catherine,' said Jenny without hesitation. It was a flat-crowned, wide-brimmed straw, with ribbons over the whole, which were tied under the chin and made the brim dip charmingly on each side. Catherine admitted silently that she did look rather well in it.

'There, my lord,' she said smilingly, 'I am quite ready now.'

'May I?' asked Sebastian, holding out his hand for her parasol. He opened it and returned it to her with a slight bow.

'I believe we shall have the most charming view if we

walk this way,' said Catherine, and as he fell into step beside her, she held her breath.

'Miss Llewellyn Morgan,' he said quietly, 'I understand you looked after Madeleine Brett before she left for Turkey, and indeed that it was entirely through your efforts that she went to the East. I wonder if you would be kind enough to tell me how you came to know her whereabouts.'

For an instant Catherine could not believe her ears, then her breath came out in a gasp and she began to speak rapidly in an effort to cover what she thought must be her too obvious chagrin. 'It was in the August; my father and I had gone to see some farmland which he contemplated buying, and when the carriage stopped, I recognized Madeleine among the field workers. I wanted to speak to her, but my father forbade me – '

'Madeleine was working in the fields!' exclaimed Sebastian, sounding amazed.

'Oh yes, harvesting. Then a week or so later, my father told me that when he had sentenced a young man to transportation that morning, Madeleine had stepped forward in court to plead for him. Father saw her in private then, and she actually went down on her knees to beg him.'

'Who was this fellow?' demanded Sebastian in an ominously quiet voice.

'He was the only son of the old woman with whom Madeleine was living and he had been caught poaching – for her, Madeleine said.'

'Are you saying that this – this peasant meant something to her?'

'Oh no, no, of course not! But she had been so ill – would not eat and was half out of her mind.'

Sebastian felt he was trying to find his way through a London pea-souper. 'Why?' he asked blankly. 'Why was she almost out of her mind?'

382

'It was the baby's death, you see – ' Catherine stopped, realizing what she had said, and drew in her breath sharply, her hand flying to her mouth.

Sebastian had stopped in his tracks and was looking down at her with great intensity. 'What baby?'

'Oh, my lord!' exclaimed Catherine in genuine distress. 'I have been guilty of the most terrible indiscretion. I beg that you will forget what I have just said!'

'Quite impossible,' replied Sebastian tersely. 'And I should be extremely grateful if you would start at the beginning and tell me *everything*.'

'No, please. Madeleine is a friend – to tell you would be such a betrayal of her trust, and – and I have already said far too much.' Catherine was almost in tears, and as agitated as her placid nature would allow, but this was the second riddle of the day for Sebastian and he knew that if he had to shake the story out of Catherine he would do so.

With a great effort of will, he softened his voice and forced himself to speak rationally. 'I hope that you will forgive me if I insist upon knowing, for Madeleine Brett was left in my family's care and I feel I am almost her next of kin and should therefore know what happened to her after she left us so mysteriously. There may be reparations I should make, among other things.'

But Catherine was as reluctant as Mr Johnson. 'My lord,' she began, 'you place me in a most difficult situation, and I must ask you again not to insist.'

'But I do insist,' said Sebastian implacably.

She knew then with absolute certainty that the massive man standing in front of her had no intention whatsoever of moving until he knew the whole story, and she gave in, but with very genuine regret. 'Very well, my lord,' she said quietly, 'but I must ask you to treat the matter with the utmost discretion and – please, please remember that I would so much have preferred to remain silent.'

Sebastian inclined his head. 'Of course,' he said, his voice very clipped.

'Madeleine must have left Bath so suddenly because – because she realized she was going to have a child – '

'Indeed?' he queried at once. 'Did she tell you this?'

'No, she said nothing.' Catherine's head was bent to hide her embarrassment; did he not realize how difficult it was for her, an unmarried girl, to be talking about childbirth?

It seemed he had no idea, for he persisted, 'Did she ever mention the father?'

'No, never. I tried once to make her, when she was so terribly grief-stricken over the baby, as I thought the father might have been able to help her, but she merely said that while she loved him and always would do so, he despised her and thought her some sort of adventuress.'

Sebastian pulled at his stock as though choking. 'Please continue.'

'So after she left your father's house, she went to Bristol.'

'Bristol!' he exclaimed. 'I felt sure it would be London!'

Catherine's patience was not endless and she thought, if he is going to keep on interrupting, this will take hours and I cannot stand it. 'Madeleine had no money,' she said almost curtly. 'She only went to Bristol because a drover agreed to take her in his cart. I believe she walked the streets all day looking for work – you see, she was desperate to find shelter for the night and was terrified of having to go to the workhouse. Eventually she was engaged by a man called George Sharpe, one of those *parvenu* merchants, who treated her and everyone else abominably. He threw her out three weeks later when he was told she was to have a child. By chance, she then met Ellen, who had been one of your father's servants, and Ellen took Madeleine to her mother – because of the pregnancy there was nowhere else for her to go – and she

384

stayed with the family in their tiny cottage. I have seen it; it is more like a hut with a lean-to thatched roof, and inside at that time there was only an old torn curtain dividing the sleeping area from the rest of the room. It was there that Madeleine gave birth, without the aid of doctor or midwife, but she apparently recovered quite well. The baby was beautiful, but too tiny because he was premature, and of course Madeleine was so poorly nourished. All the family have told me how much she adored her little boy and how heartrending it was to see her grief when he died after five days. By the time we got her here she was on the point of death.'

Sebastian *was* choking and images of her flashed before his mind's eye: her wistful expression when her face was in repose, the mute appeal in her eyes when she looked at him. He forced himself to speak at last. 'I am deeply indebted to you for all your care of Madeleine; it was an act of great charity.'

Catherine managed a little smile. 'Why, thank you, my lord, but I was only too delighted to do what I could.' She paused, gazing into the distance and thinking deeply, before adding, 'It also taught me a valuable lesson, for I now know that because we have money and a certain position in society, we are treated very differently from the poor. For instance, I was acquainted with George Sharpe and always found him most courteous in an unctuous, uncouth sort of way, yet he was a fiend to his wife and a terrible taskmaster to Madeleine and his servants. We have heard since that he went bankrupt and absconded to America, leaving his wife and children penniless. Then there was Mr Shuttleworth, a minister of the Church, whom I saw with my own eyes push Madeleine off his horse so violently that she literally flew through the air. Yet a moment later, he was smiling and bowing to me in the most charming manner.'

'He should be horsewhipped to within an inch of his

life!' said Sebastian with such savagery that Catherine retreated a step, appalled at the fury in his eyes and drawn-back lips.

'I complained to the Bishop,' she said hesitantly, 'and Mr Shuttleworth was removed from the parish very soon afterwards.'

Sebastian was shaking and his hands were clenched so tightly that the nails bit into his palms, but with the greatest possible effort, he managed to say hoarsely, 'Good. Please continue, Miss Llewellyn Morgan.'

'There is little more to tell. We are fortunate in having a very modern doctor here and he took a great interest in Madeleine's case. I must stress that she herself made a superhuman effort to recover, but Dr Kingsley and I were so worried that her mental state might deteriorate unless she had some great cause to engage upon. When Miss Nightingale wrote to me about her proposal to nurse in the Crimea, this seemed the ideal opportunity for Madeleine, and we were so delighted when she welcomed this herself.'

Catherine looked searchingly at her companion, who had obviously forgotten that she existed as a woman. 'I believe you know the rest, my lord.'

He was white to the lips and misery now replaced the fury in his fine eyes. He spoke as though with difficulty, his voice still hoarse and muffled. 'I am more grateful than I can ever express, Miss Llewellyn Morgan. Madeleine saved my life at Scutari and she means everything in the world to me. If I am ever able to render you any service, anything at all, I do most sincerely beg that you will call upon me.'

'Thank you, my lord,' said Catherine faintly. Her dream had shattered into a thousand pieces and she felt only relief when he said, 'Now, if you will excuse me, I must take my leave of you.'

After he had dashed away, Catherine remained quite

still and deep in thought. Then she sighed and made her way slowly to where her father sat in his library.

'Surely he has not gone,' Mr Llewellyn Morgan said in surprise. He had expected a radiant couple to appear and for Sebastian to ask formally for Catherine's hand. Instead, here was his daughter looking pale and abstracted.

'Papa,' she said at last, 'I believe he was the father of Madeleine's baby!'

'What!' exclaimed her father in cold anger. 'Are you sure?' and at Catherine's unhappy nod, he burst out: 'That confounded woman! I always told you she was no good – '

'No, papa, you are wrong,' Catherine said evenly. 'Sebastian de Lacey always had the reputation of being as wild as he was irresistible, and I feel that if he set out to ensnare Madeleine, she would have been quite unable to deny him – any more than I should.'

'Catherine!' exploded Mr Llewellyn Morgan. 'You appal me!'

'I am sorry, papa, but I know I am right. You never saw Madeleine's heartbreak over her baby – and you did not see the utter misery and remorse on Sebastian's face today!'

19

He remembered turning the horse's head down the long straight avenue, but after that his thoughts were blurred, and as soon as he was away from the estate, he drew up. He flung off his hat, realizing that his face was running with sweat, and the cool spring breeze ruffled his hair and fanned his burning eyes. Slowly, like a man in a trance, he wiped his face. To think he had made her suffer so much – his beautiful, tender girl – that she had starved, been hounded, and then made to labour in the fields for all those months; how could she have done it, when she was so tiny, so delicate? And to think that she had had a baby, his baby, *their* baby without any real help – Christ, anything could have happened to her: she could easily have died. At this he began to sweat again and to shake. To think that a de Lacey child had been born in such circumstances! No matter that there had been many such births down the centuries; no matter that there might be any number of his own bastards from all his nights of debauchery, for this had been *Madeleine's* child, and in his heart he thought of her as his wife and his beloved.

He never knew how long he remained there, drawn up under the shade of a huge oak, but eventually his thoughts quietened a little. He remembered his hip flask and pulled it out, uncapping it with fingers which still trembled. It was only after he had taken a long, long swig that his confidence began to return. He would renounce the title and let one of the small boy cousins succeed; then he and Madeleine would go away as he had originally planned.

'And I can make her forget,' he whispered aloud. 'I was her first man, and I was careless and cruel, but in the future it will always be wonderful for her. I can take her to the pinnacle of ecstasy, and I'll never stop telling her how much I adore her, how much I need her.' And if she wished, there could be another baby, whom they would love and bring up together. Yes, Sebastian thought as he finished the brandy, that is the way it will be.

Then he remembered Mr Johnson's strange reaction that morning, and he hastily pulled out his watch. Surely dear old Aunt Thea would have returned by now, and he might as well hear her explanation of the riddle. Fired now with brandy and new resolve, Sebastian gathered up the reins and set off at speed for Norton St Philip.

Yes, he was told, her ladyship had returned but was resting and had given instructions that she was not to be disturbed. 'Please give her ladyship my compliments and tell her that I must see her at once on a matter of the most vital and urgent importance,' said Sebastian in so authoritative a manner that the butler almost scuttled away. And if she refuses, I shall go straight up and confront her in her room, Sebastian thought with a trace of the old daredevil smile momentarily lighting his eyes. And that should surely shake her into telling me the truth!

But such action was not necessary, for within minutes Lady Frensham had appeared, looking more angular and desiccated than ever, and her opening remark was not propitious: 'Sebastian, what is the meaning of – ' But he cut her short at once.

'Let's not waste time on superfluous words, aunt,' he said as he propelled her firmly and at speed into a chair. 'I have come a long way and I just want a simple answer, which I am told you can give me. The question is this: what is it about my father's marriage to Madeleine Brett which makes old Johnson get into an immediate lather, tell me annulment does not apply, and that only you are able to speak of it?'

For an instant he saw utter astonishment in her eyes,

389

but then she at once regained her composure, inclined her head in a brief and stately fashion and announced: 'That was very right and proper of him.'

'And so?' prompted Sebastian, as she showed no signs of continuing.

Lady Frensham took out her lorgnette and polished the lenses with great concentration.

'Aunt,' said Sebastian through his teeth and advancing on her menacingly, 'I demand – '

Now it was her turn to cut him short. 'Sebastian, kindly refrain from threatening me!' she said icily. 'And remember to whom you are speaking!'

He flung away to take a quick, limping walk about the room before whirling to face her again. 'As if I could forget!' he said unkindly. 'And I am not at this moment threatening you, but by God, if you don't tell me, I swear I shall not be responsible for my actions!'

'Have you ever been?' asked Lady Frensham, apparently unmoved by his words and putting up her lorgnette to survey him with icy disdain. 'Would it be too much to ask why you appear so desperate to have this knowledge?'

'Not at all. It is because I want to marry Madeleine myself!'

That certainly shook her out of her calm. '*You* want to *marry* her?' she echoed incredulously, the lorgnette almost falling from her hand.

Sebastian looked into her eyes, which were so like his own. 'Yes, aunt, I want that more than anything else in this world.'

'But – but,' she was almost spluttering, 'I thought you did not know her whereabouts.'

'I met her again in Turkey, where she was nursing. Aunt, Madeleine saved my leg, if not my life.'

'Indeed?'

'Indeed and indeed, aunt. She nursed me day and night

390

when I was delirious and in a high fever, never leaving me but pouring liquid into me, sponging me down and – '

'Dear me, how very indelicate!' exclaimed Lady Frensham, with a sniff.

The last of his patience snapped. 'How dare you insinuate that anything about Madeleine is indelicate,' he roared, 'when she is the most sensitive, loving person in the world. If you must know, she was always careful to let the orderly look after my – my natural functions. Now, do you want anything plainer than that?'

Lady Frensham allowed herself to shudder. 'Such a boor,' she murmured as though to herself.

She is baiting me, thought Sebastian. The old devil actually wants me to lose my temper. He forced himself to saunter to the fireplace, where he put his elbow on the mantelpiece, allowing his hand to dangle, open-fingered. The other hand he thrust deeply into his trouser pocket. Then he crossed one foot over the other at the ankle, smiled brilliantly at Lady Frensham and said calmly, 'And so, my dear aunt, you were about to say?'

'May one ask if Miss Brett wishes to marry you?' was all he got in reply.

Sebastian's massive frame shook very slightly and briefly, but he managed to maintain his poise and careful tone as he answered, 'She has indicated in many ways that she loves me and would become my wife, if only I were at liberty to ask her.'

Once more the lorgnette was raised and this time Lady Frensham stared at him fixedly for some seconds until at last she appeared to reach a decision. She snapped the glasses together and said with perfect calm, 'Then you are quite free to ask her to marry you.'

He jerked upright like a marionette whose string has been given a violent pull. '*What?*' he gasped, when at last able to articulate. '*What* did you say?'

'That you are free to ask Madeleine Brett to marry you. And I now add that she is quite free to accept.'

He strode forward, eyes blazing. 'Aunt, if you are playing with me –'

It was her sudden smile which stopped him abruptly. 'As your father insisted on the marriage mainly to protect Madeleine from your sordid attentions, I had to satisfy myself about your present sincerity,' Lady Frensham said, almost gently. 'Now that you *have* convinced me, I am happy to tell you that Madeleine was never legally married to your father. When I explained the situation to Mr Johnson, we agreed that for Henry's sake we should act out a charade, and so a great-nephew of the vicar was asked to impersonate a minister of the Church and conduct the marriage service.' Lady Frensham paused dramatically and then continued, 'The stupid fellow was so nervous that he almost ruined the whole thing, but poor Henry was really too ill to realize, although I thought at one moment that he was suspicious. Of course, it was *very* fortunate that Mr Johnson did have a special licence, which a young sea captain had obtained for his own marriage that day. Mr Parsons – the great-nephew – was able to wave that in front of Henry's nose without his seeing the names shown on it – but, gracious me, how he had to hurry back to return it in time for the other wedding!'

It was amazing, unbelievable, wonderful. It was as though the whole world had burst into joyous song and brilliant light. It was as though every happy dream he'd ever had or would have had come true, and he, too, was bursting into the greatest joy he had ever known. He swooped down on Lady Frensham, not even hearing her gasped 'Sebastian, what do you think you are doing?' and lifted her bodily out of her chair, to waltz her around the room, very much as he had done with Sal almost twelve hours before.

'Aunt, you dear, wonderful old girl!' he shouted. 'You don't know, you cannot know, how unbelievably wonderful this is for me! Thank God, oh thank God! Ah, but I must get back to London tonight!' He kissed her on both cheeks, put her gently back into her chair and was across the room before she had even regained her breath. 'Goodbye for now, dear aunt, and thank you, thank you a million times – I will write to you . . .'

In the hall the butler was like a statue, silver salver in hand. 'A letter for you, my lord,' he said impassively, only his old eyes betraying that he had just overheard a most extraordinary conversation. 'Sent care of her Ladyship.'

Sebastian snatched up the letter and thrust it into his pocket; it couldn't be anything important, to be sent via his aunt. 'Thank you,' he said, and dashed out to leap into the curricle. Turning it in a shower of gravel, he started racing down the drive.

Back in the drawing room, Lady Frensham was tittering happily. No one had ever heard her titter, nor ever would, but now her usually rigid spine was bent and little sounds of 'te-he-he!' escaped her. What a couple they would make: the tall, massive man with those extravagantly good looks, and the slender, ethereal woman with her swanlike grace. Perfect bearers of one of the oldest titles in the land, and what splendid sons they would breed! Of course, there was no doubt that Sebastian was a throw-back to one of the Norman ancestors, not only because of his darkness, but also because of his deep, passionate nature; there had not been a de Lacey like him for centuries, and although he had been such a young rake-hell, she sensed that those days were gone for ever. That he was completely, intensely, in love was certain, and with marriage, a home and children the more serious side of his nature should develop. Oh yes, thought Lady

Frensham happily, it will be a wonderful marriage and our line will continue into the twentieth century.

En route for London once more, Sebastian was planning feverishly: the very first thing next morning he would be at the War Office wanting – demanding – to know when Madeleine was expected home. Then, if there were time, he would travel to meet her, either at Constantinople or Malta – he could hire a yacht! Yes, by God, that was the thing to do! He kept forgetting that he was now one of the richest men in England; of course, a yacht was the answer. How astonished she would be. How her eyes would light up and her skin take on that wonderful glow as though lit from within, which he had always marvelled at – ah, but he would go down on his knees, tell her he knew about the baby and all that she had suffered and beg her, with great humbleness, to forgive him. Then he would say: 'Beloved Madeleine, will you do me the very greatest possible honour of marrying me?' Ah, but might she not think he was just asking her in order to compensate for all the misery of the past? Might it not be better just to say: 'Beloved Madeleine, I know now that we are free to marry and I have come racing out to beg you to be my wife for I cannot live without you, and if you will have me, I swear that my entire life will be spent in trying to make you happy'? Yes, that sounded better, and it was the absolute truth. She would accept; of that he had no doubt, for deep in his heart he knew that she loved him as greatly as he did her. So they would journey together to Paris; they'd have to keep quiet about *that* because she would be unchaperoned and – here he grinned happily to himself – who in the world would believe that he, with his reputation, would keep his distance from her? But keep it he would, no matter what agony this caused him, for no hint of scandal must be attached to his future wife.

If he had not succeeded Rob, he could have suggested

an immediate wedding, but now as head of the family, he felt he owed it to them to marry in style, although nothing would induce him to have one of those fashionably long engagements; rather he would say that Madeleine had been secretly engaged to him long before he left Scutari, and that only Rob's death had caused them to delay the announcement. Aunt Thea would know better, but he had no doubt she would keep quiet.

So, Paris: he must remember to arrange for an unlimited sum to be ready for him because he felt Madeleine might like to have her trousseau made there; he'd heard – God only knew where – that there was a fellow called Worth who designed the most beautiful clothes for the Empress Eugénie, and if Madeleine wished, Worth could be commissioned to make her wedding gown – but it must be something very, very special – a fairy-tale gown for a fairy-tale bride, and one that would be remembered for years to come.

Then the actual ceremony: the obvious choice would be one of the fashionable London churches, but he felt Madeleine would prefer something quieter. A wedding in the family chapel at Royston perhaps? Yes, perfect, the chapel was a jewel of Norman architecture, and there was a sudden undeniable feeling of pride that he and Madeleine would stand beneath the banners of his ancestors, surrounded by the coats of arms of all those other brides who had married into the family. Once they knew her, the family would all love her, but initially there would be doubts and murmurings about the unknown girl who had captured him. It would be very necessary to make Rob's sister his first ally; as Wessex's wife she was powerful in many ways. Also, he would want her to present Madeleine at Court, but that could wait until after their honeymoon – ah, how wonderful, how ecstatic *that* would be! To have her all to himself, to show her by every means humanly possible that he loved and adored her!

And he *could* show her, for all the fashionable whores and all the great ladies whose lover he had been, had taught him everything there was to know about making love. Some of it he would teach Madeleine, but he loved her lack of expertise, loved the touch of her hands made tender by her own love, and the pressure of her lips – at this point Sebastian wanted to leap out of the train; the damned thing was going so slowly and he was sure he could run faster, for he couldn't wait, just could *not* wait, to put all his happy plans into being.

The train was still on the outskirts of London when he felt in a pocket for his ticket. When he drew it out he saw the letter was with it. He turned it over, noting that it was addressed to him as Major de Lacey and was in a plain envelope with an indistinguishable postmark. He decided it could not be of any importance and almost thrust it back into his pocket, but realizing that the train would be another fifteen minutes getting into Paddington, he quickly tore open the envelope and glanced at once at the signature. It was then that his world fell apart, for it was signed *Madeleine Fraser*.

20

Albert Simkin had seen many strange and unusual sights during his years as head porter at the United Services Club, but he was to remember the Earl of Wells' arrival that evening as one of the strangest. A hansom had drawn up, but no one had got out, and Albert had then watched as the cabby first peered then shouted down through the small window in the roof; still some minutes elapsed and Albert thought, Aw, my Gawd, it's one of them ninety-year-old members. But he was astonished when he saw the figure which at last descended from the cab: it appeared to be the Earl of Wells, yet instead of leaping up the steps in his usual whirlwind fashion, he walked like an old man, shoulders hunched and leaning heavily on his stick. Nor did he stop or look round when the cabby shouted, ''Ere, guv, wot about yer bag an' me fare?'

Albert ran to the top of the steps. 'My lord, are you feelin' unwell? Can I 'elp you?' only to see the Earl look up blankly. 'What?' he asked. But Albert had noticed the pain in his eyes. Aw, poor bugger is in agony from 'is wounds, he thought compassionately and, old soldier that he was, he immediately set about looking after the Earl, just as he had done when his own officer had been badly wounded during the retreat from Kabul. Quickly and without fuss he paid off the cabby, carried in the portman-teau and instructed one of his juniors to take it up to the Earl's room. Then he went into the reading room, where the Earl had slumped into a deep leather chair. Albert sucked in his breath through his teeth; wot the 'ell was the ma'er wif the man? 'E knew the rules backwards, so

397

why was 'e sittin' there wif 'is 'at an' coat still on? An' jus' gazin' into space like 'e were soft in the 'ead. 'My lord,' said Albert deferentially, but with resolution, 'may I tyke yer coat an' 'at?'

Again there was the blank stare, but this time a hoarse voice commanded: 'Brandy – a bottle at once!'

'Certainly, my lord,' said Albert, snapping his fingers authoritatively. 'Bu' naow, 'ow about yer 'at an' coat?'

'Bugger off,' said the Earl quietly but very succinctly.

'Yes, m'lord,' said Albert, pouring a glass of brandy and putting it in front of the Earl. Then he bowed, and as he passed he whipped off Sebastian's hat before retreating with dignity to his place in the hall. 'E's in a real nasty mood, Albert thought, an' I can't do nothin' more for the time bein'. Yet soon other members were appearing in evening dress and there was the Earl, still sitting, not only in his greatcoat, but in day clothes as well. Once more Albert approached him: There were no doubt abaht it: 'is nibbs 'ad got fru the brandy like it were wa'er an' naow 'e jus' kep' on readin' a bit o'paper, even though 'e mus' know it by 'eart.

'Will you be takin' dinner, my lord?' asked Albert politely.

The fine eyes looked up at him, black and opaque with pain. 'No,' said his lordship in a tone which greatly discouraged further conversation.

But Albert persisted, 'Then may I remin' yer, m'lord, that yer didn' ought to be sittin' 'ere in day clothes an' top coat,' he said, agitation making him less careful than usual about his speech. Surprisingly, the Earl struggled out of the chair, saying only, 'Then get me out of this and have a bottle of brandy sent up to my room at once.'

As Albert complied and then stood watching the tall figure walk with great deliberation towards the stairs, he thought: 'e's drunk an' all, but at that moment the Earl made a careful turn and said, 'Thank you, Simkin, you have been most thoughtful,' and Albert's soft old heart immediately melted. There's too much marryin' one wif t' other in them old families, he thought sagely, often makes 'em very eccentric . . .

Once in the privacy of his room, Sebastian tore off his neckcloth and threw it on the floor. Thank God the brandy had arrived ahead of him and he began at once to make his way towards it, shedding clothes and bumping into furniture as he walked.

Sebastian was a strong, healthy man who had been toughened by the Crimean campaign, and the fact that he had eaten very little during the previous twenty-four hours and had been dashing about almost nonstop after a night of lovemaking would not normally have upset his equilibrium too much, but this, together with the violent seesawing of his deepest emotions and hopes, had poleaxed him. Now, after drinking a bottle of brandy in record time, his capacity to feel, instead of remaining blunted, was returning like circulation to a numbed limb, and with it came total exhaustion. As he pulled out the cork with his teeth he glanced at the bed with distaste: too narrow and too lonely, he thought, frowning at it. And surely it was waving about just above the ground!

It must be wonderful to be happily married, and to share a bed with a beloved wife – not only for lovemaking, but just to fall asleep knowing that the person you adored would be with you, slender body curving into your own, and then to wake and find her head snuggled into your shoulder, her hair spilling across your chest . . . Of course it was fashionable for husbands to sleep in their dressing rooms, but he wouldn't want that and he was sure Madeleine would not banish him . . . His musing stopped abruptly when he caught sight of himself in the mirror: he was standing there stark naked, bottle in hand, and with a fatuous smile on his face – for Christ's sake, why couldn't he get it into his head that he would never share a bed with Madeleine, and that if the damnable fellow she had married had any sense, *he* would be cradling her in his arms at that moment . . . Oh, God, he thought in despair, there must be a woman somewhere who can make me forget her.

Paris, he thought, splashing brandy into the glass, he'd still go to Paris, even though he'd be alone, for they had the cleverest whores in the world there, able to make a man forget anything, and he would keep himself surrounded by champagne so that every time he even started to remember, he had only to stretch out a hand and drink himself into oblivion. Yes, that would be the thing to do . . .

Sebastian drained the glass, standing against the wardrobe to stop himself from falling over backwards. But could a man really exist solely on champagne and whores? He shook his head emphatically and reeled uncontrollably across the room. No, after a time life would be like a desert. Desert – desert? Where had he heard that before? 'Can't 'member,' he muttered. Desert . . . '*If you do not follow her your long life will be a desert. Even though you will be one of the great ones of the earth.*' The words kept on going round and round in his head, but it was no use, he could not remember.

'Lie down before you fall down,' he told himself, speaking aloud and enunciating very carefully, and he just got to the bed, where he sprawled across it, face downwards, until later in the night cold forced him to drag himself between the sheets.

He opened his eyes with the greatest possible reluctance and almost instantly closed them again. The light, the bloody light, was sending splinters of brilliance boring into his eyes, which felt gummed together . . . as though he'd cried in his sleep. 'Oh, for God's sake,' he muttered furiously and lifted his head without thinking, only to let it fall back immediately. Sweet Christ, he groaned inwardly, I've been getting drunk since I was seventeen, but I've never known anything like this before. Yet he must get up; he knew that with absolute certainty, even though he could not think why. Surely the obvious thing was to try and sleep off the worst of it. Ah, but his sleep during the night had not done much for him, for he seemed to be haunted by a woman, a black woman, with a kind, seamed face under a large black hat, who kept imploring him to remember. 'But I bloody well can't,' he muttered, frowning. Oh, God dammit, even *that* was painful. Closing his eyes again, he saw the placards that he had stared at so blankly at Paddington, placards with huge black letters: CRIMEAN HEROINE HOME. GREAT WELCOME FOR MRS SEACOLE. Seacole . . . Seacole . . . Extraordinary name, but he'd heard it before. '*My mother was a West Indian doctoress, and my father a Scot . . . I am fey . . . the information is a gift, sir* . . . Remember, please remember!' Seacole . . . a dark tartan dress, an anxious face looking up at him as he stumbled up the gangway . . . '*Remember . . . the woman you love . . . who bore your son . . . you are to be offered a second chance*.' He was suddenly alert, knowing that it was of vital importance for him to remember all she had said and, clamping his teeth together, he forced himself to get out of bed and across the room, even though to stand upright seemed impossible. But he managed to get to the washstand in a strange crouching movement, head well down. Then he levered himself upwards just sufficiently to let his head hang over the basin and, grasping the ewer, he poured the cold water over his head and neck. The iciness of the water made him gasp and splutter, but it was not enough, so dragging out the slop pail, he stood over that and tossed the basinful of water over himself again, regardless of the large amount that flowed on to the carpet. That was certainly better . . . his head, neck and shoulders were drenched and strands of curling

401

black hair were dripping into his eyes as he felt for a towel to wrap around his head. Now, try very carefully to straighten up, he told himself. Yes, yes, but slowly, for the room is spinning a bit . . . But if you can just get a cold bath – you must, God dammit, man, you bloody well must.

He did. And afterwards, although his head hurt abominably and would no doubt do so for hours, his body felt fresh and glowing. He ordered a huge pot of black coffee and scalded his tongue in an effort to drink it at once, for now there was a feeling of great urgency. He sat down, put his head in his hands and closed his eyes. Now, for God's sake, concentrate. Go back to that bleak, terrible day when they'd hustled him away from her . . . They'd hauled and pushed him into that cart, which had seemed to jolt over every stone and lurch into every hole on the way down to the quay; getting out had been difficult because his legs were trembling with weakness and his hands with shock so that he could hardly hold his sticks. Almost immediately she had appeared before him. '*I have a message . . . please remember . . . to be offered a second chance . . . because your love for each other is also very rare and very deep . . . You think now you have lost her and she will go with another to a burning land . . . but you must follow . . . she will die unless you save her . . . and your long life will be a desert.*'

Sebastian leapt up, regardless of the agony this brought to his head, and strode to where his jacket lay in a crumpled heap on the floor. The letter – where had he put the letter? He really knew the contents by heart, but he must make absolutely sure . . . Yes, here it was. He straightened the single sheet which was headed SS *Himalaya*, and began to read:

Dear Major de Lacey,
    You must think me extremely rude for not having written

before to thank you for your wonderful gift, but we have been in the throes of closing the hospital and there truly has been no time for letter writing. But now I do so want you to know how much I love the brooch; it is quite beautiful and I never thought to own anything like it. Of course, there was no need for you to send me a gift, but I very much appreciate your great generosity and do thank you.

I read the newspaper account of your investiture at Fort Pitt and felt sure it must have been a wonderful occasion. I also read of the dinner you attended at the Palace and of the very beautiful duke's daughter whom you escorted. Since then there has been no time for newspapers, but no doubt I shall see your engagement or marriage before too long. Meanwhile, you may not be too surprised to learn that I was married last week to Dr Alastair Fraser. He first asked me to marry him last Christmas, but I refused him and continued to do so until the hospital started to close, and then I realized I did not want to be alone any more. I told Alastair all about myself and he still wanted to marry me, so I am very fortunate to have found so kind and good a husband. I want only to make him as good a wife. We are now en route for India, where Alastair has obtained a post in the Indian Medical Service as assistant surgeon at Lucknow.

Just before we embarked I walked through some parts of the hospital; it was strange to see the recreation rooms which Miss Nightingale had started for the troops now so completely deserted, also all the corridors and wards, although when I came to the place where you had lain for so long, I seemed to see you still there with dear, faithful Sam beside your bed. I do so hope your leg has grown stronger during the past months and is not painful.

It is time to close now for we are about to enter Malta's Grand Harbour. I do wish you all the happiness and good fortune in the world, and thank you again for your most lovely gift. I shall wear it always and treasure it all the days of my life.

Yours sincerely,
Madeleine Fraser

The words blurred before his eyes and he realized that he was crying – crying because of the heartbreak behind her careful, formal words, just as he knew she must have cried when she read about him and Henrietta. When that account had been followed by his gift and the noncommittal message, she must have felt sure that he had ruled her out of his life. She had continued to refuse Fraser, but '*then I realized I did not want to be alone any more*' . . . Of course she did not, after what she had been through, but nowhere in the letter did she even hint that she loved her husband, only that she wanted to '*make him as good a wife*' because she had been '*very fortunate to have found so good and kind a husband*' . . . she who deserved only the very best that any man could offer her. She had '*told Alastair all about myself*' – a clear reference to the fact that she was no longer a virgin, and perhaps also that she had borne a child – but '*he still wanted to marry me*'. Ah, my darling, of course he did, as any man in his right mind would want to do. And then the last walk through the wards and the fact that she had stopped beside the spot where his bed had been: had she wept, had she thought about those wonderful, blissful, tormenting moments when they had clung together behind the precarious cover of the screens? He knew without the slightest possible doubt that she had thought, had remembered, and that she was really telling him she still cared, even though she had only a brooch from him and would '*treasure it all the days of my life*'.

Sebastian sprang to his feet once more, the violent banging inside his head forgotten. 'But I have not, will not give you up,' he said aloud. 'I never will, unless you tell me once and for all that you want to live your life without me.' For now the situation was quite different: he had immense material resources, and divorce, now their only barrier, was not insurmountable. He would go to India as Mrs Seacole had urged, tell Madeleine everything and beg her to say the word – that was all she had to do, and then he and, if necessary, an army of lawyers would sort everything out for them. He felt a momentary twinge of sympathy for her husband and suddenly saw them both as he had so often done in reality as they walked through the ward: Madeleine gliding almost noiselessly, and the tall young man in his dark blue uniform striding along beside her, his flat wooden instrument case tucked under his arm – yes, it was bloody hard on Fraser, but Madeleine had never belonged to him and no words mumbled by some fool of a clergyman could make her so. She had always been meant for him – Sebastian – and if he had not been such a God-damned stupid, cynical, cretinous bastard, none of these difficulties would ever have arisen. But, he thought with a sudden surge of confidence, all is fair in love and war, and I have not yet conceded defeat. In fact, the final battle for Madeleine's heart is only just about to begin!

One of the many things Sebastian had learned since becoming Earl of Wells was the extraordinary way money and a title smoothed one's path through life. At the War Office, when he asked to know the date the *SS Himalaya* was due at Calcutta, there had been a certain amount of reluctance, then delay, but the moment he produced his card he was told: the steamship was taking the long route around the Cape and was scheduled to end her voyage during the first week of August. The official hoped his lordship would understand that it was not possible to be more specific because of storms, breakdowns, etc., – but by then he was talking to himself, for the Earl was already across the room, striding despite his limp with great lightness and speed for so large a man.

It was the same at the offices of Messrs Thomas Cook. 'I must be in Calcutta by the end of July,' Sebastian said, and was told, 'Very sorry, sir, but all the ships, accommodation and transport for the overland route are fully booked for the next six months.'

So again the card was produced. 'Get me there,' said

his lordship tersely, 'even if I have to sleep on the deck and ride alone across the desert!'

'Oh, my lord!' exclaimed the clerk, tittering politely at such an absurdity, and within ten minutes a passage had been arranged on a ship leaving in two days' time.

The overland route took two months against four by the long voyage via the Cape, but the *Himalaya* had already been at sea for almost two of those months, so it would be a very close thing, and Sebastian, pacing the deck endlessly, was like a caged tiger. Everything moved so slowly, took such a time!

Eventually he arrived in Calcutta three days before the *Himalaya* and was waiting on the landing stage even as the ship was negotiating the deadly James and Mary sandbank. As she prepared to dock, he withdrew into the scant shade, tipping his straw wide-awake well forward, but there was little chance of his being seen by the Frasers, for the arrival of a ship from England was obviously a social event and carriages full of spectators had been arriving all the time. Sebastian had been told that it was customary for new arrivals to be given leave before proceeding to their stations, and at that moment he only wanted to know where Madeleine would be staying in the city.

As the gangway was placed in position, his heart began to race and his eyes to rake the decks: a regiment was lined up ready for disembarkation, but presumably the other passengers would be allowed off first? Surely they would have a care for the women and children in this almost unendurable heat? Ah, they were beginning to step on to the gangway now: a very large lady in – good God, a *velvet* bonnet and cape; then a heavily pregnant, exhausted-looking young woman, followed by two lively, attractive young girls – a couple of the 'spins' he had been hearing about, perhaps, coming to India to find husbands;

and then Alastair Fraser, followed by a little figure in blue.

Sebastian caught his breath sharply, fighting the sudden overwhelming urge to rush forward to her. The effort to remain still drenched him anew in sweat, and he felt for her, swathed as she no doubt was in stays, spine-pad, wire hoop and several petticoats under her long-sleeved dress. As she hesitated momentarily at the large gap between the end of the gangplank and the pavement, Alastair quickly put his hands on her waist and lifted her effortlessly, to set her down on the ground. To Sebastian, avidly watching every movement, it was only too plain that Alastair loved his wife, for there was great tenderness in the way he gently set her down, opened her parasol and handed it to her, and as he protectively put his arm loosely around her waist when they moved forward. And, Sebastian had to admit with great reluctance that the doctor cut a splendid figure. Only two or three inches shorter than himself, broad at the shoulder but narrow at the waist and hips, he stood effortlessly straight and tall: a strong young man in his prime and with an air of great resolution and steadfastness about him.

And Madeleine? There were only glimpses of her face as she raised her head in its pretty straw bonnet, but she was smiling and interested in everything around her, and her figure, in the simple blue dress trimmed with broderie anglaise, looked as slender and delicate as ever. Yes, thought Sebastian, grinding his teeth, they made a handsome couple. A couple. Man and wife. Married for over four months. For the first time Sebastian felt doubtful: was he about to 'spoil it' all for her once again? Wouldn't it be better to let her start on her new life without knowing of his presence? '*I love you enough to let you go,*' she had told him; was it now his turn to do the same?

As he struggled with his emotions, he saw an officer in the uniform of the IMS step forward and greet the couple, and then they all moved to an open carriage. When the two men began to converse, Sebastian saw Madeleine's face more clearly: in repose there was a wistfulness about her expression and her hand kept moving every few minutes to the glint of gold at her throat. With a start of surprise he realized she was wearing his brooch and kept touching it as though frightened of losing it. His indecision vanished at once: he would see her, tell her that she had never been married to his father and how desperately he himself loved and wanted to make her his wife – the choice should be entirely hers, and whatever she decided he would abide by. Surely that is fair, he thought, grinding out his cheroot with his heel and trying at the same time to grind out the small voice inside his head that was telling him to the contrary.

Untying the horse he had hired, Sebastian mounted and followed the open carriage which was now bowling along at some distance in front of him. When it drew up at the entrance to Wilson's hotel, Sebastian remained in the shade and, as he had anticipated, the two men soon emerged and drove away, no doubt for Alastair to report to Fort William. Sebastian spurred forward and handed the reins to a syce who had immediately appeared. Then, feeling less confident than he looked, he stepped inside the hotel.

On Alastair's advice, Madeleine had removed her dress, petticoats and hoop, 'but never your spine pad,' Alastair had said seriously, and she was just debating whether she could bear to keep her stays on, when there was a tiny scratching at the door.

'Who is it?' Madeleine called, hastily pulling on a cotton wrapper.

'A sahib to see you, mem,' answered a voice from the other side.

'To see me? Are you sure?' Madeleine asked, with

some apprehension. Was it a messenger from Alastair? Had something happened to him?

'Oh yes, mem, very sure,' came the voice, high-pitched and with a strange sing-song intonation.

'Then please show him into the sitting room and say I will be there in a few minutes,' Madeleine said, telling herself not to be so stupid; of course nothing had happened to Alastair! It was most likely a messenger to tell her he had been delayed, but nevertheless her fingers fumbled with the buttons on her dress and she decided not to delay by adding her hoop and petticoats. Hastily she smoothed her hair, peering into the mirror as she did so; with the grass screens covering all the windows, the light was dim, but even so the gold of Sebastian's brooch glinted and Madeleine picked it up to pin it at the neck of her dress. Already she was beginning to realize that it must be very easy to forget things in this furnace-like heat and she was terrified that the precious little jewel would be stolen if left behind at any time. Then she pushed open the door of the private sitting room adjoining her bedroom and walked forward.

She recognized the massive shoulders and the set of his head at once, and just for an instant she swayed forward as though about to run to him. Her arms moved upward, but then she checked; it must be a trick of the light, a product of her constant remembrance, aided by her having just handled his brooch. But at that moment he spoke her name very softly, with all his longing, all his joy in the word. She was turned to stone, unable to move or speak, and he came quickly forward, only now realizing what a totally devastating shock he must be to her. Taking her hands gently into his own, he peered down at her anxiously.

'Forgive me,' he said contritely. 'I was so desperate to see you that I did not stop to think.' Her fingers had begun to curl around his own.

'Sebastian.' Her voice was a mere thread of sound. 'Sebastian, is it really you?' She was looking up at him, her eyes dark with shock and her face pitiful in its mixture of amazement and joy.

Dear God, how vulnerable, how defenceless she is, Sebastian thought, longing to wrap his arms closely about her. 'Yes, it is truly I, my beloved girl,' he said softly, his voice and eyes caressing her.

'But – but I don't understand,' she said, totally bewildered now. 'Surely this is India and – and I am here with Alastair.'

'Yes, and I have followed you.'

'Here – to India? You have followed me to India?' She was looking at him now as though she expected him to vanish in a puff of smoke.

Sebastian made a great effort to pull himself together. They could so easily continue to stand, drinking in every detail of each other, but at any moment that damnable fellow might return – and before that happened he must put his case to her.

'Madeleine, darling,' he began urgently, 'I have come because I found out that you were never married to my father, and there is nothing to stop our marrying if – if you will divorce this Fraser fellow. Everything is different now. I seem to have inherited half of southwest England and am very wealthy, so it can all be arranged, if you will only say the word – ah, darling, you don't know how much I love you, how desperately I need you! I want you more than anything else in the world and, if you will let me, I shall spend the rest of my life trying to make up for all the unhappiness I've caused you. Madeleine, tell me that you will come with me . . . that you will marry me.'

It was all too much for her; she had only been able to take in a few of his words but not really to grasp their full meaning. 'But I am already married,' she said slowly, her voice expressionless.

His eyes searched her face as he realized that emotionally he was battering her, and he cursed himself for his clumsiness. Gently he grasped her shoulders. 'Madeleine,' he said again, forcing his voice to sound calm, unhurried. 'Divorce is much easier now, and with all my resources I know it can be arranged. All you have to do is to tell Fraser that you want to divorce him – or I will tell him for you, if you wish – and then we can go back to Europe together, and I promise you it will all be carried through with the least amount of pain or embarrassment to you.' He paused, wondering fleetingly if he should add that for a time they might have to live abroad; would undoubtedly be ostracized by the Court and barred from the royal enclosure at Ascot, but almost at once he cast the thought aside: she would not regard any of that as important and already had too much to grasp. 'Madeleine, my dearest darling, tell me . . . please, please tell me that we are going to be together from now on. I swear to you most solemnly that nothing will ever part us again.'

It was the note of entreaty in his voice which penetrated the layers of cottonwool in which her senses seemed surrounded; she pressed her fingertips to her temples and closed her eyes, while he waited silently. When at last she looked up, her eyes were much more alert but her voice was still only a thread. 'Have I understood . . . you are asking me to divorce Alastair and – and to marry you?'

'Yes,' Sebastian said, while the world seemed to stop as he waited for her answer.

'He loves me too,' she said at last. 'He trusts me – married me, knowing that – that I was not innocent; how could I betray him, break his heart by leaving him?'

'But we belong together, we always have, we always shall!' Sebastian said with total conviction. 'You know it, Madeleine, you know it, my darling!'

'Yes,' she whispered, 'but I cannot – oh, you don't know how kind, how good he has been to me, and he has such plans for the future – for us, and for all that he wants to do in this country.'

'He would get over it, and there are other women in the world; he is young, and he has his work.'

But she shook her head. 'I believe that Alastair will only ever love me, and to leave him would ruin his life.'

'But my darling, don't you see, you belonged to me before he even met you. We have been bound together from the very beginning, and then there was – Madeleine, I know about the baby, our baby; surely he binds us together more than anything or anyone else.'

'Thomas is dead,' she said dully.

'I know, but there could be other children – our children – whom we could love together.'

Again she shook her head. 'My future children will be Alastair's,' she said quietly, and then with a quick sob added, 'But Thomas will always be the child of my heart.'

'And you will always be the wife of my heart!' Sebastian exclaimed, his own voice near to breaking.

Then she was crying out wildly, 'Help me, oh, please help me! For you know how much I long to be with you, but I cannot! I cannot! Help me to be strong, please help me!' And she was in his arms, her face buried against his chest, her hands clinging to his back.

'Ah, Madeleine, Madeleine,' he whispered brokenly, holding her, loving her, but knowing that he had lost her.

As soon as the worst of her sobs had subsided, she stepped back to look up at him and whisper, 'I shall always remember, always treasure the fact that you came across the world to me, and there is nothing more I would ask of life than to be always with you, but I will never leave Alastair. Because if I did I would break his heart, and that would always be between us.'

Sebastian's arms dropped to his sides. 'I hope he realizes what a supremely fortunate man he is,' he said grimly.

412

'He must never know,' Madeleine answered urgently, 'for if he did guess, I should not be able to deny . . . Please, we must not meet again for I – I don't think I could bear it.'

'Nor I.' Sebastian's tone was sombre. 'I shall leave Calcutta in the morning.'

'Will you return to England straight away?'

He shrugged indifferently. 'God knows – I've not thought. No, I think I must see Harriet at Cawnpore first. But I promise you I'll not come anywhere near the environs of Lucknow.'

'Thank you,' she whispered unevenly. 'Thank you for everything.'

He still could not believe or accept that this was the end and suddenly burst out: 'My darling, darling, will you not take time to think it over – our whole future is at stake!'

But when she shook her head, he picked up his hat and came to stand before her and take her hands. He kissed them, held them against his cheek for a moment and then let them go. 'I love you, Madeleine,' he said with the utmost conviction.

'I love you too,' she whispered, not daring to look at him.

At the door he paused, then quickly swung round, unable even now to concede defeat. 'Madeleine, is there nothing I can say or do,' he began, but stopped abruptly. She was unable to speak but stood, wraith-like, with hands tightly clasped against her breast.

'Goodbye, my love,' Sebastian whispered brokenly and walked quickly from the room.

She rushed out on to the verandah in time to see the syce bring round his horse. He swung into the saddle and then turned to look up at her, his face haggard. For a long moment they looked at each other, their eyes expressing more than any words could ever do. As her

413

hands flew to her mouth, Sebastian lifted his hat, bowed with great deference and turned his horse's head. Within seconds he had disappeared from her sight.

When Alastair returned half an hour later, Madeleine rushed into his arms, sobbing and clinging tightly to him. 'Hold me,' she begged, 'please hold me.'

'Why, dearest, what is this?' Alastair asked concernedly as his arms enfolded her. When she did not reply he waited, then tried to lighten the situation, holding her a little way from him in order to see her face and saying with a smile: 'Now, what better welcome could a man have than to hear his wife asking him to hold her as soon as he appears?' But Madeleine kept her face hidden, and he realized she was shaking from head to toe. Confused thoughts rushed through his mind: was she sickening? Had she a fever? Or had something frightened her – a servant, an insect, a snake? His eyes searched the room, lingering in the dim corners and up at the ceiling; he had been told to expect cockroaches the size of mice, scorpions like young lobsters, swarms of flying ants, bats blundering into rooms, house lizards and multitudes of crawling ants, both red and white. Yet all he could see now were two small lizards halfway up one of the walls. Still with his arms around her, he led her to a chair and pressed her gently into it, then he went swiftly down on his haunches before her, covering her clasped hands with his own while he deftly felt her pulse. It was racing. 'Now, my love, tell me what has upset you,' he said gently, but with a note of the physician's authority creeping instinctively into his voice.

But to tell him was the one thing she dared not do; she shook her head, scattering teardrops. 'There is nothing,' she managed at last. 'I have just been silly. I – I think I just got a little bit frightened of being alone, with everything so new and strange and – dark.'

Relief flooded him: it was perfectly understandable and he was eager to make amends. Producing a handkerchief, he carefully wiped her eyes and then offered it to her. 'Have a little blow,' he suggested, his deep voice warm with affection. When she complied, he asked, 'Better now?'

A sigh seemed to come from the very depths of her being, but she nodded and looked down at him, searching his face. 'Oh, Alastair,' she whispered, putting her hand in a caressing movement on his temple where the red hair curled damply. 'I do so want to be a good wife . . . to make you happy and create a real home for us.'

'Why, my dearest, you are the best little wifie a man could have – you do make me happy!' he exclaimed, smiling broadly now, his dark blue eyes full of tenderness.

Still she persisted: 'Yes, but do I . . . am I . . . when we . . .' The words trailed off as Madeleine, the Victorian bride of four months, could not be more specific. She lowered her eyes, coloured brilliantly and nervously twisted her wedding ring.

And kind Alastair helped her out, as he would always do. 'More than ever at those times, my darling,' he said very softly. 'No man could have a more loving, more responsive bride, and I count myself the luckiest of fellows.'

She managed to look at him fully then, knew that he meant every word, and smiled tremulously. 'I am so glad,' she murmured.

Alastair rose in one lithe movement. 'Come and have luncheon – no, tiffin,' he said, drawing her gently to her feet. 'I believe there is a dish which we shall have to get very used to: it is called curry, and is very spicy, and it is eaten with rice. So let's try it. Afterwards everyone rests on their beds until around five o'clock, when we can open the windows. A strong wind is said to blow then and must certainly be a blessing to man and beast alike. This evening we are invited to dine with the senior doctor and his wife.'

They stayed three weeks in Calcutta, exploring the city and being entertained almost every evening by families belonging to the medical fraternity, who were always delighted to have new faces at their dinner tables. Everyone agreed that the Frasers were an exceptionally charming couple: he very attractive with his fine figure and deep voice, and she delicate as a moonflower but extremely poised – 'much more so than the majority of junior officers' wives,' remarked the most senior lady approvingly; but her brows rose high in surprise when told that the Frasers had been invited to dine at Government House. They had dutifully signed the book, thinking that was all, but Miss Nightingale had written to Lady Canning, reminding her of the young girl who had so impressed them both at her interview and giving her full details of Madeleine's marriage.

She has remained a sensible and interesting gal, thought Lady Canning when Madeleine, instead of clinging stupidly to her husband, allowed herself to be brought forward by an ADC and then conversed intelligently while so many others remained almost tongue-tied, never understanding that by being so insipid and dull they make it all very heavy going, as Lady Canning confided to a friend. And Madeleine seemed instinctively able to manage her crinoline in the armchair at dinner and to keep her elbows at a graceful angle when so many other ladies sat half-buried and hunched in their chairs. Nor did she even look up at the chandeliers as they swung and jingled in the wind, or comment as the edges of the tablecloth billowed. Instead, she quietly tucked the cloth down between her skirt and the table, and put a glass over her menu card, which was skittering around.

When the time came for departure, she did not look panic-stricken or whisper agitatedly to Alastair, but sat quietly conversing and using her fan very elegantly until the most senior lady guest rose, and then with a single glance at Alastair, Madeleine also stood and awaited her turn to make her curtsey. If she survives this awful climate, she will help her splendid-looking husband climb to the top of the Medical Service, Lady Canning thought as she nodded and smiled graciously in farewell.

'I was mighty proud of my little darling this evening,' Alastair said when they were in the hired carriage. In the darkness Madeleine bit her lip; the evening had been more of an ordeal than anyone could have realized, for in the elegance of Government House it had been impossible not to think every second of Sebastian: such a setting was his natural milieu and the Cannings, handsome, sophisticated and aristocratic, were of his world. The more Alastair praised her, the more guilty she felt and, tired as she was, she responded with even greater eagerness to his embraces that night.

'Can we not start our baby now?' she whispered against his shoulder. A baby, she thought, would cement her marriage and help to repay so much of what she felt she owed Alastair. But as always he drew away from her.

'Not yet, dearest,' he said, making his voice as gentle as possible. 'Not until we are really settled and you have become used to this climate.' For everything he had read and been told indicated that childbirth in India was extremely hazardous for European women, and the thought of losing her was unbearable. He knew she did not entirely understand his refusal as he had withheld much information for fear of frightening her. Now he put his arm across her waist and drew her close. 'I would give you the moon if I could, dearest love,' he whispered, 'but not my easiest, most natural gift – not yet, for there is plenty of time . . . We are young and we have all our lives ahead of us.'

The next morning they left for Lucknow.

PART THREE

Lucknow, 1856–7

21

The bungalow was square, with a wide pillared verandah encircling it. Under the carriage porch a short flight of steps ran down to the drive. The ground all around the building was bare, but on one side was a gold-mohur tree and at the rear, towering over the thatched roof, a giant flame-of-the-forest spread its feathery leaves and brilliant blossoms.

After Alastair had helped Madeleine down from the tonga, they stood hand in hand, gazing around before simultaneously turning to look at each other with shining eyes. Alastair produced a huge key. 'Shall we go in?' he asked. Madeleine nodded, and they walked up the steps. 'I must see if I can get these balustraded,' Alastair said at once. 'In the dark it wouldn't be too difficult for someone to miss their footing and fall sideways – easiest way in the world to break an ankle! And this needs cutting back badly.' He pushed aside the long straggly branches of bougainvillaea with which the pillars and roof of the verandah were thickly covered.

'What a perfect place to have breakfast,' exclaimed Madeleine, 'and look how nice the floor is with these red flagstones!'

Alastair had unlocked the door and, as it swung open, he quickly scooped her up in his arms. 'Who says we Scots are not romantic?' he demanded happily as he carried her over the threshold. Then he bent and kissed her ardently. 'Welcome to your first home, Mrs Fraser,' he said, grinning delightedly.

As always when he expressed his love, she responded at once, and now she returned his kiss before laying her cheek against his. 'Thank you, Dr Fraser,' she said demurely. 'I am sure we are going to be very – happy here.' Fearful that he might have noticed her hesitation, she rushed on: 'Better put me down now, as there is much to be done if we are to sleep here tonight.'

It was true: there was dust everywhere and the white-washed walls of all the rooms were dull, with many dirty outlines where pictures had hung. The furniture, such as it was, was distinctly battered, but nothing could curb the elation felt by the Frasers. 'A new wash on the walls will make all the difference,' said Alastair.

'And a good polish with plenty of linseed oil is all the furniture really needs,' said Madeleine.

They enlisted the help of Mrs Fayrer, wife of the senior civil surgeon, and within an hour a team of men had arrived to whitewash all the rooms. 'But you cannot return to the bungalow until this evening,' Mrs Fayrer insisted, 'for the tatties will need to be taken down and without them the place will be like a furnace; it is exceptionally hot just now because the rains are so very late this year. But with such high humidity I doubt whether the walls will be dry by this evening. Meanwhile, let us get on with the hiring of your servants. You will not be able to manage with less than eight, nine if you have a gardener.' When Madeleine exclaimed in astonishment, Mrs Fayrer continued: 'It's because each will only do his own job, and then their silly caste system complicates everything so much. I'm afraid, my dear, that you will find them a very lazy lot, and you will have to be *firm* with them, otherwise you will discover that they are doing the minimum amount of work and swindling you left, right and centre! All food stores have to be kept locked and precise amounts given out first thing every morning. And they are *naturally* dirty; you will find them doing the most extraordinary things with the food, if not properly supervised.'

Mrs Fayrer continued to pour dire warnings about everything into Madeleine's ear, but Madeleine's enthusiasm for her new home remained and she was to discover almost at once that Alastair, too, was a great home-lover. So they spent their first evening rearranging their few bits of furniture. 'At least the rooms appear quite spacious with so little in them,' Alastair remarked.

'Oh yes, and when we can hang our pictures and I have bought some chintz to cover the chairs and that strange contraption – is it called a punkah? – it will really be a home,' Madeleine said happily.

Alastair had been afraid she would be disappointed with so little, but now, seeing her enthusiasm, he caught her up in his arms. 'Let's go to bed,' he said, smiling down at her tenderly. 'I want our first night in our first home and in our own bed to be a long and memorable one.'

As always her response delighted him. 'Come along then, doctor dear,' she said, taking his hand and leading the way.

All the rooms led off each other and there were no doors, but Mrs Fayrer had given them a curtain to cover the doorway into their bedroom from the verandah. 'It's called a purdah curtain,' she told them, 'and most people curtain all their doorways.' The bed, wooden-framed, laced with webbing and covered with the thinnest of cotton mattresses, did not look inviting, but Alastair slipped eagerly into it, pulling the one cotton sheet over Madeleine and himself and reaching for her. Her arms had just gone around his neck when out of the total darkness a disembodied voice said softly, 'If doctor-sahib will be putting damp towels over punkah, he and mem will be spending a much happier night.'

Madeleine uttered a little strangled cry of fear and even Alastair's heart missed a beat, but he called out at once: 'Who is there?'

'It is punkah-wallah, sahib.'

Of course! They had been so engrossed all evening and the servants so invisible that they had entirely forgotten about them, and had assumed in their ignorance that the punkahs, slowly waving to and fro over their heads, were mechanically driven.

'Oh, please,' begged Madeleine in a whisper, 'tell him to go away.'

But where was the man? thought Alastair, and as though in direct answer, the voice said, 'I am sitting on verandah, sahib.'

'Ah,' said Alastair. 'Thank you for telling us, but I think we can do without the punkah tonight.'

'But, sahib,' protested the amazed voice.

'Take the night off!' said Alastair urgently.

'I am going, sahib, but – '

'That's a good fellow!' Alastair encouraged, and they both waited, but there was not a sound except for the cicadas. At last Alastair got up, lit the lamp and padded across the room to pull aside the curtain and peer out. It was completely deserted. 'Disappeared!' said Alastair joyfully and hurried back to bed, blowing out the lamp as he did so. But they were soon to realize that without the punkah the bed seemed to be on fire. Lovemaking, and even sleep, were impossible and they were both up, taking cold baths, by the time their new khidmatgar brought their tea at five o'clock.

'I do not think I want to ride this morning,' Madeleine said, wiping her face, which was already wet with sweat.

'No, dearest, neither do I,' Alastair replied, before adding gloomily, 'I suppose we shall have to get used to the fellow being there all the time.' She nodded silently, and Alastair said, 'Let's see precisely where he does sit.' They both went on to the verandah, where an old man was sitting, the long string of the punkah looped around his big toe. He salaamed deeply and grinned up at them

424

for all the world like an elderly babe, toothless and seemingly artless.

Madeleine turned back into the room and Alastair saw with relief that she was giggling helplessly; at once his deep laugh filled the room and they were still wiping their eyes when Madeleine looked through the open front door and said quickly, 'Who can this be?' Once more they both went on to the verandah to watch silently as a large man on a very small, heavily laden donkey rode confidently around to the rear. Having chosen his spot, the man began unloading his equipment: a soap board, a stick and a firebox all appeared in turn, and he then waited majestically until the bhistie appeared, carrying water. 'It must be the washerman,' whispered Madeleine and watched, fascinated, his energetic slapping and thrashing of the clothes until they were snow-white. 'But how roughly he treats them!'

'Well, at one shilling and threepence per month, dearest, we cannot complain,' said Alastair. But, although he said nothing to Madeleine, he was worried because his salary, which had seemed so enormous, would be tightly stretched to cover all the household expenses. He was told at the hospital that he would also need men to carry his instrument case, jugs and basins of water, a fan, a portable writing table, and the register of patients. Some of the doctors even employed yet another man to turn the pages of the register. Alastair decided that he could carry his own instrument case and the heavy register, and that he would do without the man to fan him, but he found at once that without this small stirring of the air, the sweat ran down into his eyes to such an extent that his vision was obscured.

Yet as he returned home at the end of that first day, he was a supremely happy man. Madeleine was adjusting wonderfully well, and the fact that they could laugh

425

together over their growing pains in this strange, fascinating country augured well for the future. His sense of wellbeing increased when he entered the living room and saw all the old furniture highly polished, and the smell of linseed oil vying with that of the kus grass of the tatties. In the bathroom the zinc bath stood ready, a pile of snowy towels beside it, and it was obvious that all the earthenware jars had just been brought in from the windward side for their water was deliciously cool. In the bedroom clean linen was laid out for him.

'How well you have done, dearest!' he said admiringly, as his arm encircled Madeleine's waist. She smiled gratefully, but there were deep circles beneath her eyes and she looked exhausted.

'I believe everyone takes an evening drive to listen to the band,' Alastair said. 'How do you feel about going this evening?'

She hesitated, and then he knew how tired she was, for she said, 'Do you mind if we do not go, just this once!'

'I should be glad not to, for the heat has been really unbearable today,' Alastair replied. 'Just look at my cap!' Although there was a cover over the crown with a neckcloth at the back, the peak had been turned into a shapeless black mass by the sun. 'But I am told the rains, which are weeks overdue, are liable to start at any time now, and so the nights at least will be cool.'

The rains did start that evening, the first heavy plops falling as the Frasers sat at dinner, and within seconds a deluge began such as they had never seen. And with it came every creature that could fly, crawl or creep. First to arrive were the flying ants, which promptly shed their wings and fell in heaps everywhere; then came a variety of beetles, moths, crickets and a multitude of one creature which to Madeleine looked like a piece of red cotton. All blundered into the lamps and descended on everything: the table, the food, the glasses.

While Alastair sat, startled but already fascinated and wanting to study them, Madeleine rose, waving her arms and flapping her table napkin in near-panic. 'Oh, Alastair, make them go away!' she cried, revulsion making her suddenly child-like.

He jumped up and waved a palm-leaf fan and his napkin energetically, even though he knew it was hopeless. 'It's all right, dearest, they are quite harmless,' he said, not quite realizing that she found the creatures so revolting to look at. He turned out the lamps except for one in the far corner, hoping its light would draw them away from the other parts of the room, and Madeleine dashed to draw the curtains over the doorways leading on to the verandah. As she reached the first, she suddenly became rigid, one arm held stiffly upright and clutching the curtain. 'What is it?' asked Alastair, and ran to her. There was still some light outside, so the dense black cloud, advancing slowly and only a few feet above the ground, was clearly visible. Pitch-black, it obliterated everything in its path and was like a huge black carpet, glittering, but with a sickening odour.

Madeleine was uttering pitiful little whimpering sounds, and even Alastair was shocked into near-panic. Then he forced himself to think coherently and almost at once recognized that the mass was coming from the river. 'Why, they're only cockchafers – flying beetles!' he exclaimed in relief, but Madeleine was now cringing away from the doorway.

'Will – will they come in?' she breathed fearfully.

'Well, perhaps just a few,' said Alastair, hastily pulling the curtain across, then he closed all the windows and shouted to the khidmatgar to have the tatties put over them. 'I want them drenched with water,' he said authoritatively, 'and please get someone working the thermantidotes at once.'

That averted the worst of the crisis, but when

427

Madeleine had gone into the bedroom to undress, she suddenly screamed and he rushed in. 'What – ' he began, and she cried out: 'It's gone down inside my bodice!' So Alastair ripped away the cotton shift only to find a tiny, pink and totally terrified house lizard trying to climb up her breasts.

Alastair's spontaneous laugh was full of intense relief. As he scooped up the little creature, he said, 'Look, dearest, it's only a lizard and a very young one at that. I expect it fell off the ceiling.' Unwisely he took it by its tail for Madeleine to see, but immediately the body fell to the ground, leaving the tail still wriggling in Alastair's fingers.

It was the last straw for Madeleine. She became completely hysterical, screaming and blundering about the room, hands over her head. Alastair caught hold of her strongly. 'Stop that screaming at once!' he ordered, but as she struggled wildly, he slapped her twice across her face, cutting off the frantic sound instantly. As she stared at him, open mouthed and stricken, he gathered her into his arms and held her warmly. 'Poor little love,' he said softly. 'I had to slap you, it was the only thing to do, and I hope you will forgive me.'

She had begun to sob quietly, her face against his chest, but now she raised her head.

'I – I've been behaving like a baby,' she said, trying hard to calm herself, but she could not repress a shudder as she admitted, 'I am so afraid of them getting entangled in my hair.'

Alastair ran his fingers through the damp chestnut strands, loosening them and looking keenly. 'Dearest, there is nothing in your hair. But just to make sure, I will brush it for you, and then I'm going to give you a sleeping draught.'

'Oh, but I mustn't sleep,' she protested, becoming agitated once more. 'They'll crawl all over me if I do!'

'No, they will not,' Alastair replied very firmly. 'I will

tuck in the mosquito net very securely around the bed, and I promise you nothing will touch you. Trust me, Madeleine.'

She was eager to please him so she submitted, swallowed the draught and was almost instantly asleep.

Alastair poured himself a stiff peg of whisky and wondered uneasily if he had been too optimistic in thinking that Madeleine had adjusted well to India. The rainy season would last for three months, and he was sure this evening was only a foretaste of what she would have to put up with. The beetles and all the other insects would be back in their multitudes, but he now realized that it was the look and feel of them which terrified her; the ever present and potentially far more dangerous mosquito had not induced such a dramatic reaction. But, he thought, she is beginning to let me see her weaknesses as well as her strengths. Her pleas to him to 'make them go away' had touched him deeply. I must be very understanding, very loving and very protective, he thought, and smiled. It was, after all, a most pleasant thought.

In the morning they found a fine film of damp on all the furniture, and there was mildew on Alastair's books and all their leather goods, but in the cool, fresh air of very early morning there were not too many insects about. When Alastair, holding her tightly, finally persuaded Madeleine to step on to the verandah, they both gasped, for all around the bungalow there was a carpet of tender green where only bare earth had been before, while shrubs which had been mounds of dusty green leaves were now like enormous bouquets of flowers.

'Just look at those!' exclaimed Madeleine, pointing to a row whose huge trumpet blossoms were of scarlet, pink and peach.

'Yes, and here's a pretty one,' said Alastair, leaning over to gather a handful of small, pale pink trumpet flowers. 'I wish we knew what they were – this white has a wonderful perfume.' He had gone to the largest of the shrubs, whose large open white flowers were like wax, and picked a blossom for her. She tucked it into her bodice and then looked beyond him.

'Oh, Alastair, look at the city!' Beyond their cantonment, the turrets, domes and cupolas of the palaces, newly washed in the night's deluge, gleamed with gold and blue, while the buildings themselves – enormous, colonnaded, and terraced in white stucco – were brilliantly outlined against the new green of the plains which stretched as far as the eye could see. 'It is like a fairy-tale city,' Madeleine said delightedly, and to add to her enchantment the air was perfumed with jasmine and orange blossom.

But Alastair had seen the curtain of rain beginning to descend in the far distance, and he took her in his arms. 'I hate to leave you, dearest, but I must. I'm afraid it will soon begin to rain again, and there may be some insects about; will you promise me that you'll try not to be too frightened of them? I know they don't look pretty, but they will not harm you, unless you let them get you into a panic.'

She shuddered involuntarily, but then lifted her chin in the characteristic gesture with which he was not yet familiar. 'If other women can bear them, then so can I,' she said, trying her hardest to sound confident.

'That's my brave girl,' he replied admiringly. 'I'll be back as soon as ever I can.'

And bear them she did, tying a large handkerchief over her hair and learning to put horn covers over glasses and cups; to check that the furniture legs always stood in saucers of water, and not to be too dismayed when bread turned to a mildewed poultice, fruit to pulp and meat became a crawling mass. The rain continued to fall almost continuously, making the atmosphere moist and suffocatingly hot; from seven in the morning until five in the

430

evening, every window and door was tightly closed against the heat, but even so the slightest movement brought a drenching of sweat.

Madeleine tried to sew, but often the needle was too hot or too slippery to hold, and so, like countless other British women throughout India, she sat alone in a semidarkened room for hours on end, listening to the incessant noise of the rain, too lethargic even to read. And there was nothing to do: every morning she would discuss the day's food with the cook and hand out precise amounts for his use and then, after carefully supervising the rest of the servants, she would retire to the sitting room, to mop her face and try to ease her skin away from its wet clothing. Sitting directly under the punkah, she would stare either at the wall or the floor, and it was inevitable that her thoughts should turn to Sebastian. While everything was new and she had things to interest and absorb her, she had managed to keep her yearnings at bay, but now they swept back irresistibly, threatening to take her over completely and to sap what vitality she still had.

Soon, within minutes of sitting down, she would not see the bare floor or the whitewashed walls, but his face – in Calcutta, Scutari, Bath, and even as she had first seen him at Paddington. She remembered his every look, every word, and she relived every incident of their few times together. It was of never-ending fascination, and inevitably she progressed to the might-have-been, which was even more absorbing, more dangerous. There were times when the small quiet voice of reason told her she should force herself to think of the present, the future, but always she returned to those other times until she yearned with all her heart, all her body and all her soul for Sebastian.

If Alastair's personality had been harsher, if he had loved her less, she would have found his attentions unbearable, but he was a kind, thoughtful, highly perceptive man and a tender lover. Sensing there was something wrong but unable to put his finger on it, he watched her carefully but very unobtrusively: she was as loving, as eager to please him as ever, and was always industriously sewing when he was in the house. Then one evening when he left the room, instead of going directly into their bedroom he turned to look back and was astonished to see that, thinking herself alone, she had dropped the sewing in her lap and was leaning back in her bamboo chair, her head resting on its tall curve, her whole body expressing such a desperate longing that Alastair was shaken. Was she homesick for England? He knew she had no family there, but many women thought wistfully of snow and soft rain, and the gentle, unpredictable climate of 'home'. Or was Madeleine yearning so much for a baby? Or was it just intense loneliness? She had made some superficial friendships, but her life had been very different from those of most other British women in Lucknow, and he knew that she thought them snobbish and very narrow in their outlook. He shuffled his feet to announce his return, and at once the sewing was taken up again, but now he realized that she had been working for weeks on the same piece of cotton, with very little progress.

Alastair settled himself in his chair and brought out his pipe. 'I think the rain is beginning to ease off a bit,' he said casually.

'Yes,' she agreed, with her usual bright smile at him. 'I thought the same earlier on.'

She had thought nothing of the kind and he knew it, but he believed she was deceiving him in order not to let him realize that something was wrong. 'I'm sure you'll be glad when it ceases altogether,' he said, busy with his pipe. 'I can't think how you fill in your time with so many hours alone.'

She made light of it: 'Oh, it takes some time to give out

the day's food and to inspect the kitchen – it is certainly true that the servants need very careful supervision – and then when that is all done, I sew or read . . . It's surprising how quickly the time does go.'

She smiled again as though to reassure him, and he said quietly, 'You're not unhappy, are you, Madeleine?'

The question took her completely by surprise, but she hesitated only fractionally. 'Why, Alastair dear, what a strange question to ask a bride of less than a year!'

He was not to be put off. 'On the contrary, the first months of a marriage are often a very testing time. After all, it stands to reason, with so many new situations to get used to.'

The grey eyes looked at him very levelly as she said, 'I would be a very ungrateful woman if I were not happy after you have given me so much.'

He leaned forward to take her hands in both of his. 'Dearest Madeleine, I have only given you what every man wants to give to the woman he loves, and it is not your gratitude I want.'

'But you will always have it,' she said, the tears bright in her eyes now.

'And your love?' queried Alastair quietly.

'Oh yes, of course, and you know I want only to make you happy.' It was actually true, for although she might be consumed by her need for Sebastian, she was also able to love Alastair for his kindness and quiet strength; he was her rock and she depended upon him completely. And if her love ever faltered, there was her intense gratitude to help her remain his devoted wife.

With this Alastair had to be content, and he said soothingly, 'Soon the rains will be over, darling, and then we shall be able to go out and about much more. And next year you must go to the hills during the hot weather.'

But that sent her into a panic. 'Go – without you?'

'Well, I should be able to take some leave to escort you

433

up there and bring you back, but I believe it is usual for husbands to remain at their stations.'

She shook her head decisively. 'No,' she said. 'Oh no, not without you.'

'Dearest, why ever not?'

'I'd be too afraid!' she said with sudden agitation, thinking: suppose *he* were there and we met? Nothing would stop me from running to him and then everything would be over and I should have betrayed all Alastair's trust. For although she had no means of knowing, her heart, her every instinct, told her that Sebastian was still somewhere in India. Seeing Alastair's astonishment, she added with perfect truth, 'I – I feel so safe here with you.'

So that's it, he thought, she's afraid of the servants. It was understandable for they were entirely silent and it *was* disconcerting to be writing or reading and suddenly to feel someone nearby, then to look up and find a servant standing just behind you; even Lady Canning was said to have expressed a wish to have a 'creaking English butler close by'. And then there were the times when he was duty medical officer and had to sleep at the hospital, leaving her entirely alone in the bungalow. Ideas raced through his mind: get her a dog; teach her how to handle a pistol; get Jeannie out next year, and he thought for the thousandth time what a very great pity it was that he had not been able to take her to meet his family; in their happy, uncomplicated presence, he felt, she would have blossomed and gained assurance. He said now with sudden conviction: 'My youngest sister, Jeannie, will be eighteen next May, and I should like to invite her out, if you would agree.'

'Oh yes,' said Madeleine, relaxing now that the crisis seemed over. 'Do let's!'

'You'll like her,' Alastair said. 'She's very pretty and lively, and will be a pleasant companion for you.'

'Then I'm sure she will be the toast of the station and will find a husband here.'

He nodded. 'Could be. It's said that every "spin" has the choice of three regiments, no matter which station she goes to, so we'll see. Of course, there is only one Queen's regiment here, but in addition there'd be all the British officers in the native regiments.'

The next day he found the dog: a tiny, starving white terrier crouched against a wall with its eyes half closed in misery. Alastair dismounted from his horse and approached it warily, for hydrophobia was a real and terrible danger. He spoke very quietly to the little creature, and when the soft dark eyes opened appealingly, Alastair tentatively held out his hand before attempting to stroke the small head. Although it was obvious that the little dog had been badly treated, it seemed to know at once that here was a friend, and Alastair was not surprised when he was able to pick it up and hold it tucked securely under his arm as he rode home.

Madeleine was enchanted, instantly sinking down in a great billow of skirts until she was kneeling beside the little animal. 'Careful, dearest,' Alastair warned. 'He's bound to be full of fleas and perhaps ticks.' But he saw at once that Madeleine and the dog were going to adore each other. So Alastair rolled up his sleeves and set about deinfesting the short white coat. When at last he was satisfied that all insect life had been dealt with, he and Madeleine knelt down together and bathed their new pet, laughing like a pair of children, while the little dog submitted quite calmly to their ministrations. Afterwards they gave him a light meal of bread and milk, which he gulped down at great speed. Then he looked up for more while a pink tongue eagerly licked the drops from his muzzle and the floor. They gave him almost as much as he wanted; 'But we must be careful as he's obviously been without food for several days,' said Alastair, who had

435

already begun to call him Jacko. Jacko then went on a short tour of investigation before returning to look up at them beseechingly, his stump of a tail still not sure whether it might wag or not. When they both spoke reassuringly to him, he first sat down, then within minutes rolled over on to his side, sighed hugely, and fell deeply asleep.

Jacko became Madeleine's shadow during the day, but when Alastair came home he was given a rapturous welcome and for the rest of the evening Jacko would either try to sit on his feet or as close to his side as he could get. 'Really, he divides his favours very equally between us,' laughed Alastair, bending to stroke Jacko behind an ear. 'Is he any better with the servants?'

Madeleine shook her head. 'No, and I don't think he will ever be.' It had been obvious from the first that Jacko hated all Indians, and even when the servants tried to coax him, he stood with lips drawn back from his small, clamped-together teeth, hackles rising from the top of his head to the tip of his tail. Soon he refused to be left at home when the Frasers went out, so Alastair frequently rode with Jacko tucked under his arm, and when Madeleine paid calls Jacko would sit under her skirt, his nose and one eye periodically peeping out.

The piano Alastair bought was almost as great a success and Madeleine, after her first anxious enquiry about whether they could really afford it, sat down and began to play at once. Soon she and Alastair were playing duets and singing together, his rich deep baritone harmonizing perfectly with her clear, bell-like soprano.

These two acquisitions, coinciding as they did with the end of the rains, saved Madeleine. Instead of hours spent sitting alone, there were early morning rides followed by breakfast on the verandah, calls to pay and receive between the hours of ten and four, then a drive to hear one of the regimental bands before returning to change for dinner. There were frequent dinner parties, and at weekends there were the races and polo matches to attend in addition to regimental dances, amateur theatricals and the more formal receptions and dinner parties at the Residency.

The Frasers were included in all the events; they had joined the Mutton Club, and when it was their turn to have a joint, they gave a dinner party, eagerly using their wedding presents of linen and cutlery, and Alastair was proud of the way Madeleine had learned to cope with the servants. She had taught them well, insisting on a very high standard, and he often heard her quiet voice saying, 'This simply is not good enough. I know you can do very much better and I shall expect a really great improvement by tomorrow morning.' It was very different from the way many British wives treated their servants. Many, beaten by the sun, were too lethargic to take any interest at all, while others, knowing there was an inexhaustible supply of labour available, instantly dismissed staff for any quite petty misdemeanour.

Alastair's own fascination with the country and its native inhabitants continued to grow. Without their knowing it, he and Madeleine soon gained two reputations – among the Europeans for giving lively parties at which simple food was extremely well cooked and served, and among the Indians for their kindness. They only learned of the latter when one evening their khidmatgar announced 'A rissaldar of 3rd Cavalry is asking for you, sahib.'

Madeleine looked at her husband, who shrugged very slightly and said, 'Please show him in.'

A tall, thin Indian in the French grey uniform of the Cavalry entered and saluted punctiliously, but then stood silently as though uncertain of how to proceed.

'Good evening, rissaldar-sahib,' said Alastair politely. 'What can I do for you?'

'Good evening memsahib, good evening sahib,' the man replied, and then with his face puckered in distress, he burst out: 'It is my son, my only son, he is very sick and I am coming to ask if doctor-sahib will help me, for the child burns and will be dying without help.'

'What exactly is the matter with the child?' asked Alastair quietly.

'His throat, sahib, since this morning he is not speaking or eating and is crying with pain.'

'And you say he feels very hot?'

'Yes, yes, sahib, burning to the touch, and all the time is tossing and turning.'

'Has any other doctor seen him?'

'I am asking Indian doctor who is telling me that my child will be dead by morning.'

'I will certainly look at your son, rissaldar-sahib, although you must understand that if the Indian doctor cannot help, it is unlikely that I will be able to do so, either.'

'Thank you, sahib, thank you, thank you. Everyone is telling me to come to Fraser-sahib as he and mem are so kind and good to Indians.'

Alastair's eyes briefly held Madeleine's: a nice bit of soft soap, they said, and met an understanding gleam in return. He went immediately to pick up his instrument case and Madeleine said gently, 'I do hope your son will recover, rissaldar-sahib.'

It was forty-eight hours before Alastair returned, exhausted and unshaven. Both Madeleine and Jacko ran to meet him, Madeleine exclaiming, 'Oh, Alastair darling, I am so glad to see you! I've been so worried!'

He held her off. 'I'm filthy. Unwashed and with a stubble guaranteed to graze your cheek.'

'I don't care,' she replied, putting her arms around his neck and kissing him. 'But I'm sure you *are* worn out, so

438

I'll let you go now and you can tell me about the child when you're ready.'

'It was a bad case of putrid throat,' Alastair said as he bent down to Jacko, who had flung his front paws against Alastair's leg and was uttering little attention-seeking barks. 'All right, little fellow, all right! I took the child into hospital and did a trachie, but I didn't dare leave him, for if the staff didn't kill him off with their attentions, his mother would have. As soon as I've bathed and shaved I must go back before their combined efforts undo all the good work. If only we had a decent nursing staff!'

Madeleine followed him into the bedroom, where he began to peel off his uniform. 'Alastair, could I help?' she asked tentatively. 'At least I could faithfully carry out your instructions.'

Alastair's tousled red head appeared from the folds of his shirt. 'What a marvellous idea! But I wonder how it would go down with Scott and the others? I'm only an assistant surgeon, and to bring in my wife to nurse . . .' But he did, and between them they saved the child. It was all a nine days' wonder which might have led to opposition, if the garrison had not very soon found a more disturbing topic.

It all started with the widely circulated story of the sweeper at the Dum-Dum arsenal who had asked a sepoy for water from his drinking bowl, known as a lota. The request had been refused on the grounds that the sweeper, being of low caste, would defile the lota. 'But you are about to lose your caste, anyway,' the sweeper was reported to have replied, 'because the British will order you to bite the new cartridges which are wrapped in the fat of cows and pigs.' Soon British officers throughout all the stations were endeavouring to reassure their men that the cartridges were greased with a mixture of wax and mutton fat, but the sepoys remained unconvinced, and even suspected the feel of the paper in which the cartridges were wrapped. In February the Native Infantry Regiment at Barrackpore openly showed their mistrust of both cartridges and paper wrapping, although at the Court of Enquiry held two days' later, the troops admitted that most of their information emanated from the bazaars.

'It is a tragedy because the new Enfield rifle, for which the cartridges are to be used, is a splendid weapon,' said Colonel Inglis at the Frasers' dinner table, 'and we must have it to secure our borders. Apart from Afghanistan, which is always on the boil, there is China and our greatest threat – Russia.'

'But sir, are the cartridges the only reason for the unrest?' asked Alastair, who knew the answer but was anxious to have a senior Army officer's opinion since so many of the military were said to be closing their eyes and ears to the situation.

Colonel Inglis answered at once: 'No, they are not. They are certainly one, if not the main reason, but there is also this most pernicious rumour that we are about to force the Army to become Christian.' Colonel Inglis paused to take a sip of wine before continuing, 'While this, of course, is nonsense, it has to be admitted that certain individuals are making definite efforts to convert their people. Do you not agree, Case?'

Colonel Case nodded. 'Most certainly, although I personally think that another factor has been the Dalhousie reforms, which were pushed through too quickly and must appear harsh not only to the army, but to farmers, landowners and princes alike. Then there has been the abolition of suttee – '

'Oh, but my dear, surely you cannot think *that* custom other than monstrous!', exclaimed his wife with a slight shudder. 'To make widows throw themselves on their husbands' funeral pyres!'

'Of course it seems so to us,' agreed her huband, 'but

not to orthodox Hindus. The further law allowing Hindu widows to remarry is, I think, insensitive, to say the least.'

'I wonder how we shall be seen by posterity?' Madeleine mused, and Alastair said quickly, 'I suspect as well meaning, but generally insensitive – '

'Why, Dr Fraser, you speak as though our remaining in India is doubtful,' said Mrs Inglis in surprise. 'Surely India will always be the greatest triumph of our Empire?'

Alastair looked at her from under frowning red brows. 'I do not know, Mrs Inglis. Although I hesitate to voice an opinion, it does seem to me that over the past fifty years or so there have been subtle yet distinct changes in our relationship with the Indians.'

'Go on, Dr Fraser, blame it all on the coming of the memsahibs!' said Maria Germon with a little laugh.

'Well . . .' Alastair began uncertainly, as though he agreed but was afraid of offending the four women present, but before he could go on Madeleine said quickly, 'We have become far too serious for such a warm evening. Shall we not adjourn and have a little music?'

As they later broke up, Maria Germon said, 'Clever of you to invite senior and junior couples together.'

'Well, I *did* wonder,' Madeleine answered, 'but Mrs Inglis is young and Mrs Case is a bride.'

'Madeleine, you must give me the recipe for your navarin; it was a gorgeous meal – lovely veggies, home grown, I suppose?'

'Yes, and the flowers too. Alastair is so proud of his garden!'

Maria sighed. 'You are lucky. My dear old Charlie is no gardener, and although we have a mali he just sits and looks at the ground. I go out to give him a prod now and then, but consider my complexion more important than anything he can produce. Don't you find it just impossible to keep your skin *absolutely* pale in this climate? I've sent

441

for some Bridal Bouquet Lotion from home but fear I shall be quite yellow by the time it arrives!'

Colonel Case held Madeleine's hand in farewell and said, 'I do hope we have not alarmed you, Mrs Fraser. You may be sure that whatever happens elsewhere, my regiment will never mutiny; I know each and every one of the men and can vouch that they will remain true to their salt.'

But Captain Germon said sotto voce to Alastair, 'We are sitting on a powder keg, and to add to our danger, we have this inability of senior officers everywhere to believe their men capable of mutiny, even though it has happened before.'

Alastair nodded. 'I know we have only one Queen's regiment here, but how many others are there between ourselves and Calcutta?'

'One,' said Charles Germon, 'in seven hundred miles! Goodnight.'

'Did it go all right, do you think?' Madeleine asked anxiously when their guests had departed.

'Perfectly, dearest,' Alastair answered proudly. 'The meal was excellent and you did the table and flowers so well.'

'Maria Germon was full of praise for the flowers and vegetables,' Madeleine mused, as she moved around the room plumping up cushions, 'but I wonder if we let the conversation become a little too sombre.' Madeleine looked at him concernedly. 'Just how serious is the situation?'

As Alastair paused, uncertain whether to tell her or not, she added firmly, 'I want to know.'

'Then I have to tell you, my dearest, that potentially it is very serious indeed. Mutiny is by no means unknown in the Indian Army, and now that the Company has expanded so greatly, many of the best regimental officers are being induced to change to the civil service, in which pay and promotion chances are much more favourable. And there have been stupid changes; the General Service Enlistment Act, for instance, which stipulates that all recruits to the Bengal Army must be prepared to serve overseas – when it is known that a Hindu cannot do so because in a wooden ship permission for him to cook his own food could not be granted. Also, there would be no provision for the daily ablutions which the faithful need to perform. No one seems to have taken into account that those Hindus who have served overseas already have been treated as outcasts when they've returned to their villages.' Alastair stopped abruptly as he realized that Madeleine looked very tired. He went swiftly across the room to put his arm warmly around her waist. 'Forgive me, darling, for spouting on and on,' he said contritely, 'you must be worn out after such a hectic day. And don't let anything I've said upset you for, don't forget, next month we have Sir Henry Lawrence coming to us as Chief Commissioner of Oudh. He is a man of outstanding ability, with years of experience in this country, and is said to understand and respect Indians as people – something which some of us British seem to have forgotten.'

'Well,' said Madeleine tiredly, 'I certainly hope he will be an improvement on Mr Jackson and that he will be able to control Mr Gubbins, whom I really cannot *stand*.'

'I know. Apart from his awful temper, there's something about the fellow . . .'

The appointment of Sir Henry Lawrence was universally popular. 'Such a dear old man,' said Maria Germon, regardless of the fact that Lawrence was only fifty-one. From the start, while contending with the internal feuding among the city's hierarchy, Lawrence prepared for disaster. Within days of Coverly Jackson's departure, Lawrence called a meeting of all European officers, both civil and military. When he rose to speak, few doubted that he was indeed an old man, for his thin face was sunken and deeply lined. A long straggly beard and an obvious disregard for dress added to the impression of age, and it was only his eyes that made people realize their mistake, for they were alert, missing nothing, and with a curious blend of sadness and spiritual intensity lurking in their narrow depths.

'Gentlemen,' he said now, 'for many years I have been aware that mutiny in the native army was a distinct possibility and I am now convinced that we are on the brink of catastrophe; there are many signs pointing to this, perhaps the most serious being this rumour that we are about to force the army to become Christian. You have only to listen to any village drum at night to be aware of this, and no speech, denial or proclamation appears able to quash the notion; there is even a wild rumour that the widows of the Crimean dead are to be brought to India where they and the chief landowners are to be forced into marriage so that in time the estates will be handed over to Christians.'

A ripple of laughter greeted this, and even Sir Henry smiled. 'Yes, I agree, it is quite absurd,' he said, 'but together with all the other rumours it adds considerably to the sepoy's confusion and doubt. Gentlemen, it appears to be quite plain to me that all these rumours originated, and are now being fanned, by agents provocateurs and fakirs in the bazaars. Many of you will be aware of the old prophecy that our rule in India will last only until the centenary of Plassey, and this year is that centenary; I believe this is also being whispered in the bazaars, together with the mysterious phrase that "all will become red". Other signs are the widespread outbreaks of arson in army buildings and the distribution of chupatties, which I consider to be most sinister.

'It is almost three months since the first reports of these were received, and the procedure always appears to be the same: a village watchman being approached in the early dawn by a watchman from a neighbouring village, clutching a number of chupatties in his right hand, with the instruction to "take two and make ten more", eight of which are to be passed on to another village. No one knows who ordered the distribution in the first instance, but the chupatties have now travelled over tremendous distances at very great speed, and always with the message "from the north to the south, from the east to the west". I am convinced, gentlemen, that many villagers do not know the true meaning themselves – indeed, some of them wonder if *we* started it all, merely to ascertain how quickly news can be spread; but the more sophisticated hint that it means trouble.'

Sir Henry paused to take a sip of water. 'I am sure I do not need to tell you, gentlemen, that if and when that trouble comes, we, in Lucknow, will be in the midst of it . . . for the greatest dissatisfaction is in the Bengal Army and most of its sepoys were recruited from Oudh. I personally think that the annexation of this kingdom was a mistake, that it, too, has added to the present situation, and the fact that this happened only last year means that it is still very much in the forefront of the sepoy's mind.'

Sir Henry paused again and passed a handkerchief over his face; the weather was beginning to warm up very considerably and in the enclosed room the atmosphere was already hot and heavy. 'In view of what I have told you, gentlemen, I am proposing to fortify, so far as I am able, the Residency, the Machi Bhawan fort and the surrounding environs. Then, at the first sign of serious trouble, I shall order all the women and children into this compound and, if necessary, the Queen's Regiment and those native troops who positively demonstrate their loyalty to the Queen. Immediate steps must therefore be taken to fill every cellar, court and outhouse with munitions and foodstuffs – the latter not only for ourselves, but for our livestock as well. However, I would ask you to remember that there is also a great need for tact and discretion; if the populace see too many signs of defensive measures or any other indication of panic, they may well be induced to take action before we are ready. Although this compound is on only slightly sloping ground, it is the one commanding site in the city and I have asked Major Anderson, our chief engineer, to prepare a line of defence and to demolish all buildings which obstruct this line, be they palaces or mud huts.' Sir Henry cleared his throat. 'However, I am insisting on the preservation of the holy places in the vicinity. Now, I shall expect every able-bodied man to report at sunrise every morning for arms drill, and all officers will be issued with arms with which to defend their homes. Are there any questions, gentlemen?'

There was a short pause while men in tight uniforms shifted in their chairs, mopped their faces and murmured to their neighbours. Then one of the senior civilians, Mr Ommaney, rose. 'I should be obliged if you would tell us, sir, how long you think we could hold out, if besieged?'

Sir Henry allowed himself a slight, wintry smile. 'I hope, Mr Ommaney, that should a crisis arise, we would be reinforced before an actual siege became reality. In the unhappy event of this not occurring, I would estimate that we could hold out for a month.'

Louder murmurings broke out then as the full implication of Sir Henry's words struck his listeners. Then Alastair rose. 'Sir,' he began in his deep and exceptionally pleasant voice, 'I have only been in India for just over seven months, so I hope you will forgive me, but surely if the sepoys *really* trusted and *liked* us, they would believe what we say about the cartridges and the idea of mass conversion to Christianity?'

Sir Henry's eyes gleamed. Here was a young man after

446

his own heart, he thought as he rose again. 'You are perfectly correct about the underlying reasons,' he said, his voice rising a little, 'and we have only ourselves to blame. In the last century – or even thirty, forty years ago – there were close ties between British officers and their native troops. There was stern discipline, but also much laughter between all ranks – in those days most British officers spoke Hindustani quite fluently, no doubt because almost all had Indian mistresses and, perhaps because of these ladies, they were given some insight into the Indian mind. But later discipline became very lax; newly arrived officers from England frequently behaved with arrogant, often insulting ways towards their troops and servants, and the senior officers were often too lethargic or too indifferent to correct their disgraceful attitude. So it snowballed until we have the present situation!'

When he finished speaking there was complete silence and he became aware that while all the faces before him bore an expression of astonishment, there were many who also appeared actually hostile.

A gleam of humour lit Sir Henry's eyes as he said: 'The fact that the attitude I have described still exists today makes me very sad, not only for our two nations, but for all those officers and men who *have* tried to understand, befriend and counsel their Indian brethren. You do not need me to tell you, gentleman, that there have been – and still are – many such officers and men.'

Not for nothing, thought Alastair, is Sir Henry noted for his tact and diplomacy.

22

Now that the time for caution was over, Alastair urged Madeleine to learn to handle a pistol. 'Just as a precaution, dearest,' he said, trying to sound reassuring. 'Such knowledge can only be beneficial, not only in the present troubled time, but wherever we are in India.' To his relief, she readily agreed, so every day they rode out together into the moffusal, where in a quiet spot he began to teach her to load, cock and fire, hanging a large melon from the branch of a huge peepal tree for her to aim at. She became proficient in a very short time and Alastair was soon replacing the melon with an orange.

'Well done!' he exclaimed when, standing with legs slightly apart and holding the pistol in both hands at arm's length, Madeleine hit the orange, pulping it into flying fragments. 'That was splendid, darling!' Alastair said, his warm smile enveloping her, 'and it is a great relief to me, for I know that you are now able to defend yourself, although God forbid you should ever have to. I suggest you sleep with the pistol under your pillow, especially when I am duty medical officer – oh, damn these mosquitoes!' He slapped the back of his neck, where already several large bites were becoming visible.

Madeleine took a handkerchief and a small bottle from her reticule. 'Let me put some eau de Cologne on your neck,' she said, 'and then do let's go home, for I really believe you are attacked much more out here than in town.'

'I don't know,' Alastair said, as he bent forward so that she could dab his neck, 'the beastly creatures are everywhere – ah, that feels nice and cool.' Ever since their arrival in India, he had been plagued by mosquitoes, whereas Madeleine was rarely bitten. 'Interesting that,' Alastair had said. 'I should like to find out why . . .'

But there had never been time, and now all his thoughts were concentrated on other things, for on 10 May the native troops, together with units of the police, had mutinied at Meerut, setting fire to their lines, murdering their officers and all the European women they could find before setting off, some two thousand strong, for Delhi.

'But,' said Alastair reassuringly, 'they'll not get far, for Sir Henry has told us very emphatically that they will be pursued from Meerut.' He paused to make sure that she was taking it calmly.

Madeleine had blanched instantly, but now she said quietly, 'Please go on, Alastair.'

'Well, I was only going to add that if a mutiny had to break out, Meerut was one of the places best able to deal with it, for I'm told they have more Queen's regiments there than at any other station.'

Madeleine frowned. 'But,' she said thoughtfully, 'if that is so, does it not seem strange that the sepoys should choose to mutiny there, of all stations?'

'Yes. But I rather wonder whether they did actually *choose*, for from what I can make out, a blustery fellow called Carmichael Smyth ordered his regiment on parade and was convinced that once they knew they could tear off the ends of the cartridges – instead of biting them – the sepoys would accept them. Instead, all except five men of the regiment refused; they were later court-martialled and sentenced to ten years' hard labour and, as if that were not enough, the entire garrison was paraded to watch the eighty-five men being stripped of their uniforms and then shackled. I'm told a lot of them were old soldiers who had fought with us in many battles and had medals to show for them – how degrading, how bitter for them, not only to have such harsh sentences, but to lose their pensions and end their service in such a way. No wonder many were said to be in tears and to have begged their British officers to save them, but of course nothing could be done, and the very next day the mutiny started – with the freeing of those prisoners.'

Madeleine was instantly reminded of Jem shuffling along in his leg irons, the fetters around his wrists so tight that he was hardly able to grasp her Bible. 'Oh,' she said in distress, 'surely it could have been handled in a kinder, more understanding way.'

Alastair sighed. 'I know, dearest. But perhaps it's just that you and I are so new to this country, we don't fully understand . . . anyway, you can rest assured that the mutineers will be pursued, especially as Major General Hewitt, the Divisional Commander, was on the spot, and Delhi also comes within his command.'

But General Hewitt refused to order such action and the mutineers crossed the Jumna. The troops within Delhi and the riffraff from the bazaars – the badmashes – rose in a frenzied orgy of murder and no one was spared: neither Indian merchant, nor British woman and child; neither civilian nor military. A detachment of the 54th Native Infantry Regiment was sent to parley with the mutineers, and immediately the rebels mowed down the British officers. Their Colonel was bayoneted repeatedly by his own men, who then rushed to join the mob crowding the streets and howling for blood.

In Lucknow, Sir Henry Lawrence told his secretary that the whole army throughout the country would now rise in rebellion. Already, by his unique blend of conciliation, diplomacy and resolution, he had averted one uprising at Lucknow, but rumour was rife throughout the bazaars, and many Europeans complained that there was a sullenness about their servants and the majority of other Indians with whom they had to deal.

'I've not noticed this with our servants, have you, dear?' asked Alastair one evening in late May.

Madeleine thought for a moment, 'No . . . with ours it's more a reluctance to look one in the eye, and I think there sometimes seems to be an expression of regret.'

'H'm. I wonder if it would be a good idea for you to pack a few essentials of clothing, soap, etc., in your carpetbag and I will store it in my room at the hospital. It certainly won't stay fresh very long kept like that, but at least if you should have to come into the Residency suddenly, it will mean that you have a few changes.'

'Do you really think it will come to that?'

Alastair busied himself with getting his pipe alight as he pondered. Only that morning Sir Henry had gathered his officers together and told them that there had been mutinies at ten other large stations and countless smaller ones following the capture of Delhi, and he now considered that if Lucknow fell the whole of the Ganges Plain would be engulfed. As Alastair was about to give a watered-down version of this to Madeleine, he remembered that the following night he would be duty medical officer and so she would be alone in the bungalow for all of twenty-four hours; he decided not to tell her, but said instead, 'No one knows, dear, but I think we should be prepared, in view of what has already happened at Meerut and Delhi, don't you?'

Madeleine nodded and rose. 'I'll go now and pack bags for us both.'

'How will you ever ride with them?' Madeleine asked the next morning as she surveyed the two bulging carpetbags which Alastair was knotting at each end of a length of rope.

'Don't worry about that,' he said. 'Poor old Rambler might not be too keen to have them draped over his sides, but it's only for three miles.' Alastair turned and put his hands on Madeleine's shoulders, his concerned eyes searching her face. 'It's you I'm worried about,' he admitted. 'I do so hate to leave you alone for so long.'

She tried to make light of it. 'Then don't think about it, my dear doctor!' she said, smiling up at him, a finger moving to smooth his anxious frown. 'After all, I can sleep and do what I want during the day, but you have to be on duty all the time.'

'Oh, I can rest on a bed during the night, so long as it's quiet,' Alastair said. 'Now, promise me, my dearest, that you will keep the pistol beside you during the day and under your pillow tonight.'

'I promise, sir,' she said, still smiling.

'And that if . . . if anything untoward happens, or if you feel uneasy about *anything*, you will go straight across to the Germons, no matter what time it is?'

'Cross my heart,' she said, doing so exaggeratedly.

Alastair gathered her into his arms. 'Then goodbye, darling, I'll be back as soon as I can tomorrow.' He kissed her deeply, laid his freshly shaved cheek against hers and then tore himself reluctantly away. She took his hands as they slid from her waist, held them lovingly for a moment, then slowly let them slip apart.

As he leapt down the steps, she called out, 'Take care, and don't work too hard.'

He turned to smile up at her, his eyes moving in a caress over her slender figure as she stood with Jacko at her side. 'I love you,' he said. Then he swung into the saddle, turned Rambler's head and trotted down the drive. At the gate, he waved and she blew him a kiss.

She was glad when the night passed uneventfully. She had been apprehensive and had slept little, her hand frequently moving beneath her pillow to find the pistol and the little velvet case containing Sebastian's brooch. Every night, the last thing she did was to put the case under her pillow, and the first thing every morning was to remove it, even taking it with her when she went to her bath; during the day she was never seen without the brooch pinned at her throat. Often she would take it in her hand and gaze at it before closing her fingers protectively over it. She thought of Sebastian as constantly as ever, but the intense yearning she had felt during the idle months of rain had at last given way to a wistful sadness, a hurt deep within her heart that she would never know where he was, whether he was happy, whether he had found someone to replace her. Yet at the same time she dreaded that in some way she would hear, would know, for then her present precarious contentment would vanish like the morning mist. So she tried never to ask questions of those who had returned from other parts of India.

In some nebulous way Madeleine felt that if she could remain cocooned in her own little world she would be safe, that her tranquil life with Alastair was to be her ration of happiness and must be guarded. And, when she looked back at the hardships she had endured, she was immensely grateful for her present contentment and good fortune, acknowledging that she owed it all to Alastair, who had loved her sufficiently to marry her. In a way which she did not fully understand, she knew that she loved him too – not in the desperate, all-consuming way that she loved Sebastian, but nevertheless with real warmth and a tremendous desire to make him happy.

So on that morning of 28 May, she was smiling and patient with the Afghan trader who had appeared on the verandah and insisted upon unrolling the most lovely Persian rugs and Kashmir shawls for her to see. 'They are all beautiful,' she told him, 'but quite, quite beyond anything I could afford. Come back in twenty-five years' time when my husband will be retiring and perhaps he will be able to buy me a shawl.' She looked round quickly as a gig drove up beneath the porch and she saw Dr

Fayrer descend. 'Why, Dr Fayrer, good morning,' she said, moving to the top of the steps. 'This is a pleasant surprise! Do come and sit down; would you care for coffee or a lime sherbet?'

Dr Fayrer was the senior civilian physician at the hospital, a kindly man who took as great an interest in his staff as in his patients. 'Neither, thank you, Mrs Fraser,' he said almost hoarsely. 'I am afraid I am not here on a social call.'

Madeleine looked at him more closely and saw that he was stooping as though over-burdened by tiredness or sorrow, and the first chill feeling of dread touched her heart. 'Dr Fayrer,' she said, her voice suddenly serious, 'is anything wrong?'

He nodded slowly. 'I deeply regret to say that I have very bad news – '

'Oh, not . . . Alastair?'

'Yes, I am afraid your husband is gravely ill,' he replied, watching her carefully.

'Gravely ill?' she echoed, totally unable to believe the words. 'But . . . he left here yesterday morning in perfect health!'

Again there was the quiet nod. 'Yes, but during the day a high fever developed and severe erysipelas was diagnosed last night. He refused to let us tell you, but this morning my colleagues and I agree that septicaemia has set in.'

'Septicaemia,' she echoed again, frantically trying to think, to remember.

'Blood poisoning,' Dr Fayrer said gently, reading her thoughts.

'Oh, dear God, dear God,' Madeleine whispered, hands flying to cover her face for a second. 'But are you sure? Can it develop so quickly?'

Dr Fayrer nodded a third time. 'Always in this climate,' he confirmed.

'How bad is it?' Only a tiny part of her brain was still functioning; the rest was too panic-stricken for coherent thought.

'I am afraid . . . very bad indeed – ' he broke off abruptly as Madeleine was suddenly rushing past him and down the steps. After a moment's stupefaction he realized that she was intending to run all the way to the hospital, in the heat of midday and without parasol or bonnet. 'Mrs Fraser – wait!' he shouted, but panic had now taken over completely and she was deaf to every sound, her one thought being that she must get to Alastair. As Dr Fayrer moved to follow her, he saw that a tiny white dog was running by her side, whimpering and looking up at her with tongue already lolling. Dr Fayrer caught up with them within minutes, but by then he was breathing hard. He grasped Madeleine strongly by the arm. 'Mrs Fraser, please collect yourself,' he said sternly. 'I have a gig here to take you to the hospital, but I insist that you fetch a bonnet and parasol first!'

'No, no, let me go!' Madeleine shouted, struggling within his hold. 'I must go to him – I must be there to help in some way!'

'Of course, of course,' Dr Fayrer soothed. 'But what is the use of becoming ill yourself – with sunstroke?' As she quietened, he added: 'Now, please oblige me by getting some covering for your head so that I may drive you with all speed to your husband.'

She went then, running as she had done with the milk for Thomas and the ointment for Sebastian, running on legs that threatened to give way any second, driven on solely by her desperation. Within minutes she reappeared, frantically knotting the bonnet ribbons under her chin. As she lifted her skirts to step up into the gig, she remembered Jacko and bent to tuck him under her arm. 'Please hurry,' she said when she and the doctor were both seated. 'Oh, please, please hurry!'

As soon as the gig drew up before the hospital she jumped down, still clutching Jacko, and without waiting for Dr Fayrer she rushed into the building, calling out wildly to Dr Hadow, who had just appeared, 'Where is he – where is Alastair?'

Dr Hadow, who had just left Alastair's bedside, now took her arm. 'This way, Mrs Fraser.'

Still running blindly along, she turned to look at him. 'How is he?' she whispered.

Dr Hadow lengthened his stride to keep up with her. 'There appears to be no change,' he said, speaking as gently as he could. Only half an hour before Alastair had opened his eyes so far as he was able and asked quite lucidly, 'What am I suffering from?' When told, he had said very calmly, 'Then I am done for,' and had tried to smile when they had all said, 'Not if we can help it.' Then he'd asked for Gilbert Hadow and in an urgent whisper had said, 'Hadow, will you look after my wife? I'm afraid she'll take it very badly for she has only me, and with her tremendous capacity for *feeling*, it will be so hard for her. Will you . . . see her through, then get her on a ship as soon as possible? I have a brother at the Cape; she may want to go to him and his wife, but if not, then to my family at Edinburgh. And, Hadow, please . . . will you make sure she has every comfort . . . there will be no shortage of money and my father will reimburse anything you have to spend . . . you can contact him at Edinburgh Royal . . .' Alastair's voice had trailed away and Dr Hadow had said at once, 'My dear fellow, you may depend upon my doing everything possible for your wife – if necessary.'

Seeing Madeleine's distraught face now and conscious of her violent trembling, Dr Hadow said: 'Are you familiar with the effects of septicaemia, Mrs Fraser?'

'Yes – at Scutari,' she replied in a panting whisper.

'Then you will be prepared to find your husband very changed.'

She could only nod, smothering a sob, but when she first caught sight of Alastair, her instinctive reaction was to say, 'This is not my husband,' for his face was red and twice the size, the nose flattened by swelling, the eyes mere slits and the lips puffed to shapelessness. Then she saw the hair, and with a sudden rush, she had darted forward to sink beside the bed, her hand moving to raise the wet red strands from his brow. 'Alastair . . . my darling, darling,' she whispered, agonized, but he had slipped into unconsciousness. She turned to speak to Dr Hadow, and found them all there: Fayrer, Scott, Brydon, Partridge, Darby and even Wells from the 48th Regiment, all looking at her with deep compassion and concern. 'There must be something,' she begged, her terrified eyes moving from face to face. 'Dr Brydon, you were on the march from Kabul . . . you must have had to deal – '

'Dear lady,' Dr Brydon said, 'if it were humanly possible to do more, none of us would hesitate. I believe you understand this, being a doctor's wife and the daughter of a doctor.'

'Yes,' she whispered, and turned back to Alastair.

'But there is always prayer,' Dr Fayrer said, feeling she must be given something to cling to.

She saw Sister Benedicta's face then, heard her words, and remembered how she herself had prayed at Sebastian's bedside when his condition had also seemed hopeless. Dear Mother of God, she implored silently now, please help Alastair. Please don't let him die . . . not now, when he is in the prime of life and when there is so much he wants to do for this country. You know how great the suffering is here, how valuable his skill and knowledge can be.

Some time later Alastair did appear to rally; the fever dropped very suddenly and he became conscious, his slit eyes opening with considerable effort. 'Madeleine,' he whispered hoarsely.

'I am here, my dearest,' she said, forcing herself to speak quietly and calmly. 'Let me give you some lime juice.' With the utmost tenderness she raised his head and held a glass to his lips. Alastair gulped down the deliciously cool liquid, but then sank back as though in complete exhaustion. 'Thank . . . you . . . darling.'

'Rest now, dearest,' she begged.

'Must . . . talk,' he muttered, 'must . . . tell . . . you . . .'

But she laid her fingertips lightly over his swollen lips. 'When you are stronger; sleep now and there will – will be plenty of time for talk later. I shall be here with you . . .'

'Madeleine . . . little love . . . remember all those at Scutari – '

She *had* been remembering, remembering only too vividly the agonizing deaths of those suffering from septicaemia, and the memories had drenched her in the ice-cold sweat of terror. But now she said urgently, 'It was quite different for them – they had been days, even weeks, without attention, food or warmth – you are so strong, so healthy, Alastair, if you will just try to conserve your strength, you will soon get over this.'

He tried to smile, but it only made his face more grotesque. 'Will . . . try,' he murmured dreamily and then, as though struggling to remain alert, he said more strongly, 'Listen, Madeleine . . . if I should not . . . recover . . . you must go . . . to the family . . . They will look after you . . . Promise me you will . . . let them care for you . . . until . . . until . . . there is someone else.'

'But I don't want anyone else!' she cried brokenly, and at that moment it was the absolute truth. 'I want to stay here with you!'

'Yes . . . yes, we've been so happy, haven't we? The

458

best little wife a man could ever have . . .' The voice was sinking again, but with the last of his strength, Alastair said, 'You have . . . so much to give . . . must not spend . . . your life alone . . . you need to love . . . and be loved.'

'Oh, hush, Alastair, please hush!' she begged, unable now to stop the tears. 'We'll be together always and – and in a few weeks we shall be able to say how silly we were to talk like this. When you are better, we will go together to Simla or Missourie, where you will soon be quite yourself again. They say it is lovely in Simla, and perhaps you may even be reminded of Scotland, with the pines and the mountains . . .' The words, like her tears, had been flowing nonstop and Dr Hadow, watching quietly from across the room, realized that she was trying to convince herself as much as Alastair. Yet even before she had finished speaking he had sunk back into unconsciousness and was soon muttering in delirium and high fever. 'Shall I sponge him down?' she asked, turning her piteous eyes on each of the doctors in turn.

Dr Fayrer shook his head. 'It is best to let him be.'

Madeleine began to wring her hands in terrible distress. 'But the fever is so high – his heart . . .'

Quietly Dr Fayrer lifted the sheet which covered Alastair and she saw that his body was covered with open abscesses in which there was already some movement . . . Her thin scream was cut off only as she fell in a merciful faint.

But nothing would keep her from him. As soon as she could stand, she was back beside his bed, working desperately to clean the great open sores, but even as she swabbed one, so another would burst into being, oozing thick droplets of pus and filling the room with a powerful stench.

'He is dying by inches,' Dr Fayrer told his wife, 'and I am very apprehensive for her; except to answer calls of nature, she has not left his side for three days, not sleeping, and having taken only liquid in all that time. I fear her collapse, when it comes, will be total.'

'Is she tearful or hysterical?' asked Bassie Fayrer, whose own health was not good, and she could not repress a shudder as she thought: Madeleine Fraser today, perhaps myself tomorrow.

'No, not now,' Dr Fayrer said in answer to her question. 'She is completely calm, totally silent, with her face set in utter determination as she attends to him. I confess that in all my years of experience I have never seen such complete devotion or such strength of will, and there is no doubt that if willpower could save him, hers would do so. She is fighting like a tigress for his life.'

But in the afternoon of the third day, even Madeleine could not wish Alastair to live longer, for his suffering was too great; the battle had been lost and she could only sit numbly beside the bed, listening to his stentorian breathing. When this suddenly stopped, she did not move, and Dr Hadow went briefly to Alastair before saying very gently, 'It is over now.'

She looked up quite blankly, hearing only Sister Benedicta's voice saying, 'Sometimes God demands a sacrifice of us . . .' But when Dr Hadow explained that the funeral must take place at once, Madeleine came briefly back from her private hell to say, 'Oh, but supposing – supposing he is only deeply unconscious . . . Supposing he were to wake and find himself hidden in a black, airless box . . . Oh, think! No, we must wait . . .' So all the doctors came and examined Alastair in turn, and Dr Brydon said, 'Come and see for yourself, Mrs Fraser, he is gone.' Dr Fayrer added with a note of urgency in his voice, 'The city is in an uproar, and there is a rumour that the mutiny will start here when the nine o'clock gun is fired tonight . . . Mrs Fraser, I beg you, be reasonable, there is only about another hour of daylight left. And who knows what tomorrow will bring?'

They were all busy men, and the long-awaited catastrophe was almost upon them, yet they hated to harass her. She rose to her feet, twisting her hands in agonized indecision, but then Jacko, who had remained forgotten in a far corner with his head resting on his front paws, his great sad eyes swivelling to watch everyone as they came and went, suddenly sat up, raised his head and howled eerily. Everyone started and turned to look at the little animal. Madeleine felt a crawling sensation at her nape and she moved on stiff legs to pick up Jacko, who immediately became silent but continued to tremble violently in her arms. Quietly then Madeleine said to Dr Fayrer, 'What do I have to do?' and there was an almost audible sigh of relief from the five medical men as Dr Fayrer replied, 'Leave everything to me. Let me take you to my wife now so that you can rest until I come for you. But, perhaps, first a moment alone . . .?'

Slowly she shook her head and turned away from the bed. What was the good of praying now? She had been praying nonstop for three days, but none of her pleas had been heard, and now there was nothing, nothing here, nothing anywhere in the world . . . She tried to make an effort for Mrs Fayrer's sake, but when the doctor reappeared and said very quietly, 'We are ready now, Mrs Fraser,' he thought her like a complete automaton, and behind Madeleine's back his wife spread her hands, palms upwards in a gesture of hopelessness.

If there had been more time, if the situation had been normal, everyone would have attended the funeral, probably even Sir Henry himself, for Alastair had been extremely popular; but instead only the five doctors and Mr Harris, the senior chaplain, were there. However, Madeleine did not seem to notice as she stood, absolutely silent and still clutching Jacko, throughout the service.

461

There were oblique sideways glances at her as the coffin was lowered into the bare, dusty earth, but she remained gazing ahead dully. Both Dr Fayrer and his wife had previously told her she must come to them and stay for as long as she wished and until the situation quietened. With a ghost of a smile Madeleine had thanked them politely, and now, as Mr Harris and three of the doctors came to murmur condolences before hurrying away, she held out her hand to each in turn, thanking them for all they had done, and then turned to Dr Fayrer and Dr Hadow to say, 'Please, I should just like to remain for a little while . . .' Both men hesitated; it was a reasonable request, but she was too calm, too composed, and already the Indian dusk was falling. 'You will be sure to come to us when you leave, won't you, Mrs Fraser?' Dr Fayrer said.

Madeleine nodded. 'Thank you, yes.'

'And, my dear, I beg you not to linger here for more than a few minutes – it will be dark in a very short while, and I should like you to be safely indoors before then.'

Again she nodded. 'In a very short while,' she echoed, making it sound like a promise.

They turned away reluctantly. 'I don't much like leaving her alone,' Dr Fayrer muttered.

'Nor I,' his colleague agreed. 'Poor young woman, it must be like a nightmare to her, for Fraser always appeared so strong.'

'He *was* strong,' Dr Fayrer said decisively. 'Surely that is why he took three days to die; but who could withstand such an onslaught of infection? Until we find something to kill that, we shall continue to die like flies, especially out here –'

A nightmare, yes, that's all it really was, a particularly vivid and terrible nightmare, and the jagged flashes of light in her eyes surely confirmed that she was not really awake; yet how could she be up and dressed when it was

462

a nightmare? 'Must rest,' she murmured, one hand covering her left eye . . . such pain in her head, and the light obscuring her vision . . . Must get home . . . must.

She stumbled back to the Residency area, seeming not to notice the tremendous movement and bustle of men and beasts all around her, then out through a gate and along the dusty road. It was almost dark now and people jostled her on all sides, so that at times she almost staggered, yet somehow she managed to continue until at last, drenched in sweat and trembling with exhaustion, she turned in at the garden gate and almost crawled up the steps, which Alastair had not been able to have balustraded after all. The bungalow was dark and silent, but she did not notice. She did not even think to remove her bonnet before falling across the bed, where she lay completely inert, and within minutes was deeply asleep.

She might not have wakened had it not been for Jacko's barking close to her ear and his front paws scratching frantically at her shoulder and arm, but when she did open her eyes it was to brightness and red light dancing on the wall opposite; and there was noise, tremendous noise of shouting and banging, as though close by a vast crowd was assembled. Madeleine half raised her head, listening and looking around but not comprehending until she noticed that the punkah was not moving over her head. She frowned. Why was it still, and why was Jacko behaving as though trying to tell her something very urgently? Where was everyone – the servants? Alastair . . . oh, oh, dear God, Alastair! Had it really been true then? Muzzy as her head felt, she knew now with great conviction that Alastair was dead, that she was alone in the bungalow and that it was night.

She pulled herself to her feet, swaying for a few moments while her heart began to thump with an unknown fear; then she forced herself to cross the room and go out on to the verandah, where a gurgling scream rose within her. It was as bright as day because all the bungalows were blazing, and everywhere figures were running, some with flaming torches, some with their arms full of silver objects which gleamed in the light, and others clutching babies and with children running by their sides, pursued by figures whose raised arms held long curved swords. Then a torchbearer sprinted across to Madeleine's side of the road; she saw him dash into a nearby bungalow, and the reflection of his torch as he ran from room to room; within seconds he was back on the verandah, yelling to the crowd, who swarmed across – the *pad, pad* of their bare feet sounding even above the roar and crackle of the flames. The bungalow was empty, but the crowd found numerous articles to take and small fights developed between two or three who wanted the same items.

In five minutes or less, she knew, they would be storming into *her* bungalow and a curved sword would come slashing down on *her*, yet still she could only stand and stare. Until Jacko growled deeply, menacingly, hackles rising along the entire length of his little body. Madeleine did swing round then and instantly screamed, for a tall Indian was standing in the doorway, tulwar in hand.

'Do not be afraid, mem,' a voice said quickly, 'I am Rissaldar Nathan Ram, and I am coming to take you to Residency. But hurry, mem, hurry, the badmashes will be here in a minute.'

As she still remained incapable of movement, Rissaldar Ram came forward to take her arm in a firm grip, and as she cringed away in terror, he said, 'I am a friend, mem, doctor-sahib saved my son and now I am saving sahib's memsahib. But please to hurry, for I am not being able to hold back the bad men.'

Fleetingly she remembered the child with his huge,

kohl-rimmed eyes, and the way his father had gone down on his knees to touch Alastair's boots with his forehead in gratitude for saving his son's life. That, and the fact that the rissaldar had done the unthinkable by taking hold of her arm, made Madeleine move then, only pausing to scoop up Jacko. With his thin fingers still holding her arm above the elbow, she ran with Nathan Ram through the rear of the bungalow and into the back garden. He moved with extreme speed, motioning her to bend low as they raced towards the shelter of the cookhouse, and then to the shadow of the huge flame-of-the-forest. Now they were out in the back road, passing the rear of the next bungalow even as the mob stormed in at the front. From there on all the buildings were blazing, turning night into day, but the tall hedges bordering the gardens were not yet alight, and so, by bending close to these, Rissaldar Ram and Madeleine were able to put some distance between themselves and the great majority of the mob.

Eventually she had to stop, for it had been like running through a furnace and her breath was coming in gasping sobs. Reluctantly Ram let her rest for a few moments and, as she stood desperately trying to clear her smoke-filled lungs, she looked back. A little animal cry of anguish escaped her, for the figures were running all over Alastair's garden, trampling it into dust; and even as she watched, others were pushing the piano down the steps, where it bounced with loudly protesting jangles. Then with a *woosh*! the thatch became a ball of flame, and within minutes only the smoking walls were left of the home she had shared so happily with Alastair. Her will almost snapped then, but the rissaldar was saying urgently, 'If they are finding us, mem, we shall both be hacked to pieces.' And she realized that he had risked – *was* risking – his life for her.

'I am ready now,' she said, her breathing still ragged. But she kept up with him, and as soon as they left the cantonment, the brilliant light was replaced by velvety blackness; now the streets were narrow and tightly packed with buildings all shuttered and dark. There was an overpowering stench of open drains and their contents, mixed with the smells of cumin, garlic, curry and jasmin. Madeleine wondered how anyone could find his way through this labyrinth without light, but Rissaldar Ram never hesitated. Normally the streets would be full of shoving, shouting humanity, but now they were almost entirely deserted except for the many beggars sleeping close to the buildings and the roaming, scavenging dogs. Nathan Ram guided her into the middle of the road and slowed from his quick, effortless trot to a rapid walk. She was glad of his strong hold on her arm, for she was constantly stumbling now, not only from intense weariness, but because of the many obstacles in her path; her feet, shod only in soft leather house slippers, were stubbed against rock-like objects, yielding objects, and soft squashy mounds into which they sank and stuck while liquid overlapped them.

Then suddenly the Baillie Guard was before them, well lit, heavily manned, but not yet barricaded, and an unmistakably British voice was shouting the time-honoured phrase: '*Halt! Who goes there?*'

Rissaldar Ram briefly shook Madeleine's arm, urging her to speak, but her throat had closed with dryness, emotion and exhaustion. So it was he who replied loudly, 'I am Rissaldar Nathan Ram of the 7th Cavalry and I am bringing in Memsahib Fraser from Mariaon Cantonment.'

There was a series of muffled exclamations then, and a lantern was brought to shine in Madeleine's face.

'Why, Mrs Fraser!' exclaimed the officer of the guard. 'Come in, come in. We had thought all women and children were safely in already. You must be exhausted.' Another hand took her arm now, and as she stumbled forward, the hand went quickly around her waist. 'Can

466

you walk the last few yards, or shall we carry you?' the same solicitous voice asked, and a head bent low to hear her hoarse whisper, 'Can walk,' then as she passed through the gate, she stopped and turned to thank the man who had saved her life. But there was no sign of Rissaldar Ram; as silently as he had appeared, so had he vanished into the blackness.

Madeleine never knew how she managed to get to the Fayrers' house, but as she was half carried up the steps she dimly heard Maria Germon's gay voice saying, 'Captain Green would not let me bring in my piano, was it not very unkind of him?' And then all the sounds of a crowded room were abruptly cut off as Madeleine appeared in the doorway, her dress in ribbons around the hem, her bonnet and hair hanging down her back, and her face streaked with dirt. Still clasped in her arms was Jacko, whose huge dark eyes looked imploringly from face to face. As her legs finally buckled, Madeleine faintly heard Bassie Fayrer's voice saying, 'Oh, my dear, my poor dear!' and her husband's deep-toned, 'Thank God, we've found her at last!'

For the next two days she slept almost without a break, and when she did waken there was a haziness, a reluctance to think, to remember, even to open her eyes. So she remained in a twilight world, knowing that periodically hands sponged her hot body and changed her nightgown; that she was helped into a sitting position, where strong arms supported her on both sides 'because she is like a rag doll and immediately falls over, either sideways or forward, if we do not hold her when she is fed' – that from a soft feminine voice, followed by another in deep male tones: 'Don't forget she has taken a terrible emotional battering and is now completely worn out – mentally, physically and emotionally. Rest, sleep and frequent light nourishment is all you can do for her . . .'

The words sounded strangely familiar and Madeleine frowned, unwillingly seeing in her mind's eye Catherine and Dr Kingsley at the foot of her bed, and the de Lacey arms set in the middle of each mullioned pane . . . and Thomas, wrapped in the rabbit skins and put into that terrible box – no, not Thomas, but a box, definitely a box, being lowered into curiously red earth, very dry and hard, and everywhere so dark, as though almost night . . . But who was it in the box? Thomas? Sebastian? Her memory shied and bucked away from the truth until it burst from her lips in a scream: 'ALASTAIR!' But her eyes, fully open now and focusing, saw his tall figure in the familiar blue uniform standing above her. With a sob of joy, she shakily pulled herself into a sitting position and held out her arms.

'Oh, Alastair, I've had such a terrible, terrible nightmare!' she cried, tears raining unheeded down her cheeks. 'I am so glad . . . so very *grateful* that you are here. It was so vivid, I thought it was real . . .'

He moved slightly and went down on his haunches facing her. 'I am Dr Hadow,' a voice said very quietly, very gently, 'and I am sorry to say that it *was* real – you already know that it was not a nightmare, don't you, Mrs Fraser?' As Madeleine, silent and slack-mouthed, shook her head vigorously, he continued, 'I want you now to face the truth: you fought with all your strength to save your husband, but none of us could, and it was a mercy when his suffering ended.'

'Why?' she whispered. 'Why did he die?'

'You know that too,' the patient voice said. 'It was blood poisoning.'

Again her head was vigorously shaken. 'No. He was perfectly fit.'

'The mosquito bites on the back of his neck: we think he must have scratched them, perhaps after doing a dressing, causing erysipelas to develop and, from that,

468

septicaemia. You know, you must know, that many surgeons fall victim to this – it only needs the prick of a finger during an operation and there is nothing to be done for the sufferer except to administer brandy, laudanum and beef tea – all of which you gave to Alastair yourself, Mrs Fraser.'

Dr Hadow paused to allow his words to sink in while he watched her carefully. She was hunched into a broken-down, curving figure of grief, her head sunk on her breast, but when he persisted softly, 'You do remember that, don't you?' she nodded. 'Then I also want you to remember what happened in the cantonment that night and to realize that we – all of us here, in the Residency compound – might have to face a far worse crisis any time now, just as we British are having to do at many other stations, for there are uprisings throughout Oudh. So I want you to make a conscious effort to become fit and strong again and to put behind you the tragedy of Alastair's death. It will not be easy for you, I know, but he asked me to look after you until you could leave India, and so I am speaking very plainly: if we have to evacuate Lucknow; if we have to travel for days, weeks in the moffusil, it will obviously make my task easier if I am not looking after a semi-invalid.'

It was indeed plain speaking, but she had raised her head and now, as she flushed and the tears stood bright in her eyes, she lifted her chin in a small proud gesture. 'Very well, Dr Hadow,' she said, surprising him by the steadiness of her voice. 'I will start getting up from now on and, although it was very kind of you to promise to look after me, I would prefer you not to do so. I really can manage alone, and as soon as the roads are safe, I shall make my own way to Calcutta and find a ship to take – take me somewhere.' Despite her brave words, she could not quite control the tremor in her voice at the end, for where in the world was she to go?

Dr Hadow stood up. 'Good,' he said briskly. 'I suggest you dress now and go into the open air. The other ladies are sitting on the verandah and I want you to join them. It is essential for you to rest, but in company and fresh air, not alone in this stifling room. I'll be on my way now, but you know where to find me if I can help in any way.' Silently he thought, I can understand her attraction now, for apart from that enchanting face, there is so much vulnerability that every male must instinctively want to protect her; and then, just when one thinks her totally dependent, she shows considerable hidden strength and spirit.

It was only after Dr Hadow had left that Madeleine realized she was lying on the floor, with only a charpoy between her and the stone; also that there were ten other such charpoys and seven smaller ones strewn around the otherwise completely bare room. How dark it is, she thought, hot and airless! Then she saw the room was windowless, and although a punkah moved lazily over the middle of the room, there were no signs of the other occupants.

Madeleine got shakily to her feet, one hand pressed to the wall for support, and then she heard a little soft whimper and a tiny rough tongue began to lick her toes. 'Jacko! Oh, Jacko!' she exclaimed, as she bent to pick him up. 'I should have known you would still be here, you dear little dog. Yes, yes, it's all right, you needn't look so anxious, and I don't want to be licked, thank you!' The little animal was ecstatic and his joy warmed her grieving heart. As she stroked him and laid her cheek against the top of his head, she whispered, 'Master has gone, Jacko. You knew that before I did, but he loved us both and would want us to try and survive, so we'll just have to look after each other, won't we?' Her tears rained down on Jacko, but as his soft nose butted her throat,

Madeleine raised her head. 'And I won't let anyone see me cry from now on!'

So when Bassie Fayrer came in a little later she was surprised to find Madeleine dressed and trying to deal with her hair without brush or comb. 'Why, my dear,' exclaimed Mrs Fayrer, 'I am so pleased to see you are up and dressed. I was just bringing you some broth, but instead I hope you will take it upstairs with the rest of us. Dr Partridge has been kindly reading *Guy Mannering* to us as we sew.'

'Thank you, Mrs Fayrer, but where am I?'

'In the taikhana of my house,' was the quiet reply. 'All we occupants of the Residency area have naturally taken in you poor refugees, and my husband thought this underground room would be the safest place for all of you. There are ten other women in addition to yourself, and seven children, so you will never be lonely!' Mrs Fayrer's small smile faded as she looked around. 'But I am afraid it will be very uncomfortable for you all.'

This was to be only too true in the near future, but at that stage the women and children merely used the room for sleeping.

After the burning of the cantonment the city had quietened, so the Baillie Guard remained open and some wives still took short drives into the city, Maria Germon among them. 'But I do not relish it,' she told the assembled sewing party, 'for some of the native troops are now very insolent.'

'In what way?' asked Madeleine quietly.

'Oh – by remaining slouched on the ground as one passes, instead of rising and saluting as they always used to do at once. And then some spit in the dust just where one is about to put one's foot.'

'Is it true,' asked another anxious-looking woman, 'that the sepoys are walking through the bazaars with dolls dressed as English children whose heads they slice off in front of the crowds?'

There was a long, agonized silence and several women instinctively drew their children close. Then Maria said firmly, 'One certainly hears such stories, but I rather doubt their authenticity. What do you think, Madeleine?'

Madeleine invariably sat with head bent silently over her sewing, but she knew Maria was trying increasingly hard to draw her into the conversation. She looked up only briefly to say, 'I do not know if the stories are true or not, but I *do* know only too well that my life was saved by a rissaldar of the 7th Cavalry, who took great risks to find me and bring me here.'

There was another, shorter pause, and several covert glances were directed at Madeleine, whom many found rather enigmatic. 'And I,' said Mrs Bruere at last, beginning to shake as she spoke, 'I have to say that I am alive only because some friendly sepoys dragged me through a hole in the wall of my house, even as their companions were bursting into the front. Oh dear, oh dear, when I think of it – and my poor husband – I – I – ' Mrs Bruere dissolved into tears, trembling violently, and could not be comforted.

Then Katherine Bartrum spoke. 'Yes,' she said shyly, 'I, too, was brought to safety by sepoys, for after my husband had to leave us at Secrora, we were entirely at the mercy of the sepoys who accompanied us . . . Robert did not have much confidence in them, and Mrs Clarke and I were very apprehensive, but they looked after us very well, even getting milk for Bobbie on the way and bringing us safely here.'

Madeleine looked up to smile gently at Katherine; they had met once before when the Frasers first arrived and it had been a bad moment for both women when they had first come face to face in the compound, for Katherine had not known about Alastair's death. Speaking with all

472

the intensity of the shy who have gained confidence, she had said, 'I begged and pleaded with Robert to let me stay and die with him, but he eventually persuaded me to leave for Bobbie's sake . . . I did so long for him to come with us, but as medical officer he felt he should remain with his regiment, and now I – I wonder if we shall ever meet again.'

Madeleine had already given up uttering platitudes; the stories were too numerous and too harrowing. So she had said simply, 'I hope with all my heart that you will be reunited soon.'

'Oh, how lucky you are to have your husband with you!' Katherine had burst out, and then looked horrified when Madeleine answered very quietly, 'Alastair died last month.'

Since then they had met frequently and Madeleine always tried to reassure Katherine, whom she felt had never forgiven herself for her gaffe. Her own composure remained fragile, but it was only in the darkness of the communal bedroom that she ever gave way to silent tears. Dr Hadow, who had every intention of keeping his promise to Alastair, made a point of meeting her casually every day, and of allowing his admiration for her courage to show in his eyes, for she always mustered a smile to reassure him – until the day she remembered the carpet-bags of clothing Alastair had brought to the hospital. Necessity made her go to collect them, but she was not prepared for the overwhelming grief the room caused her: it was tiny and bare except for a plain deal table and chair, yet Alastair's personality lingered there – in the shelf of medical books, the ink-stained blotter and the small velvet case standing on the table. When she opened the case, she saw it contained the miniature of herself painted on ivory by a Turkish artist in Constantinople the week following her marriage; she was shown wearing the wedding bonnet for which Miss Nightingale had sent urgently to Malta, and the artist had even included the brooch at her throat.

Madeleine closed the case quickly, swinging away from it and its memories, but then there was his uniform, neatly folded on the chair. Hesitantly she took the dark blue coat in her hands, noting that there was still a red hair on the collar. Alastair, oh Alastair, her heart cried, and she suddenly clasped the coat to her, arms tightly wound around it, cheek laid against the collar. Dr Hadow, pushing open the door, found her thus, and she knew that just this once she could not pretend. 'I hurt,' she said brokenly, and he nodded understandingly. Yet almost at once she rallied, took the coat by the shoulders and folded it. 'I wonder, Dr Hadow, if you would very kindly put this and Alastair's bag somewhere else. I am sure the room must be needed and perhaps, if we are besieged, the clothes may be useful to someone.'

'Of course,' he said, and then, taking this rare opportunity of speaking to her when her defences were down, he asked quietly, 'How are you managing, Mrs Fraser?'

'Well enough,' she answered at once, dashing away the tears on her cheeks. 'There are too many other heartbreaking stories for me to pity myself.' She even managed the faintest glimmer of a smile as she added, 'I am sure in a very short while the wound will begin to close and by the time we are able to leave here it will have healed, even if the skin over it is very thin.' She paused and ran her fingers very lightly over the ink-stained blotter. 'Although I shall never forget what has happened here for as long as I live.'

News of the fall of Cawnpore and subsequent massacres there reached Lucknow towards the end of June and engendered a sense of urgency in the garrison; there was a general feeling that time was running out for them, and work on the defences continued night and day. By now the few Britishers still arriving from the outstations did not recognize the Residency, for instead of the brilliant flower beds, creepers and beautiful trees, the gardens had deep trenches and gun emplacements; where the wall ended, palisades, bamboo stakes and earthworks topped with huge iron spikes had been erected. There were two guns outside the Fayrers' house and four others at the nearby post office.

Sir Henry, much against his better judgement, rode out with six hundred men to engage the mutineers at Chinat, some six miles from Lucknow. Within an hour of engaging the enemy, the native gunners had deserted, the cavalry had fled and the British troops, demoralized by the death of Colonel Case, were in retreat. All the native infantry remained loyal to their masters, and more than one wounded British soldier owed his life to a native infantry-man who carried him from the field. As they fell back on Lucknow, the army was harassed by enemy cavalry, and the wounded who were unable to go on, both British and Indian, fought to the last man.

In the Residency compound conditions were chaotic: in addition to the returning troops, who were being hurriedly redeployed, there were wounded arriving on foot, in litters and on gun carriages; strings of camels, horses, bullocks and even the huge grey shapes of elephants, all pulling and straining at guns and every variety of cart. Suddenly, like rats leaving a sinking ship, all the coolies vanished, while in the city itself every vehicle and every available animal was used to convey its citizens at breakneck speed as far as possible from the Residency.

As rebel cavalry began to splash down into the river wherever fordable, so boats were frantically pushed off from the shore. The inhabitants of Lucknow were leaving the British and their loyal native regiments to their fate.

That night the Baillie Guard was closed and barricaded; the Residency area was now totally surrounded on all sides by rebel forces whose guns had already started to blaze and roar.

23

Madeleine had been standing with many other women near the Baillie Guard to give the weary troops water, but when she saw the enormous number of wounded, she hesitated only briefly before slipping away to the hospital. Although there was no shortage of doctors, that afternoon all were working nonstop in sweltering heat. Dr Fayrer had just placed a bunch of silk ligatures in his buttonhole, when he looked up and saw Madeleine. 'Mrs Fraser,' he began, fervently hoping she was not going to bother any of them with some trifling problem at such a time, when she cut in quietly, 'I know how to dress stumps, and I should so like to help, if you will allow me.'

Dr Fayrer's eyes briefly met those of Dr Hadow, and then he said cordially, 'We should be more than delighted, Mrs Fraser.'

So Madeleine rolled up her sleeves and within minutes was attending to an amputee. Since the day when she collected her belongings, she had avoided the hospital, the very sight of it sharpening her grief, but once she began to work her thoughts revolved entirely around her patients. It was already dark when Dr Fayrer came and told her she must return to the house.

'Oh, but I was used to working until midnight at Scutari,' Madeleine protested, 'and there is still so much to do.'

'Nevertheless, I must insist that you return to the taikhana. Although the shelling and gunfire have ceased at last, we do not know what is to happen during the night and you will be much safer in the underground room.'

Dr Hadow insisted upon escorting her, despite her

protests, and when they stepped into the starlit night both came to an abrupt halt: all the houses held by the rebels in the near vicinity of the compound had been loopholed, while on their own side many buildings were already pockmarked by shell and gunfire, the verandah of one being completely wrecked.

At daybreak the onslaught started again, followed by an attempt to rush the Baillie Guard which was eventually beaten off. Throughout the compound the women were ordered to remain indoors, and for those in underground rooms the day was particularly trying for they were without light or air, their children screamed almost non-stop at the terrifying noise, and all expected that their final hour was upon them.

Madeleine had pleaded with Dr Fayrer to be allowed to go to the hospital, but he was adamant: 'Not while this shelling lasts, Mrs Fraser. Those devils are using our eight-inch howitzer which they captured yesterday, and while the Residency itself is their main target, many shells are falling elsewhere. No, Mrs Fraser; I said no, and I mean no!' But later in the day he rushed back. 'Mrs Fraser, can you come now? Miss Palmer has had her leg shot off and I should be glad if you could attend her.'

So Madeleine ran with him through the hail of bullets to where the eighteen-year-old daughter of Colonel Palmer was recovering from the chloroform. 'The leg was almost completely severed,' Dr Fayrer explained to Madeleine, 'so the actual amputation was very soon over and I am hoping against hope that she will recover.' But Miss Palmer was slowly but calmly dying when at midnight there was a tremendous explosion which broke every window within the compound, shook walls and sent down showers of mortar and brick dust.

There was instant pandemonium. Above the frenzied shouts and blaring of bugles could be heard the screams of children wakened from their first uneasy sleep, and the various sounds of terror uttered by the large assortment of animals. The entire garrison was convinced that the rebels had blown up the defences and were about to pour through. Madeleine, who had been allowed to remain throughout the night with Miss Palmer, was choked by the clouds of dust, which were so thick that she could not see across the room. At last Dr Hadow dashed in, hardly recognizable through the layer of grime and dust which completely covered him. Madeleine was fanning her patient with desperate urgency and Dr Hadow bent to look at her; she was barely conscious and breathing with extreme difficulty.

'I fear it will be the end for her,' Gilbert Hadow whispered. 'Her father has just been told about her and will be here any minute.'

'But whatever has happened?' asked Madeleine as she continued to fan Miss Palmer.

'Oh, the Machi Bhawan fort was blown up on Sir Henry's orders and the garrison has just arrived. They all got through the enemy lines safely, but at our own gate there was almost a disaster when Colonel Palmer's order to open the gate was mistaken by our people for "Open with grape". They were very nearly fired upon by the guard and then, when that was averted, no one could find the man with the key to the gate! All in all, I think it's a miracle that they're here, but I understand they've got a lot of sick and wounded, so we can expect an influx any minute now.'

There was no question of Madeleine returning to Dr Fayrer's house; she remained on duty throughout the night, only going back to the *taikhana* next morning to wash away the worst of the dust. She was on the point of setting off once more when George Lawrence, Sir Henry's nephew, rushed in shouting for Dr Fayrer. 'My uncle has been hit!' he cried, 'and I think he is dying!'

Dr Fayrer, striving for calm in this worst of crises, said tersely to Madeleine, 'Come with us!'

When they arrived at the Residency they found that soldiers of the 32nd had carried Sir Henry downstairs and laid him upon a table. 'Help me to cut away his clothing,' Dr Fayrer ordered Madeleine, and together they worked in silence; when the wound was uncovered it was obvious that there was no hope: the upper thigh had been shattered and there was extensive injury to the abdomen. Waxen-faced but conscious, Sir Henry asked, 'How long have I got to live?' and at first Dr Fayrer could not bring himself to tell the gallant old man the absolute truth, but when Lawrence said, 'I want a definite answer for I have a great deal to do,' Dr Fayrer answered, 'Forty-eight hours, sir.'

Sir Henry was moved for safety to Dr Fayrer's house and Madeleine was asked to help nurse him.

'How is he?' 'Is he conscious?' 'What hope has he?' were the questions asked constantly of the staff. There was little to be said or done for Lawrence, whose agony was great throughout the remaining hours of his life. However, he remained conscious until almost the end, urging that every man should die at his post rather than surrender and his last clear words were: 'God help the poor women and children'.

He was buried after dark in a communal grave with those others who had died that day, the service being conducted to the accompaniment of bursting shells and a hail of bullets.

Dr Fayrer ordered Madeleine to rest and not to return to duty for at least twenty-four hours. She slept for twelve, but then insisted upon dressing and resuming her share of duty, both in the house and the hospital. In later years, whenever she was asked about the siege, Madeleine always said that she thought it really began after Sir Henry's death: when the immense shock of this had passed, people started to realize how desperate their plight was. The constant bombardment terminated the semblance of gaiety, the little parties and the visiting which many had tried to maintain. With the disappearance of servants, ladies who had never boiled a kettle had to make meals from rock-hard ship's biscuits and tough meat from the carcases of gun-bullocks. To add to their misery, there was the deluging rain and insufferably hot weather, the multitudes of mosquitoes – and the terrible flies. After swarming in huge black masses on the bodies of dead animals, the flies would invade rooms, clustering on the eyelids of sleeping children, around the corners of mouths, crawling up nostrils and other orifices of the body, and covering the food as people ate it.

'I wonder that any of us survived,' Madeleine would say, 'for there were no coolies to empty the latrines, and dead animals sometimes lay for days before a makeshift burial could be arranged, while the human dead were buried in only shallow graves because all the diggers had fled.' Inevitably disease flourished, particularly cholera, smallpox and ague. Babies died in great numbers from gastroenteritis, or starvation because their mothers had died or lost their milk. Madeleine never forgot the heart-rending way these babies had turned their tiny open mouths instinctively to the breast of any female who held them; how the strong ones at first cried loudly and persistently for nourishment and how this had changed to a soft whimper as they weakened, until at the end they were silent and still in total apathy. Their deaths were like so many blows over the heart to Madeleine, for they reopened the wound of Thomas's death, but determined not to give way, she threw herself into work with desperation, only leaving the hospital to snatch a few hours' sleep at infrequent intervals.

Other women now worked at the hospital, but Madeleine and Mrs Polehampton were the only ones with any training, so the greatest responsibility fell to them and they moved into a room in the former banqueting hall, which had been turned into an additional hospital. Unfortunately, it had been necessary to barricade all the windows, so the rooms were stifling and airless; the sick and wounded lay, not only on every available kind of sofa, mattress or bed, but in rows upon the floor. It was Scutari all over again, on a different scale and in a different setting, but the pain and the suffering were the same, so were the dirt and the shortages of all medical supplies.

Bobbie Bartrum had cholera and Katherine was nursing him devotedly, although she was almost too weak to hold him, and there were times when she secretly gave up all hope. Madeleine spent as much time as she could with her, and together they kept up each other's spirits. 'But,' said Madeleine, 'you do too much,' for Katherine, although suffering from boils on her hands, was the self-appointed maid of all work for her room. In filthy, tightly packed lodgings with fifteen other women and children, it was she who made the most determined effort to keep the room in some semblance of order, as well as doing most of the cooking. Bobbie recovered, but Mrs Clarke, who had come with Katherine on the journey from Secrora, died in childbirth, her baby following her immediately, her little boy some three weeks later. Fortunately, just when Katherine felt she could bear no more, she was moved into a house where she shared a room with only one other young woman.

'At least,' Madeleine said, trying to cheer her, 'we do not have to sleep at our posts in all weathers and under constant fire, and we *are* able to change our clothes sometimes. Besides,' she added with a shudder, 'I just could not burrow down under the earth and stay down there for hours looking for mines, as our men have to do, so we *are* luckier than they!' She rose wearily. 'I must go and see how little Louisa Henderson is.'

'Oh – the little girl who has dysentery and an ulcerated throat?'

'Yes. I fear for her; she is so terribly wasted and pallid. If – if anything should happen to her, I just don't know how her poor mother would be able to bear it; having seen her husband killed before her very eyes, I don't believe she could survive any more grief.'

But Mrs Henderson greeted Madeleine with a radiant smile. 'My darling child is better today,' she exclaimed joyfully. 'I managed to get her a little milk, which she was able to swallow and then she actually sat up and began to *talk* and *laugh* in her own dear pretty little way! I think I'll take her up from this hateful room and into the sunshine for a short while.'

Louisa Henderson died two days later after her throat had closed completely. Madeleine stayed with Mrs Henderson, sharing her agony, and later stood, herself choked with grief, as Mrs Henderson laid her baby in a small box which a private in the 32nd had made for her, just as Jem had made for Thomas . . .

'There are so many little orphans who need all the love and care we can give them,' Madeleine said some days later to Mrs Henderson. 'Will you not try to help some of them? Most have witnessed their mothers' deaths and are grieving terribly.' So Mrs Henderson made a gallant effort, and was soon to be seen reading and talking to groups of pale, unsmiling children. 'I think she is going to be all right,' Madeleine confided to Dr Fayrer.

'Well done,' he said, smiling and patting her briefly on the shoulder. 'I know how hard you've tried to give her some incentive to go on living.'

But it was not to be: Mrs Henderson, at Madeleine's suggestion visiting a woman who had recently given birth, arrived as a round shot came bursting into the room, tearing off the mother's head as she sat with her baby at her breast. The infant died of starvation and Mrs Henderson spent the next few days wandering around the cantonment blank-eyed and totally silent, before being found dead in the early morning rain. She was thought to have been trying to make her way to where her child was buried, but had fallen in the mud and lain there until death claimed her.

There were others who died by their own hand, or who went out of their minds, unable any longer to bear the strain of the terrible noise, the filth, smells and tragedy.

Yet for those who did endure, the news brought on 22 September was what they had been waiting, hoping and praying for: a relief force under General Havelock had crossed the Ganges and was on its way.

By the twenty-fifth the thunder of Havelock's guns could be clearly heard coming from the east, and the flag which had so constantly been shot at, shot through and shot down from the Residency roof was hastily sewn together yet again and hauled to the top of the battered pole, so that the relieving force could see it. But first that force had to fight its way through the narrow twisting streets of the city, where at every window and on every roof a murderous fire rained down upon it. To the wild skirling of their pipes, the Highlanders led the advance, running and cheering as they went, until in the late afternoon the Baillie Guard was opened and through it they streamed – bearded, dirty, wet, many covered in blood, all in mud, to be greeted by rapturous cheers from the garrison. Many men and all the women wept. Madeleine, down at the gate with countless other women to offer the men water or weak tea, had no idea that tears were streaming down her face.

Katherine Bartrum, with Bobbie in her arms, rushed to the gate with all the others, and could not believe her ears when an officer told her that he had shared the same litter with her husband the previous night. 'Dr Bartrum will be here very soon now. He is in the rearguard with an artillery battery.'

So Katherine waited at the gate, her eyes darting from face to face, turning constantly to peer into the middle distance, but there was no sign of Robert. It was long after midnight when she eventually ceased her endless pacing and quietly, without fuss, took Bobbie back to their room.

For Madeleine, after the first joyous hours, there was a great deal of work to be done: casualties had been extremely heavy and they now began to pour in. The staff worked through the night, amputating, gouging out bullets, sewing up wounds and bandaging, but every man, no matter how mortal his wounds, managed to smile and murmur, 'We got here in time, we saved them.' Only those in command knew the bitter truth: the relieving force was too small to raise the siege or make evacuation of the garrison possible.

The next morning Katherine dressed Bobbie in the one clean dress which she had been saving for the occasion and took him outside, where she stood, looking eagerly about her. Later she took Bobbie to the top of the Residency tower, where she stood until dark, watching the road.

The following day it was left to Mrs Polehampton, whose own husband had recently died of cholera, to tell Katherine that Robert had been killed within sight of the Residency while tending the wounded of his unit. For a time Katherine's courage deserted her and constantly she would say to Madeleine, 'To think he was shot through the head, his beautiful head.' But gradually, on the urgent entreaties of all her friends, Katherine gathered her forces together once more to look after Bobbie, for hadn't Robert's last words to her been, 'Look after my little darling'? And she had tried so hard to do so, nursing him through cholera and several lesser illnesses, keeping him warmly shielded against her breast through all the bombardments, and seeing him change from a chubby, fifteen-month-old baby to a little wizened, huge-eyed child who only smiled when he played with Jacko or was able to watch the monkeys swinging through the skeletal trees. As Katherine lay weeping in Madeleine's arms, she said over and over again, 'He is all I have left to love and live for.'

A feverish gaiety began when it was realized that the siege was to continue, for nothing appeared changed, yet now men and women hardly noticed the constant noise of cannon, round shot and musket, barely started at the sudden huge explosions of mines, or looked at the amputated limbs piled up outside the hospital. The frequent urgent shrilling of bugles was largely heard only by those for whom it was intended, and few even noticed men scrambling out of one defensive post to rush and reinforce another as an assault began.

It became normal for men formerly used to the finest cigars and cheroots to smoke chopped straw or leaves. Children played war games, while women ground dhal between stones to make a substitute for soap, mended clothing with any scrap of material, sewed shirts from floor cloths or even made a suit from the green baize of a billiard table – all by the light of a twist of cotton soaked in oil. When head lice were first discovered, women cut off their hair and covered their heads with caps or handkerchiefs and spoke laughingly of the arrival of 'light infantry'. When hordes of howling sepoys attacked one or more of the posts which men – *their* men – defended in mere handfuls, the women gathered round a piano to sing hymns or retired to a quiet corner for prayer.

As soon as she was able, Madeleine went from group to group of the relieving force asking if there was a list of British women and children who had been in Cawnpore at the time of the uprising, but all heads were shaken and she was given the same answer: conditions had been too chaotic and the need to push on had precluded the force from learning more. Turning away with a shudder, Madeleine could only pray that Harriet had been elsewhere and had survived.

The almost telepathic feeling she had once had that Sebastian was still in India had long since left her, and she was now sure that he had returned to England months previously. In rare moments of reverie she thought, I am a very fortunate woman, for I have been loved by two wonderful men: the first, who came across the world to me even after he had inherited 'half of southwest England' and could have any woman, and the other who married me, knowing that I was not innocent and had borne an illegitimate child. If I die tomorrow, I shall have known the heights and the depths, and perhaps have experienced more than many of the other women here. And it was all because that awful man swindled papa out of his money; if he had not done that, papa might still have left me in General de Lacey's care, but I should have been a well-to-do young woman and Sebastian would have thought of me quite differently. There would have been no Thomas, but then I should never have known dear little Mam, Ellen would have remained just a loyal servant and poor Jem might never have been caught; I should never have known that people like the Sharpes and Mr Shuttleworth *could* exist, and I would never have met Miss Nightingale or Alastair, or gone to Turkey. And I certainly would not be in Lucknow at this time! Yes, she thought, I have gained very valuable experience from all the people I have met, and most of them have enriched my life too.

Yet even as Madeleine acknowledged all that, she also realized that none of her past aroused much emotion in her: Sebastian was a figure from the very distant past, a past she could hardly believe in, while Alastair's death now seemed to have occurred *years* before, and the memory of their brief life together had a flimsy, dream-like quality. The sight of his clothes being sold at one of the regular auctions brought only a momentary stab of pain. 'I don't think this scarlet and my hair were meant to be together,' he had said laughingly the first time he wore his full-dress uniform, but she had told him he looked splendid in the scarlet coat with its white facings and gold epaulettes, even though at that moment another figure in blue and cherry red had been superimposed on the scarlet and white . . . Ah, well, they had both gone from her now and she would remain alone. Surprisingly this no longer held any terrors for her, but she clung to Jacko. Most pets had long since been put down, but Madeleine shared her meagre rations with Jacko and he accompanied her everywhere. When she ran through a hail of bullets she held him tightly against her breast as other women held their children; he slept on her bed at night and hid under her skirts during the day; she often talked softly to him, sharing her thoughts, and he knew her every mood, every tone of voice, and was completely devoted to her.

In a rare moment Madeleine confided to Dr Hadow: 'I don't know why it is, but I cannot seem to *feel* any more. Although I lost Alastair, I have had less to bear than so many others who have seen husbands and two, even three, children die, yet they can still laugh, cry, mourn or rejoice, but I can do none of these.'

But, thought Dr Hadow, there is no other woman who has worked so hard for days and nights on end, bandaging, swabbing, sponging, comforting, and he had seen her face during amputations when she stood so quietly in the background; she had been pouring out her compassion, tenderness and care for months and now she was drained. And he suspected there had been other tragedies in her life, for he had seen how shadowed her eyes could often be.

'Don't worry,' he told her. 'Emotion will return. Meanwhile, accept the lack of it as a blessing in the present sad circumstances. I know it seems as though we shall never get out of here, but now that Delhi has fallen, I feel much more optimistic and am certain that forces are being mustered to relieve us. I promise you, when they do come, you will be able to experience much emotion and all of it happy!'

And those forces were coming: from England, from Scotland, Burma and China, Hong Kong and the Cape, coming with their guns, their camel trains and their elephants, marching at a steady three miles per hour to the skirl of the pipes. The vast plain, green now after the rains, slashed with the vibrant yellow of mustard and hazed with the delicate blue of flax, made a suitable backcloth for the heterogeneous uniforms, which included the Sutherland kilts of Sir Colin Campbell and the 93rd, the men and their Commander who had held the Balaclava road in that thin red line. Now they were swinging along proudly to the strains of 'The Campbells Are Coming' and 'On wi' the Tartan', the Crimean medal pinned to their brown cotton blouses, which had been issued to them in anticipation of service in China. Each and every man knew that the eyes of the Empire were upon him and that he was walking into history, for a storm of fury had swept through Britain when the stories of Delhi, Allahabad, Agra, Cawnpore, Lucknow and scores of tiny outstations had become known. The clamour for revenge was universal, but most important of all, every man knew he was marching to save the lives of nearly seven thousand men, women and children, whose food supply was believed to be nearly gone.

By early November, those in the Residency knew that relief was very near.

* * *

489

Madeleine, emerging from the hospital at first light to gather firewood, paused on the verandah to breathe in the cold morning air, and immediately noticed the old Indian who sat cross-legged and hunched on the tiled floor. His turbanned head was sunk on to his breast, but she saw that a thick grey beard enveloped his cheeks and the lower half of his face, while his eyes were covered by a dirty white cloth. A small bowl containing a handful of rice was beside him and Jacko immediately ran to this. 'Oh, Jacko, no, no!' exclaimed Madeleine, 'Oh, you naughty little dog, come here at once!' She ran to gather up her seemingly deaf pet and turned agitatedly to the blind man. 'I am so sorry, but I'm afraid my little dog has gobbled up your rice. If you can wait a while, I will bring you some chupattis.'

To her surprise, the Indian shook his head. 'Please, mem, do not be worrying,' he said in a high-pitched, trembling voice. 'My grandson can bring me more rice.'

Madeleine frowned, finding this hard to believe, 'Are you sure?'

'Oh yes, mem, very sure, mem.'

'I don't remember seeing you here before.'

'No, mem, I am only coming here since one hour from other hospital.'

'Oh – are you needing attention?'

He did not answer, but said instead, 'Mem's husband is doctor-sahib, perhaps?'

For a few seconds Madeleine did not answer, then she said softly, 'He was, but he is not here any longer.'

'Doctor-sahib not here in Lucknow with mem!' It was an exclamation rather than a question, uttered with such surprise that Madeleine felt constrained to explain.

'My husband died six months ago.'

'Ah.'

'Madeleine! Madeleine!' It was Mrs Polehampton,

490

running out from the hospital, her thin face wreathed in smiles. 'They've got through to the Alambagh!'

The mutineers were maintaining a constant barrage of fire and Madeleine, setting off at last to collect the firewood, noticed that already a thick haze, caused by dust and gunfire, lay over the city.

Many women took it in turns to forage for firewood and, as this became increasingly scarce, it was necessary to go nearer and nearer the outer wall to find any timber at all. But by now the majority of the defenders gave little thought to walking through gunfire and Madeleine, wrapped in a dark shawl against the November chill, soon became immersed in her task. It was only when Jacko began to growl that she looked up, and then she was transfixed: immediately ahead of her there was a small hole in the wall through which an enemy sepoy was wriggling, while two others began to walk noiselessly towards her, naked tulwars in their hands. Very slowly Madeleine straightened, still clutching the bundle of firewood, while her eyes, dilated with terror, were fixed on the grinning faces. At her feet Jacko was barking so frantically that he was almost choking and his whole tiny body was rigid, hackles erect along its entire length.

It was then that, with a rush of air, a figure shot past them, a huge sword whipping and cutting before him, while a voice shouted, 'Run, Madeleine! Run!'

But if she was transfixed with terror before, she was equally transfixed now with amazement, for the voice was the one that she knew better than any other in the world, the one she had never thought to hear again. The figure was turbanned and clad in loose Indian clothing, but the voice was Sebastian's. In spite of his damaged leg, he was moving at incredible speed and uttering wild yells as the three sepoys rushed him. The great sword, glinting in the pale sunlight, swished down and hacked off the hand of the first man to reach him. A second later he had half turned, and the sword swung again to slice off the head of the second sepoy. The third raced towards him, tulwar held horizontally to run him through, but instantly the massive figure side-stepped and instead his own sword drove into the man's side. But a fourth sepoy had now squeezed through the wall and was running towards Sebastian, who turned fleetingly to look back.

'For God's sake run, Madeleine!' he repeated hoarsely, and at that moment his thonged sandal caught in a trailing root and he fell flat on his back, his head hitting the rock-hard ground and momentarily stunning him. But in falling, his loose jacket opened, revealing the revolver thrust into his waistband. As the sepoy rushed towards him, Madeleine dropped the firewood and also rushed forward. Then, acting entirely on instinct, she snatched hold of the Adams and, cocking it with frantic haste, fired upward from where she crouched over Sebastian. The sepoy uttered a gurgling scream and staggered, yet came on, with tulwar ready to slash, but in that instant Madeleine felt herself grasped strongly around the waist and rolled over and over out of the dying enemy's path.

'By God, you're a marvellous girl!' said the figure poised above her, and she found herself looking up at the blind old Indian, except that he was not blind at all but smiling at her with Sebastian's eyes. 'But don't faint on me now, darling,' he was saying as he scrambled to his feet, and then realizing she was dazed with shock and horror, he grasped her arm firmly and pulled her to her feet. 'Can you run, Madeleine?'

She nodded, unable to speak or take her eyes off him.

'Then quickly, darling, we have about ten seconds' start to run for our lives!' His hand slid down to hold hers and then he was off, moving with the great speed for which he was so well known, even though now his movements were lopsided. And Madeleine ran with him; unhampered by hoop or petticoats, she was able to keep up, while Jacko, thinking this must be some new game, raced happily beside her.

Sebastian did not stop until they reached the verandah of the hospital, where they both fell panting against the wall. For a few seconds they could only look at each other, and then he raised her hand, which he still held, to his lips. 'Well done, my brave and wonderful darling!' he exclaimed, his eyes velvety with tenderness. But before she could speak, he had released her hand and moved to the steps. As he raced down them, he shouted over his shoulder, 'I must warn them about the hole, but I'll be back as soon as I can!'

I've gone out of my mind, Madeleine thought as she looked first at her hand and then all around her. There was not another person in sight. Yes, that's it, I've gone crazy and imagined that Sebastian was here – *here*! How absurd, how impossible, yet – yet, where was the firewood? It must have been a kind of hallucination, she thought fearfully. I thought I saw him and the sepoys, and so of course I dropped the wood, and I must have imagined that I shot that man! She looked down at Jacko, who was gazing up hopefully, tongue lolling and thin sides heaving. 'Oh, Jacko dear,' she whispered, 'if only you could talk and tell me what really happened.' Automatically she walked into the building, where Mrs Polehampton, catching sight of her stiff-limbed movements and staring eyes, came quickly towards her.

'Madeleine, are you all right?' she enquired anxiously.

The girl looked like an automaton and her words, when she managed to speak, did nothing to reassure the older woman: 'I didn't get the wood; I – I had a bit of a shock.'

'Well, never mind, my dear,' said Mrs Polehampton soothingly. 'Come and sit down and I'll somehow make us a cup of tea.' No use pressing her for details now, she thought, but how on earth can I heat anything without fuel? 'I'll be back in a few minutes,' she said to Madeleine, who had sat down and was now staring straight ahead, with lips slightly parted and huge eyes fixed on the opposite wall.

But when Mrs Polehampton returned and said, 'Madeleine, there is a man outside asking for you,' Madeleine leapt to her feet, looking, Mrs Polehampton thought, afraid and yet on the verge of radiance.

'Who is he?' she whispered, and Mrs Polehampton said, 'I don't know; he's dressed as an Indian, but speaks like an English gentleman – ' she broke off with a gasp as Madeleine rushed past her, the radiance now breaking through her shock.

On the verandah a huge figure was outlined against the light and, as she gazed up at him, the old mischievous smile parted his heavily bearded lips. 'Please, ma'am, I've brought the firewood,' he said, and his tender look was like a warm cloak enveloping her.

'Sebastian,' she whispered haltingly, 'are you – can you be *real*?'

'Why yes, my darling angel girl, I can assure you that I'm very real,' he replied happily. 'And if you will just tell me where you want this wood so that I can free my arms, I'll convince you in no time at all!'

Mrs Polehampton, concerned about Madeleine, had run to Dr Hadow and he, ever mindful of his promise to Alastair, now appeared, only to stop abruptly before the strange figure, whose hair was black and curling around his ears, yet who sported an enormous, almost white beard. His face looked even stranger, for it too was black, except where sweat had run down from his forehead, thus giving his skin a striped effect. Fine dark eyes looked Dr Hadow over coolly without a hint of embarrassment at his own odd appearance.

'Good morning,' said the doctor, involuntarily becoming very British.

A gleam of amusement showed in the other man's eyes. "Morning to you,' he said blithely as he bent to put down the firewood.

'May I know who you are, sir?' enquired Dr Hadow, now speaking more sharply.

'Major the Earl of Wells, formerly of the Eleventh Hussars,' Sebastian said, bowing. Beside him Madeleine gasped, and he gave her the slightest sideways glance, eyes dancing now, as he straightened. 'And who might you be, sir?' he enquired casually of the amazed doctor.

That gentleman gathered himself together. 'I am Dr Hadow,' he said with quiet dignity, 'and I am here because Mrs Fraser's late husband asked me to look after her for as long as she remains in India.'

Not another of those damnable doctor fellows! thought Sebastian. I can tell it is high time this one was sent about his business. 'Indeed?' he said aloud, and although the black brows had risen, his tone was surprisingly cordial. 'Well now, I am most happy to be able to relieve you of your very pleasant task, doctor, since I intend to look after Mrs Fraser from this moment on.'

But Dr Hadow was not so easily put off; after all, he reasoned silently, although the fellow *said* he was an earl and he certainly possessed all the supreme confidence of the aristocratic, no one had heard of him until now. 'Really, my lord?' he said politely but stiffly. 'But may I suggest that we ask Mrs Fraser for her views before we come to any arbitrary decision?'

'Oh – oh,' said Madeleine hastily, as she instinctively moved a little nearer to Sebastian. 'Thank you very much, Dr Hadow, but I should like to be with – his lordship.'

'Mrs Fraser was left in my family's care long before her marriage, you see,' Sebastian added smoothly.

'I see,' echoed Dr Hadow without conviction, but as he looked at Madeleine, his eyes widened: she was transformed into a most beautiful woman with great eyes shining like twin lamps and a delicate blush suffusing her gaunt cheeks; he remembered his own assurance to her that, when the moment came, she would be able to feel emotion 'and all of it happy'. There was absolutely no doubt that such a moment *had* arrived, and his face softened into a smile of genuine warmth. It was also obvious that this huge man, this so-called earl, could hardly take his eyes off her. 'Well,' said Dr Hadow, nervously clearing his throat, 'if you will excuse me, I must return to my patients.'

'Yes, of course,' said Sebastian, his tone now hearty, and as soon as the doctor and Mrs Polehampton had gone back into the building, he turned to Madeleine, his arm going around her shoulders and drawing her gently against his side. For a moment they remained silent, letting their eyes express all the joy and love they felt for each other. 'Let's sit down,' Sebastian suggested at last, thinking that, for all her radiance, she looked as though she might fall down at any minute. He drew her to an ancient, rickety bench and she took his free hand in both of hers, looking at it, running her fingers over the warm dry flesh, but then shaking her head slightly as she whispered, 'I still cannot believe you are really here.'

'I don't wonder, my darling, seeing me like this, covered in lamp black and with this awful beard full of ash!'

'I thought – I felt so sure you had left India long ago,' she said, not having taken in a word he said.

'I did leave, but I came back as quickly as I could –' he broke off, thinking he must not spoil this moment by telling her, but instantly she knew that something was terribly wrong, and that now it was he who needed her support.

'Please tell me,' she said simply.

The words came out in a rush then, for this was to be the first time he had spoken about the memory which was seared into his brain. 'I was in Calcutta when the news came through that everyone in Cawnpore had been taken into the Bibighur entrenchment. Willie was with me, but Harriet had not been at all well after the birth of their twin daughters and was pregnant again, so Willie didn't want her to move until after the birth . . . We both went at once to Havelock and begged to be allowed to join his force, but we arrived just one day too late to save the women and children . . . I was one of the first in. I tried to stop Willie, but he was close behind. We found Harriet – ' Sebastian's voice broke, and his fingers convulsively clenched around Madeleine's, but almost immediately he regained control. She was holding his hand warmly against her breast, but he couldn't tell her now, not while she was so weak, and with so many other tragedies around her. When he spoke his voice was once again strong and calm. 'Willie, poor fellow, went out of his mind – raving, and trying to run amok among the loyal native troops who had marched with us. I was the only one who had some measure of control over him, so I had to get him out of India, even though I was half out of my own mind with worry about you. By keeping him in an almost continuously drugged state and travelling only by night, I got him to Bombay and we took the overland route. When we reached Malta I was able to leave him at the military hospital, and I came straight back here. I swear, Madeleine, that if' – he broke off, still unable to say 'your husband' – 'if Fraser had been alive and well, I would have kept my promise and faded into the background, but as it is, I'm not going to let you out of my sight again!'

Everything was happening too quickly for her to fully assimilate in her dazed state; later she would weep over Harriet and ponder all that Sebastian had omitted, but now she could only exclaim in astonishment, 'You came all the way back to India for *me*?'

He looked at her very seriously, tenderness almost entirely obliterating the tragedy in his eyes. 'Didn't you once say that you would go to the ends of the earth to be with me?' he asked very softly.

The news that an English earl had suddenly materialized in their midst certainly created a diversion, and for some hours Sebastian was closeted with the commanders, giving them up-to-date information on the relieving force and the state of the country in general. After that he attached himself to the brigade mess, where, as a crack shot, he was greatly welcomed.

So Madeleine joined Maria Germon and the other wives who took weak tea and brandy in the early mornings to the men who had done duty throughout the night; in no time it became part of her normal routine, but always on arrival she would look anxiously about her until Sebastian appeared, and he sensed that she still could not quite believe in his reality. They tried to be very discreet, but it was soon obvious that when together they retreated into a world of their own.

Although Sebastian never formally asked her to marry him, he began to talk about their future. 'We'll go by the overland route and stay awhile in Italy so that you can choose whether to be married somewhere there or in Paris. I had originally intended that we should marry in the chapel at Royston, but with your being quite recently widowed, I think perhaps a very private ceremony on the Continent would be better; and then a honeymoon in the good air of Switzerland before we go home to Wells. You'll love the castle, darling, it's even older than Summerleigh and is surrounded by beautiful old woods. This little chap will enjoy rambling through them' – this to Jacko, who had become almost as devoted to him as he was to Madeleine. 'But, of course, if you'd prefer Summerleigh, I'm sure Llewellyn Morgan would sell it back to me now that Catherine has become engaged to Templecombe's heir . . . We could make our home there until we have our babies, but then I think we'd find it too small.'

Madeleine would look at him through her lashes and smile secretly. Was this the same man who had once told her that 'hordes of puking babies' were not for him? She would invariably stop him there by putting the tips of her fingers against his mouth; he was so certain, so confident, but she remembered Alastair and all the plans he had made. So although her eyes would shine, there would be tears in them too, and she would say, 'We have to get out of here first.'

But by now it was obvious that they would get out, for the guns of the relieving force were becoming louder and louder, and the kilts and bonnets of the Highlanders were clearly visible a thousand yards from the Residency compound. Yet the battle continued until after dark, turning night into brilliant day with all the buildings on fire, the guns blazing, shells and rockets exploding into splinters of light. Until, suddenly, the rebel guns fell silent, and a scouting party of Highlanders creeping into the Shah Najaf mosque with fixed bayonets found it empty. The rebels, fearing that the combined firepower of the British would ignite all the gunpowder stored there, had silently melted away through the gate to the river.

Sebastian, rushing back to the hospital, could only say with a catch in his voice, 'It's over, darling. We move out tomorrow,' before enfolding Madeleine in his arms. They stood silently, holding each other in quiet thanksgiving that each had come through unscathed.

But Madeleine had not forgotten Alastair, and that evening, just before the evacuation was due to begin, she asked a piper if he would come with her to the cemetery. He readily agreed, although there was still danger from the powerful enemy forces remaining in the vicinity and able to fire on sight. So, standing beneath a bare tree in the pale winter sunset, Madeleine watched as the piper slowly marched around Alastair's grave playing 'The Flowers of the Forest'. The tune, played as a dead march, was extraordinarily impressive in that shattered place where so many lay in shallow communal graves, and Madeleine wept for them all. Most of all, she wept for Alastair, because now she realized that the sacrifice which she thought she was being asked to make had really been his – his life, so that she could be with Sebastian. As the last notes died away, she whispered, 'I will never, never forget you, and if it had been humanly possible to save you, I would never have left you. But thank you, thank you . . .' With a final, lingering look at the grave, she turned away to where Sebastian waited. He came forward silently to put an arm closely about her shoulders and together they walked to where the long line was assembling.

So at long last they began to move out: first the wounded, the women and children and the civilians, under strong escort.

At great expense Sebastian had bought a half-starved pony for Madeleine to ride. 'But Mrs Inglis is determined to walk,' Madeleine protested, 'and I think I ought to do the same. Why – oh, Sebastian!' for without any hesitation he had put his hands on her waist and lifted her on to the pony.

'I am sure Mrs Inglis is a splendid woman,' he said firmly, 'but I wonder if she has spent every day and most nights at the hospital as you have – she certainly looks stronger than you. And anyway, so long as I am able to procure some kind of beast, I will not allow the future Countess of Wells to walk!'

So Madeleine remained unfamiliarly astride the bony animal, her old carpetbag hanging on one side and Jacko in a long narrow carrier made from an old mat on the other. She saw Maria Germon, wearing all the clothes she owned, plus all her other possessions, having to be hauled on to a pony by Charlie and two other officers amid loud laughter. Madeleine, looking anxiously around for Katherine and Bobbie, saw instead Mrs Inglis walking beside an ancient, broken-down carriage pulled by coolies. Her children and a small white hen were in this while Mrs Case – who had come as a bride to Lucknow and was leaving as a widow – followed on foot.

Just when Madeleine had given up hope of locating Katherine, she saw a tiny hand waving to her from a tonga and realized it was Bobbie. Then there was Mrs Polehampton, also waving and smiling through her tears and clutching, as a treasured possession, her late husband's harmonium, which had been presented to him long before by the 32nd.

So many familiar faces, Madeleine thought, so many tragedies shared, yet all the scarecrow figures were walking quietly and proudly now and most were trying to smile.

As she passed through the Baillie Guard, Madeleine looked back: the flag was still flying, but the compound, like the riverside palaces lining their route, was a scene of total devastation, with walls and buildings crumbling and shot to pieces. Her eyes narrowed, straining to see beyond them to the original hospital where Alastair had died, and then beyond again to the cemetery, searching for his grave, but the haze and too many shattered buildings obscured it. '*You must not spend your life alone,*' he had said. '*You need to love and be loved . . .*' It seemed a lifetime since he had died, but she knew now that she had loved him too, and had made him happy. Goodbye, dear, dear Alastair, she said silently but from the depths of her being. I *have* found someone and I will be happy as I believe you truly wanted, but your goodness and your love will always live in my heart.

501

She felt Sebastian's hand cover her own as he said quietly, 'Don't look back any more, darling.' Madeleine nodded, unable to speak. Yet I am so lucky, she thought as she blinked back tears, for Sebastian is with me – how should I be able to bear this if I were leaving him behind, as so many other women are having to leave their men, not knowing even now when they will see them again.

It was to be another three days before the Residency was finally evacuated. The garrison left at midnight, to the roar of the naval guns which had kept up a continuous bombardment upon the still heavily defended areas. Then, at the Baillie Guard, both General Outram and Brigadier Inglis paused. The last of the troops had already passed them, marching unevenly to delude the enemy, and both commanders stood looking back; all the shattered buildings were lit from within by lanterns and bits of rag soaked in oil in a final bid to outwit the mutineers, and it was an eerie sight, for always before there had been movement, the many sounds of men and animals, bugles blaring the alarm, together with the roar and rattle of gunfire; but now, as the naval guns momentarily ceased, there was nothing but the small noises of emerging rats and the flapping of discarded canvas in the breeze. In the flickering light of the lanterns the mounds of fallen masonry and the spiked guns were outlined against the night sky.

Silently both commanders lifted their caps in a last tribute to all the suffering, gallantry and endurance they had witnessed. Then they, too, turned and hurried away.

More and more of that endurance was still to be demanded of the refugees, for their six-mile-long procession was creating clouds of choking dust which settled in ears, noses and mouths, caused near-blindness, and so dried throats that speech was almost impossible and the craving for liquid desperate. All were constantly drenched in sweat and those who walked did so on hugely swollen feet and legs frequently knotted by cramps. When they finally reached the Alambagh it was found that many of the eleven hundred wounded had not survived.

'How tragic, how cruel,' Madeleine rasped, 'that they should die *now*, because of the jolting and the dust, after living through so many other dangers.'

Sebastian nodded. 'Yes, and I've just heard that Havelock has died of dysentery.'

There were ample medical supplies stored at the Alambagh and every able-bodied man and woman volunteered to help the overworked doctors. It was late at night when Madeleine said, 'I must stop now for my sight is blurring and I might measure out something incorrectly,' and as Sebastian drew her gently against him, she murmured, 'It is *so* wonderful to have you here' – and fell asleep on her feet, her head resting on his chest.

He scooped her up as her legs began to fold, holding her with all the love and tenderness he felt for her. And as he looked down at her small face, serene in sleep, he prayed silently, O God, I beg You, whatever my life is to be, long or short, successful or disastrous, let it be spent with this one woman; whatever You wish us to bear, in joy and in sorrow, let us bear it together.

Then he took her to a small tent which his name and air of authority had procured and put her gently down on to a camp bed; smilingly he undid his brooch and the buttons at her throat and took off her worn-out boots; her small feet looked puffy and sore and he would have massaged them except that he was afraid of waking her. Jacko, with eyes fixed on her and body quivering, had been carefully estimating the height of the bed, and he now launched himself on to it, turned a complete circle and then flopped down, snuggling into the small of Madeleine's back, his pink tongue curling in a jaw-splitting yawn as he watched Sebastian fetch a blanket.

'You're a lucky little fellow,' Sebastian whispered to him smilingly as he covered Madeleine and her pet. Then, wrapping himself in a ground sheet, he lay down outside, rifle by his side. He was taking no chances.

Yet their greatest danger was to lie ahead at Cawnpore, for as the procession neared the city, they heard heavy firing and saw columns of smoke rising in the still air. Soon the bitter truth became known: the city was under attack by huge forces and the garrison had withdrawn to an entrenchment erected after the first catastrophe. To the weaker spirits it seemed the end, for if the bridge of boats over the Ganges had been seized they would all be stranded in hostile countryside. A ragged cheer went up when it was confirmed that the bridge was still intact but under such heavy fire that they would not be able to cross until the naval guns could silence the enemy. So the haggard, worn-out men limped forward to help haul the huge guns into position, and many of their womenfolk went also to give them the last of the column's water.

It needed the concerted efforts of men and beasts to manoeuvre the guns, but by sunset the following day they had done so and wiped out the rebel batteries. Then at long last the procession began to move forward across the river: huge, plodding elephants, emaciated bullocks, heavily laden camels raucously protesting as ever; guns and horses; cavalry and infantry; native servants and British memsahibs; litters and carts; the living and the dead, all crossing the sacred river in a cloud of thick dust, to halt close to the entrenchment where six months previously so many had been taken out to their death. Evidence of their agony was all around – in the blackened walls of roofless bungalows, the charred remains of furniture and trees, and in the overwhelming atmosphere of pain and death.

Sebastian had lapsed into long silences, his eyes, narrowed and hard, only softening when they rested on

Madeleine. She could see that he was in torment and thought it must be the memory of Harriet's death, so although privacy was almost impossible, she tried to reach him by showing her tenderness and compassion.

On the third day, Sir Colin announced that the women and children must be ready to leave the next morning for Allahabad, and thence to Calcutta. Madeleine, going in search of Sebastian, found him pacing endlessly to and fro, the glowing tip of a cheroot clamped between his teeth. 'Sebastian darling,' she whispered, her heart going out to him, 'please won't you let me share this grief with you?'

He strode quickly across to her then, tossing away the cheroot, to wrap his arms tightly around her. 'Madeleine, my dearest darling, my beloved girl, you know that I love you more than anything else in the world, more than life itself, and that I would do anything to save you hurt.'

'Yes,' she said softly, 'I know that, my darling.'

'So – will you forgive me when I tell you that I cannot come with you tomorrow?' He held her away from him, trying to see her expression in the moonlight.

This was something for which she was totally unprepared. 'Oh,' she breathed, 'oh, please, no.'

He drew her down to sit beside him on a huge upended tree trunk. 'Madeleine, Sir Colin is planning a battle to rid Cawnpore once and for all of rebel forces and I think I must take part in that.'

She began to tremble. 'No,' she said. 'No, no, he has a large army now – you don't have to – I'm sure the other men from Lucknow will not be expected to fight another battle.'

Sebastian took both her hands in his. 'Listen, darling, please listen. I am volunteering because of Harrie and her two babies, and because Willie is dead – there was a letter waiting for me here from Malta: they had tried to keep him locked up at the military hospital because he was so violent, but somehow he got out after killing an orderly, and then he took his own life.'

'Oh,' whispered Madeleine again, 'oh, dear God! But – but what good . . .?'

'Madeleine, I'd hoped not to tell you, but I have to avenge her death because Harriet was not killed quickly by a bullet or even a sword thrust. When we stormed in there was great evidence of a massacre but few bodies – they'd all been thrown down the well – but we found Harrie . . . She was lying on her back in a far corner against the wall and – and, Madeleine, they had delivered her by slashing her with their *tulwars*; her unborn child was exposed, but its head was – was smashed . . . Even as she died, she must have flung out an arm, for it lay across two tiny pairs of shoes . . . the shoes of her twin baby girls . . . which *had the feet, with their little socks, still in them* – ' He broke off abruptly and turned away to bury his head in his hands, remembering the two frail little girls who had clung to his trouser legs and gurgled with delight whenever he had scooped them up, one in each arm. When Madeleine heard the first of his sobs, she rose on legs that seemed barely capable of movement and went to him, taking his head and holding it tightly against her breast; she felt his arms go round her waist, and thus they remained, holding each other in a moment of total love and trust.

When his harsh racking sobs had stopped at last, Madeleine slid to her knees before him so that his face was on a level with her own. 'You see,' Sebastian said hoarsely, 'I kept thinking: suppose it had been you, with our babies – first in the river massacre, trying to hold two terrified toddlers, then thinking yourself saved only . . . only to be butchered in that way.' She kissed him then, deeply and longingly, her arms sliding around his neck, her fingers buried in his short curling hair. He responded at once, his arms enveloping her, his lips ravishing her with all his passion and hunger. They longed to make love to each other then, but were surrounded by thousands of people, many of whom might even now be listening. So at last Sebastian reluctantly got to his feet and gently raised Madeleine; with his mouth against her ear he whispered, 'I would give anything to spend this night with you and show you how much I adore you, if it were only possible . . . but I promise you that for this one lost night, there will be hundreds of others throughout our lives when we shall be together.'

But that made her shiver in fear – fear that death might prevent him from keeping that promise, and they were now so deeply attuned to each other that he felt her apprehension at once and said simply, 'I will come immediately after the battle, whatever the outcome. Will you wait for me at Allahabad, darling?'

'Oh yes,' she whispered. 'I will wait.'

His resolution wavered the next morning when the convoy was about to set off yet again; she looked so small and frail in her tattered dress and ancient bonnet, so vulnerable, standing there alone except for Jacko whom she held in her arms as other women held their children. What the hell am I doing, thought Sebastian wildly, avenging the dead when I should be protecting the living? But at that moment she smiled and raised her hand.

'God go with you, my love,' she said, not caring who heard, and then she turned and climbed into a bullock cart, even as it started to move.

The good ladies of Allahabad, who, after all, had had their own baptism of fire, could not quite understand their sisters from Lucknow. The survivors of the great siege were expected to show signs of the tremendous physical and emotional ordeal through which they had passed, but instead most managed to smile and appear cheerful. 'Of course,' explained the charitable, 'after such an experience, their feelings must be blunted.' But in fact the women of Lucknow had done with tears and grief and were determined to win their next battle: a return to normal life. So they exclaimed joyfully over baths and clean hair and the new dresses which every *derzi* in the city was frantically stitching. When they ran to listen to the band and laughed, few realized that they were remembering when the mutineers had mocked them by playing English airs, even the anthem, just outside the compound. Naturally, though, almost everyone started at the smallest unexpected sound, and there were a very great many who suffered nightmares, but the deepest emotion was roused when people spoke of 'the fort at Lucknow'.

'It was never a fort,' the survivors said. 'The compound consisted of several houses in what was once a large garden, bordered by a low wall on one side and on the other by a parapet made of earth, bamboo and iron spikes . . . and it was all situated in the heart of India's second largest city.'

Madeleine had at last met up again with Katherine Bartrum and was shocked at Bobbie's appearance: he had the huge-eyed, wasted look of so many of the children who had died, and Katherine was desperate to get him away to a more temperate climate. 'But now the doctors tell me that he is too frail to go home by the overland route and that the sea air is what he needs most.' She could not bear to be parted from him for an instant, and he even rode with her in the evenings whenever she was invited out in someone's carriage. Madeleine's heart ached for her; so many of the babies had been born with dysentery and everyone knew they could not live, but Bobbie had been so healthy.

Madeleine spent as much time as she could with Katherine, trying to keep up her spirits, and each day when she found them both sitting in the garden, she would put her arms around Bobbie and lay her cheek against the top of his small head in silent thanksgiving that he was still alive. Yet Bobbie was to die on board ship, a few hours before it was due to sail for England, and Dr Fayrer was to carry his tiny coffin for burial beneath a mango tree in Calcutta's Lower Circular Road Cemetery. And Katherine, to whom fate had been so terribly harsh, was to marry another doctor and bear a son and two daughters before her own death in 1866 from consumption.

News of Sir Colin Campbell's success at Cawnpore on 6 December reached Madeleine soon after her arrival at Allahabad, and chill struck at her heart: supposing Sebastian were already dead, or desperately wounded? Supposing, supposing . . . her thoughts revolved entirely around him, even to the extent of blocking Harriet's death from her mind.

It had taken the convoy five days to reach Allahabad, but a lone horseman, even riding a half-starved horse, would surely take less time. Unable to disguise her feelings any longer, Madeleine took to walking on the battlements of the fort to view the road and the river. From early morning until the light faded she would be there, sometimes not even leaving for food and drink, but still there was no sign of him.

By the tenth day after the battle she had almost given up all hope as she climbed the innumerable steps, her heart thudding with the desperate wish that perhaps she might see his figure far below, riding towards her. The sun was surprisingly hot and in her haste she had forgotten her parasol, but her eyes, straining against the glare, saw that the road was quite empty. Then it all blurred as tears rushed to her eyes; something terrible had happened to him, and why hadn't she insisted on remaining in Cawnpore? How *could* she have left, knowing what horrific wounds were inflicted and how great was the suffering they caused – and how long would it be before she knew?

'Are you Blanche de Lacey, waiting for her Hugh to return from the crusades, or Margaret her Richard from Agincourt, or even Mary her John from Blenheim?' The words were softly spoken and she was not even sure she had actually heard them, but she whirled and there he was, holding out his arms, his eyes alight with happiness, a tender smile creasing his tired face.

'Sebastian!' she screamed and flew to him, moulding herself against him, her hands clutching the back of his shirt. For a few seconds she looked up at him speechlessly, and then buried her face against his chest as the tears rained down. He rested his chin on the top of her head and closed his eyes. My dearest darling, he thought, you'll never know what you're doing to me by standing so close . . . But almost at once she stepped back to raise her head and look at him again through drowned eyes.

'I cannot bear to see you cry,' he said tenderly, 'and I swear this is the last time in our lives that I will ever make you do so.'

'But I'm so happy!' she exclaimed.

Happy? With tears streaming down her face? He carefully suppressed a laugh, but his eyes danced. A breed apart indeed!

'I can't believe it,' she said, impatiently dashing away the tears now. 'I heard about the battle, but I'd almost given up hope.'

'I told you I would come back, my darling angel girl, and here I am.'

'Will – will you have to go away again?' she asked fearfully.

He took her small gaunt face in his hands then and looked down into her eyes with great tenderness. 'I'm never going away from you again,' he said. 'Never. Ever.'

And in all their long life together, he never did.

Epilogue

Visitors to the beautiful and magnificently preserved castle at Royston Lacey (given to the National Trust in 1976) will find a whole room devoted to memorabilia of the twenty-fourth Earl and his Countess: one wall is covered with Crimean War photographs and drawings, together with a large oil painting of the famous Charge. In a glass cabinet the Earl's blood-stained cape is displayed, with his huge sword beside it, and a small statue, cast in bronze, of his favourite charger, Rollo. On a purple velvet cushion are his Victoria Cross and the Crimean Medal with its silver clasps of Sebastopol, Inkerman, Balaclava and Alma, while on another similar cushion there are the foreign orders and decorations he accumulated over the years.

In the same cabinet are the Countess's shoulder sash, a faded strip of material with the words '*Scutari Hospital*' in pidery red letters; the carpetbag which she took first to Turkey and later to India; the medal of the Royal Red Cross awarded her in 1883; and a framed hand-written letter from Florence Nightingale congratulating the couple on their marriage in 1858.

On another wall are drawings graphically illustrating the siege of Lucknow, while in the family chapel there are memorials to William and Harriet Frensham and their infant daughters, and one which reads simply:

Sacred to the Memory
of
Dr Alastair Fraser, IMS,
who died at Lucknow on 30 May 1857,
in the twenty-ninth year of his life
Never Forgotten

511

But it is the portraits which fascinate most visitors: in the Blue Drawing Room there is the famous Winterhalter, painted shortly before the Earl and Countess returned to England from their honeymoon; they are depicted standing against a pastoral background, with the Earl wearing formal black only relieved by his linen and the white rose in his buttonhole. He appears a supremely happy man, and the artist has captured not only his splendid looks, but the great magnetism he possessed all his life. Beside him is his Countess, ethereal and swan-like in her grace, with dazzling skin and luminous eyes in which there is an expression of wonder, as if she cannot quite believe that life could be so joyous. The Earl clasps her hand, which is resting on his arm, and the otherwise formal portrait is relieved by the sight of a tiny white dog peeping out from beneath the hem of the Countess's gown.

There are many splendid portraits in the house: the Sargent, painted in 1885 of the Earl and his sons, is a fashionable and sophisticated study of four handsome, extremely elegant men; the full-length Renoir of Lady Harriet de Lacey depicts not only her youthful beauty but a hint of her father's early wildness; while Hellieu's head and shoulders of the Countess shows that even in age she retained her grace and delicate beauty. But it is to the Winterhalter that the visitor most frequently returns, for there is a kind of magic about that portrait of the Earl and Countess painted in 1858. In the springtime of their love.